BLOODAXE

BLOODAXE

ERIK HARALDSSON

C. R. MAY

COPYRIGHT

This novel is a work of fiction. The names, characters and incidents portrayed in it, while at times based on real figures, are purely the work of the author's imagination.

It is sold subject to the condition that it shall not by way of trade or otherwise, be lent, resold, hired out, or otherwise circulated without the writer's prior consent, electronically or in any form of binding or cover other than the form in which it is published and without a similar condition including this condition being imposed on the subsequent purchaser. Replication or distribution of any part is strictly prohibited without the written permission of the copyright holder.

ISBN: 978-1-9996695-0-8

Bloodaxe is for Henry, my own Berserk

GLOSSARY

Bonder - A freeman, typically a yeoman farmer, who pledged allegiance to a lord in return for legal and if necessary armed support.

Drekkar - A large warship similar to a skei but heavily ornamented. A dragon ship.

Faering - A four-ing, a small rowboat with four oars.

Hersir - A landowner and local chieftain who owed tax collecting duties and military service to his jarl and king.

Hird - The armed retinue of a warlord or king.

Huskarl - House-man. A bodyguard or retainer to a powerful chieftain, jarl or king.

Jarl - A regional lord responsible for administrating a province on behalf of the king for whom he collected taxes, duties and owed military service.

Karvi - A ship typically mounting sixteen to twenty oars, used to carry cargo and/or fighting men. Wider in the beam than the more specialised skei and snekkja, the ships excavated from Oseberg and Gokstad are examples.

Knarr - An ocean-going cargo ship.

Skat - Tax, tribute.

Skei - 'that which cuts through water.' A large sleek warship mounting thirty oars and above.

Snekkja - 'thin and projecting.' A small warship mounting twenty to thirty oars.

Styrisman - The helmsman on a ship.

Thing - An open air assembly of freemen, where matters of law and politics were debated and a ruling made by the lawspeaker.

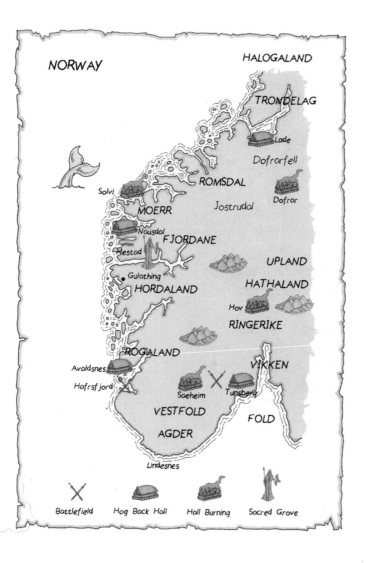

PART I

VIKING

1

Wimborne Mynster
The year of our Lord 955

H is work begun, the scribe looked up and flashed a smile brimming with youthful innocence. 'Tell me about King Erik, Your Grace.'

The archbishop blew the froth from his ale and peered across the rim, chuckling softly as he took a sip. 'Bloodaxe?' The man sat before him looked too young to scrape the down from his cheeks, at times he felt as old as the hills, a relic from another age; he had been a kingmaker, negotiating as an equal with foreign kings on the borders of Northumbria like a Caesar of old. 'You have to be more precise with Norsemen,' he gently chided the youth. 'They have more kings and sea kings at any given moment than have ever been pontiff in Rome!'

The hearth flared as a log settled to send tongues of flame curling upward, and Wulfstan crossed to the window with a sigh as his attempt to add a touch of jollity to the conversation failed to alter the lad's beatific expression. Taking

3

another pull from his cup the old churchman looked out across the fields. The days were shortening quickly as the year wound down. Soon it would be time to chant the Christ Mass, and his eyes ran down to the water meadow and the River Stour beyond as his mind began to drift back across the years. Trees reached skyward, skeletal in their winter slumber beneath a dark cap of rooks; somewhere in the distance the harsh bark of a vixen set the dogs to yapping in the nearby kennels.

'Bloodaxe,' he said with a disarming smile: 'Erik Blood-axe. You know if a young cherub like you had called him that to his face, he would have taken his axe and split you like a log.' The old Northumbrian flicked a look at the West Saxon and was gratified to see that the name of his friend still carried power, despite the year that had gone over since his passing. 'Erik Haraldsson, most favoured son of King Harald Fairhair,' he went on as the scribe lowered his head and began scratching his marks onto the vellum before him. 'If it is an undeniable fact that Harald was the greatest Norseman, his son Erik was perhaps the greatest Viking, although he too was a king five times over to my certain knowledge. I will tell you all that I know for it will add to his reputation, and reputation, as all men of worth are aware is what fighting men crave above all. But if you are to understand my tale you will need to do more than form letters of ink.' He waved a dismissive hand at the lush greens and gentle slopes of Dorsetshire. 'You will have to work your mind's eye to people a land where snow capped peaks reach the clouds, the seas roar and boil and men are as hard as the rock which surrounds them.'

Wulfstan looked across the room. The clerk was scribbling dutifully away; he doubted that the young man possessed the imagination to carry his thoughts beyond the minster walls, but his mind settled to the task as the fire sputtered, the warmth seeped into his bones, and the ale worked its spell.

'Erik was sent north to foster when he was a lad of seven winters, to a hersir named Thorir Kolbeinsson in a region the Norsemen call Fjordane. This hersir was a great warrior, one of Harald's greatest fighters in the days of his youth, days when they had riven shield walls in a brotherhood of spearmen and axemen, driven all who dared to oppose them from the land and forged the first kingdom of the Nor' Way in the crucible of war...'

THE BLADE WAILED like a banshee as it cut the air. The young Norseman skipped backwards and dropped his shield to deflect the blow but the axeman knew his work, and a heart-beat later the heel had hooked the rim and sent it spinning from his grasp.

Erik's eyes darted from side to side as he judged the distance to the board, but the men before him only laughed and closed in for the kill. 'What are you going to do now? Nowhere to hide, outnumbered and cut off from your friends.' The spearman dropped the tip of his weapon and glared above the rim of his own shield as the pair circled.

Erik swung in slow deliberate arcs as his attackers searched for a way to unlock his stubborn defence, his eyes flicking from spear point to axe blade as he attempted to keep both men in view. Even deprived of the protection of his shield both attackers knew that they had a cornered a wolf, and a wolf at bay was as dangerous a thing as any man was likely to meet on Midgard.

A quick look was all that was needed, and Erik knew that the hand grip was beyond his reach. Years of training imposed themselves upon him and he discounted the thing, pushing it from his mind as he concentrated on the figures before him. They were splitting up, circling, spear and axe jabbing forward as they tested his makeshift defence and sought a weakness.

Arinbjorn attacked first, the silvered blade of his spear flashing in the pale sunlight as it stabbed low; but Erik was ready, and a skip of his feet sent the lunge darting past his calf. Perfectly balanced his own spear was already in motion, the point of the blade cutting an arc in the still air of the morning as it scythed towards the attacker's face. Arinbjorn pulled his head back at the last moment, the blade whistling through as he steadied himself to counter.

The older man made a move as he spotted an opening, and his war axe stabbed forward even as the boy swung around to face the attack. But before the blade could connect Thorir was gasping with surprise and admiration as Erik, at his mercy a moment before leapt forward, turned somersault and rolled back to his feet. The boy's spear was already moving as the pair sought to shepherd him between them, and the base of the shaft shot out to strike Arinbjorn's knee with a loud *crack* which resounded around the field. As the spearman crumpled under the blow, Thorir came back again. Opening his body, the veteran snatched his shield aside as he moved in for the kill.

The last attack had disabled one opponent but it had left Erik wide open to the counter, and Thorir sensing final victory put his all into the jab. The joy which lit his features lasted little more than a heartbeat, and he stared in disbelief as the point of the boy's spear whirred through the air to prick at his throat. As Thorir froze, Erik flashed him a grin. 'Was that fast enough foster-father?'

The tension drained away as the men lowered their weapons, and the pair shared a laugh as Erik dropped the spear point and took a step back. Arinbjorn hobbled across, his expression a curious mix of pain and amusement as he flexed his knee and grimaced. 'Did you have to hit me so hard foster-brother?'

Erik smiled again. 'Just be thankful that we had bound the ends of the spears with wool cloth.' He glanced down at the bloody tear in his friend's breeks. 'Or you would have been hobbling for the rest of your days.'

Thorir clapped the boy on the shoulder. 'Then it is good thing that we shall always be friends.' He raised his head and called across to one of the thralls as he went about his work. 'Amlab!' The slave was halfway across the courtyard, water slopping from the pails as the yoke at his shoulders swung and lost momentum; he paused and turned his head. 'Yes, Master?'

The hersir took a deep breath and rubbed the growl from his belly. 'Tell them that we will eat outside this morning.'

The thrall bobbed his head, waddling away with his charge as they ambled across to the knoll. It was a good place to break their fast, grass covered and dry for the most part despite the morning dew, and they lowered themselves to the ground with a sigh as the slave disappeared inside. Thorir spoke first, and the younger men shared a smirk as Arinbjorn mouthed the words in time as they came from his father's mouth.

'I never tire of this view, lads.'

Erik followed Thorir's gaze to the West, out beyond the naust, the boat sheds which had given the settlement of Naustdal its name, down the waters of the fjord to the distant peaks. The wolf grey rock capped the higher ground, matching ribbons streaking the clefts and crevices as scree channelled down to the shore. The early morning sun had cleared the higher ground away to the East and the waters of the fjord shone sword blade bright.

It was almost a ritual now, and a good one Erik thought, that the three of them would finish morning practice at this place. The sound of hammering drifted up from the boat sheds on the strand as men went to work; Thorir's carter and his boy were yoking the ox in the field below as the day's toil began. Arinbjorn straightened his leg with a grimace as a woman ducked through the door of the hall with a jug of ale.

Thorir screwed up his face and peered at the sky. High up mare's tails flecked the heavens, drifting towards the snow capped peaks of Jostrudal; lower down a scattering of leaden clouds were ambling due east. Even in high summer a downpour was never far away in Fjordane. The drink arrived, and the girl knelt before them to fill the cups as the men waited impatiently. Morning practice was thirsty work; parched throats made it difficult to talk, and the first cupful disappeared in moments. Arinbjorn flicked the tip of his tongue as he licked the drops from his moustache, holding the cup forward for a refill as another thrall approached with warm bread and hot sausage.

Erik pulled his knife, wiping the blade clean on the leg of his trews as the platter was placed before them. A snort and a nod from the elder at their eagerness, and the younger men were stuffing the food into their mouths before the woman could straighten her back.

Thorir tore at a loaf as he threw his son a look of mischief. 'So,' he said. 'Do we think that the lad has the balls to go Viking?'

'Of course father,' Arinbjorn shot back. 'We are always in need of ballast.'

The trio chuckled as Erik moved forward to top up the cups. Thorir watched the liquid turn from dun to gold as the

morning sunlight caught the flow. Slapping his lips in anticipation he waited until the jug had moved on before sinking a
mouthful with relish. 'It may be sometime yet until our young
lad becomes full-grown, but he will attain the legal status of a
man at harvest time.' He fixed Erik with a look before he
went on. 'A young huskarl, Helgrim Smiter, came from your
father the king this summer at the Gulathing.'

Erik's cup fell from his lips in surprise at the revelation,
and his eyes went from father to son as the pair exchanged
looks of amusement. The huskarls were a lord's closest
companions, the best of the best. He looked at his foster-
brother, and the twinkle he saw in his eye confirmed Erik's
suspicion. 'You knew, you bastard!'

Thorir chuckled happily as Erik made to poke his son's
swollen knee with the toe of a boot, before revealing the
reason for the visit. 'This Helgrim is one of your father's
most promising young fighters, a lad who had already carved
himself a reputation as a fearless warrior in the South.'

The inference was clear, the king was taking a special
interest in Erik's progress as manhood approached, and Erik
listened intently as Thorir confirmed his suspicion. 'King
Harald wanted to know my thoughts on your king-worthi-
ness. Naturally, I told him that you were a hopeless arse.' He
paused to let the words sink in, before flashing a grin at his
crestfallen young foster. 'But a big arse, who fights like any
two men and eats like three.'

'Part of it was true at least,' Arinbjorn cut in. 'I will leave
you to guess which part I mean!'

Erik's hopes rose again as Thorir speared a length of
sausage with his knife. Erik was hanging on every word now.
It was not the custom for a boy at foster to meet with or even
set eyes upon his natural father until he had come of age.
Communication between the two had been nonexistent since

9

he had travelled up from his father's hall at Avaldsnes four long winters before, but men told him that he had grown into the very likeness of King Harald: tall; broad shouldered; fair of face beneath a shock of honey-blond hair. His father was the greatest Norseman that had ever lived, the man who had grasped the disparate people of the North Way and forced them together for the first time by sheer willpower and force of arms. Others expected great things of him, but none expected more than he did himself.

'However, an arse who has yet to kill a man, or even sail to foreign lands,' Erik countered as he began to recover his grit. 'That needs to be put right foster-father.'

Thorir nodded. 'That it does. That is why I rode over to Hestad, to the grove there. Offerings were made to Óðinn, gold and precious things: the Allfather spoke.' The old hersir moved a hand to his neck. Withdrawing it he looked at the spots of blood from Erik's spear strike and shrugged. 'The priests said that there will be blood and fire in the North lands before the crops are sown in the spring. That's why I have stepped up our training.' He looked from one to the other: 'blood, fire and death.'

2

BOLLI SIGURDSSON'S CHALLENGE

T he knarr cut the waters of the sound as Hisaroy came
up broad on the starboard bow, and Erik hauled the
tiller to his chest as he guided the ship into the channel. The
Gulathing was only a few miles ahead now, and oars slid free
of the hull as the winds dropped to a whisper in the lee of the
island. As the sail was hauled and sheets made fast, Arinbjorn
hopped up onto the steering platform and frowned. 'Hopefully the calmer water will do the trick. Who would have
thought that he would get seasick?'

The pair lowered their eyes to peer down into the cargo
hold amidships. The stallion was raising its head as it sought
the breeze, its great nostrils flaring as it gulped down the tang
of the nearby land. Erik nodded in agreement. 'Let us hope
that he has not been too weakened. Bolli Sigurdsson is insuf-
ferable at the best of times. If his nag wins this contest, we
shall never hear the last of it.'

The challenge had been made a few days before. Warning
horns had blared on the strand, and the men had hurried from
the hall to watch the drekkar as it coasted down Sunnfjord
with lazy strokes of the oars. The dragon ship carried no beast

head atop its stem post and the white shield of peace hung at its masthead but it always paid to be sure, and before the ship was halfway to Naustdal the men of Thorir's hird were set in their war gear and deployed for battle on the field below the hall known as the *vang*. It had been an uncomfortable day spent entertaining the boorish son of the jarl, he and Arinbjorn had never been friends and Erik had inherited his dislike, but all had agreed that the prospect of a horse fight at the autumn Thing would add spice to the week. Most of the important business that year had already been decided at the great summer Thing, and the final gathering of the year was often a dreary affair. The contest would offer a final flash of excitement before men hunkered down in their halls and the dark months of winter cloaked the northern land.

The *Helga* rounded the final ness, and a shout from the lookout drew Erik's mind back from its meanderings. Gulen was in sight, the strand wooded by the masts of the early arrivals, and Erik pointed the bows inshore as he sought out the landing place. Arinbjorn gave him a nudge and raised his arm. 'There he is!'

Erik lifted his eyes, nodding as he made out the signalman on the crowded shoreline. 'I see him.'

One of Thorir's men was perched in the upswept stern of the hersir's drekkar, the scarlet of his cloak flame-bright in the sun as he held it high and guided them to their berth. Erik was gratified to see that his foster-father had thought to leave him plenty of room to manoeuvre; with a final tug at the tiller the bows of the *Helga* came about, and oars were shipped as the knarr coasted the final few feet to land. The crew spilled into the shallows as the keel plate grounded, and within moments the ship was being hauled beam-on to the shore.

Arinbjorn clapped his foster-brother on the shoulder and flicked him a look. 'That was nicely done. Let's get Bram ashore: the sooner his belly settles, the sooner we can fill it with oats. Nobody fights well on an empty stomach.'

Crewmen were already running out the gangway amidships, bridging the gap down to the stony strand as others slipped ropes through iron rings and released the horse from its tethers. As the crew made the ship fast the friends made their way ashore. A last glance back across his shoulder told him that Bram was on the ramp, and the pair shared a look as men came down to guide the stallion to the corral. 'Come on brother,' Arinbjorn said with a smile. 'Let us take ourselves off to my father's booth. We have a busy night ahead.'

ERIK CAST another look down the meadow. Arinbjorn gave him a playful dig with the goad and handed it across. 'Here, you shouldn't need this, but it is as well to have it to hand.' He followed his foster-brother's gaze and shook his head. 'If they don't hurry along, they shall miss the fun. It doesn't look like the horses are prepared to wait!'

The pair turned back towards the corral. Bram was straining against the rope as he caught the scent of his opponent, the eagerness sending a buzz of excitement sweeping through the crowd as men lay wagers and crowded the paling. 'It's a pity,' Erik frowned, 'I should have liked Thorir to see my victory.'

Erik looked back towards the Thing. His foster-father was clearly visible on the Law Rock sat alongside Rognvald Eysteinsson, jarl of Moerr; men were thronging the roped off halidom which was the heart of the thingstead itself as the advocates for each man in dispute argued their client's case in law. No weapons were allowed within the hallowed ground marked by the ropes and hazel withies, and Erik allowed himself a snort of amusement despite the pre-fight nerves which were beginning to build within him as the supporters of those in dispute gesticulated and argued their man's case. It would be some time before Thorir would be free from his duties there and Erik clapped Arinbjorn on the shoulder. 'Yes, you are right,' he agreed. 'Let us begin.'

The pair made their way through the crush, and Erik lifted his chin as he spied Bram's opponent for the first time. At the far end of the enclosure Bolli Sigurdsson's men were struggling to restrain a magnificent piebald stallion as it bucked and snorted, its nostrils flaring as it struggled to reach Bram. Arinbjorn smiled. 'There is your boy, he looks a bit of a beast. Are you sure you still fancy it?'

Erik's mouth turned up into a grin as he stooped low to slide between the rungs of the corral: 'Bram can take him, just you watch!'

The noise from the men crowding the paling rose again as they saw Erik enter the ring, and the boy strode towards the centre as a cheer filled the air and Bolli too finally made an appearance. The man vaulted the top rung with ease, and his followers chanted his name as Bolli acknowledged the crowd and made his way down. Erik planted his feet just short of the midpoint and waited. To his surprise and anger Sigurdsson strode beyond the centre of the ring and came to a halt only inches from the toes of his own boots. Brays of asinine laughter came from Bolli's henchmen at the far end of the corral as the jarl's son towered above the son of the king. At nineteen Bolli was already a full-grown man, and his lips curled into a snarl as he stared down his nose at the eleven year old beneath him. Erik felt his cheeks flush at the deliberate humiliation, and he struggled against the overwhelming desire to take a backward step as he craned his neck to look his opponent in the eye.

Despite the forced laughter from Bolli's lickspittles and

the men come down from Lade, Erik stood his ground. Isolated from King Harald's power base in the South by the mountains of the Uplands, the men of the Trondelag had always considered themselves to be a breed apart from the rest of Norway, and despite the friendship which existed between jarl and king, the potential for conflict ran beneath the surface like a dangerous riptide; unseen for the most part, but ready to sweep the unwary away to a grisly death before they could recover their wits.

Erik knew that to react to the deliberate provocation would only invite greater humiliation upon himself before help could arrive; he forced down the shame as he spat through gritted teeth. 'I believe that you have a challenge to issue, jarl's son?' Erik saw disappointment flash across Bolli's features that his adversary had failed to rise to the bait, but he recovered to give a mocking smile as he pushed again to draw a reaction from his young opponent. 'Let us see if your horse has better breeding than yourself, king's runt. Consider that challenge enough.'

Erik's temper flared at the insult, and he managed to control it with difficulty as he snarled a reply. 'Those words have cost you your life, but that is a matter for another day.' He indicated the nearby crowd with a jerk of his head. 'You may as well die wealthy, I suggest that you take the opportunity to wager silver on my victory. I understand that the odds are heavily in my favour.'

A sidelong glance told him that the watching men of Sogn and Hordaland, the other districts which sent representatives to the Gulathing, were as scathing in their opinion as those at his back, Arinbjorn and the men of Fjordane. But his comments drew a ripple of laughter, and Bolli had revealed himself to be little more than a braggart and a bully. It had been the first small victory of the day, and Erik's open handed gesture of incomprehension towards those watching as he made his way back to the horse brought forth the first cries of support from the crowd.

To his satisfaction the mood of the onlookers seemed to have stirred Bram to an even greater degree, and the horse bucked against the restraining ropes as Erik threw his foster-brother a wink. The look of thunder fell from Arinbjorn's face as he saw that Erik had turned Bolli's intended insult against him, and his face came alight with anticipation as Erik indicated that he slip the ropes to begin the fight.

It took a moment for the horse to realise that it was finally free, but a slap on the rump set it in motion and Erik danced aside as the animal shot past him towards his foe. Milking the crowd as he sought to drum up support Bolli had taken a little longer to regain his friends, and Erik watched gleefully as his men hesitated to release the beast while their lord was still between the pair. The excited cries of the crowd finally sent Bolli scrambling aside, but Erik's quick thinking had not only caused him to lose face but left his horse at a disadvantage. Bram was almost up with them, and the added momentum told as he slammed into the flank of his opponent before the horse could turn to face him. Bolli's men were sent flying backwards as the great bulk of the horse crashed into the paling; unequal to the task it gave way in a crack of splintering wood, and Bolli's mouth gaped in horror as Bram rose onto his hind legs, poised to crash down on the vulnerable belly of his horse. The crowd sensed a quick end to the fight, and their cries fell away as the shadow of Erik's horse darkened the body of his opponent; but a heartbeat later the silence was broken as a whip cracked out, and Bram, his attack forgotten amidst the pain, wheeled away.

Erik's eyes went from Bram to Bolli as the victory was snatched from his grasp. It was expressly forbidden to take anything other than a goad into the fighting space, but the look of satisfaction on the face of the jarl's son told them all that he was the type of man who thought that rules and convention belonged to other, lesser, folk. The men watching from the sidelines finally recovered from their shock, and the stillness which had hung over the battleground was shattered as they voiced their outrage.

Bolli's horse was attempting to rise and his men rushed forward to help it back to its feet before Bram could return, but as they rolled the great body back on an even keel it was obvious to all that the fight was over. Blood pooled where the horse had lain amid the broken fencing, and Erik saw the cause for the first time as the horse struggled upright. Bolli had seen it too, and the man's shoulders slumped as he realised that his efforts to prolong the fight had been in vain. Men were entering the corral now as they too saw Bolli's horse impaled on the broken shaft, the blood pumping out to redden the grass all the confirmation they needed that the fight was already over.

A familiar voice sounded at his side, and Erik threw a final glare of hatred at Bolli before turning away. He gave Arinbjorn a look of puzzlement as he realised what his friend was asking of him. 'What do I want done? What do you mean? Every man here can see that Sigurdsson has no honour; the tale of it will go back to the halls with their owners. Bolli is disgraced, there is no need for me to add anything in the eyes of the men here.'

Arinbjorn indicated Bram with a sigh. Erik looked across for the first time and saw that Thorir's huskarl Horse Hair Gisli had come up from the halidom and was leading Bram across. As men parted before them they exchanged looks of disquiet; others were drifting away casting fearful looks back across their shoulders, sensing the trouble to come. Arinbjorn spoke again, and Erik looked at him in bemusement. 'Men are going to fetch their weapons, brother. Will you accept compensation, or will the matter be decided at spear point?'

Gisli reached them before he could reply, and Erik saw for the first time what had prompted Arinbjorn's question. Bram's left eye had been destroyed by the tip of the scourge; all that remained was a gory mash set within a dark pit. He shook his head in reply. 'Take an axe to the horse.' He flicked a look back up the field. Bolli was back among his men, and it was clear now why he had brought two shiploads to witness a simple horse fight. Erik shook his head as Thorir's words from the knoll came back to him. 'Your father said that the Allfather spoke to him as he sacrificed at the grove at Hestad, remember?'

Arinbjorn thought for a moment before the light of understanding came into his eyes. 'There will be blood, fire and death before the crops are sown in the spring.'

Erik nodded. 'I will accept no compensation for that which has been done here: it was Óðinn's will. Come,' he said. 'Let us talk to Thorir. He will know what form our retribution must take.'

ERIK STOOD ON THE BANK, and a gentle laughter rolled from him as he watched the girl at her work. Gytha looked up as she noticed that he was there for the first time, the flash of her smile causing a flicker of happiness to run through him. Erik returned the smile as he ambled across and lowered himself at her side. 'You are a long way from the strand fishwife,' he said jokingly. Gytha picked another codfish from the basket at her side and tossed it across. 'Here,' she said, 'there is plenty of work for two. I have to help prepare for the coming of age feast for the king's son when I am through here, and the guests are already beginning to arrive.'

Erik snatched the fish from the air and slid his short seax from its scabbard. Gytha shook her head, pouting her lips in mock exasperation. 'You can't use the same knife that you would take to gut a man, the blade is too thick.' She snatched up a spare knife and flung it onto the grass at his side. 'Here, use this.' Erik turned the short blade this way and that as he examined the cutting edge. Barely more than the thickness of a leaf, the knife tapered down to a wickedly sharp point. Gytha had a fish in her hand, and she held it belly side up as she explained the finer points of fish gutting to the son of Harald Fairhair, king of the Norwegians. 'A flick of the wrist to open up the belly, slide your thumb inside like this and scoop out the innards.' The fish guts slid into the pail between her feet as she made a sideways cut just behind the gills and lopped off the head. 'The heads are collected in the pan to be made into stock, then a quick swish in the bucket of seawater to rinse the muck from the body of the fish and into the pail ready for hanging on the *hjell*. She shot him an impish smile. 'They will be the wooden drying racks you may have noticed lining the foreshore when you beach your longship, lord.'

Erik looked at the fish in his hand, tossed it back into the bucket and pulled a face as he rubbed his hands clean on the grass. 'Why is the daughter of a hersir gutting fish like a thrall woman?'

Gytha stopped what she was doing and crinkled her brow. 'You mean that I should be inside at my loom with the other women of good stock, acting coy as I listen in and they trade tales of their menfolk's battle cunning and bravery.'

Gytha picked up another fish and the blade flashed again. 'I like learning all the things which make the household func-tion as it should. One day soon I shall have a hall of my own, and I will know how to tell the difference between those who are pulling their weight and those who are slacking.' She lowered her hands and looked back again. 'You know me Erik, better than anyone else. I am not like them,' she said, casting a glance back across her shoulder towards the hall.

Erik sidled across as he recognised the melancholy in her voice. 'Yes, I know. That's why I want us to be together.' They had spent most afternoons these last few years exploring the hills and dales together or sailing the faering across the choppy waters of the fjord. His foster-sister was more than a friend, and he knew that she felt the same way towards him.

She put down the knife, and Erik was surprised to see the sadness in her eyes. 'The other women,' she said. 'They want their husbands to be men of reputation; feared and admired wherever they go.' She laid a hand on his sleeve. 'If I were to allow myself to believe that we could be together I would have to wish for the opposite.' He looked at her in confusion and she explained. 'Erik, you are a Haraldsson, the son of the king. If you become a great man you will be too important to marry the daughter of a hersir from Fjordane, and if you fail to live up to the expectations of the king you will very likely not live at all. I hear that the king's consort is producing a new son every year to add to those by-blows which are born to kitchen maids and the like.' She shook her head sadly as the realisation that her words were true showed on Erik's face. 'Besides,' she continued with a pointed look. 'I over-heard some of what my father and Horse Hair Gisli were saying one night, after they had returned from sacrificing at Óðinn's Grove.' She placed a hand on his cheek, leaned forward and kissed him tenderly. 'It was as well they jour-neyed to Hestad. You will need the gods at your side if you are to survive the task they have set you.'

3

JOSTRUDAL

The hubbub in the hall had dropped to a murmur as the warriors crowded the benches, hanging on every word as the skald paced the hearth-side and wove his tale. Erik glanced across from his place at the top table, pride shining in his eyes as the wordsmith leaned into his staff and swept the room with his gaze:

> *The berserks were roaring,*
> *THIS was their battle!*
> *The wolf-coated warriors howling,*
> *iron clattering...*

The young prince had heard the tale of the ship fight at Hafrsfjord many times, but the treasure never lost its lustre. It had been the final great battle in his father's bid to overcome the kings of the North Way, the last stand of those who opposed his will. Harald had pledged years before that he would neither cut nor comb his hair until the country was one under his kingship. With this victory his enemies were either dead or fleeing the land never to return, and Erik's father had fulfilled his promise: Harald Lufa, Shaggy Harald became Harald Fairhair, the first king of Norway.

Arinbjorn laid a hand on his sleeve, and Erik turned aside as the skald chirruped on. 'Father asks that we join him outside.' Erik turned and furrowed his brow in question, reluctant to leave before the tale was concluded, but he saw the excitement in his foster-brother's eyes and he drained his cup as he stood to go. 'I thought that this was meant to be a celebration of my coming of age?' he replied, but Arinbjorn was already out of earshot and Erik shrugged his shoulders and followed on. A wolfhound moved aside with an expectant look, hopeful of a morsel from the table; Erik tossed it a meaty bone, running his fingertips through the wiry coat as he passed. The cold air on his cheek told him that Arinbjorn was through the doorway, and Erik hesitated as he felt the tension rise in the room and even whispered conversations trail away:

> *He stopped the ships*
> *when the strife he expected,*
> *blows struck on shields;*
> *ere Haklang was fallen…*

It was the start of the battle. Most of the men in the room had hefted their shields and ringed their lord as he had led them over the prow, clearing the deck of the enemy ship; driving its crew back beyond the mast. Eyvind Glum had made his stand, at the stern with those men who were true to their oaths, and Thorir had earned his own foster-brother's lifelong gratitude when he had sent the king's enemy to Óðinn's hall that day. It was a good tale but it was a tale of other men, and Erik snorted as he ducked through the doorway as he sensed the chance to weave the first stanza of his own.

Thorir was on the far side of the yard with Horse Hair Gisli, deep in conversation with a full bearded man he had never seen before and he wondered at it. Away to the south-east the new moon shone bright from a vault sprinkled with stars, bathing the hillside with its steely light and turning night to day. In full view of the comings and goings of thralls as they went about their work, men would see them clearly as they came from the hall to use the piss trench which had been dug for the occasion. Before his disappointment could make itself fully felt, Erik and Arinbjorn were up on the group. Thorir raised his eyes as they drew up, and the hersir indicated the visitor with a roll of his head. 'This man is Kari Hallsson, a hunter and tracker who works the highlands of Jostrudal and the valleys and woodlands to the East. His brother is a bonder of ours who farms further up the Nausta Valley, paying *skat* as did his father before him.' He clapped the man on the shoulder. 'They have always been among the first to send tribute and answer the war arrow's call when the hird has need of bolstering. They are an honourable and trust-worthy family.'

The man inclined his head in gratitude at the respect shown towards his clan, the great bush of his beard splaying on his chest like a breaking wave as he did so. 'It is *my* honour to be in your presence lords,' he said. He turned his head towards Erik and dipped his chin a little further. 'And to be of use to a son of the king on such a day as this.'

Erik acknowledged the greeting with a nod before turning his eyes to his foster-father. 'Kari has the right of it. What could be so important that it would call me away from my own coming of age festivities?' A thrall woman passed by with a cheese from the store, and Kari surprised the younger men by turning back to the others and raising his voice a notch. 'Yes, lord,' he said earnestly, 'a wolf it was, a big one too, an old grey muzzle. He must have been driven out of the pack, or he is just a loner; either way he is helping himself to a meal from our traps and he has no fear of us. Something needs to be done.'

The woman stole a glance back across her shoulder, and her pace increased just a touch as she approached the door to the hall. Thorir and Gisli shared a look, and the pair snorted as a flash of buttery light played upon the sets before the door closed with a thump. 'That should do it, lord,' Gisli said. 'She has a mouth on her like Sognefjord that one.'

Erik and Arinbjorn were clearly bemused, and Gisli began to explain. 'Kari *is* a huntsman, but it is not old grey muzzles which are to be our prey but young bucks.' He flicked a look at Thorir, and the hersir continued with the explanation. 'I have been doing more than gathering in the crops and preparing for winter since we returned from the autumn Thing. I had men travel up to Nidaros and Lade to see what they could discover about the movements and habits of the jarl and his boy.' He flashed them a look of triumph as Arinbjorn and Erik began to hope that retribution for the humiliation at the Gulathing was at hand after all. 'Bolli Sigurdsson and three score of Sigurd's huskarls left the Trondelag to spend this Jule with his favourite leman at a hall near Dofrar.'

Erik looked crestfallen. 'Whether Sigurdsson intends to spend a cosy Jule at this place with his mistress or not, we will never be able to attack him before he is forewarned. Dofrar is too far from the sea and the roads inland are snowbound at this time of year.'

Arinbjorn shook his head. 'You are too easily dissuaded brother.' He turned his gaze to the man at his side. 'No man who could spend all winter on the hills and fells would need the help of his lord to chase away a toothless old wolf.' He shared a smile with his father before turning back. 'Kari knows a way; Bolli thought that making you look a fool at the corral would be a fine thing, but you made him a promise that the jest will cost him his life and we mean to help you keep it.'

THE HORSEMEN WAVED in farewell as they guided their mounts back to the track. Kari gave his sister-in-law a parting hug, clapped his brother on the shoulder and vaulted into the saddle. Within moments the guide had exited the yard and cantered to the head of the column. The iron grey light of the false dawn drew a line on the heights to the east, but darkness still held sway in the depths of the dale. *Gormánuður,* Slaughter Month, was drawing to a close, soon it would be *Jólnir*, the month of Jule; the sun would rise midmorning and set little more than four hours later. Blizzards could be expected on the fells, some lasting for days, further delaying their progress; it was the reason why they had left a full month to make the journey to Dofrar and why the wolf story had been so vital to their quest. People gossiped, and tales of powerfully armed groups taking to the hills at this time of year required an explanation. Thorir had provided his foster with a party of forty men, good fighters, men proven in battle; enough to set tongues wagging, but not so great that untrustworthy eyes would count it an army. It was the reason why they had made such a show with the heavy hunting spears as they had left Thorir's hall at Naustdal; despite the season ships came and went via the North Way, the channel which sheltered in the lee of the string of offshore islands and skerries and gave the country its name. Even during the season of storms, Sigurd Jarl's hall at Lade was little more than a few days' sail to the North; traders came and went: men talked.

Erik glanced across as the horses picked their way eastwards in the gloom. 'That was a good meal and better company. Thorir was right, you have a fine family Kari.' The guide beamed at the praise from the king's son and pulled a cheeky smile. 'You were expecting salmon then lord?'

He raised a brow at the man's cockiness before his mouth curled into a smile. Self-assurance was a valuable trait in a guide, and he replied with a chuckle. 'This close to the Hove-foss, yes,' he admitted, 'I did. I know that most of the bonder downstream of the waterfall stock up on salmon and sea trout in late summer. I daresay that elk meat is one of the benefits of having a huntsman as a brother.'

Erik looked through the trees to the dark line of the River Naust. Following its course the shredded waters which marked the position of the foss came into view, gleaming as they cut the vale despite the gloom. 'How long will it be before we can expect to encounter deep snow?'

Kari screwed up his face. 'A dozen miles or so yet, lord.' He looked at the sky. The band of grey which marked the returning sun had widened, but the stars still reigned in a sky as cold and hard as iron. The guide turned back with a smile. 'This weather is perfect for our journey. We will be in the foothills tonight and on Jostrudal itself around midday tomorrow. There is a hut at the head of the valley where we can rest up before then, and then it is up onto the high fells.'

It was the first time that Erik had trodden the mountain paths at midwinter and the young prince pumped the guide for information as he sought to order his mind. Despite Thorir's recommendation it was his own life on the line, and he knew that he needed all the details he could gather before they came into any danger. 'Snow would have been falling for months up in the highlands. How can we expect the horses to carry us through with only a few hours of daylight?'

'Þórr himself helps us, lord,' Kari explained in reply. 'We

sacrifice and dedicate our kills to old red beard and he makes it possible for us to work the highlands during the months when the animals wear their best winter coats.' Erik cocked his head in question and Kari fished inside the pouch at his side. Withdrawing a small figure, he held it up for all to see as he continued with his explanation. 'If you look, lord,' he said, 'you can see Þórr grasping his whiskers, pulling them apart as he blows through to create the wind.' Erik looked at the small bronze figure as the guide held it up to the wan light and turned its face to him. 'Because the mountains are so high they are nearer to his hall, *Bilskirnir,* lightning strike, up in Asgard, so the winds are fierce.' He gave a chuckle. 'You wait until we reach it, lord. If you think that the gales at sea are strong, you might be in for a surprise if we are out of luck. But,' he added with a look of triumph. 'Because the winds are so strong they compact the snow, pushing it together harder and harder with each and every blow until by this time of year it will bear the weight of men and even horses.' Kari glanced at the sky again. 'With the clear skies we have had over the last few days, it will be as cold as Hel's dark hall up there. If we rope the horses together to help them travel across the slippery surface, we should be able to make good time.'

Erik remained unconvinced, but his foster-father seemed content to place his life in the hands of this mountain man and it would be unbecoming in a son of Harald Fairhair to show fear. The uplands men called Jostrudal contained some of the highest peaks in the whole of Norway; if a storm did hit while they were exposed up there, Þórr could very well finish what Bolli Sigurdsson had started, back at the horse fight.

The conversation had taken his mind away from the pathway ahead, and Erik looked up as the roar of water on rock broke into his consciousness. The track rose as it skirted the thundering waters of Hovefoss, and the little column climbed up out of the shadows and into the pale light of a northern winter. Free from the confines of the woodland, Erik could just make out the crescent of the sun as it peeked above the crinkled crags on the skyline to the South.

Within the hour the path was rising again, the incline increasing steadily now as the foothills of Jostrudal itself hove into view in the distance. The temperature fell with each mile travelled, but the increasing elevation lengthened the hours of daylight available to them as they cleared the shadow filled confines of the valley floor. A dusting of snow became a fall, and very soon the drifts were above the hocks of the animals as they trudged steadily towards their destination. Conversations lessened as the cold seeped into tired bodies and minds, and it was with a sense of joy that the hut which was to be their home for that night came into view.

Kari turned back with a smile. 'Another early start tomorrow lord, and we will be up on the fells long before sunset.' The guide twisted in the saddle, squinting as he peered back westwards. Erik followed his gaze. The sun had left the sky long before, but the pale glow which marked its passing still blushed the horizon. The temperature had plummeted in the last hour, but the skies remained clear and the threat of fresh snow seemed remote for now at least. Kari confirmed his thoughts as they turned the head of their mounts away from the path and pointed them towards the shelter. 'Best we make the most of the good going,' he said. 'The mood can change quicker than a she-bear in heat up there.' He hawked and spat into the snow. 'And be just as dangerous.'

.   .   .

ERIK GAVE two sharp tugs on the rope which bound him to the mountain man and urged his mount forward with a press of his knees. It was the agreed signal that he wished to talk, and Kari drew rein, bringing his own horse to a halt as he waited for Harald's son to come up. Erik moved forward, craning his neck as he bellowed above the roar of the gale. 'How much further?'

Kari attempted a smile of reassurance, but both men knew that it was half-hearted and he quickly thought better of it. Erik's hopes dropped a little more at the thought that there was a good chance that the man was lost, and he knew that he would have felt far more confident had he never tried; if he *was* lost they were very likely dead men. Kari was speaking again, and Erik strained to listen as the wind snatched up the words and threw them away to the East. 'There should be a gentle dip ahead, lord, not much more than a short bow shot away. There is a low ridge as you come up the far side, the shelter is in the lee of that.'

Erik nodded that he understood and spoke again, the concern obvious from his tone. 'How close are we to the edge?'

Kari grimaced. 'Close enough.' He pinned him with a look, and Erik felt the first reassurance that day as he recognised the heft in Kari's words. 'Don't worry lord, I will not take you over the edge.' The white line of a smile showed in Kari's beard again, but this time the confidence contained in the man's reply lifted Erik's spirits as he offered a joke despite the mayhem all around them. 'I have never gone over the side before, lord, and I don't mean to start now!' The wind redoubled as he spoke, and he cupped a hand to his mouth as he bawled out again. 'Besides, roped together as we are you boys will all land on top of me if we do go: it would spoil my good looks!'

Erik snorted as he recalled the name which Thorir's man Helgi had called the guide, Elk Kari, back at the hut. It was said that he had hunted elk on the high fells so long that he had begun to resemble one. A bulbous nose and widely spaced eyes did nothing to quash the rumour among the more superstitious folk back in Naustdal that he had been sired by one of the great animals, and if that was the case Erik thought, he could think of no other he would rather lead them at this moment.

Reassured, Erik clapped the guide on the shoulder as he fell back into line. He made sure to catch the eye of the men immediately to his rear as he did so, throwing them what he hoped would be taken as a reassuring wink. Only the nearest men's eyes were visible in the near whiteout, red-rimmed and sore as they battled against the effects of the wind driven snow. Hooded travelling cloaks of the densest weave were pulled tight, while even breeks of wool-backed leather struggled to hold the worst of the bone chilling wind and damp at bay. On top of it all the upper body of each man was swathed in fur, bear for Erik less noble animals for the huskarls, the side facing windward as snow covered as the peaks which surrounded them.

Kari's reference to the nearby precipice caused Erik's mind to wander back across the day as the men lowered their eyes once again and the horses struggled forward. They had been in the saddle as the first light flared in the eastern sky. Long before the sun had appeared, the track had left the valley floor and plunged into the wildwood. Slowly, as the light returned, oak and elm had been replaced by fir and beech and by midday they were clear of the tree line, the snowy path dog-legging as it climbed the valley side, skirting waterfalls which tumbled down to mist the air from the heights above.

At first the journey had been uneventful, the stillness of the high fells broken only by the soft crunch of freshly fallen snow beneath hooves and the occasional snort or whinny from the animals themselves. Half a mile to the West the far side of the vale had shone in its seasonal cloak, with only the odd grey slash where bare rock showed through to taint the flawlessness of the white wall which greeted their looks. Golden eagles soared as they rode the updraft, away to the North the pale winter sunlight shimmered from the icebound waters of Oldevatnet.

By early afternoon the clouds had swept in from the West and the first flakes of snow, as large as silver coins, had begun to fall. Very soon the sun was little more than an indistinct smear, low down to the West; the wind rose by degrees, and before they could reach their destination for that day land and sky had merged and the soft-as-a-feather snowflakes had become arrowheads as a full scale blizzard drove them at man and beast alike.

A jolt and the column had stopped again. Kari was out of the saddle, boar spear in hand as he probed the surface, and the relief which washed through the men in the column was palpable as the elk-man turned back and threw them a smile of triumph.

4

A BURNING

'Either I am going deaf or the storm is finally blowing itself out.' Erik heaved himself up onto the narrow stone shelf, licked a fingertip and held it to the flow. He turned back with a smile. 'I thought so, it's no longer screaming death: the wind has dropped to a gale.'

The others, despite the discomfort, raised a smile in return. Thorir Hersir had always said that you could never tell a man's real worth until he was faced with adversity; the past two days had been that and more.

If the storm which had burst upon them had caused them on occasion to doubt the abilities of their guide, the manner in which he led the party directly to the mountaintop shelter had fully restored the men's faith in him. Wind driven snow had completely buried the refuge, but the guide had led them unerringly to it despite the whiteout which had smothered the little band. Two walls of stone had been constructed in a crisscross fashion in such a way that at least one part of the haven must always be sheltered from the direction of the wind. Kari had explained as the men set to work digging out the packed snow, that it was an unspoken duty of all men who habitually travelled the highlands that they collect mosses and lichen from the route and deposit them at the shelters for use in time of need. A fire was soon blazing that night, small and delicate, but enough to warm a little broth for each man. It had thrown back the darkness, and the men had hunkered down to see out the worst of the gale as the wind howled and shrieked about them.

The horses had suffered the most, but although they were exposed to a greater degree to the violence of the storm, the remaining walls had offered shelter from the worst of it and their sheer bulk and habit of bunching together had saved them. By periodically switching the horse's place in the line each had only spent a short time exposed to the worst ravages of the storm, and with the gale clearly blowing itself out Erik was pleased to see that they seemed none the worse for their ordeal.

As soon as they were sure that the worst was behind them Erik led the group from their refuge, and men stretched and flexed weary limbs for the first time in days. Elk Kari came across as the men crossed to make a fuss of their mounts. 'We need to grab this chance to cross the highlands with both hands lord,' he said. 'The storms up here have a habit of coming in pairs.' He gnawed at his lip as he switched his gaze out to the West. Erik's own eyes were drawn across as he did so. The outline of the far side of the valley was beginning to harden from clouds still heavy with snow, and a glance away to the South told him that it was coming up to midday. The higher elevation up on the fells would give them a little more time before the long northern night closed in about them once again, and Erik turned back with a frown. 'You say that the storms often come in pairs.'

'That they do lord.'

'How long do we have if that is the case here?'

The guide clicked his tongue as his eyes scanned the lightening sky. 'It's not always easy to say,' he replied finally. 'But it does look like it's clearing away for now.' He scratched at his chin as he thought; finally Kari reached a conclusion. 'More than half a day, I would say. Hopefully more like two. If we do get two full days we will be dropping down into Ottadal, but if the weather looks like closing in again we can take one of the gullies which lead to the East and be back on lower ground before it really hits.' He cuffed a drip from the tip of his nose and sniffed. 'I would rather keep to the high fells if I can, there are a few scattered settlements in the valleys to the East and the drifts will cause us problems. I doubt that they could warn our friends up ahead that we were on the way, but why take the chance?'

Erik nodded. 'Up here, though. Will the fresh snow slow us down?'

'In the valleys it would.' Kari walked a few paces from the dead ground beyond the shelter. As the men watched in amusement, he jumped up and down and shot them a smile. 'Not on the high fells though. As I said before, lord. The wind packs the snow together as it lands. Any that does not get blown away is as hard as stone in moments. It's another reason why we would be far better travelling the highlands if we can, there are no drifts and hidden potholes to slow us down.'

Erik felt his confidence returning for the first time since the storm had hit. 'Let's get moving then, the sooner we start the better.' The men had been working the horses as the pair spoke, and Helgi handed his own reins across as the men mounted up.

Kari's judgement had been sound and they made good time that day. As the last of the light paled in the West men tore strips from their cloaks to wind around the base of their spears. In the gathering gloom the spears became torches, the party snaking forward towards their destination under an oval of light. Kari led, the guide's horse as at home in the mountains as any elk or hare, picking out the path unerringly as they closed in on their goal. A rocky outcrop became the next rest point, the war band gathering in its lee as the stars looked down and the moon waxed to first quarter. Barely rested, the men were on the move again as the first line of grey cut the skyline to the East, and by midday on the fourth day the great shoulder of rock which was Jostrudal was trending downwards. As the sun lowered that day to become an indistinct glimmer and the clouds returned to bunch up in the West, Kari was leading the column down into the sheltered valley of Ottadal.

A shepherd's hut, abandoned now to the winter snow sheltered the party that night, and daybreak revealed a sky cloaked in grey. Erik looked back as the column made their way down to the long line of Lake Vaga. The peaks which edged the fells like twin sentinels brooding over the upper valley, Glittering and White Spear, were lost now as a ribbon of greyness sat on the roof of Midgard, and the horses breasted the snow as they made their way down into the main valley.

The going was tough and the light had all but left the sky when the banks of the great lake were reached, but as the long night deepened its hue the clouds cleared away to reveal the spectral glow which men called the Northern Lights illuminating the way ahead. By using the frozen foreshore as a pathway, Kari had led Erik and his men to the outlying farmstead which had been marked to host the war party during the short daylight hours prior to the attack, and the men snatched what rest they could in the manner of warriors everywhere as their hosts strove to fill empty bellies with fresh bread and hot broth.

As the shadows on the snow lengthened once more and moved around to the East, Erik called the men together.

'I don't intend to outline what we are about to do, nor how we will go about it.' His face tightened into a smile. 'Anymore than I would tell your grandmother how to use a needle and thread. As you know, Elk Kari and I rode a few miles along our intended route earlier and the way ahead is clear. That means,' he said, 'that we can leave the skis where they are on the spare mounts.'

The men exchanged looks of relief as the rumours were confirmed. Every man there was an experienced skier, but they were all well aware that even a minor injury sustained during the assault could result in them being left behind.

Horses of course were also a far quicker and less tiring means of travelling. They had already experienced the savagery of a highland storm and had no wish to repeat it. If the weather denied them a quick return across Jostrudal following the attack they could very quickly find themselves outnumbered in a friendless country, and no man there harboured any illusions as to their chances of surviving such a thing.

Erik was pleased to see that they were all attending his words. This was the moment he had feared, more than traversing the roof of the world in midwinter, more than the attack itself. He had taken Thorir Hersir's advice on how to conduct himself and was thankful for it, but every man before him was an experienced huskarl and he was a man of twelve winters; although they were well aware of his lineage and respectful of it, his own worth would have to be won, his own reputation wrought in the hard game of war. He glanced across to the square of calf gut which allowed the pale winter light to lift some of the gloom from the interior. The skin was darkening rapidly as the sunlight left the valley, soon it would be time to fix the wooden shutters into place; it was time to go. 'To our horses then,' he said finally. 'Let us do this thing and take ourselves home.'

Erik threw the door ajar as the men gathered up their spears and shields and bunched in his wake. Stepping outside into the wan light of mid afternoon, Erik made his way across to the barn. He allowed himself a smile as he recalled the happy snorts and whinnies of the animals as they had been led into the shelter that morning. They had had a tougher time of the journey, far more so than the men and that had been hard enough, and he could sense their disappointment that the rest was over as he hauled at the great doors and equine heads turned his way. His own mount sidled across and Erik teased an ear, moving the hand down to stroke the animal's neck. Helgi had already saddled the beast, and Erik led it out into the courtyard as the others saddled their own. Soon all was ready, and Erik stole a look at the bonder and his family as they stood and watched them prepare to depart. He threw Kari a look as the guide moved his own horse to his side. 'You are sure that they can be trusted?'

'Yes, lord,' he replied. 'I have known Odd for years. My men and I have always stayed here if we are ever stranded by bad weather on this side of Jostrudal. He is kin to one of the lads; he knows how to keep his mouth shut.'

Odd had a son, a young man of fourteen or fifteen by the look of it, and Erik called him across as the last riders moved into place behind him. 'Here,' he said, as the nervous lad approached and dipped his head, 'take this.' Erik slipped a silver ring from his arm and tossed it across to the moon faced karl. 'One day you can tell your own son that you received the ring from Erik Haraldsson, the day he came to stay.'

A quick tally and Erik led the party out of the yard and turned the head of his horse to the North. They had twenty miles or so to travel until they reached the hall which contained his enemy, but they now knew that the snows around Ottadal had been late in coming that year and the way ahead was clear. Within a few miles a flicker drew their eyes skyward, and soon they were riding forth beneath a witches brew as the Northern Lights returned to weave their patterns of green and red. Erik glanced back along the column as the ghostly lights danced above their heads, and his heart leapt as he recognised that the men had drawn the same conclusion; Óðinn himself was lighting the path to their destination, and Erik thought on the tales he had heard around Thorir's hearth as the frost covered snow crunched beneath his horse's hooves. Most men said that the shimmering light was the bridge from Midgard to Asgard opening up to receive the spirit of a hero; but he had always favoured the other, that the lights were the reflections made by moonlight playing on the mail, helm and spear point of a valkyrie. It mattered little, he knew; both explanations indicated that a man of high rank was about to make the journey from which no man returned.

With the gods-light showing the way the miles went beneath their hooves, and long before the first trace of grey-ness entered the eastern sky Erik was leading the war band out of the mouth of the valley, following the course of the frozen beck as it snaked down into Gudbrandal. After a few miles Kari urged his mount alongside and pointed away to the north-west. 'There it is, lord, that is the hall.'

Erik's gaze followed the guide's outstretched arm. Gudbrandal was broad and deep: away to the North the high-lands of Dofrarfell shone white beneath a mantle of snow.

The valkyrie still stood poised above, bathing all in her flickering light as she waited for the moment to swoop down and gather in Bolli's soul, but the vale was thickly wooded and Erik struggled to pick out the building from the gloom.

Kari noticed and moved his hand down to point at the valley floor. 'Down there is the settlement of Dofrar itself,' he explained, before slowly moving his arm across. 'Follow the line of that low ridge, and just before you reach the tree line you can just make it out.'

Erik did as he was bid, and he nodded as the hall finally revealed itself as a solid shape within the wider gloom. He flashed the guide a triumphal grin: 'I have it.'

ERIK CHEWED at his lip as his eyes flicked from side to side, searching out the shadows. 'You are sure?'

Helgi nodded, the glint of his helm bright in the gloom. 'Yes lord, I have circled the hall; there are no dogs and not a soul abroad.'

Erik flicked a look across his shoulder. Elk Kari was still there, and the guide's deliberate nod told him that both men knew the reason for the look. Erik pushed down the shame he felt that he had doubted the man, but the truth was that the attack seemed to be going just a little bit *too* well.

Deep snow drifts had denied the fields which flanked the valley side to them, forcing Erik to travel the roadway which snaked along the foot of Gudbrandal itself. At every settlement or collection of huts he had expected to receive a challenge, but either the hour was too late, the distance from potential enemies too great or the sight of so many armed men abroad in the depths of the witching hours too alarming to draw men from their hearth or bed. Doors had remained resolutely closed as they put the final few miles behind them, and soon they were guiding their horses along the track which led to the hall itself. Hobbling the horses in the lee of a woodland outlier they had come forward to discover that the gods were still smiling on their enterprise; neither palisade nor ditch ringed the buildings, and with the confirmation that any dogs must also be warming themselves at the hearth side Erik suspected a trap.

Helgi shared his worry, but the huskarl spoke again as Erik hesitated. 'The men are in position, lord. If this is a trap we are already snared. If not we need to do this thing and be far away before daylight.' His gaze shifted back down to Dofrar. 'We have no idea how many fighting men the town contains. As soon as the town watch sees our flames the place will come alive.'

Erik nodded that he understood. The man was a seasoned warrior, a veteran of raids and fights from Dublin to Wolin, a leader of men: it was the reason that Thorir had sent him along after all. Erik ran his eyes around the compound a final time and gave the order: 'light the brands.'

Sparks flashed at his side as fire-steels were struck, and soon the hall was enclosed by a ring of flame. As the torches were lit, Erik drew his sword and strode free of the shadows. Planting his feet foursquare before the doorway, he filled his lungs as men all around hurried forward beneath comet tails to touch flame to thatch.

'Bolli Sigurdsson!'

The challenge was met by the first dog barks from within as the animals finally fulfilled their duty to their masters, but no storm of arrows had met them as they had walked free of the shadows and Erik allowed himself a smile as he came to know that he had his enemy at his mercy. The sound of men rushing to their arms came from the hall at last, the gruff calls of fighting men mixing with the panicked cries of thralls and women as the fire took hold and smoke began to fill the building.

The door was pulled inward, and Erik heard the unmistakable sound of sinew straining against horn to either side as arrows were nocked and bows raised and sighted at the opening. Erik's men crowded the flanks, shields and spears raised as they dared any occupant to attempt to flee as the voice Erik knew so well came from the blackness.

'I am Bolli Sigurdsson. Who seeks to burn me in?'

The fire flared as a sudden wind gusted up the valley, the roar of the flames causing Erik to delay his reply. Despite the lateness of the year the deeper layers of thatch were as dry as old bones from the heat of the long hearth, and the faces of the attackers were revealed as the flames rolled and licked above the ridge line. Despite the growl of the flames, Erik thought that he heard the intake of breath from the man inside as the flickering light revealed him to his victim. Helgi recognised the danger in an instant, and the huskarl's shield came up to protect the king's son from an arrow loosed from within.

Erik took the opportunity to announce himself as the breeze lessened and the flames settled once again.

'I am Erik, King Harald's son: I give you leave to send out women and thralls, but you are fated to die here Bolli.' Despite the danger from spear or arrow, Erik could not help but flick a look up at the night sky. The lights had flared since the attack began and a thought entered his mind as he spoke again. 'The Rainbow Bridge awaits you Bolli, though I doubt your worth. Go, prepare yourself for the journey for you shall not leave this place alive.'

The first women and thralls were hurrying through the doorway, and Erik was pleased to see that his men were moving among them, flicking at clothing and head coverings with the tips of their spears. It was not unknown for those trapped inside to try to escape disguised as women or slaves, and although it was the action of a *nithing*, Bolli had already proven himself to be such at the Thing. Besides, the very public slight to his honour which he had suffered at the horse fight had driven any feelings of mercy from Erik's heart. As the flames redoubled in intensity a roof beam gave way with a crack to send the last of the women tumbling through the doorway. Satisfied that all those who wished to take up his offer of quarter had now left the hall, Erik indicated with a flick of his head that the doorway be sealed. As the contents of the woodpile and debris of the yard were heaped up, Bolli Sigurdsson's final words carried to them through the smoke:

> *'The flame thirsty warriors,*
> *Will boast of the burning:*
> *When wood sweated smoke;*
> *Their zeal will be repaid,*
> *When ravens gorge on Erik's flesh.'*

5

DRAGONS

W ind howl and a stab of chill air announced that the door to the outside world had been opened to the occupants of the hall. A flash of light lit the space beyond the wooden screen which divided the cross passage from the great room of the hall itself, blinked and went out as the door was closed again to the storm. It could only be the watchmen returning from their stint atop the nearby headland, and Erik tagged along as Thorir and Bergthora rose from their high seats and crossed to the inner door. It was as they thought, the men struggling from bearskins as they looked forward to a place at their lord's hearth. Bergthora showed the men honour by presenting them with the first well-earned cups of the evening, and smiles broke out on wind blasted faces as they gulped down the warm brew. Puddles quickly began to collect on the stone floor as the outer clothes were suspended from wooden pegs to dry, and Thorir led them through into the fustiness of the main room after they confirmed to him that the new watch was safely in place and all was well.

Three months had passed since Erik had burned in Bolli Sigurdsson in far off Dofrar, and despite the severity of the winter which had gripped the land, a revenge attack had to be expected at any time. Snow had fallen steadily since Jule, but the same drifts which had closed the mountain paths and valleys to vengeful jarls would also keep the bulk of Thorir's hird from fulfilling their oaths should the jarl come by sea. The threat was very real. The belts and waterways which lent the country the name Norway were sheltered from the roaring ocean beyond by the string of islands which girded the coast like a shield wall. The fjords which made up the region known as the Trondelag were more extensive than the steep sided lands of Fjordane and men could travel freely about the district however impassable the roads and vales became. Thorir knew that he would lay beneath Sigurd's avenging sword blade until the spring thaw could open the way for the war arrow to travel his lands; it was an anxious time. That Erik's raid had not only met with complete success but had managed to return flush with victory was one of the things which gave the men at Nausdal hope that all would yet be well. The storms had held off in their fury just long enough for the band to transit the wild fells of Jostrudal, and despite the difficulties Thorir had led the boys back to the grove at Hestad to offer sacrifice for their deliverance.

A mournful howl filled the air as a strong gust found the smoke hole, and the men sat at the benches shared a look and a smile as they called for more ale. If the winds were strong enough to worry the foundations of a hall as great as Nausdal, even the North Way would be a horror of white horses and spindrift. They were safe for now.

Gytha was moving among them, topping up cups and lifting the winter gloom with her smiles. Erik reached up and pulled her to his side as she came up, laughing along with the rest as the action was met with good-natured catcalls and laments. 'Come and talk,' he said with a smile. 'The men have had enough of your father's ale for now.' At almost fifteen, Erik's foster-sister was only a few years older than he was himself. Universally loved by the warriors of her father's hird, Erik had grown as close as any to the girl in the five years he had spent in Thorir's hall. 'Sit down, have a drink and tell me about your day,' he said with a twinkle in his eye. Gytha laughed, and Erik pulled a face as the men nearby snorted into their ale.

'My day?' the girl said. 'You very know well how my day went, Erik Haraldsson!'

He pressed a cup to her and flashed a smile. 'Tell me anyway.'

'Well,' she replied with mock excitement, 'I just don't know where to begin.'

Erik chuckled as she took a sip from her cup and another gust shook the building. He knew full well that her days were even more mundane than those of the men if that were possible. Cooped up like chicks in a hen house by the winter blow, the months before the spring thaw could seem to stretch without end. A log settled in the long hearth, the resultant glow blushing the young girl's cheeks as she began to rattle off the events of her day. 'After overseeing the work in the kitchen,' she leaned in and dug him playfully in the ribs with a finger, 'so that the men could wake from their drunken slumber to a hearty breakfast, I set to with my needle. Apparently,' she said, 'there is a new Sigurd the Dragon Killer hereabouts, whose first act of manhood was to set the North aflame. I, of course, have been given the duty of helping my mother record the deed for all time with our needlework so that this hero will be remembered for all days, while the wielder of the needle itself will be little more than dust.'

Erik attempted to hide his smile behind his cup as he

questioned her again but his eyes betrayed his amusement. 'Is that all? That seems very little for a strong girl like you.'

As a reply he received a sharp intake of breath, and Gytha gave him a playful slap as rumbles of laughter came from the men within earshot. 'And then I poured ale for men who had little better to do than boast of their manliness, drink, belch and sit around scratching their balls!'

Erik gave her an affectionate hug. Despite the fact that he was now a man and a prince of Norway, his early time at Thorir's hall had been carefree days of fun and laughter as Bergthora had smothered him in the love the death of his own mother had denied him. Harald his father was a man with a voracious appetite where women were concerned, and although he was now the eldest surviving son of the king, even at a tender age Erik had quickly realised that the gods had smiled upon him the day that he had been sent to foster among the close-knit family. The shared triumphs and disappointments of the years had forged a bond between Thorir and Bergthora which, even as a small child, had been obvious to him.

'So, as you can see, my day has been much the same as yesterday and the day before that, and the day before that...' Erik laid a hand on her sleeve as Gytha's voice brought him back and smiled again. 'Yes,' he said, 'I think that I understand.'

She took another sip of her ale and fixed her gaze upon him. 'Erik,' she said earnestly, 'we have always been the best of friends, ever since the day I watched you leap into the shallows from the prow of the ship which carried you north to us.' She dropped her voice so that none but he could hear. 'I ask you this because I know that you will answer me truthfully, without hiding the truth of it from me however grim. My mother and father think that smiling and making light of our situation will stop me from worrying, but it does the opposite.' Her brows drooped as the frown which he knew so well came to her face. Erik stifled a smile of affection; he well-knew all of her moods and knew her to be a girl who chafed to be treated as an adult. He nodded that he would do so.

'Jarl Sigurd will come against soon, either overland, by way of the straits or even both.'

He pursed his lips and gave her a nod.

'Is there no chance that the jarl will accept wergild for the death of his son?'

Erik shook his head. 'If I was unwilling to accept compensation for the death of a horse at the Gulathing, then no, I doubt very much that Sigurd Jarl will be open to a payment in gold and silver for the lives of his son and three score of his finest huskarls.'

A look of disappointment clouded Gytha's face and Erik felt a stab of remorse that his actions had placed all those that were dearest to her in danger, but she recovered quickly to lean in and brush his cheek with a kiss. 'Thank you,' she said, 'for your honesty.'

Arinbjorn was passing, and he knitted his brows in question. Erik shrugged. 'I am a hero. All the girls love a hero.'

Erik and Gytha returned to their drink as he ducked through the doorway, each one unsure how to continue the conversation now that the truth had been spoken aloud. Luckily Gytha's brother had only gone to piss, and he reappeared before the silence became too uncomfortable. 'It was a summer well spent when father had the midden built on the back of the hall.' Another gust howled at the smoke hole and he pulled a face. 'I daresay that the women are even happier about it than the men, especially in weather such as this.'

'They are certainly happier that they no longer have to

watch men who can't be bothered to make the trek to the outhouse piss into the hearth night after night,' Gytha replied.

Arinbjorn snorted. 'You are just envious, there is nowt wrong with a bucket if you don't fancy the walk. Come on,' he said, 'shift up. I want to hear what is so deserving of a kiss on a bleak day like today.'

Erik shuffled along the bench and Arinbjorn settled down next to his sister. Gytha was the first to speak. 'As nobody else thinks that I am strong enough to hear the truth, I asked Erik whether he thought that Sigurd Jarl would accept compensation for his loss.'

Arinbjorn looked across the front of his sister. 'You got a kiss for telling her that we are all dead in the spring?'

'No,' she said. 'He got a kiss for treating me like an adult and giving me an honest answer.' She raised herself to kiss her brother on the cheek. 'And you can have one too for confirming it. We shan't all die anyway, only the men. I shall be taken as a thrall and spend the rest of my life milking cows.'

Erik and Arinbjorn shared a look. 'It looks as if we got the best of the deal then.'

As the cups were refilled, Erik gazed about the hall. Thorir's household warriors lined the benches, their cups and ale horns nestling amid the slops on the tables before them. Each man's shield, spear and sword hung from the wall to his rear, Thorir Hersir's emblem of the black horse proudly proclaiming his allegiance. Twin posts marched the length of the hall, each decorated with tales of gods and men: Þórr and the Midgard Serpent; Baldr's death and Óðinn's ride to Hel. At the head of the hall sat Thorir Hersir on his high seat beneath the *sigil* war flag which flew above him in battle, and beyond that the twin gods-pillars carved into the images of Þórr and Óðinn and the entrance to the lord's private quarters.

Sconces set into the side walls threw out a greasy light, although what little they emitted was almost matched by the amount of smoke from the whale blubber candles they contained.

The days were lengthening now; each and every time that the clouds cleared away to reveal the pale orb of the sun it had risen a little higher in the southern sky. Very soon the weather must break, the snows melt and the first buds of spring scent the air. It was usually a time of joy in the North, as ploughmen toiled, halls were aired and frozen rivers became torrents of icy meltwater. This year it would be different; spear and sword would replace hoe and adze. Erik looked around the hall at the faces before him and wondered who among them would pay the blood price.

THE SPEARMAN DUCKED his head inside the hall, his gaze flitting from face to face as he searched out his lord. Erik was sitting with Arinbjorn and Horse Hair Gisli, and the trio shared a look as they recognised the interruption for what it was. Arinbjorn was the senior, and he caught the man's eye to ask the question which had come into their minds the instant that he had appeared. 'Is this it?'

The huskarl hesitated, but gave a slight nod of confirmation to the hersir's son before he turned to find Thorir. As the men in the hall leapt to their feet, Arinbjorn called after the departing sentinel. 'You will find my father down by the river.'

Men were already taking down their shields from the wall, resting the great boards against the wainscoting as they retrieved mail and helm from their personal chests. Erik's everyday sark and breeks were already on the floor as he went to fetch his own, and he called across to Gytha as she emerged from the women's room to see the cause of the commotion, oblivious to his nakedness. 'Here,' he said, 'you are just in time. Help me into my war clothes. If I am going to meet my ancestors I want to look my best.'

The girl knelt and pulled the trunk from its place below the benches, flipping up the lid with a clatter. 'Which breeks do you want?'

Helgi was already struggling into his mail shirt and he gave Erik a dig. 'Whatever you do, do it quickly.' He dropped his gaze for a moment and winked at the girl. 'You are right breeks would be a good place to start, he is not going to scare anyone off with that.'

Gytha chuckled, despite the tension which crackled in the air about them and reached into the chest. 'Red or blue?'

'Red…no blue,' he replied, 'the ones with the gold braiding at the sides and bottom; and the padded undershirt.'

As the clothes came flying his way, Erik's mind raced. If the men on watch high above the waterway had lit the warning beacon the moment that ships had entered the fjord they should still have plenty of time to prepare to receive the attack. As was usual the wind was in the West, and although it had dropped in strength significantly from earlier that winter, the sleek hull of a longship needed very little tailwind to cleave the waters like a ploughshare. He rattled off the clothing he had decided upon as Gytha continued to rummage in the chest: the red and silver gaiters, red tunic, and knee-length mail shirt.

Gytha paused and raised a brow, her reply dripping with sarcasm: 'yes lord.'

Erik snorted and gave her a wink. 'And don't forget the purple cloak, the one edged with marten fur.' His weapons were still in place on the wall above his chest space, and Erik ran through the best combination of arms before he shrugged and decided that he would take them all: sword; seax; spear; bearded axe.

As the first of the men began to file from the hall, Erik was being helped into his *brynja*, the close-linked mail shirt of a warrior. As it unrolled down his body to fetch up against his knees, Gytha was already holding out his sword belt. He was buckling it around his waist in a trice, and he placed his battle helm upon his head as the young woman retrieved his shield from the wall with a grunt of effort.

'Set?'

Erik glanced aside, and was grateful to see that Helgi had waited until he was ready. The room was almost empty of men now, but the news had reached Bergthora and her women and they were filing from the women's bower, their expressions betraying their anxiety as they went to watch the men decide all their fates.

Erik hefted his shield, and Helgi stood aside to let the son of King Harald lead him to the battlefield. The last men to come filed in his wake as Erik left the smoky building and filled his lungs with the salty tang of the fjord. A quick look to the West told him that the enemy ships were yet to round the final headland, and his eyes swept the area as he strode down to take up his position in the shield wall. Thorir was already on place, bent forward with arms outstretched as Horse Hair Gisli helped him into his own brynja; Arinbjorn was pacing the line, checking that nothing had been forgotten in the rush and offering words of encouragement. Beyond them the waters of Sunnfjord gleamed in the sun. He glanced at Helgi, still stood at his side: 'come on,' he said, 'let us find our place in the wall.'

Ahead the fjord was still free of ships, and Erik felt like a king as he strode down the length of the hayfield towards the men he had come to know so well. Thorir was lifting his chin as he fixed the ties which held his helm in place, and he called across as his foster-son reached the battle line:

'Erik! I want you with me.'

Erik's heart sank, but the hersir was already stomping across before he had a chance to make his feelings known. 'I know that you want to be in the frontline, but accept that I may know what I am doing and follow my orders,' he said with the ghost of a smile, 'just this once. Here,' he said, 'stand beside me on the knoll and tell me what you see. This is your first fight, if you survive it you will learn more in the next hour than I have been able to teach you in the last five years.'

Helgi went away to join the defenders, and Erik cast a longing glance in their direction before he followed Thorir with leaden feet. The grassy mound, the same place where they often breakfasted after weapons practice had been kept clear of the plough for just this reason, and Erik turned and looked out across the heads of the shield wall to the flatter land of the vang and the fjord beyond. Gisli was banner man, and the black horse sigil snapped in the breeze as Erik began to go over the dispositions before them. 'The men are drawn up two deep the length of the lower wall, on the inner side so that they can benefit from its protection. Arinbjorn has placed himself at the centre of the roadway where it cuts the wall with his closest companions to defend the weakest part of the defences.' He turned back and looked at Thorir. 'We are twenty paces back from the main battle line where we can oversee the fight and quickly come to the aid of any place where the enemy are threatening to break through.'

A growl went through the men lined up in their ranks below him; it could only mean one thing, and Erik's head followed the others as they looked towards the sea. A magnificent drekkar was clearing the headland, and within moments the waters were a cloud of sail as the enemy fleet swept into view. It was an overwhelming force, and Erik pushed down the feelings of guilt with difficulty as they threatened to overcome him and he came to know that those he had grown to love, the people who had welcomed him into their hall and made a man of a callow boy, now faced annihilation as a result of his pride.

6

FIVE KEELS

The blaze sawed with each fresh gust; spear points became flames, helms aglow in the firelight as Erik reached the end. He sank the horn of mead and dashed it to the ground, and a heartbeat later the king was on his feet. Harald reached down as Thorir leapt up at his side, and the sound of a thousand spears beating against a thousand shield rims thundered about the vang as Fairhair raised the hersir's arm and made his gratitude plain.

Giddy with pride Erik drank in the atmosphere as the recital came to an end and his father Harald, king of the Norse, came across and flashed a smile. 'Come,' he said, 'walk with me.'

Harald led Erik down towards the strand as his men began to erect tents and start blazes of their own to warm themselves during the night ahead. A cool breeze was blowing in from the fjord, and Erik pulled his cloak a little tighter about his shoulders as he waited for his father to speak.

'You have caused me a problem,' the king began. 'A very big one, and one I could well do without.'

Erik listened as his father went on, unsure which direction the conversation would take. Was he about to bear the blame for the events of the winter?

'Sigurd Jarl is an old friend of mine, a shield brother from the wars of unification. A powerful man, the headman of a powerful region; his support is crucial to me.' To Erik's surprise a rumble of laughter came from the king, and his face broke into a grin. 'And you killed his rat of a son!' The king laughed again. 'The looks on the faces of Thorir's men when we fetched up on the strand; all riled up and nobody to fight!' Harald glanced down at his son. 'How did we look?'

Erik beamed with pride as he recalled the sight. 'Magnificent father. The big drekkar came clear of the headland, and before we even had time to realise that it carried no beast head at the prow our eyes widened at the sight of a fjord filled with snekkjur, the smaller warships bounding along like wolfhounds around the huntsman. And then,' he added with a sense of wonder, 'when you all struck your sails together, wheeled prow on to the shore and ran out the oars.' Erik paused as the sight replayed in his mind. Finally he shook his head, and his voice wavered with emotion as his minds-eye saw again the long blades rising and falling in time. 'I was overawed, lord.'

It was the king's turn to look overjoyed, and he balled a fist and gave his son a light punch on the shoulder. 'That's good,' he said, 'that's what a king of Norway needs to be.' He stopped and looked at Erik, studying his son as he thought. The boy felt the power of the man as he withered beneath his icy blue gaze, but the king nodded as a decision was made. 'You saw how the men reacted as you described the horse fight and Bolli's burning in.' The king shook his head. 'And that trip across Jostrudal in midwinter, even my heart was in my mouth,' he chuckled. He opened his great hand and looked at Erik again. 'You held them there,' he said proudly, 'every one of them hanging on your every word. These are not mild men, Erik, these are men of war; hard men, men who go Viking, men who know what it is to face overwhelming numbers, heft their weapons and bravely march forward.'

Erik looked up. His father was tall even for a Norseman, but the conversation was going well, and he craned his neck as he risked a question of his own. 'How did you know that we were about to come under attack?'

Harald snorted. 'A king who does not know all that goes on, both within the bounds of his kingdom and beyond, rarely remains so; especially in such a kingdom as my own. By leaps and bounds, one short journey after another from one hall to the next, the news of Bolli's death had passed over Upland to the Vestfold and the South in a matter of weeks. Thorir is not so wet behind the ears not to have sent a fast boat south the moment that the weather allowed either. Even as you slogged your way north, my hersir was preparing for the consequences of your actions.'

They had reached the strand, and the king's boots scrunched on the shingle as he raised a hand in reply to the acclamation of the ship guard. High above the first stars were hardening as the sinking sun blushed the western skyline.

Suddenly the king's features brightened, and a smile lit his face as he too recalled the past. 'You have a touch of your mother about you,' he said. Turning his face to his son, Erik felt a thrill course through his blood as he recognised the light of pride shining in his father's eyes. 'I have had a few wives,' the king snorted, 'and I daresay that I will have a few more before Óðinn decides that it is time for me to take my place alongside our ancestors on the family bench. But Ragnhild was the best of them and probably always shall be.' Harald looked again at his son, and Erik was surprised to see sadness there. 'It was a hard time when she died. Do you recall anything of her?'

Erik confirmed that he didn't. He had only been two years old when his mother had died, but he did recall snatches of the journey north. It was the first time that he had travelled on a longship, and the sights, sounds and smells of the sea had thrilled the boy even then.

'I only had her with me for three years,' Harald continued, 'and you were our only bairn. A king has to have a consort and I married Snofrid soon after.' The king glanced down at his son and blew out. 'It's the way of the Finns that their women don't take too kindly to bringing up other women's sons, especially if they are older than their own. They tend to be...' Harald sucked his teeth as his mind searched for the right way to explain the danger he had been in as a child, without making unsubstantiated allegations. Finally he had it, and Erik nodded that he understood why he had been packed off to distant Fjordane with such haste. 'They tend to be, less protective,' the king said. 'Accidents can happen: ships sink; young lads stray in front of bowmen while hunting, that kind of thing.' King Harald changed tack as the conversation threatened to stray from the path he had intended. 'Did you know that Guttorm is dead, and you are now my eldest son?'

Erik confirmed that he did. 'My brother was killed fighting Solvi the Splitter, down on the Gota River. I will kill him for it father,' Erik said earnestly.

Harald nodded. 'Thorir has done his work well, as I knew he would. It is time to reward my own foster-brother's loyalty, and for you to move on to the next part of your life.'

They had reached the place where the big drekkar was moored, and the pair ran their eyes across its sleek lines as the king's guard hovered at a respectful distance. Erik had never seen such a fine ship, and he marvelled at the workmanship as the pair stood in silence. He counted up the oar ports and gasped. Thirty a side meant that with a double crew the warship could bring over a hundred warriors to the place of battle: an army. The prow curled above them, its timber a frieze of serpentine carvings, and although the beast head had been removed lest it frighten the spirits on a friendly shore it seemed clear to Erik that it could only be a dragon.

'It was meant as a gift to your mother's father, the man who you were named for, King Erik down in Jutland.' The king shot his son a wink. 'He is a man I want to keep on good terms with. Not only does he keep the other kings down there busy and away from the Vikken with his constant warring, it seems that the gods intend to keep him in a good supply of daughters. As I seem to produce only sons, we make a good match. The ship will have to go to Sigurd Jarl now,' he said with a shrug. 'Along with a chest of gold and silver.' King Harald clapped his son on the shoulder. 'It is a price worth paying. You cannot make a kingdom without cracking a few heads, but Sigurd fears my power and the way that you took care of his son tells me that you too have the making of a king of Norway Erik. Take yourself off now, back to Thorir's hall and say your farewells. Your time as a prince at foster is over; tomorrow you become a sea king.'

'WHERE IS IT?'

Kolbein Herjolfsson leaned in and pointed. 'You see that arm of rock? The one wearing a crown of cormorants?'

Erik narrowed his eyes, sighting down the man's outstretched limb. A small arm of rock came off the skerry, thrusting through the surging waves like a line of rotting teeth. 'Yes, I see it.'

'Well, there is a small channel which runs between the islands there. It's a tight fit, but it will save us half a day's sailing at this time of year if we don't have to go the long way.'

Erik turned back and regarded his little fleet with pride as they followed on in line astern. In addition to his own ship *Isbjorn, Ice Bear,* four snekkjur breasted the swell, *Bison, Okse, Reindyr* and *Fjord-Ulf.* With each ship carrying twenty rowers a side plus the styrisman and other leaders, Erik commanded a force of over two hundred battle hardened fighting men with which to amass treasure and reputation in the softer lands to the south. After years of drift as he learned the ways of a warrior under the tutelage of two of the best, the boy had suddenly become a man.

A herring gull's piercing cry cut the air, and Erik watched the grey backed bird riding the air current mere feet to starboard as it regarded him with a flaxen eye. Kolbein was heaving the steering oar to his chest as he guided the *Isbjorn* towards the turn, and Erik's mind wandered as the styrisman called instructions to the crewmen working the sheets. It had been two days now since Sigurd Jarl's fleet had appeared in Sunnfjord, and although the presence of the king and his war fleet had meant that Bolli's father had had no option but to accept the compensation offered for the life of his son, they all knew that it was prudent to put as many miles between themselves and the Trondelag as quickly as they could. The hatred he had witnessed in the jarl's eyes as he had been forced to watch Erik lead the ships down towards the open sea had been obvious, and he recalled his father's words of advice as they parted that day with a shiver: *"use the remaining years which the gods grant me to become the hardest man you can Erik. You have made a powerful enemy for life, I cannot protect you from beyond the grave."*

The bows began their swing to starboard, and Erik came back from his thoughts. The teeth were petering out to reveal the mouth itself, whitecaps dotting the narrow channel as the conflicting currents thrashed and boiled. Kolbein saw the look on Erik's face as the swirling waters of the channel were obscured by the upsweep of the prow, and he gave a chuckle of amusement. 'That's nothing,' he said. 'One day I will take you through the Moskstraumen, a great tidal eddy up in the Lofotens. Some people say that the sea god *Njörðr* has his hall beneath the spot, and he sucks down seafarers who lack the skill to cross it. Here,' he said, releasing the tiller and skipping down from the steering platform, 'you take us through, and I will guide you from the bows.'

Erik's jaw dropped as Kolbein continued for'ard, his arm shooting out as he issued his orders to the crew. As he grabbed the tiller and steadied the ship the sail was already being brailed, and the way came off the ship as oars slid proud of the hull. The sail was sheeted home, and it quickly became obvious why they were to shoot the gap under oar power alone. Erik rolled on the balls of his feet, his eyes darting from side to side as he tried to take in as much of the view ahead before the prow blotted it out completely. Kolbein was in the bows, his cloak billowing like a cloud as the wind snatched it up and threw it way to the North, and Erik blinked the windblown spray from his eyes as he attempted to watch for the sign. As the dark outline of the skerry rose up on the starboard side, Kolbein's right arm stabbed out. In an instant Erik had the tiller to his chest, his gaze pinning the man in the bows as the rowers drove her forward. Erik felt the long, sleek hull of the *Isbjorn* give a shudder as the currents threatened to spin her on her keel, but the youth gritted his teeth, braced his feet against the wale and held on tight. A heartbeat later Kolbein was waving to larboard, and Erik pushed the big steering oar away as the ship pivoted on its axis. As the prow came about, sunlight was snuffed out as the ship entered the channel; dark rock towered to either side as Erik fixed the man in the bows with his gaze, but his heart leapt with pride and relief as he turned and flashed him a grin. Erik's belly gave a lurch as the undertow picked up the little hull and funnelled her through, but he allowed himself a smile of satisfaction as he saw the crewmen exchange nods and smiles at his helmsmanship.

Kolbein was walking the deck as oars were shipped and the sail lowered halfway down the mast, and he shot Erik a wink as he came alongside him. 'Now the boys know that you are not just a passenger.'

The waterway beyond the islands was broad and calm, all the choppiness of the open ocean left beyond, and the pair turned back to watch as the other ships made the channel. *Reindyr* shot the gap in a welter of spray quickly followed by *Okse,* and as men whooped and called in their excitement the little flotilla began to gather in the lee of the skerry. Soon the tall prows of the *Fjord-Ulf* and *Bison* emerged from the shadows, and Kolbein shielded his eyes as he raised his chin to the sky. The sun still lit the crest of the island off to larboard, but the smaller island to the West was little more than a dark outline; the day was all but spent, it was time that they searched out a good landing place in which to spend the night. Kolbein raised his arm as he indicated a sheltered cove a mile or so ahead. 'That's a good place to rest up,' he said. 'There is enough room to beach all five ships, and the hill there will shelter us from the westerlies. The prevailing current there-abouts tends to fetch driftwood up on the shore too, so we should have the fires roaring before it gets too dark.'

The wind was fitful in the lee of the island, but up ahead another patch of choppy water showed where the sea poured through a narrower gap in the land. They would have to row if they were to make a landfall beyond it, and Erik ordered the sail brailed up as the other ships laboured to come back into line astern. Erik was overjoyed to see that the crew were turning their faces to him as they awaited the order to run out the oars, and he glimpsed the satisfaction on the face of Kolbein that his ploy had worked. Everyman aboard knew that there had been a dozen ways in which disaster could have overtaken the longship as it shot the narrow channel, but Erik's helmsmanship had carried them through and they had seen for themselves that he was more than the pampered son of a king. He called the command, the blades slid proud of the hull, and the eyes of thirty-two oarsmen fixed upon him as they curled their backs and tensed.

A flash of grey caught his eye, and Erik snorted as he saw that the gull had returned, riding the air current to starboard as it too seemed to await his command. Despite the delay the faces of the men were intent, fixing him with their stares like faithful hounds, and he felt the thrill of the moment as he gave them the order to get underway for the very first time.

'On my mark...'

He raised his boot, paused for a heartbeat, and brought it down onto the boards with a crash.

'Row!'

A grunt came from the men as the oars bit the waves and the *Isbjorn* began to creep forward. Soon the ship was gathering speed, the prow rising and falling as it reached the land breach and breasted the swell, seawater hissing as it sluiced alongside. The gull had taken its leave, finally content that this boy could handle a snekkja as well as any weather-beaten mariner, and Erik laughed as the spray necklaced the prow and he saw that the other ships were making a race of it. 'Come on lads,' he called as prow beasts ranged outboard. 'The *Isbjorn* leads, others follow!'

Kolbein was alongside him, and Erik concentrated on holding his course as the styrisman beat time with his foot. Before him backs straightened and curled again as the rowers redoubled their efforts, and Erik shared a look of triumph with the huskarl as the ship began to draw ahead. The sheltered waters of the cove were drawing closer with each stroke of the oar, and as the ship pulled ahead once again Erik looked about his little fleet with pride. The ships were leaping the waves, seawater streaming from their flanks in silvered rills before they buried their heads in the next wave in a mantle of spray, and his eyes shone with excitement as an image came into his mind. He had been out in the faering working on his ship craft, manning two of the four oars which had lent the little rowboat its name with Arinbjorn two summers past. His foster-brother had been working the rudder when his expression had come alive as he pointed out a pod of *morder-hval* crossing the wide bay of Stavfjord. The murder-whales were hunting, chasing down a shoal as they harvested the deep; black and white flanks streaming beneath a cloud of spray as they broke the surface and drove their prey before them.

The bay was coming up off the starboard wale and Erik tugged the tiller to his chest as the memory faded, the prow sweeping around as he aimed for the shore. Hummocky dunes led back to a ridge of grey rock, its dips and gullies hazed with green where grasses and sea thrift sheltered from the worst of the weather.

Kolbein was back in the bow, guiding him in with a sweep of his arms, and the smiles of the crewmen mirrored his own as the keel grated on sand. As men tumbled into the surf, wading ashore with tents, barrels and cooking pots, Erik secured the steering oar and followed on.

7

THE SOUTH WAY

E rik cursed under his breath as he stumbled again. This far from the fireside the night was as dark as the pitch they used to caulk the ships, and he paused for a moment, lifting his head to gain his bearings. Despite the blackness the ridge top stood out as a jagged line against the lighter clouds beyond; he was almost at the summit, and he suppressed the desire to call out for directions with difficulty. Despite the fact that the chances of an enemy finding their lair was remote Thorir and Arinbjorn had taught him well, and he smiled to himself as the memory of one of the big hersir's no-nonsense sayings came to mind: *only a milkmaid or a thrall worries about trolls and night-gangers, so keep your mouth shut and trust to your instincts.*

He ran his eyes along the summit as he couched his spear, hooking the small bag back onto his shoulder for what felt like the hundredth time on the short trip. Finally the point of rock hardened from the gloom; it was little more than fifty paces to the right of him, and Erik set off again across the slippery rock face. He was soon there, and he returned the smile of the guards as he slipped down beside them: 'food for hungry men, lads!'

Erik handed the hot parcels across to the grateful men and reached back into the knapsack. 'And a ewer of ale to keep your spirits up.'

Erik snorted as he saw the whites of the men's eyes widen, despite the all-enveloping darkness. 'Thank you, lord,' the lookout replied through a mouthful of food, 'that will go down nicely.'

Erik switched his gaze out to sea as the men munched contentedly at his side. The cloud cover was total with not a glimpse of the moon or a star to cast its light on Midgard, but the sea was as calm as a mountain lake, all the choppiness of earlier forgotten. Despite the inky darkness, any ship brave or foolhardy enough to risk the skerries on a moonless night would leave an obvious wake.

'It's just a taste,' he replied. 'On a night like this, I thought that you could use a little cheer.' The smell of the hot bacon was tantalising, and Erik nodded towards it as another mouthful disappeared into Kjartan's mouth. 'Does it taste as good as it smells?'

The men looked horrified as they realised for the first time that Erik had not yet eaten. He held up a hand and chuckled as they both offered up their half chewed remnants. 'It is fine, I have my own waiting for me when I get back. I will have a sip of that though,' he added with a smile. 'It's thirsty work trying to find a way up here in the dark!'

Erik sank a mouthful as his eyes followed the coastline. The islands trailed away to the North, dark stones set into a green sea, each skerry ringed by a halo of white as the waves lapped the shore. Thorir had always drummed into him that a lord led by example, and despite his own hunger Erik knew that his small sacrifice would not be lost on the men before him. Before the ships could be shouldered back into the surf in the morning, the story would have swept the ranks. The king's son put their own welfare above his own; he was one of them, a lord worthy of their loyalty and respect. Erik took another mouthful of the ale as the sentinels finished off their meal, and was pleased to see that their eyes never left the straits and channels below them for more than a moment, despite the distraction of his presence.

The silence was broken as a growl came from his empty belly, and the trio shared a laugh. 'It is best that you take yourself off lord,' Kjartan said with a smile. 'A half starved sea king will be no use to anyone!'

Erik nodded and stood to go. As he did so he saw the anxiety on the faces of the watchmen as their eyes dropped to his side and they realised that he was still holding the ewer of ale. Slinging the leather bag onto his shoulder, Erik make a great show of slowly upending the container as he drank the contents. Looking back, he stifled a smile as the guards struggled to hide their disappointment. He slapped his lips as he popped the bottle back into the sack. 'That was good ale,' he said as he rummaged inside the sack. 'It's as well for you that I brought two.'

THE WIND HAD RISEN as they talked, and the high prows and wide bellies of the ships flickered in the reflected firelight from the strand. Kolbein was speaking, and Erik listened in as the other ship's styrismen added their own thoughts and advice. 'So, what do we think? Gotland? Visby is always full of shipping.'

Alf Karisson, skipper of the fleet and shipmaster of the *Fjord-Ulf* shook his head. 'Not this early in the year, Kolbein, it would be pointless. The traders are on their way south full of furs, amber and ivory: we can get that anywhere.'

'The towns are rich though,' Kolbein countered, 'full of silver.'

'And well guarded,' Skipper Alf replied. 'The richer they have become on the eastern trade, the higher the walls have risen. All the silver is safely stored in the towns these days. Also,' he added with a look, 'we are not a couple of hulls filled with a lowly hersir and his hird, out seeking plunder until the summer is over and it is time to go home and make hay. We have the king's son with us, remember? I doubt that King Harald will thank us for upsetting the king in Uppsala.'

'Vindland then? Take as many captives as we can and head straight up to the slave market at Novgorod. They pay good silver for Vinds, strong men and even stronger women the Slavs.'

Alf shook his head: 'not worth the hassle.'

They all turned their heads to the shipmaster, and he gave a shrug. 'All the rivers are blocked by forts. I was up there a couple of years ago with Arne Gunnarsson from Hordaland. We spent a day and a half storming this fort,' he took a sip of ale and raised a brow. 'It was a hard fight too, we lost a couple of lads, and when we took it all they had there was a few iron pots and pans. All the valuable stuff is too far inland.'

'England? The Danes have grown fat sucking on that teat.'

Alf rolled his eyes, and Erik snorted into his cup as he watched the other shipmasters let out a sigh.

'What's wrong with raiding England then?'

Alf gave them all a look of pity. 'Not any longer they don't. That tit has shrivelled up and run dry, ever since Edward Alfredsson took the king helm they have been fighting to keep the land they took in their father's day. And that sister of his…' He shook his head.

'Athelthing?' Kolbein offered.

'Athelflaed,' Alf corrected him. 'Athelflaed Alfredsdottir, the Lady of the Mercians. She's a valkyrie; I spoke to a Dane once, a trader out of York, who claimed to have seen her riding into battle on the back of an enormous ram. The Danes and a few of the old Dublin Norse tried an invasion a couple of years back; it cost them the lives of three kings and half a dozen of their jarls in a big battle at a place called Tettenhall. You will get nowt but a spear in the guts these days in England.'

'Frankia?'

'Not now that Hrolf the Ganger has been ceded the land around the Seine estuary.'

'Ireland?'

'Maybe,' Alf conceded with a shrug. 'Although Thorstein and his brother Sigtrygg the Squint-eyed have been run out of Dublin for a few years now and settled in Waterford, Man and the Wirral.' He shrugged. 'Most of the Norwegians in the area are only there because they were unhappy under King Harald's rule.' He glanced at Erik. 'I am not casting any doubts on your courage lord, but there are plenty of men sailing the Irish Sea who would love to come across Fairhair's son, men who could darken the sea with ships.'

Erik had heard enough. Leaning forward he fixed each man with a stare as he recharged the cups. The conversation fell away, and the shipmasters, experienced raiders, trusted huskarls of the king waited for the man they now regarded as their leader to speak. He let the silence stretch until he was sure that he had their attention and pulled a smile. A wolf-grey light washed across the beach as the clouds finally parted and the moon shone in the southern sky. Away to the

East, the waters of the North Way took on a steely hue. 'I want to sail due south,' he said finally. He cast his eyes beyond the small group sat before him, out beyond the fire-light where the men drank and joked. Three hundred Norsemen: axemen; swordsmen; bear shirts and wolf coats had been placed under his sole command. He knew, even at the age of twelve, that this was a test; Harald Fairhair had created a kingdom where before there had only been a disparate collection of chiefdoms and petty kings. His father had told him on the strand, back in Nausdal, that he fathered boys; if his life's work had been the creation of a kingdom of Norway, he would be looking for a successor. There could only be one, and Erik knew the likely fate which would await those who failed to gain the prize.

His brother Guttorm had proven unequal to the task, hacked down by an enemy of their clan down in Gotaland. He was the eldest now, but the king's new consort was producing a new son every year; he had been given the means to carve a future, to be the one king, and he meant to grasp the opportunity with both hands. His first act had been to take the life of Bolli Sigurdsson, the son of the king's leading jarl. The next had taken even his father, the king by surprise. The men had expected him to take his place alongside Alf on the steering platform of the *Fjord-Ulf* as he learned the ways of the sea, but he had insisted that he travel on another ship. He was no longer a child to be wet nursed through life, and he thought that he had seen a flash of pride illuminate the face of the king as they had parted that day.

'South,' Erik said finally, 'I want to go south. Not to Ireland, not to King Edward's land of burhs, fyrdmen and craven Danes. Not to Vindland,' he raised a brow, and a ripple of laughter rolled around the shipmasters as he finished his sentence; 'despite the impressive strength of their women.

And not to Scotland,' he added, 'before anyone suggests it. From what I hear it is all midges, damp sheep and porridge; we may as well stay in Norway. What lies to the south of Hrolf the Ganger's lands? Alf?'

'Brittany lies immediately to the South lord,' the skipper answered with a raised brow. 'It is well worth a look. There is a nice fat monastery there that I have had my eye on for a while now.' His lips pulled back into a lupine smile which was slowly reflected in the faces surrounding him. 'Yes,' he said finally. 'With five keels full of King Harald's men, Brittany would be a fine choice.'

THE SHIPS WALLOWED in the swell like fat bellied gulls as Erik stood in the bow and raised the knife. One of the first lambs of the year kicked and squirmed in his fist until a slash of the blade opened the belly, and the watching men fingered gods charms as blue-grey ropes of gut slid free and lifeblood gushed to redden the waves. Kolbein Herjolfsson at his side emptied a barrel of ale into the waters as the carcass fell with a splash, and the sacrifices to Njörðr the sea god completed, Erik indicated that the crewmen move forward to fix the beast head into place.

The rest of the crew watched with pride as the fang toothed head of a bear, the *Isbjorn* itself, was lowered into place on the prow and the retaining peg hammered into place. It was the first time that Erik had seen the snarling beast head atop the prow, and he wondered again at the transformation it wrought to a ship. No longer merely a means of travelling from one place to another, the ship had taken on a persona of its own. All around them the ships were coming to life as the sound of mallet on wooden pin echoed across the waves: the shaggy head and sweeping horns of the *Bison*; *Fjord-Ulf* -

wolfish fangs and glint of eye; *Reindyr* - majestic, its golden antlers wooding the air; *Okse* - power, muscle and bullishness personified.

The ceremony complete, Erik ordered the spar hoist and the great sail shaken out and sheeted home. As the yard inched upwards men were looking at the weathervane, high up in the mast head, hauling at the braces as they angled the sail to catch the wind. Kolbein had the steering oar, and Erik hopped up alongside the big man as they watched the first breath of wind pluck at the sail. Moments later the great sheet billowed, and the crewmen exchanged smiles as the *Isbjorn* took its first great breath and shook itself free of the land. Erik hung from the backstay as he watched the other ships set their own sails, the crack as the great woollen sheets filled carrying to him across the waves despite the rush of the wind. Very soon they were flying south, the island of Kormt hazing astern as the snowcapped peaks of Rogaland came up on the beam.

The wind sang in the shrouds as the great bay which held Hafrsfjord opened up to larboard, and Kolbein showed him honour as he recalled his father's great victory there. The crew joined in as they lounged amidships, beating the rhythm with their boots as they belted out the Lay of Harald:

> '*Did you hear in Hafrsfjord*
> *how hard they fought*
> *the high born king*
> *against Kjotve the Rich?*
>
> *Ships came from the east*
> *craving battle,*
> *with gaping heads*
> *and prows sculpted.*'

That evening they were off the coast of Agder; Lindesnes, the southernmost landfall in Norway was a line to the East as Erik took the watch and pointed their prow to the South.

'STRANGE FRUIT.'

Erik shared a look with Kolbein and snorted. 'Who said that Vikings don't grow on trees!'

The men were crowding the wale as the *Isbjorn* lost way, and Erik turned back. 'I would like to take a closer look.' He shot the styrisman a smile. 'Let us see if the shore guard are as brave when faced with five snekkjur.' He looked up at the weather vane. The sealskin tassels which hung along the lower edge were blowing steadily southwestwards. The gods were with them, if ships appeared they could lower the sail and be off in moments.

'Brail the sheet, lads,' Erik called as he made his way amidships. 'We are going in to see what Hrolf the Ganger's men have been up to.'

It had taken them a full month of easy sailing and harder rowing to reach the mouth of the river which the Franks called Seine, but with every mile of seawater which passed beneath their hulls the days grew a little warmer and a little longer as the southern spring cloaked the land in green. The wandering birds were in the sky, a full two months before they could be expected in far off Fjordane; swifts and swallows cut and dashed, clouds of starlings swept to and fro and the first puffins and gannets skimmed the waves.

The first lands which they had passed had, Erik had had to admit to himself, been a grave disappointment. There had seemed to be little to tell between the lands of the Frisians and the Flemings and the grey waters which were carrying them south. The sandy dunes and salt marsh which reigned everywhere along the bleak coastline appeared little higher than the sea itself to a man brought up among the steep fjords and high peaks of Fjordane. Wise men, men knowledgeable of things which had passed beyond the memory of most, told that this was a land which long ago had contained great trading centres: towns of stone buildings and high walls; jetties and wharfs piled high with exotic goods from the southern sea and beyond when the empire of Rome held sway hereabouts. But the days of greatness had passed, and a century of warfare and plundering by Northmen and others had left little more than the occasional rude hut or stone ruin visible in a land rinsed free of colour and men.

Passing the estuary of the Rhine things began to look up. Crosses appeared above the shoreline and perched on promontories as they reached the lands which had long been Christian; towns appeared, glowering behind their defences as they passed, and ships moved about at a respectful distance as the golden headed snekkjur arrowed south. By the time that the little fleet had reached the narrows where the high chalk cliffs of England and Frankia cast envious looks at each other's wealth the clouds had cleared away, and the sun shone from a clear blue sky.

Skipper Alf had brought the *Fjord-Ulf* up on the beam, cupping his hands to his mouth as he called that they would do well to keep to mid channel and away from the English coast. Kolbein had agreed that they follow their friend's advice. Alf's love of raiding went to his very bones; it was a reason why King Harald had chosen him as Skipper of the fleet, and Erik knew that his father would be as interested in Alf's reports as to his decision making as he would any other aspect of his leadership. As unlikely as it had been that King Edward's ships would have left port to challenge his powerful flotilla, Erik knew that it would have been foolhardy to take the chance.

The men pulled the *Isbjorn* towards the wreck with easy strokes of the oars as the other ships stood off to windward, ready to come quickly to their aid if the need arose. Soon they were a short spear throw off, and Erik ran his gaze across the ship as the oarsmen worked the blades to keep station in the current. At ten oars a side the ship was smaller than his own, and a quick tally of the cadavers festooning the yard, prow and stern post told him that it was still fully manned by a crew of the dead. He had seen dead men before, that was not why he had closed on the wreck, but a comment from one of the men caused him to raise his eyes to the shore. A horseman had appeared on the dunes, and as he watched a dozen more came into view. He had the answer to his question, and he ordered the sail set as the oars were shipped and the sleek hull carved the waves. Alf had been right again, Hrolf the Ganger was taking his new duties seriously; it would seem that the kingdom of the Franks was safe for now.

8

STRANDHOGG

The haunting call drifted from the tree line, and Erik stifled a snigger as Kolbein gave an involuntary start and hissed under his breath. 'Bastard owl: I will give him something to hoot about when I get ashore!'

Nerves were as taut as harp strings as the steering oar was worked and the *Isbjorn* turned its prow to the beach. Erik glanced up as a shadow fell across the ship, but the clouds were cobweb thin and the full light returned in moments. Behind them the *Reindyr* was making its turn, the oars causing barely a ripple as they stroked the glassy surface of the water as the tide stilled and prepared to ebb. Low to the water the hulls of the snekkjur should be all but invisible against the solid darkness of the land; the mast had been lowered and lay along the cross trees amidships, the brightly coloured sails safely stowed, but the prow beasts still glared landward to frighten away the spirits of the place and snarl their warlike intent.

The huge stone cross was just where Alf had said it would be, and Erik sent a plea to his own gods that the Christians would never realise just how helpful their displays of faith were to those who meant them harm.

Kjartan was in the bow, and the styrisman watched the man intently as he guided the craft through the rocky shallows. Erik glanced aside as the antlered head of their companion's prow beast came up on the starboard beam, and he laid a hand on Kolbein's shoulder as a gods-luck gesture as he took up his spear and began to move forward. The soft metallic chink of brynjur filled the air as the mail clad men who would follow him onto the beach rose from their sea chests and funnelled in his wake, and Erik saw Kjartan turn and flash a final smile and a thumbs up that all was well, before he too snatched up his spear and hefted his shield.

A last look ahead, and Erik was pleased to see that they were close enough now to make out the trunks and boughs of individual trees, and he drew back his arm and launched his spear into the darkness as the keel grated on land. Óðinn, Allfather, had done the same when he had hurled his own spear at his foemen to start the very first war, and despite the warmth of the night and the dangers which lay before him Erik found that his mind was back in Thorir's hall. A blizzard was raging as the skald stalked the benches; but the fire pit blazed, food and drink were plentiful, and the words had seared themselves into the young boy's memory as he had hugged his knees to his chest and dreamt of the day he would do the same:

> *Óðinn hurled down*
> *and shot over the warriors,*
> *that was yet the onslaught*
> *of the world's first battle.*

The stockades were broken
of the High One's fortress,
the Vanir stamped the ground
with their chants of battle.

The spear shaft was swallowed by the darkness and Erik drew his sword, vaulting the bulwark as the *Isbjorn* shuddered to a halt in the shallows. Before he could take a pace forward men were dropping from the bows to splash into the surf all around him, throwing their shields into a defensive ring around their king before any arrows could snicker from the shadows. Erik raised his own shield, hunkering down behind the boards as he waded the few yards to the strand. As the men from the *Reindýr* arrived at his side, Erik set off at a trot. The spring tide was at its high point, and within a few yards they were pushing their way through the lower branches and into the woodland itself. Ankle deep in last autumn's leafage the smell of the land, sappy wood, the musky smell of the earth itself, was like a half remembered tale after so long at sea, and Erik paused as the others fanned out to either side and searched the gloom for any signs of opposition.

To his surprise his mind began to swirl, and he reached out a steadying hand as his legs threatened to buckle beneath him, but he allowed himself a snort of amusement as a glance to either side told him that he was not alone. A deep breath was all it took to drive off the feeling of nausea which had threatened to overwhelm him, and he exchanged looks of amusement with a few of the others as they did the same. He regained his land legs as the memory of the rise and fall of the deck began to fade, and he began to relax for the first time in hours as he made his way back to the strand. Kolbein was ashore, deep in conversation with Thorfinn Kettilsson the styrisman of the *Reindyr,* and the pair looked across with a smile as he emerged from the tree line and stomped across. 'Nothing,' he said as he returned the smile. 'No opposition at all, even Kolbein's owl has seen sense and taken flight!'

The shipmasters exchanged a look, and Kolbein shrugged his shoulders. 'It's a long story.'

Erik flicked a look at the moon. It was beyond its zenith, and a quick calculation told him that they could expect to have no more than a couple of hours of darkness in which to get in position to launch the attack at dawn. The bay had been larger than he had expected, almost as wide and long as those of the fjords back home, and it had taken more time than he had allowed for to reach the cove. Hugging the southern shore the flood tide had carried them safely over the rocks and sandbanks as the snekkjur had attempted to melt into the shadows, but it had been a close-run thing. Thankfully Alf's diversion seemed to be working, and the nocturnal hunter which had frayed Kolbein's nerves had been the only sign of life they had come across that night. Holed up in a nearby creek, the crews of the two ships had watched from cover as the lines of smoke which marked the passage of the *Fjord-Ulf, Bison* and *Okse* rose into the Breton sky as they ravaged the settlements surrounding the adjoining bay.

The three leaders shouldered their shields and hefted their spears as the last of the assault party disappeared into the trees. A last word of encouragement with the ship guard and they were off, leaving the glum faced men behind them as they plunged into the trees. Twenty men had been left behind, a quarter part of each ship's crew; chosen by drawing lots twenty men was a sizeable force, more than he would have liked to have taken from the attacking force, but they were enough to mount a stout defence of the ships or row the hulls into deeper water should they be discovered. The first sign of dawn would see them fixing the mast and hoisting the sail; if the winds were favourable they should be at the beach below the monastery in time to recover the raiders and their booty long before a counter-attack could be organised from any Christian forces still in the area.

Kjartan was waiting for them, and the huskarl nodded in greeting as they came up. 'We have reached the road, lord,' he reported. 'It's just beyond that fallen oak.'

'Just where the Skipper said it would be.' Erik shook his head. 'Remind me to stand him an ale or three when we meet up again.'

The road shone in the moonlight, the ancient stones polished smooth by the tramping feet of men long since gone to dust. Skipper Alf, who Erik had by now concluded must know everything worth knowing about the southern lands, had told them that the old roadway had originally been built to connect the ancient lookout station which guarded the entrance to the river ahead with the nearest town. The old stone tower had been converted by the Christ priests to build the bolthole which was their ultimate goal that night, and Erik counted down the mile markers as the moon dipped and the first hint of grey lit the eastern sky.

The roadway rose before them, and Erik raised a hand to bring the column to a halt before they reached the crest. 'Wait here lads,' he said as they grabbed the chance to sip from their water skins. 'The monastery should lie on the far side of this hill. We will take a quick look.' Erik indicated that Kolbein and Thorfinn come along, and the trio slipped their shields from their shoulders and propped them against a tree as they began to push their way back into the greenwood. Within a few yards the cover was dense enough to conceal them from any early risers on the lee, and the Vikings pushed through the underbrush until the woodland opened out onto a scrubby meadow before them.

As they had expected men were moving about, despite the early hour, and Erik ran his eyes across the buildings before him as he began to formulate his plan of attack. This was the moment that he had trained for, years of spear and sword work in the hayfield before Thorir's hall, all the stories of past raids; words of advice and guidance which had come from his foster-father and brother as they had broken their fast on the grassy knoll. The three shared a smile as they saw that their brothers in arms had done their work well. Every armed freeman for miles around would be rushing towards the smoke stained sky as they sought to drive the heathen attackers from their land.

Kolbein leaned in and lowered his voice to a murmur. 'The old watch tower is where they will keep the best stuff lord. You can see the stone walls lighten in colour where they have raised the height. You can't see from here but the original door will have been sealed. The only way in now will be through that door halfway up the side.' He sighed. 'If we don't reach that before the ladder is pulled up we won't have time to winkle them out before we have to leave, we can't risk being trapped in the bay.'

The monastery lay undefended before them, and Erik nodded that he understood. He had seen enough. The light on the eastern horizon had taken on a blush of pink as the sky horse *Skinfaxi*, Shining Mane, pulled the sun towards the world of men; the ships would be shaking out their sails and poling themselves into deeper water about now. He would have liked the cover of full darkness, but the months of early summer were firmly in the southern lands and the nights were shortening by the day. There had simply been no time to reach the anchorage, come ashore and get the men within striking distance of the monastery walls before the dawn was upon them. Ideally he would have had the hours of darkness in which to encircle the walls, sealing off each gateway before moving in to take the main prize, but he had an idea that he thought might work and he itched to set it in motion. But they would have to move, and move quickly. The moment that the ships appeared around the headland surprise would be lost, and the raid would fail.

Pushing their way back through the undergrowth they were soon back at the road, and Erik allowed himself a smile as he saw the mien of the wolf on every face there. 'Right,' he said. 'I will outline what you will see when you crest this rise and then Kolbein Herjolfsson will assign each man his part in the attack.' He noticed a few of the men exchange looks of surprise that their young king was to plan the assault, and he noted their faces and pushed on. They may have expected or even hoped that a more experienced man would take command at this point but this was his hird and, although he would always be open to well meaning advice like any wise lord, he would lead from the front. 'The road runs as straight as a spear from the crest behind me to the monastery itself. There is a low wattle fence around the perimeter but no gate, so once we are through spread out and cause mayhem. The main building lies nearest the bay on the left and the dormitories where the monks sleep come off it at each end forming what they call a cloister; the road leads directly to this.'

Erik ran his gaze around the group. 'I need the fastest half a dozen runners. Who thinks that they are up to it?' Erik began to untie his helm as the men stepped forward. He nodded in satisfaction as he saw that he had pretty much guessed who they would be from their build. Two were shipmates, Thorstein Egilsson and Anlaf Crow, the others from the *Reindyr*. He was beginning to learn the names of those on the other ships in the fleet but these were unknown to him, and he committed their names to memory before he gave his instructions. 'Right lads. Leave anything which will slow you down here: helms, brynja and ask a friend to look after your sword, we don't want them to get in the way when we run. We shouldn't encounter armed opposition but if we do we will hold them off with a little spear work before the rest come up and take care of them.' He pinned them with a stare. 'We must reach the old signal tower before they can raise the ladder to the doorway. The quickest of us grabs it and holds on tight.' The corners of his mouth curled into a smile, and the men chuckled as he made a prediction. Years of racing Arinbjorn, Helgi and other members of Thorir's hird across the fells above Nausdal had bequeathed him the strength of a man far beyond his years: 'that man will be me.'

Erik was already pulling the mail shirt over his head to fall with a chink alongside his sword and helm at the road's edge as Kolbein spoke. 'Shall I detail a man to take care of the shepherd boy, lord? He will carry a horn and blow a warning the moment that we appear on the roadway.' Erik's mind raced. It was obvious that he had seen no shepherd when they had spied out the monastery buildings from the tree line and that his huskarl was attempting to spare him any embarrassment. But if it was plain to him, then it would be just as obvious to an experienced war band; he decided that attempting to conceal the fact would do more harm to his reputation than admitting that he had missed the lad. 'You are right,' he said as he felt himself flush, 'I did miss him.'

Kolbein nodded. 'It was easily done, lord. The boy was sitting in the deep shadow, I could hardly make him out myself.'

'But you had the wisdom to realise that a field full of sheep would very likely be under guard, I didn't.' He looked at the men of his hird and could see that he had made the right choice between bluffing it out and admitting his oversight. 'I made a mistake, but I promise you all that I will never make the same one twice.' As the men rechecked straps and fittings, Erik turned back to Kolbein. 'Yes, hurry a man over there to take care of our friend.'

Kolbein jerked his head and a dark shape plunged back into the trees. 'Thorfinn saw him too, lord. He will be there in no time.'

'You know the men better than me. Assign the leaders to each group and let them know their target.' He clapped the man on the shoulder and threw him a parting smile. 'Let's go and stir things up!'

The last of the men who would accompany him in the mad dash to the stone tower were placing their brynjur and helms in the underwood, scooping up handfuls of dun coloured leaves to hide the costly items from view. Erik began to do the same as he realised the sense of it. A well made mail shirt such as his own was worth twenty ounces of silver; a sword would cost double that to replace, but the loss of what may very well be a family heirloom would be a thing of shame. It was the reason why they had handed their swords to another man for safekeeping but brynja were just too heavy, they would have to take the chance.

As he stood again, Erik could see that the skyline was now feathered pink and scarlet as *Skinfaxi* approached. The ships would be on their way, the monks in the clearing below beginning to make their way to the next of their interminable devotions, and he made his way to the centre of the road as the rest of the hird gathered in their own groups, rolling their shoulders, warming blood and muscles after the chill of the night for the work ahead.

A glance to either side to check that his men were in position and Erik hefted his spear and broke into a run. Bearded faces, grim and alert; wide boards, the bosses a dull silver in the gloom flashed past on either side, and before he could get into his stride Erik gained the brow and came out into the full light of dawn. The roadway fell away in a gentle slope as it ran down to the simple gateway he had seen from the tree line, and Erik gathered speed quickly as his legs pumped for all they were worth. As he thundered down the back-slope the sun disappeared from view; he was back in the shadows, and he swept the area before him as he closed in.

The first faces were beginning to turn their way as Kolbein led the rest of the hird out into the wolf light of dawn and Erik recognised the moment when the first of the monks realised that they were under attack, but he was through the gateway now and closing quickly. The nearest Breton was cupping a hand to his mouth as he prepared to shout a warning and Erik raised his spear to skewer him, but he thought better of it as he came closer and he dropped a shoulder to send the man spinning away. Any loss of momentum now could cost them their prize, and he scanned his surroundings as they broke out into the courtyard. Grey robed figures were scattering about the space like a flock of startled hens, but Erik's heart leapt as he raised his eyes to look beyond them and saw that the ladder which was their goal was still in place.

A face appeared at the doorway just as he looked, its mouth gaping in surprise, and Erik redoubled his efforts as he saw the monks hands move towards the rungs of the ladder. They still had twenty yards to go as the gangway jerked into the air and the thought that he could aim his spear at the man flashed through his mind, but the Christian was no fool and Erik could only look on in despair as he pulled back into the interior.

Anlaf came past him, and Erik watched as Thorstein speared another, but the ladder was already above head height and one more heave would leave them stranded at the base of the tower. Erik's heart sank. His very first raid had left him looking like a fool.

9

THE RED KING

As he started to check his stride, Erik realised that Anlaf was still running full pelt towards the sheer face of the tower. A heartbeat before the hirdman dashed himself against the stone wall, his spear clattered to the ground and he launched himself into the air. Erik watched as the ladder began to move upwards again but Anlaf was as tall as any in the hird, and he willed the man's outstretched hand to grab the ladder before it could be heaved out of reach. Despite the mayhem all around, Erik's world narrowed down to encompass only the diminishing gap between the bottom rung of the ladder and the warrior's fingertips. Sure now of their success, the monks in the tower paused as they moved their hands down the side rails for the final heave which would see the ladder safely stowed within; but Anlaf's palm was closing around the bottom rung, and Erik thrilled to the sight as he saw the huskarl's fingers curl and his knuckles whiten as they tightened their grip.

Thorstein shouted at his side, *'get ready!'* and Erik let his own spear drop to the ground as his men formed a protective screen around him. Anlaf was dropping back to the courtyard, and Erik had the madcap sight of one of the monks from the tower arrowing through the air etched into his memory as the unexpected downward movement plucked him from his eyrie.

The ladder crashed to the courtyard, and Anlaf moved to hold it steady as Erik began to move forward. Half a dozen paces and he leapt into the air to land with a crash midway up the ladder. A moment of panic as he began to fall back, but his hand fixed itself to a rung and he grasped it with sweaty fingers as his feet scrabbled for purchase. A face appeared above him, the horror of the situation writ large upon it, and Erik began to climb as he felt the ladder shudder as his men threw themselves against it below him. Sandalled feet appeared above him as the remaining Christian sought to kick the ladder away, but the weight of those below him held it in place. It was the action of a desperate man, and Erik saw the fear on the monk's face as he reached the doorway and threw himself inside. Rolling to his feet Erik bunched his fists as he prepared to take on the holy man unarmed, but the man had backed away and he spun on the balls of his feet as he searched the room for an unseen opponent. The room was bare, but for a coil of rope and a single chair placed against one of the white washed walls. It was obviously used for little more than a place to store the ladder in times of need such as this, and Erik's eyes moved from the unmoving monk to the dark portal at his side. A staircase curled away there, and a shaft of light confirmed that there was a further room above.

'Don't worry, lord,' a voice came from behind him, 'once you break in they all stand stock still like frightened mice.'

Erik looked across as Thorstein's face appeared at the top of the ladder. A moment later he had heaved himself into the room and stood there grinning widely. 'You ran like a hare, but I think that Anlaf had the beating of you lord.'

Erik snorted. 'It's as well that he did. I would never have

jumped high enough to grasp the ladder, and even if I did I doubt that I have the weight yet to winkle these Christians out of their shell.' He looked back at the monk and wondered to see the look of calm acceptance on the man's face. Thorstein had noticed his surprise, and he moved to explain. 'Christian monks never put up a fight, they usually make do calling down curses from their God and the like. Even if you give them a good working over they rarely tell you where the treasures are kept. They believe that by suffering on his behalf, their God will admit them to heaven.'

Erik raised a brow and Thorstein gave an explanation. 'Heaven is a bit like Valhöll without the drinking and fighting.' He shrugged. 'Not every man is a fighter, lord. At least this one is quiet, I can't do with flying spittle and curses. If I wanted to hear that all day I would have settled down with a woman!'

A bell began to toll, irregular and muted at first, but the unseen bell ringer soon got into his stride and the sound rolled across the surrounding countryside. 'It looks like they managed to close the door to the bell tower before our lads could reach it, lord. It is best we get a move on before horsemen turn up.'

Thorstein had drawn his seax, the short bladed stabbing sword which most warriors wore at their waists, and pointed across the room with it. 'Best we get upstairs, lord. Grab what you can see and toss it out of the window. The lads in the cloisters can sift through it, there are more of them and it will be quicker.'

Erik drew his own seax and crossed the room. The monk was still standing next to the inner doorway, the joy in his eyes plain to see as the sound of the warning bells filled the air outside and Erik shot him a look of warning as he approached. The man backed away, and Erik ducked through and began to mount the staircase as Thorstein ordered him down the ladder to the courtyard before following on.

The staircase was not much more than the height of two men, and Erik stole a look and quickly drew back his head as the room above opened out. Despite Thorstein's assurances even a man with little weapon skill or bravery would have him at their mercy as he climbed; without even a shield to protect him, any attacker would not even have to come close to loose an arrow as he emerged into the light. But the quick glance had been all that he needed to see that the room was empty of life, and he climbed up into the room and looked around him. Small square shelves lined the far wall, each cavity containing a tightly rolled scroll; in the far corner a heavy chest rested against the wall. Several staves were stacked in one corner, each one topped by a silver cross, and a large book, the binding embellished with gold and gemstones shone in the wan light of the early dawn. Windows had been cut in each of the four walls, but their narrowness made it obvious that they had been made more for observation than allowing light to lift the oppressive gloom in the room. A wooden staircase led upwards to a hatchway in the ceiling, and Erik was about to cross to it as Thorstein came up into the room. The huskarl's eyes lit up at the amount of booty there, and he shot Erik a smile as he came across. 'Let's make sure that we are alone, and then we can start chucking this little lot down the stairs, lord.'

Erik nodded. 'Make a start and I will check the next level.' He crossed to the hatchway as the first of the staves clattered down the stairwell and paused beneath it. Constructed from thick oak planks, the hatch was hinged on one side and secured on the other by a pair of heavy iron bolts. Erik examined the ironwork as the sound of the chest being dragged across the floor filled the room. All were coated with a fine patina of rust, cobwebs and the husks of long dead insects filled the cracks between the boards. It was clear that the hatchway was rarely used, and Erik relaxed a touch as he lifted his arm and began to work the first of the bolts. They grated back in a cloud of fine red dust, and he jumped down to the floor as he let the cover swing down to hang into the room on its hinges. Immediately the room was flooded with light, and it became clear that the next level up must be the roof of the tower itself. He climbed the stairs, bobbing his head in the hatchway as he ensured that the space really was clear of men. Satisfied that he was alone, Erik mounted the steps and came out onto a flat roof and into the full light of the early morning. A crenelated bulwark ringed the space and Erik walked to the edge, eager to see just how well the raid was going.

The bulk of the monastery church lay to the North, and Erik ground his teeth in frustration as he watched the great bronze bell swinging to and fro at the top of the bell tower as it alerted the countryside for miles around to their presence. Running along each side of the cloisters were the low buildings which catered for the more day-to-day activities of the inhabitants: dormitories; kitchens; scriptoria; even a piggery and smithy in the part furthest from the sanctity of the church building itself. In the open space below, his men were beginning to sort the inhabitants into those who could fetch a price and those whose futures were less obvious and possibly far shorter. Others were making a pile of anything else of value as two of the hird drove an ox drawn cart into the cloister.

The first whiff of smoke came to him as he raised his gaze to the northwest, and his heart lifted as the golden prows of *Isbjorn* and *Reindyr* sailed into view. The first fronds of flame were beginning to show in the thatch of the roofs below him, and Erik watched the smoke thicken to cleave the roof line as the same morning breeze which was bringing the ships carried it eastwards. He nodded to himself in satisfaction. Skipper Alf and the men in the other ships would soon see the signal and abandon their own depredations, backtracking to the meeting place and leaving the army which had gathered against them aghast as they looked to the South, saw the pall of smoke hanging over their land and realised that they had been outwitted.

In the cloisters below, the monks were now sorted into those who could fetch a good price in the slave markets and those whose future was arguably grimmer still. The monastery itself was almost a town made small: shepherds; stock men; brewers; smiths; it seemed as if there was very little that was not produced within the community. A large proportion of the men were young and fit, well fed and disease free, perfect for the market. In the midst of it all Erik saw the figure which he knew must be the Abbot himself. The man was attempting to put a brave face on the calamity which had overtaken them all in the dawn, and Erik found to his surprise that he admired him all the more for it. Despite what he had heard at home, Christians and the kingdoms they inhabited seemed surprisingly strong: wealthy, well ordered and thriving, despite more than a century of attacks by his own countrymen and others. Maybe he would find out more while he was in the South? Wise men always found room in their lives to accommodate another God.

The muffled sound of splintering wood drew his attention back to the church, and Erik watched as his men poured into the building. Thorstein called from below that the room was clear, and Erik sheathed his seax as the tolling of the bell grew erratic and fell silent. He snorted at the wanderings of his mind. Óðinn had given them the victory, and he asked nothing in return but that men recognise his existence and pledge to fight by his side at the end of days. What kind of God would expect men to grovel on their knees, day after day, and bask in his glory? He leaned forward and let a ball of spittle fall from his lips, watching as it tumbled end over end until it became a starburst in the dust. He had loitered long enough, it was time to go.

'HOW ARE WE DOING?'

The crewman looked up from his work and gave a curt nod. 'Almost done, lord. That was a good haul, we needed to ditch some of the ballast before we loaded it aboard. It all being mostly metals, I have stowed it down near the keel. She's a well found ship,' he said, patting the side strakes with a hand made as rough as the oak itself by years of rowing. 'But all ships leak a little, and she's no different. Metals don't care how wet they get, but you still need to balance the ship.'

Erik nodded that he understood. Gold and silver were heavy; only the gods yet knew how long they would be away from home and which seas they would sail before they returned to Norway to share out the loot. Up on the headland the monastery was a sea of flame, long tongues of red and orange licking the now silent bell tower as greasy black smoke billowed high above. Away to the East the sun had long ago cleared the wooded hills, and Erik raised a hand as he estimated how much time had elapsed since his mad dash in the dawn. He looked back up the beach, up beyond the place where the men of his hird had thrown a shield wall across the place where a woodland outlier narrowed the meadow, to the rapidly growing number of spearmen who were gathering there. Kolbein was shepherding the sullen looking captives into line as they prepared to frogmarch them aboard, and Erik called across as the distinctive clatter of wood told him that the deck planking was being refitted to the ship. 'Is there any sign of movement yet?'

His question was rewarded with a smile, and the huskarl shook his head as he replied. 'They still have less than half our number lord. They'll not make a move until they outnumber us at least two to one, however important the churchman thinks he is. Of course, that could change in a moment if a local lord turns up with his levy.' A voice came from the bows: 'we are all set, lord, bring them up!' Erik indicated that they start loading the captives with a jerk of his head.

The Bretons at the head of the field began to grow agitated as they saw the holy men being bundled aboard the ships but everyman there, locals and Viking alike, knew that they had neither the numbers nor the weapon skill to intervene. Erik began to cross the shore, and Kolbein came to his side as he neared the defensive line. 'Congratulations lord,' he said. Erik threw him a look and his styrisman explained: 'on the success of your first strandhogg.'

Erik snorted. The practice of shipborne raiding had been prohibited within the regions of Norway by his father the king. It was one of the few things which Thórir Hersir and Arinbjorn had been unable to prepare him for, but raiding for slaves was a profitable business and a staple of their raids overseas. He raised his eyes to look beyond the defensive line. The enemy were still fixed to the hilltop but a number of them were moving backwards and forwards now, cajoling those whose bravery was found wanting as the departure of the raiders grew closer. 'Shouldn't we chase them away, it would only take a moment?' he spat in disgust. 'Standing down here while they try to pluck up the courage to face two ships' crews. Either they want to save their priests or they don't. If they lack courage they should have stayed at home with the women!'

Kolbein plucked at Erik's sleeve, drawing to a halt before they came within earshot of the defensive line. 'Forgive me if I speak plainly lord, but I have been charged by the king with more than just honing your battle-craft. Your father did not become the first king to hold sway over all the lands of the Norse because he was the largest, meanest warrior.' He gave a chuckle. 'Although that helped!'

Erik looked and saw that Kolbein's gaze was still drinking in the details before him. The huskarl continued as his eyes darted about the field. 'You'd have played tafl at foster?' It was more a statement than a question; all boys of quality were taught the board game, but Erik confirmed that he had. 'Then you know strategy. When you are the red player, what is the object of the game?'

Erik shrugged. 'To get safely to the corner of the board.'

Kolbein nodded. 'Outnumbered and surrounded by white pieces, the king and his plucky little army have to fight their way to safety.' The huskarl lowered his eyes and looked at his lord. 'And do you remember your greatest victories?'

Erik nodded as he began to understand which way the conversation was going. 'The times when I reached the corner of the board without losing a man.'

Kolbein's face lit up in a smile, and Erik could see that the man was recalling some of his own games as his voice drifted. 'White pieces swarming all around you, probing, offering a chance to trade one of your men for two of theirs because they could afford the loss: attempting to draw you out; whittle down your defence. But you kept your discipline and won through; all together. It's why some men call it *hnefatafl*, fist-table; the victory is not in killing the enemy or amassing loot, but in punching through their defences in a brotherhood of warriors. You are right,' he went on as he raised his chin to look at the Breton spearmen again. 'We *could* run these men off, that's even if the collection of cobblers, thatchers and assorted shit shovellers stayed to fight once they saw us coming up the hill. But we could lose a man to a javelin before we reached them, another to a lucky spear thrust.' He moved the point of his own spear towards the tree line in the West. 'What if they have men hidden among the trees, or on the back slope where we gathered before the attack? How do we know that the local lord is not about to clatter down the road at the head of fifty horsemen? Either could cut us off from our ships, and then our position could begin to get very sticky, very quickly.'

Erik nodded that he understood. 'Just like tafl, do what you came to do and get the men away in one piece before they have to fight to keep what they have already gained by stealth?'

Kolbein clapped him on the shoulder and gave a nod. 'Make the men wealthy in gold, silver and reputation but value their lives above all and they will love you for it, lord. The time will come soon enough when Óðinn sends his battle-maidens to carry off a soul or two. Show the men how much you value them, and when that time does arrive you'll not find any shortage of men willing to take your place on old one-eye's benches.'

10

KARVI

A rumble of laughter rose into the balmy air as the men watched the Breton oarsmen stroke the sea. 'That's not a ship! Look at the tumblehome on the hull, that is a barrel!'

'It's as well for you that they are,' Kolbein chided his friend. 'Or we could be arranging to pay *them* to get *your* sorry arse back!' Despite Alf's scathing judgement the Breton ship was leaping the waves as it came on, a scattering of pearls girdling the prow as it fought to make headway against a freshening wind. Erik was the next to speak as he pointed to the masthead. 'Why the branch?'

'It's their way letting us know that they come with peaceful intent, lord,' Alf answered. 'We used to do the same, back when my father was a lad, but now we use the white shield as you know.' He gave a shrug. 'I like it.'

Erik stole a look back across his shoulder at the captives and tried to imagine what was going through their minds. He doubted that the men sat hunched in their forlorn group got the chance to discover their real worth, just how much value in hard, shiny silver their lord placed upon their head but that day had arrived; they were about to find out.

His mind drifted back over the last few days as the Breton ship came close, and his heart lifted with pride as he reflected on the success of his first raid. They had boarded the ships and cast off from the beach below the burning monastery as soon as the captives had been loaded aboard. Pulling away from the headland they had watched as the roadway disgorged spearmen, and he had exchanged a look and a smile with Kolbein at his side that the king had punched his way through after all, the tafl game won. By the time that the sun was at its high point the broad waters of the bay had opened up before them, and obscenities and good-natured shouts had flown between the crews as Alf had brought the other ships out from the side bay to join them. They had left word with the monks who were deemed to be too old or infirm to fetch a price, back at the strand, that they would remain at the shield shaped island at the mouth of the bay for five days before sailing on. Now it would seem, their patience was to be rewarded.

Erik turned to Kolbein as the Breton ship entered the calmer water in the lee of the island and the crew shipped their oars. Men leapt into the shallows as the hull made the shingle, and the Vikings lining the high water mark painted their faces with their fiercest scowls as the first men ashore tried not to cast nervous glances their way.

Erik spoke sidelong as the Breton ship was hauled beam on to the shore and a gangplank splashed into the surf. 'How much shall I ask for our friends?'

Kolbein watched as the men who would do the negoti-ating appeared at the head of the gangway. 'Take a moment to study those they have sent to broker a deal, lord,' he replied. 'We will set our price accordingly. If they look men of worth, we have a managed to nab a man they prize. If not we may as well cut the hands, nose and ears off the old abbott and ditch him on the beach. Then we replace him with the fittest men among this lot and set a course for the slave markets. Recall what I said last night and you can't go wrong.'

'About linking the value to the price of a well made helm?'

'That's right, lord, it's the key to successful negotiation for men like us. By lucky coincidence the price of a good sturdy helm, one made of the best steel with a one piece nose guard that won't get pushed back into your face the first time that it is struck, is roughly a pound weight of silver.' He looked across his shoulder to the place where the men of the hird were lining the high water line and gave a smirk. 'Tough bastards, and not all of them the cleverest that you will meet; but every man there knows the price of his kit and they can relate to it. If you manage to wring five hundred pounds of silver from these Bretons, they will know that not only have you filled the hull of the *Isbjorn* with gold and silver from the raid itself, you will have added the value of a new helm for each man here plus a hefty bonus by use of words alone.'

Erik watched as the crew of the Breton vessel moved aside, and Kolbein purred at his side as the man sent by the local ruler to negotiate for the return of the captives was revealed. A pale blue tunic and leggings were edged in golden braid, and a cloak of midsummer blue was pinned at the shoulder by a large silver brooch of exquisite workmanship. If not a man of wealth and influence himself it was certain that he had been sent as the representative of such a man, and Erik could feel the satisfaction that they had managed to snare a prize worthy of such a reaction sweep through the men at his side.

Kolbein spoke out of the corner of his mouth as the

nobleman leapt the final few feet to land with a crunch on the shingle. 'Two hundred and fifty pounds of silver for the abbott and as much as you can get for his monks, lord. That will make it a nice day's work.'

The Breton lost no time, striding along the beach as his companions struggled to negotiate the wobbly plank, and Erik smiled to himself as he suspected the mettle of the man he was about to face. The five styrismen in Erik's little fleet: Kolbein Herjolfsson; Skipper Alf; *Okse's* Ulfar Whistle-tooth; Thorfinn Kettilsson of the *Reindyr;* Gauti Thorodsson of the *Bison,* were at his side, and Erik watched with interest to see if the man would make the mistake he fully expected him to do.

The prisoners were on their feet, the mixture of hope and excitement plain as their hoped-for earthly saviour approached, and Erik watched with amusement as the Breton stopped ten paces before them and his eyes flicked from face to face as he sought the likely leader. He saw the man's gaze linger upon him for a moment before it moved swiftly on, and he snorted gently beneath his breath that he had likely predicted the opening move of this tafl game correctly.

Alf was the eldest there, the telltale signs of a lifetime spent at sea etched into every inch of his hide, and Erik watched as the man's gaze settled upon him and he began to make his introductions. 'My name is Gwenneg seneschal; I am here as a representative of my lord, Alan, King of Brit-tany,' he began. 'I have been authorised by the king to conduct negotiations on his behalf regarding the return of the Most Holy Abbot, Huw of Landevennec, and of the brothers of his order.'

A large rock stood at the waters edge, and Erik settled himself down to watch as amusement began to radiate from his companions. This man Huw seneschal may look the part of the experienced negotiator he mused as the man awaited a reply to his declaration, but he had already made an elementary mistake which would cost his king dear. He had looked at the group before him and seen what he had expected to see; a hardened band of cutthroats led by a gnarled and weather-beaten old pirate. He had not the wit to realise that the youngest in the group looked out of place among them. The mere fact that Erik was barely more than a boy despite his great size, would indicate to any experienced negotiator that he must someone of importance; only a fool would have discounted him so quickly.

The silence which had greeted the Breton's announcement stretched on, and the man himself was beginning to look around as he realised that he may have made a mistake. Kolbein had begun to suspect Erik's ploy, and he was the first to break the silence. 'Two hundred and fifty pounds of silver and you may have your Abbot back in one piece. A further two hundred and fifty and you can take the younger priests also.'

Erik's mind wandered as the Breton turned to his helmsman and began to argue the price with the special kind of oily charm which seemed to be a feature of courtiers everywhere. Twenty warriors had at last managed to disembark from the Breton ship and were waiting for their lord, a dozen paces away. It was the first time that Erik had seen Christian warriors up close, and he studied the men who were his natural enemies as Kolbein and Huw played out their word game. Tall and broad of shoulder, only the nut-brown hair, the lack of beards and the long droopy moustaches set them physically apart from the men of his hird, and Erik found that he was impressed by the quality of the arms they carried. Well led, they could prove a worthy foe.

Beyond the men, the wide bay which formed the backdrop to the haggling was not unlike those of home, though the hills which ringed it had little of the majesty of the snow capped peaks there. The early summer weather was already as warm as the hottest days in Fjordane and the men had told him that the lands further south were hotter still. His countrymen were already raiding and trading southward, beyond the River Loire to the Christian kingdoms of Navarre and Leon. Beyond that he knew lay the lands of the Umayyad where the god of the East held sway and men were the colour of autumn leaves.

The negotiations were coming to a close, and Erik gave a snort of amusement as he saw the look of satisfaction on Kolbein's face. The price was about to be fixed, his styrisman had got the full five hundred pounds of silver, and he felt the merest pang of guilt as he finally added his first words to the negotiation. 'No, that is not enough. The price is five hundred pounds of silver for the Abbot alone. You have two days to return here with the ransom or we sail with your precious churchman on board; the priests come with us.'

IF IT HAD NOT BEEN for the early start they would never have spotted them. As it was, the gilt weathervane on the leading ship glinted like ice as the sun lay low in the eastern sky. 'Edge us over there,' Erik said. 'Let us get a better idea of their numbers before we commit ourselves.' He shot Kolbein a wan smile. 'It would be a shame to lose all of our hard won loot so soon, after all!'

They had left the island which had sheltered them for the best part of a week as the first blush of dawn painted the eastern skyline. The Bretons had finally delivered the silver and taken their Abbot away as the sun had slipped beneath the western horizon the night before. The tide had been in full flow, and Erik had wondered at the timing as the crewmen on the southern craft laboured to make headway against the force of the incoming current. Kolbein and the rest of the men, hoary Vikings to a man had no illusions however, and the first pale light of the false dawn had revealed the sails of an avenging fleet appearing at the head of the bay as they rode the ebbing tide and had shaken out their own sails to quickly put the island behind them. Now, little more than an hour into the day, the danger had been left astern and the little fleet had become the hunters again. Pal was looking his way, and a nod from Erik sent the lithe young crewman scurrying up the mast. The other ships were closing up on the *Isbjorn* as they awaited his orders and Erik cocked his head as Pal's face turned back. 'Three ships, lord,' he called as the following wind did its best to snatch the words away. 'I don't think that they have seen us yet.'

Pal lifted his head, peering back to the West, and Erik shared the sense of anticipation with the other members of the crew as they waited for their friend to add flesh to the bones of his report. He shot a glance at the weathervane on his own ship as he waited. They were upwind, the sealskin tassels snaking away to the Northwest, and Erik ordered Kolbein to bring the ship about as he sought to close the distance between them before they were spotted against the glare of the sun. The other ships had bounded up on either beam of the *Isbjorn,* and Erik felt an overwhelming pride as he saw the experienced raiders aboard them hauling on war gear and fitting strings to bows.

He looked back to the mast top as Pal cuffed the spray from his eyes and turned his face back to the deck. 'I can see them clearly now, lord' he said. 'I thought that they were knarrs, but they are not: they are karvi.'

Erik exchanged a look with Kolbein. Knarrs were the

deep water traders of the North. Wide bellied and seaworthy, they were primarily sailing ships whose use of oar power was restricted to manoeuvring when beaching or in a port. They typically carried a crew of half a dozen or so; just enough to work the ship, but not so many that any profits need be split too many ways. Karvi were similar in outline, but whereas the space amidships on a knarr was taken up by an open hold, a karvi had one continuous deck running fore and aft with fifteen or sixteen oar ports a side and the crew to work them. Their versatility made them the ideal ship type for transporting high value cargo and the men to guard it, and both men recognised the glint in the other's eye as they mentally totted up how much loot three such ships could be carrying.

Any hopes that Erik's fleet could close with the three vessels unseen were dashed a moment later as Pal called down from the masthead that they were bearing away to the West, and Erik began to feel the now familiar thrill of the chase course through his blood as the ship came about and the wind began to blow steadily from astern. Sails billowed, shroud lines thrummed as the five snekkjur crested the waves and bounded after their prey, and Erik called Pal back to the deck as the distance quickly closed and the hulls of the karvi grew on the horizon.

Less than half a mile separated the two flotillas when Erik saw the moment when the opposing leader realised that they would never outrun his sleek warships, and he watched as the karvi shortened sail and began to lash themselves together as they prepared to fight the ship. Erik ordered his own sail shortened as they approached, and he walked past the prisoners towards the bow as the way came off the ship. Each of the five ships carried three of the crestfallen priests, men who had seen their last hopes of salvation receding astern only a short time before. Manacled to the mast, Erik could only imagine the fear among them as they prepared to become the helpless witnesses to a battle at sea.

Skipper Alf was leading *Fjord-Ulf* out to starboard, and a quick look to larboard told Erik that the *Reindyr* was mirroring his action there. If it came to a fight, the numbers were perfect for the type of attack he had in mind; two ships to force their bows between the stern posts of the enemy, *Fjord-Ulf* and *Reindyr* to lay themselves alongside the outermost hulls with Gauti in the *Bison* free to exploit any opportunity which presented itself.

The *Isbjorn* began to wallow as the ship slowed to a crawl, and Erik hauled himself up alongside the fang-toothed beast head, cupping a hand to his mouth as he hailed the ships ahead. 'I am Erik Haraldsson: who has your oath and what is your business?'

A helmeted head appeared at the stern of the karvi, and Erik thought that he could feel the crackle of anticipation at the closeness of action even through his own back as the skipper answered with a snarl. 'My name is Asbjorn Einarsson; Sigurd Jarl has my oath, hall burner. My business is my own.'

'If you know my lineage, you also know that your lord owes skat to my father on the goods you carry,' Erik smiled in reply. 'It must be your lucky day, Asbjorn, for I can easily steer a course for King Harald's hall; transfer the third part of your cargo which rightfully belongs to the king and I will see that it is safely delivered.'

Asbjorn lowered his head, sent a gobbet of phlegm spinning into the waves, looked up and scowled. 'I would not give the king's runt the breath from my arse.' He raised his gaze and ran his eyes across Erik's fleet. Alf and Thorfinn Ketilsson had already second guessed which way the exchange would go, and oars were stroking the waves as the long sleek shapes of the *Fjord-Ulf* and *Reindyr* moved around to outflank him. 'I have heard it said that fate sometimes withholds a man's doom when his courage holds.' Asbjorn gave a fatalistic snort. 'Let us see if that is true.'

As the final word left his mouth, Asbjorn drew his shoulder aside. Before Erik could react a spearman leapt into the space and hurled his dart but Erik's own men were faster, and he heard the thunk as Anlaf's shield moved across to pluck it from the air. As he took a pace back, Thorstein and Anlaf Crow moved forward to shield him from further attack as the ship was oared forward and the wolf coats moved forward into the bow. Kolbein was steering the Isbjorn directly between the tall stern posts of two of the three ships before him, and Erik watched with satisfaction as grappling lines arced through the air and the ships were hauled together. Faces appeared at Asbjorn's side, yelling their battle cries as the ships closed, and the moment that they touched Erik's men surged forward.

Erik looked to either side as the sound of fighting came from the front. Both of the flanking attacks were in progress, and although he could see that boarding the higher sided karvi was proving troublesome, superior numbers were telling and the first of Alf's men were already aboard and fighting hard.

'Come on,' Erik said to his shield men. 'I know that my place is directing the fighting, but if we dally here we will miss it completely!' He stepped forward into the crush, raising his spear above his head as he attempted to bring it to bear on the enemy. The wolf coats were gaining a foothold despite fighting with the disadvantage of height, and a heartbeat later a cry of victory filled the air as Asbjorn was skewered and heaved overboard. With the death of their leader the heart went out of the enemy, and soon Erik was scrambling over the stern of the karvi and surveying his prize. Skipper Alf came up, a swelling above his eye already as large and shiny as a harvest apple and darkening by the moment. 'It looks like we have wine, lord,' he said with a lopsided grin; 'lots of it.'

PART II

SHIP ARMY

11

OSWALD THANE

Erik and Kolbein shared a look, and the sea king saw the pain in his friend's eyes as he spoke the words which every styrisman the world over hoped would never pass his lips: 'Are we abandoning her, lord?' Erik snorted a reply. 'Not if I can help it. It's been nigh on twenty years since I first stepped aboard, that day back in Nausdal when I was little more than a lad. We have watched too many miles go under her keel to give the old girl up without a fight. Let's see what Thorstein has to say first, and then we can decide what to do.' Kolbein clapped Erik on the shoulder as his worse fear was chased away, shooting out as he turned to go. 'You see to the ropes, and I will see how much more room Gauti has on the *Bison.*'

It had all seemed like great fun at first as some of the worst ideas often do, but now they were at serious risk of foundering and the smiles had been well and truly driven from the faces of the men on the *Isbjorn. Bison* had come alongside, and Erik waited amidships as the crew frantically transferred the heaviest of the treasure in an effort to lighten the load. Erik chewed his lip in worry as he stretched to look past the great curve of the bow. The other ships were beating back towards them but it would be some time yet before they could come to their aid, and Erik's fingertips drummed impatiently on the sheer strake as he waited for Thorstein to reappear.

An indistinct paleness shimmered in the depths, and moments later the huskarl popped to the surface in a gout of spray. Thorstein gulped down air before sweeping the hair away from his face with the wave of a hand. He took a moment to knuckle the water from his eyes, but when he moved his hands away Erik's guts tightened as he saw the concern written there. Thorstein coughed up the last of the seawater as he held up a shard of oak. 'Snapped, lord,' he blurted out as he tossed the thing aside.

Kolbein had heard the verdict and hurried across. The styrisman rested his elbows on the wale, and he shot off a question as the experienced swimmer made his way back to the ship with easy strokes despite the choppiness of the waves. 'Thorstein, is it a clean break?'

The man in the sea had reached the ship's side, and he trod water as he splayed the fingers on both hands and wove them together. 'Gnarled up,' he coughed as a wave slapped against his face. 'All knitted together like a twisted stick, bang amidships.'

Erik was already running his eyes across the deck as he reached down to help Thorstein clamber back on board. Before he could yell the first command Erik realised that the crew were ahead of him, and he watched with satisfaction as two men worked the halyard, gingerly lowering the spar and the sail it supported to the deck. Willing hands reached up to take the weight off the yard as it came down, and Erik held his breath as the rakke bracket scraped down the mast and the hull gave a tortured groan beneath their feet. As the weighty woollen sail was released and bundled across the gap to the *Bison* and the yard made fast, Erik crouched and peered below deck. 'How does it look?'

Kolbein glanced up and pulled a face. 'The good news is that the keelson is in one piece; it's a hefty piece of oak, and it spans the place where Thorstein said the damage is.' Two men were at his side, passing buckets of seawater up to willing hands on deck. As the water level dropped Kolbein pointed at the side strakes. 'We have popped a few treenails but the strakes themselves are undamaged, so I can have a couple of lads down here replacing them as soon as the water level drops enough to let them see what they are doing.' He blew out, raising his chin to study the clouds as the men worked at his side. 'The weather looks like it should remain calm for the next few days. If the keelson can take the strain and we tighten up the fore and back stays, the standing rigging should hold her together.' He shook his head and flashed a smile as the immediate fear that they were sinking began to recede. 'Whales! he said. Let's race them, it will be fun!'

Erik snorted. 'How was I to know they had calves with them? By the time I saw them it was too late.'

A familiar voice hailed them and Erik stood and looked to larboard. The *Fjord-Ulf* was reefing its sail, and oars slid proud of the hull as the way bled off the ship and the prow began to turn. 'Need a hand?'

Erik grimaced. 'The keel's busted, but we think that we can make land.' He watched as the Skipper ran a practiced eye across the hull. Finally Alf cupped his hand and called across. 'She has settled a bit low in the water but there is no sign of hogging; let us hope that you are right.'

Erik glanced fore and aft. The tops of the bow and stern posts still looked about the same distance from the water so

Alf's observation was encouraging. It seemed that the combined efforts of the keelson and the rigging were preventing the ends of the hull from drooping and taking on the distinctive arched pig back which seamen called hogging.

The *Fjord-Ulf* came alongside and Alf asked for permission to board. In a moment he was on the steering platform, and Erik watched as he took in the state of the ship with an experienced sweep of the eye. Alf nodded, and Erik suppressed a smile despite the gravity of the moment as the man gave a grudging thumbs up to their efforts at keeping afloat. 'Not bad; I had this happen to a ship with me once, off the coast of Frisia. Not mine of course,' he added with a hasty sniff. 'One of my lads grounded on a sandbank going at full clip. He was never in danger of foundering of course, so we had more time to think. What we did come up with though before we hauled her off and made for the coast, was removing the running rigging and using the ropes to pull the hull together.'

Erik knitted his brow in question, and Alf skipped down from the steering platform. 'Like this, lord.' Moving to starboard, he unwound one of the seal skin ropes from a cleat and threaded one end through oar hole amidships. Moving along the deck, he threaded the rope back through the next, pulled it taut and reefed it off. 'Repeat that all along both sides of the hull and it will pull the two halves of the ship together; it will help to keep the keel from pulling apart.' He indicated to the Northwest with a flick of his head. 'Northumbria is half a day's sail in that direction, so we should reach it tomorrow; I can have Svein look at her then and see what he can do. He's no shipwright as you know, lord,' he said, 'but he can fix most things up until we can get to a ship yard. If we lash the *Fjord-Ulf* to larboard and the *Bison* to starboard we will give you greater buoyancy. Of course,' he sniffed again. 'We will not be able use the sails, the speed would put too much strain on the keel. But even with only one bank of oars in use on both ships we should get there. Straight in, get her beached, and we can see how we stand.' He raised a brow. 'And hope that the man who happens to be king of Northumbria this month either never gets to learn of our presence, or has nothing against Haraldssons if he does.'

THE NIGHT HAD BEEN cold but the sea had remained calm, and the crew began to stir as the coastline began to harden from the gloom. Soon Skinfaxi had hauled the sun above the horizon, and the men on the ships scanned the place where they would make landfall for any signs of life as the shrill cries of gulls filled the air. 'As dour as it looks, I have rarely seen a more welcome sight, lord.'

Erik nodded as they began to believe that they would make it. Relieved of the need to steer or work the ship by their companions alongside, the overnight journey had been one of boredom for the most part, despite the fact that possible catastrophe lay only a heartbeat away. Men had sat beside the ropes which lashed the *Isbjorn* to her sister ships all night, the hand axe at their side testament to the speed with which they would have to sever the cord should the keelson give way under the pressure and the cold waters of the North Sea flood in. Everyman there knew that the ship would go under in moments, but men had kept baling as others used mallet and wedge to drive back the tarred rope which caulked the seams. 'Let's hope that the locals are friendly. It would be a shame to go to all this trouble, just to abandon the ship on the beach.'

Kolbein pointed northwards. 'Well, we will soon find out.'

Erik looked. A bevy of small fishing boats had put their sterns to the wind and were racing for a small settlement nearby. 'Gone to raise the alarm.' He patted the sword at his side. 'Well, they had better think twice if they think that we are going to be a pushover. It looks to be a reasonable size place, with any luck a shipwright will have his yard there; it will save us the trouble of trying to find one if we need to.'

Within the hour they were splashing in the surf, lines of men hauling at bowlines as they heaved the *Isbjorn* clear of the sea. *Bison* and *Reindyr* rode at anchor below the low water mark, and although half of the crew had come ashore with Erik and his men, enough had been left aboard to remove the ships from danger should other warships hove into view or enemy spearmen appear on the low cliffs overlooking the beach in overwhelming numbers. Away to the north the *Fjord-Ulf* and the *Okse* were close inshore, following the curve of the coastline as Skipper Alf went in to investigate the nearby town.

Between them, the ships now contained more than three years' worth of booty gained from this voyage alone, raiding all along the coastline of southern Frankia and beyond; although it seemed unlikely that a back of beyond place like this could put enough men into the field at such short notice that they could threaten almost two hundred experienced fighters, it always paid to be sure.

With the *Isbjorn* now clear of the sea and the likelihood that they would live to tell the tale of their great escape from the monster of the deep looking increasingly likely, the men crowded around to take their first look at the whale damaged keel as others lent their weight to tip the hull on its side. The last of the seawater was still draining onto the shingle from the damaged hull, but it was clear to them all just how close they had come to disaster. The heavy oak beam was as

Thorstein had said, cracked and splintered where the great humped back of the animal had crashed into it, and Erik waited for Alf's crewman to give him the verdict. Svein ran his hand along the splintered oak and turned back with a frown. 'I was hoping that it was a cleaner break than this, then I could fit an oak plate to either side of the break, bore through the lot and treenail them together.' He shook his head as he picked a strip of splintered oak from the *Isbjorn's* keel and held it up for examination. 'Not like this lord, Thorstein was right; it's all mashed up. There is no way that the wooden pins would hold together long enough for us to reach home. Our hulls are made to flex with the sea, they would soon pop out and then you would be swimming before you knew it.' Svein took a few paces back, his hand worrying his beard as he thought and his gaze flicking from stem to stern. 'What I can do,' he said finally. 'Is cut a length from the stern post and scarf that in; after all it's already been cut and shaped to match, it's just a projection of the keel itself. I will have to be careful that I don't damage any of the garboard strakes, the planks which are attached to the keel itself, or we could be back were we started.' He pursed his lips and blew out through his nose as he worked through his plan again. Finally Svein nodded. 'It will take me the good part of a day, but I think that I can get you home, lord.'

They had feared the worst but Svein seemed confident enough, and the men on the beach exchanged smiles as they began to hone their stories in preparation for a lifetime retelling any that would listen of the day they had battled the Midgard Serpent *Jormungandr* and lived to tell the tale.

Erik left Svein to it and rounded the hull. Peering inside he could see the smaller pieces of treasure beginning to emerge from the muck which had collected there in the years since the ship had last been overhauled, and Erik wrinkled his nose at the smell as he began to toss the sodden remains of looted wall hangings and spoilt supplies onto the beach. The sun was higher now and the men were beginning to set fires as they prepared to cook the first food of the day. Kolbein had already led fifty men to the top of the low sandy cliff which edged the beach, and Erik watched as they made their way to the higher points to get a better view inland. Satisfied that all seemed well there, he called to those remaining with him. 'Crew mates!' As the men turned his way he shot them a mischievous smile. 'We have been given the opportunity to give the *Isbjorn* a good clean. Let's not let it go to waste, we don't know how much time we have.'

'STILL ONLY FIVE THEN? There are no signs of others hiding in the shadows?'

Kolbein shaded his eyes with the sill of his hand and swept the forest edge from left to right. 'It certainly looks that way. Five horsemen riding straight towards us, with their shields hanging at the crupper and the points of their spears pointing to the ground indicating that they come with peaceful intent.'

Erik cocked a brow. 'It's what…half a mile between here and the tree line?'

Kolbein shrugged: 'about that.'

'Well,' Erik said, 'as soon as they get far enough that we can be sure that it is not a trap I will go and see what they want.' The styrismen of the *Bison* and *Reindyr* had come ashore with most of their men, and Erik called to them as he walked proud of the line. 'Gauti, Thorfinn; I am going to meet them with an equal number and see what they are up to. Hold your position here at the top of the cliffs, but keep an eye on the beach in case they are drawing our attention away from a flanking attack. Alf and Ulfar Whistle-tooth will be back with the other ships soon. Let them know what is happening.' He called to four of his spearmen to follow as he threw a smile back across his shoulder. 'Oh…and someone run down and tell Svein to hurry up with his woodwork. We may have to make a quick escape after all.'

The four outriders accompanying the central figure were clad in mail and helm, and Erik ordered those following him to do likewise as the distance between the two groups closed. Erik ran his eyes across the horsemen as they came together, and was pleased to see that they appeared to be Englishmen. Ironically fellow Norsemen were far more likely to be a threat due to the actions of his father, back in the homeland. The leading figure's round face was clean shaven in the manner of a Christian priest, and while one of his escort sported a full beard, the other three had shaved their cheeks leaving just the distinctive full moustache of the southern warrior class. The clothing and weapons clearly told of their wealth, and Erik was intrigued to discover the reason for their visit as the men dismounted fifty yards away.

The leader handed his reins to a companion, surprising the big sea king as he walked forward alone and greeted them with an open smile. 'My name is Oswald Thane, lord. Have I the honour to be addressing the atheling, Erik Haraldsson?' Erik confirmed that he had. 'I bring greetings from my own lord, Wulfstan, Archbishop. He has asked me to convey his disappointment that he is unable to leave York at this time to greet you in person, but hopes that that happy day may come in the near future.' As Erik looked at the man in astonishment, he continued. 'My lord also asks that you receive this small gift to share among your men as you see fit.' The Englishman raised his arm, and Erik sensed the men at his rear stiffen as a cart rumbled forward into view from the shadows of the trees. The land was a little higher where Erik stood, and he moved to calm his guard with a flick of his hand as he saw that the cart was piled high with tuns of ale and flitch of bacon. 'You must be our guests of course,' he said as the ox drew nearer. The food and ale were welcome gifts for men who had just spent weeks at sea, but he was long enough in the tooth to realise that they could easily be poisoned. He studied the man before him and saw to his satisfaction that no hint of fear crossed his features.

'That would be an honour, lord.' Oswald beamed before continuing, the first part of the task set him by his master obviously accomplished. 'If I may be so bold, we have much to discuss.'

GULLS SKIMMED THE BREAKERS, the harshness of their cries at odds with the mood as Erik splashed through the shallows. Willing hands reached down to haul their king aboard, and he turned to give a parting wave to the small party of men lining the clifftop. Reaching the mast fish he jumped up and down, shooting the men a smile as he saw their confusion. 'If Svein's workmanship is to be found wanting, I would rather it happened in the shallows than the deep! Come on,' he said as the oarsmen sat braced at their stations, 'let us go and join our friends.' He gave Kolbein the nod, and the ship began to inch away from the land as the styrisman called time. In deeper water the steering oar gained traction, and Kolbein hauled the great blade, swinging the prow seaward as the men in the other ships whooped and called.

By midday the coastline was lost in the haze astern, and Erik reflected on his conversation with the friendly Northumbrian as the *Isbjorn* cleaved the waves. In the years that he had been away his brothers had grown to manhood; now they were beginning to push for the kingship of the Norwegians itself. He had no doubt that he could quash their ambitions, he was a warrior of reputation, even a churchman in York had known who his ships contained from the description of their prow beasts alone.

Twenty years raiding along the shores of Frankia, Wendland and beyond had filled his hall with treasure; soon it seemed the time would come when he would need a land army at his back and he smiled a rapacious smile as he looked forward to the fight for the ultimate prize, Fairhair's king helm itself. Just one fly floated amid the suds that topped his ale horn; Hakon, his youngest half-brother now at foster with the king of the southern English. King Edward had left Midgard to simper at Christ's feet if the Christian priests were to be believed and a new king ruled there now, his son Athelstan. Men said that he was just as warlike as his father and grandfather and more pious too; they were testing times for Norse and Danes alike.

Sigurd Jarl still ruled at Lade and he had had a hand in the boy's removal from the kingdom. There was scheming there Erik knew, he would have to keep an eye on the situation. Oswald had held out the offer of an alliance with Northumbria who already felt the power of this Athelstan, should Erik inherit his father's gift stool. In the hazy workings of his mind an idea began to harden from the miasma. The dream of a kingdom stretching from Dublin in the West to Finnmark in the North began to form, a realm to surpass the greatness of his father. Erik's eyes flashed fame-bright as the ship crested the waves and the tafl pieces began to move in his mind's eye.

12

THE HUSTING

The raven banner was brought forward as the body of the stallion was hauled away, reddening the grass in a bloody trail as it was dragged towards the cauldron.

Kolbein spoke with reverence as the ceremony approached its climax. 'The oath ring from Þórr's temple was a good idea.'

Erik shot the huskarl a smile. 'Yes, I thought so too. A man thinks twice before he makes a pledge if the thunderer has come among us.'

Kolbein snorted. 'Or your father. A man thinks thrice or more when he comes under Harald Fairhair's eyes.'

Erik looked across, back towards the hall. A high seat had been brought out, and Erik looked with pride upon the burly figure of his father as he regained his place surrounded by guardsmen. Even at almost four score years of age the king still dominated those around him by the force of his presence alone. As king and father of the nation King Harald had shown honour to his eldest son by performing the *blóð*, beheading the horse with one crushing sweep of a magnificent bearded axe before skirting the perimeter of the hustings, the house Thing, flicking the sacrifice's lifeblood onto the hazel wands which marked the limits of the sacred space. Between King Harald and the war banner the prow beasts of the fleet had been set up to overlook the sanctified area, each golden face a snarl as the firelight danced across fang, bull neck or antler.

Anlaf Crow was ready and waiting, and Erik gave his huskarl a nod as others covered the ground with hides. As the man put the battle horn to his lips, Erik looked out across the waters of the fjord to the grey capped peaks beyond. The summer was all but spent, the harvest newly gathered; soon the uplands would wear their cape of snow. But before they did so, one last duty remained for the men who had returned from abroad that autumn. The length of Norway, ship's crews would be gathering in scenes such as this, parcelling out the year's gains before they dispersed to gather in smoggy rooms as the wind howled and roared to swap tales of another summer spent raiding or trading in the rich lands to the South.

As the doleful note trailed away men appeared on the foreshore: singly and in pairs; knots of friends; full ship's companies. His most trusted warriors, his personal guard the huskarls: other men of the hird. Struggling beneath the weight of booty or walking swiftly to the gathering as their luck, skill or duty that year had ordained.

The hustings hallowed, the pair moved across to the shrine as the warriors gathered under their styrismen. Seeing the men in their divisions Erik gripped the silver ring on its pediment, the first to speak the oath as was right:

'I, Erik Haraldsson, king of this company, swear under Þórr's eyes that the treasure which I place before you all is the complete and full amount which I have gathered on this season's Viking. I vow that I have hidden away nothing for my own use, and I further pledge my word that I have no knowledge that any other man here has done, or intends to conceal that which belongs to us all for his own use and pleasure.' Tightening his grip, Erik swept the gathering with his gaze before continuing with a look of pride. 'Furthermore I submit myself to your judgement, by offering to lead everyman here who will pledge the oath of fastness to me in next season's raids.'

Erik turned and made his way back to the place where the booty which he had accrued over the past summer's raiding was piled high. Unaided as was the custom, he shifted the pile across until all was littering the ground before the raven standard. As he took a pace back Kolbein moved in to grip the temple ring and repeat the oath, adding his own pledge of allegiance and becoming the first man in the hird to renew his vows for the coming year. The men came forward in order of seniority to mirror his actions: Skipper Alf; Ulfar Whistle-Tooth; Thorfinn Ketilsson; Gauti Thorodsson, styrisman of the *Bison*. Soon the hoard was knee high, and Erik looked on with pride as man followed man and they had reached the fluffiest cheeked warrior without losing a single man.

As the men returned to their companies the air began to crackle with anticipation as Erik ran his eyes across their number. He had spent a heady evening the night before with his leading men, retelling the tales of the summer raids; choosing who had shown valour or distinguished themselves in such a way that they stood head and shoulders above their companions. He had seen most of their actions with his own eyes of course and had his own ideas, but he was happy to accommodate the views and opinions of his most trusted underlings as any good leader should. As the ale had flowed the names of the chosen dozen had been hammered out under the roof of his hall, and Erik let the tension in the hustings rise as he lingered over the announcement. Twelve men were chosen, the hirdmen stepping forward proudly from the throng as their names were called to cries of joy and back slapping from their shipmates. These were the men who had proven their trustworthiness by their actions and battle fury, and as the warriors came forward to begin the task of dividing up the loot the styrismen began to do likewise with the men under their command.

First the treasure and men were divided into two equal lots, and then divided again as the scales clanged and groaned under the weight of silver. Erik's fourth part was set aside, and he basked under the proud gaze of his father as the pile grew higher. No man begrudged him the greater part which had been gained by their collective efforts. All men knew that a leader's duty to them went far beyond leading them in battle and they would receive the majority of it back, either directly by way of the gift stool or less obviously through the food which they would eat, the ale they would sink, the provision of a sturdy keel beneath their feet or a roof above their head.

The quarter part which would be divided among the styrismen was removed, and as the remainder was divided again into five equal parts by the chosen men the ceremonial cloth known as *skaut* was brought forward and laid before the banner. In his final act of the ceremony Erik moved forward and placed five plumb weights, one for each of the ships under his command, onto the centre of the skaut. Each was angled towards the place where a single ship's company had gathered together, and Alf as skipper to the fleet moved forward to point out the order in which the crews would come to choose which pile to carry away for distribution among themselves.

As the last crew carried away their share Erik raised the first horn of the evening, and the hustings shook as the answering cry of *skál* came back in a full throated roar. The styrismen came together as the ale barrels were tapped, and Erik showed them honour as he filled each man's horn in turn. The vessels came together, and each man drained his drink in one as they toasted their success. At the edge of the clearing the sacrifice had already been butchered, and the tantalising smell of the meat drifted across the hustings as it simmered in great iron kettles.

Laughter swept the group as they jostled at the tap, ale sloshing from horn rims as a hand gripped his shoulder and Erik recognised the voice of the king. 'You will excuse me if I spirit away your lord for a short while lads. I have a great deal to discuss with my son.' The men pulled themselves up as they recognised to whom the voice belonged, and Erik and his father shared a laugh as they saw the ill disguised impatience written on their faces as their eyes roamed from king to ale tap. 'Don't stop for us,' Harald snorted. 'But make sure you leave a drop or two!'

Harald led Erik towards the foreshore as thralls hurried away with buckets of sacrificial blood. Mixed with oats they would be brought out again as a treat at the yuletide feast along with the blood sausage they would produce. The king inhaled deeply as the aroma of simmering horse flesh drifted across the hustings. 'That was a fine display,' he said wistfully as they walked. 'Oh, to be a young man again.'

Erik made to tell his father that he still had many years left in him but stopped himself. It was becoming clearer with each visit to the homelands that the king was ailing and the man had never been a fool; he would not insult his intelligence to suggest otherwise and he waited patiently for his father to continue. Down on the beach faces turned their way as they passed, the smiles, boozing and lighthearted banter a universal feature of men who had just been paid. Smiths had set up their camps on the strand, and already they were doing a steady trade as men handed over their silver: coin clippings; rings cut from dead fingers; a winged woman prised from a Christian book cover, and had them smelted down and recast as arm rings and small ingots. Further along the shingle women loitered, ready to relieve the men of a little silver in exchange for something altogether more fleeting. Harald snorted at the sight. 'Women have always been my weakness.' He turned his head, and Erik was surprised to see a look of regret flit across the king's features; 'and now you will have to deal with the results of that appetite.'

'In what way father?'

'While you have been away, raiding and forging a reputation, and even before that,' he chuckled as he rediscovered his humour. 'I have been producing sons. Some of them are already dead,' he conceded with a shrug. 'Guttorm we have spoken of before, killed down in Gotaland by that bastard Solvi the Splitter. Frodi and Thorgisl were killed long ago in Ireland.' He raised a brow. 'Never trust a man from one of the Irish tribes. If there are no enemies at hand, he will pick a fight with himself!'

The pair shared a laugh. Erik's second voyage had taken him as far as the islands of the Sudreys, off the western coast of Scotland. He had sighted the northern tip of Ireland but Skipper Alf had cautioned against landing there as the place had become hostile to Haraldssons since Sigtrygg the Squint-Eyed had retaken Dublin from the natives.

'Others too have died,' the king went on. 'Halfdan Highleg was blood eagled by Torf-Einar the Orkney Jarl and a good thing it was too.' King Harald spat his contempt. 'All of my sons by that Finnish witch are a bad lot.' He flicked a look at Erik. 'But I am getting ahead of myself. You will know that he burned in Torf-Einar's father, Rognvald Eysteinsson, jarl of Moerr and sixty of his men. Rognvald and I were great friends, it was he who finally cut my hair so that I earned my eke name Fairhair. Now I am growing old it is becoming harder and harder to keep the survivors under control.'

King Harald opened the palm of his right hand and flexed it. Erik was surprised to see that the king could barely uncurl his fingers. 'It's something that my father had and his father before him,' Harald explained with a sigh. 'Don't ask me what it is, it must be the work of a witch or a god-curse on the men of our family from long ago. As you age you develop these gristly lines in your hands, and as they grow so your hand begins to curl into a claw.' He sighed. 'I can just about grip a sword, but my days of fighting are in the past.' He fixed Erik with a stare. 'So I would like to name you as my heir. I think that you are the only one who has the strength in body and will to hold the kingdom together when I am gone. I have given most of my surviving sons king-doms to rule on my behalf, but I have kept the best for you: Halogaland, Moerr and Romsdal.' He looked at Erik and saw the pride there. 'It will honour my own foster-brother Thorir Hersir; he and Arinbjorn will gladly rule Fjordane and collect the skat. Bring your own household down to Avaldsnes. I have a hall there which you can use, and we can rule together from Rogaland until you lay me in my barrow.'

Erik was electrified as he realised the importance of the conversation, but he was experienced enough now in the ways of men to know that the offer would come with a price attached. Harald looked at his son, and Erik saw the cold gleam in his father's eyes which betrayed the hard man within. No ordinary man could have defeated the kings and jarls and forged the first kingdom of the Norwegians. It took ruthlessness towards his enemies as well as open handedness towards his friends to achieve such a great thing, and Erik listened intently as his father continued.

'Before I go to my grave there is one thing remaining which I wish to accomplish, a debt which needs repaying. Many years ago I was bewitched by Snofrid, a daughter of a king of Finns, and tricked into marrying her. King Svasi was a guest at the midwinter feast, and I provided one of the halls at Avaldsnes for his use as any good host would. On midwinter eve as we sat at our cups, Svasi told me that he had brought a fine gift south and it was waiting for me at his hall. My guards went across and could find no sign of treachery, so I accompanied him there.' King Harald spat in disgust as he recalled the night and its consequences. 'When we came to the place it was barely lit, but mindful of the reassurances of my men and trusting to my sword arm should they have missed any threat I went in. A scent permeated the hall, sweet smelling, the sort of cloying smell which sticks in your craw.' The king sighed. 'Just like the smell of death; I should have known then that there was more to this gift than I should like, especially with the Finnish reputation for *seith*.'

Erik nodded. All men knew that the Finns were accomplished in the ways of the dark sorcery men called seith, and he could see the regret which his father still felt reflected in his eyes as he continued the tale. 'A young woman was standing before the hearth, the light from the flames glossing hair as black and burnished as a raven's. She smiled and held up a silver chased cup as I came towards her and I was smitten. The movement had caused her shift to tighten across her body, and with the backlight provided by the hearth fire…' He shook his head and pulled a wry smile. 'It was as if she was wearing nothing at all. A voice in my head told me not to drink from the cup, that the moment I did I would be lost, but…'

Despite the gravity of the subject they shared a smirk as Erik formed his father's thoughts into words before adding a question of his own. 'Women have more subtle ways than seith to cast their spells over a man. And this king Svasi still lives?'

Harald nodded. 'In a region known as Bjarmaland, far to the North, beyond the place where the coast of Finnmark trends to the East.'

Erik looked away to the West as he thought. Skinfaxi the sun horse had almost done its work for the day and the sky there was the colour of an angry bruise. 'I will send forth the war arrow in the spring. Bjarmaland will be looking for a new king before the next harvest is gathered.'

Harald beamed before twisting to beckon forward one of his guardsmen. The man hurried across, passing the king's own war axe to his lord before retiring back into the shadows. 'Here,' Harald said. 'Accept this blade; carry it always and tell men that it was a gift from Harald Fairhair to his favourite son.' The king cradled the axe, still smeared with the blood of the sacrificial stallion, and held it forward.

Erik took it from his hands and studied it with pride. The body of the blade had been chased by smith cunning into a mass of writhing *ormr*, the black infill which men called niello causing the serpents to leap forth from the blade. He had already witnessed the effectiveness of the hardened steel cutting edge, back at the *blóð*, and he smiled again as he felt the heft of the weapon and found it to be perfectly weighted. 'Thank you father,' he said. 'I shall treasure it always.'

'If you can,' the king was saying, 'try to take that bastard Svasi's head with it.'

Erik glanced up from his prize. 'I shall.'

Harald laid a hand on his son's shoulder. 'I know that you will. That's why I have gifted it to you of all my sons.' The sounds of carousing men drifted down to them from the field before the hall, and the king snorted as his mind drifted back to the gatherings of his own youth. But he had found his successor, he was sure of it, and Harald stood and brushed the earth from the seat of his breeks. The mood had grown reverential with the giving of the gift, and the king sought to lighten it again before they retraced their steps and rejoined the throng. 'You will need a name, one to cower your enemies.'

Erik looked up. 'Haraldsson has always worked in the past, father.'

Harald snorted again. 'But there are still a dozen or so Haraldssons…' He thought for a moment and gave a shrug, 'that come immediately to mind at least. I did say earlier that women were my weakness! You will need a distinctive name, one which men will remember and set you apart.'

Erik rose, and the shingle crunched beneath their feet as king and under king began to make their way back along the strand. 'If I throw a name at you, forgetting your own men for the moment,' Harald said as they walked, 'what nickname springs into your mind?'

'Bjorn?'

'Ironside.'

Harald nodded. 'And Magnus?'

'Barelegs.'

Their eyes met, and they both saw the amusement there as Erik realised the importance of his father's lesson. Harald rattled off another few names as they walked, and Erik supplied the answers.

'Ragnar?'

'Shaggy-breeches.'

'Ivor?'

'The Boneless.'

'So what's it to be,' the king said. 'Which name shall Erik Haraldsson bear as he forges his name as the king of Norse?'

Erik shrugged. 'It's not for me to say father. A man cannot give himself an eke name.'

'That is true,' Harald conceded with a nod. 'I daresay that the Jarl in Orkney would have been met with laughter if he had sent word instructing everyone that he wished to be called Skull-splitter.' Harald glanced down. 'It will need to strike terror in the hearts and minds of your enemies when I am gone. Something distinctive,' he mused, 'something worthy of the Fairhair's chosen son.' He pointed at the gift with his chin. 'How about War-Axe?'

Erik was about to agree, but a look of inspiration lit his father's features as the last of the day's light flashed to add a crimson sheen to the bloody blade. 'No,' he said, 'I have it. The next king of Norway will be known as *Erikr Blóðøx:*Erik Bloodaxe.' Before Erik could answer the king slapped his thigh and beamed as he repeated the name, obviously well pleased with his choice, but it was Harald's following statement which caused his son to gape like a freshly landed codfish. 'Yes,' he said, 'Erik Bloodaxe will do just fine. You will also be pleased to learn that I have arranged for you to marry the daughter of a Dane king, Gorm the Languid, down in Jutland. You are to leave for Jelling to negotiate the dowry and set the date of the betrothal before the winter storms can interfere with the crossing.'

13

GUNNHILD

Harald Gormsson paused, raised his chin to look out beyond the lip of the pool and let out a sigh. 'It's certainly a magnificent looking country,' He shot Erik a look, and the Norwegian snorted as he recognised the twinkle of mischief in the Dane's eyes. 'Hard work for farmers though.'

'It's as well that I am not a tiller of soil then,' Erik replied. 'Somehow I doubt that you would have delivered your sister up to her grisly fate if I was.'

The Dane laughed. 'I think that you would be the one fated to meet a grisly end if that was the case. My sister has led a charmed life where marriage is concerned, she only dodged a betrothal to a prince of the East Franks because they decided that they would rather attack us instead.' Harald smirked. 'I doubt that the two were linked, but you never know! There was talk at one time of her being married off to an Englishman, a thane from Mercia, but the poor man met with an accident while out hunting.'

It was Erik's turn to spring a surprise on his guest, and Harald gave a nod of recognition that the man who was destined to become his brother-in-law in a few short hours was not lacking in knowledge of the world beyond his own shores. 'That would be Hereweald, thane of Tamworth. It's a funny thing, but Hereweald is the English equivalent of your own name, Harald. I thought that you would have liked him. True,' he added with a look. 'The union would have brought the whole of the upper valley of the River Trent firmly under English control, maybe beyond Repton up to the walls of Derby, or even Nottingham itself. Very close to your own estates at Torksey.'

The Danish king sniggered with delight, and the two men, both under-kings and intended heirs to their father's wider kingdoms shared a look of mutual satisfaction with the other. If their families were to be joined together in kinship it was always desirable that the two men who would one day head those dynasties liked and respected the other. It was the reason why King Gorm in Jelling had encouraged the two young men to spend so much time together while Erik was in the South the previous autumn. Hunting in the forests and moorlands of Jutland had forged feelings of mutual respect between them, a bond further strengthened by the Viking raid they had undertaken against the lands of Gnupa, son of Olof the Brash, the Swedish warlord who had overrun Danish lands in Scania a decade before. Erik continued with his explanation as the pair idly watched the wakes made by yet another rowing race cream the glassy waters of Karmsund.

'Is it true that Þórr himself wades across the strait on his way to visit Yggdrasil each dawn?'

Erik chuckled. 'So they say, but if he does I have yet to witness it.' He cocked a brow. 'A good attempt, but I am not finished with our conversation about poor Hereweald yet. If I am to marry Gunnhild, I need to know if I will have to sleep with one eye open for the rest of my days!'

Harald gave a shrug. 'If a man loses his life during a hunt

he has proven himself to be unworthy of marrying into the family of Gorm Hardeknudsson.'

'So, this accident was nothing to do with the man the English call Harald Blue-thane?'

If Erik had hoped to surprise the Dane with his knowledge of the far off land he was about to be surprised in turn.

'Is that what Oswald told you?'

Much to the Danish prince's delight Erik gave Harald a blank look, unable to conceal the fact that he could not place the name. Suddenly he had it, and his face lit up as he recalled the man from the Northumbrian beach. 'Oswald Thane, archbishop Wulfstan's linkman!' He laughed again. 'No, I have other sources of information. They tell me that the English near the border live in fear of this Harald Blue-thane, the Dark-thane; mothers hush troublesome children with the threat of his coming to carry them off in the night.'

It was Harald's turn to laugh at the description, and he gave a shrug of his powerful shoulders as he conceded that it was he. 'It's a reputation that I am trying to lose,' he admitted. 'Before someone decides to call me Harald Child-bane. Blue-thane is bad enough, by the time that it gets spoken of in the Danish tongue the thane has often become tan, tooth.' He pulled his lips back into a lupine snarl and spoke through his teeth. 'Can you see any blue teeth there? I catch just about every man I speak to looking to snatch a glimpse of a blue tooth when I open my mouth to speak.'

'So, what can you tell me about this archbishop?' Erik asked. 'You have estates in England.'

'Wulfstan?' Harald replied with a snort. 'The archbishop is as wily as a fox and as sharp as a blade.' He shook his head, but Erik could see the admiration in the Dane's eyes. 'For a Christian to cling on to power and even prosper in that madhouse of a kingdom must be like holding a wolf by the tail; let go and you will end your days in a whirl of gnashing teeth and slashing claws. Northumbria is a hotchpotch of people: English; Norse; Dane. Even Irish and Scots. But the thing to remember is they fall into two factions. The landowners headed by Wulfstan the kingmaker want above all else to keep the country independent of the southern English. The traders based in York don't care who calls themselves king so long as they make a tidy profit from their dealings. They want York to be the centre of a trading hub which runs from Dublin in the West to the North lands, Christendom and beyond. What's more they are the ones who bring prosperity to the good folk of York; they spend more silver in the town because their wealth is more easily spent and not tied up in land and hall. They tend to have the support of the townsfolk in any showdown and they are not afraid to use that power. Take my advice,' Harald said earnestly. 'Keep away from Northumbria, they have grave fields full of kings.'

Erik looked back across the strait. The ships had finished the final race and were heading in as the sun hung low in the western sky; the guests would be itching to get started with the wedding feast after a full week of games, trials and events. 'It is time to head back I think, before this waterhole develops a crust of ice. If we spend much longer here they will be calling you Harald blue-prick,' he said, flicking a look at the knot of guardsmen nearby. Danes and Norwegian, Erik was pleased to see that the men were beginning to mingle at last. Traditional enemies it was understandable of course, but if the upcoming kinship between the houses of Hardeknudsson and Fairhair was to work at all the men would need to lay their prejudices aside. The kings hauled themselves back onto the grass, shaking the icy water from their hair and bodies like hounds caught in a downpour. Erik looked across as they began to dress. 'Come north with me next summer, we can campaign together. There is nothing like warfare to forge a bond between fighting men, it will stand us in good stead when we are full kings.'

Harald snorted. 'That sounds like a fine thing, but the truth is that I cannot afford to go on adventures. We are fighting the Swedes in the East and Henry the Fowler and his Saxons in the South. Add to that the chances that this new king in England will overrun our remaining settlements there and we will be faced with powerful men returning home with their followers.' He gave a shrug, and Erik saw the concern in Harald's face for the first time. It was clear that the Danes needed this alliance more than they did themselves, and he stashed the thought away for future use. The lands which owed his father allegiance stopped at the Gota River; maybe that could be pushed further south? The problem was the number of half brothers his father had sired over the course of his lengthy lifetime. It was true that a few were already dead, but the surly demeanour of those who had attended the wedding feast told of their dislike for the close relationship which had developed between Erik and their father. Erik's sworn enemy, Sigurd Jarl up in Lade, had sent his apologies; the coastal districts were under attack from Vikings and he would be failing in his duty to the king if he were to abandon the rich lands at such a critical time. To be truthful he was relieved that the man had stayed away, but he had doubled the number of his bodyguards as it became clear that time had still not dulled the jarl's thirst for vengeance.

Erik clapped Harald on the shoulder as they walked. The shadows were stretching before them now as the sun sank in a brawl of reds. 'This English King Athelstan has my youngest half-brother at foster, a brat called Hakon. We have common cause, Harald. Maybe we can teach him a lesson?' Erik looked at him with a gleam in his eye. 'Erik Bloodaxe and

Harald Blue-prick, carrying fire and sword to the over proud English.'

Harald laughed as the comment lightened the mood as it had been intended to do. 'Maybe Bluetooth is not so bad after all!'

The guards fell in behind them as they scaled a low rise and the halls came into view. People stopped to look, conversations fell away as they came, and it was obvious that all were eager for the night's carousing to begin in earnest as the Norwegian spoke again. 'Erik Bloodaxe and Harald Bluetooth it is then; names that will resonate down the centuries.'

'So did the folk of Geatland, his hearth
companions, mourn for the lord who had
been laid low.

They said that of all the kings upon Midgard
he was the most open-handed and beloved,
gracious to his people and keenest for fame.'

A LONG DRAWN-OUT silence fell upon the hall as the recital reached its conclusion, the speaker taking up the proffered ale horn with a grateful nod to quench his thirst. King Harald Fairhair was the first to react, reaching forward to beat the tabletop with a ham like fist. Slowly at first the beating was joined by others, faster and faster, until the rafters of the hall shook with the sound.

As the thunderous boom made by hundreds of fists began to subside, Fairhair, king of the Norse, raised himself from the high chair and swept the hall with his gaze. Within moments the air was still, and men turned their faces to the king and waited to hear his words.

'King Harald Gormsson you honour not only this occasion, but your father and the Danish people with your skill at word play.' Erik and Gunnhild, the groom and bride, were sat to either side of the great king, and Harald placed a hand on each before continuing with his praise. 'My heart soars that I have lived long enough to witness the joining of our clans in the form of these fine young people. Tell me,' he said, 'where you first heard such a tale. It is new to us here and believe me,' he said as he cast a cheery eye along the benches packed with warriors, 'when you reach my age it is a notable day in itself when you discover something that *is* new.'

Harald Bluetooth bowed his head in recognition of the praise as a rumble of laughter at the high king's words rolled around the benches. 'It is a tale I first heard when I was little more than a lad growing up in Britain, from an English skald lord. It comes from a kingdom they still call East Anglia, although the last of their native English kings fell fighting against my countrymen around the time that a mighty king was driving the last of his enemies from these lands at a place called Hafrsfjord.'

It was the turn of the Norwegian king to acknowledge praise with a dip of his head, and the walls of the hall echoed once again to the staccato beat of pumping fists and booming voices as the spearmen acclaimed their venerable lord. 'And this Beowulf,' he replied. 'He was a king of Geats, down by the River Gota?'

'Legend has it he was the last and greatest of their kings, but many still believe that he was none other than Óðinn himself in the guise of a man.'

King Harald raised a brow, and the Dane explained. 'The Angles and Saxons have long been Christians lord, but they still hold their ancestors in high esteem. Even the pious West

Saxons are at pains to trace the ancestry of their kings back to the Allfather.'

Fairhair nodded, satisfied that the true gods still clung to a place of honour, even at the heart of the lands claimed by the Christ. Many merchants he knew had already prime signed, a half conversion which allowed them to trade in Christian lands, and he had received embassies from the Saxons both in Britain and Germany promising great rewards in return for allowing Christian priests to preach in his own kingdom. He had allowed them free rein and reaped the rewards. As long as men paid their taxes and answered the war arrow it was of little consequence; every free man belonged bodily to the king, his soul was his own. 'Well,' the king beamed, 'that was a tale fit to end the evening.' He rubbed his hands with glee as he ran his eyes across the treasures piled high in the centre of the hall. 'Harald has delivered the dowry and Erik has added the bride price.' He smiled again. 'And a goodly amount it is.' He raised his voice to carry as men hastily charged their cups. 'Have we all eaten well?'

'*Yes!*'

'Have we drunk our fill?'

'*No!*' came the answering cry, and although the reply was expected thunderous laughter still filled the hall as the men pummelled the tables again.

'Well,' the king smiled, 'that can be rectified shortly. But for now it is time to invite the goddess into our company.' The hall fell silent once again as the culmination of the week-long festivities reached its conclusion. Harald took up a large silver hammer, the head a gleaming knotwork of interlaced serpents inlaid with gold. Turning to face the couple he led those in the hall as they chanted the words which would invite the goddess of oaths and the thunder god to witness the union :

'Bring in the hammer
to hallow the bride;
On the maiden's knees
let Mjollnir lie,
That both the hand
of Var may bless.'

Harald moved forward to place the hammer onto Gunnhild's lap, looping the handfasting ribbon around their wrists as they exchanged their vows. The oath taken he turned back to the room with a grin. 'Is that it then?'

An answering cry and a smattering of ribald suggestions assured him that there was still one important ritual which remained to be completed. The king looked nonplussed and the guests lining the women's benches covered their faces with their hands to hide their bashfulness, but their shoulders shook to betray their mirth as he held his hands wide and replied. 'Well, she will soon have that on the move, what with all the poking and prodding she is about to get down there.'

Erik sought out the figure of Gytha among the women at the far end of the hall as the king entertained them. Their eyes met, and they exchanged a look which told them that they were both feeling the passing of the years as Erik's mind drifted back to recall a few of their adventures together as children. At that time he had naively hoped that she would be the one bound to him by the wrist, but both of them had known all along that he was too important to marry the daughter of a hersir, even one as highly thought of as his foster-father. Thorir was swapping a comment with his son only a few feet from his side, both men laughing at the king's jesting, and Erik gave a snort as Arinbjorn shot him a smile and a wink. Gytha was long married herself now, to a son of the jarl of Moerr; it was a happy union by all accounts and he found that he was joyful for it.

King Harald was still holding the room in thrall with his descriptions of the ongoing nuptials, and Erik's mind came back as he listened in again. A huskarl called out from a side bench, and the hall looked on gleefully as the king leaned in, poked a finger into his ear and gave it a good waggle. Removing it he gave the tip a look, screwed up his face in disgust and wiped the finger against the side of his breeks as he cocked an ear and replied. 'What?'

The spearman stood and jerked his hips back and forth as his friends egged him on, and the king's face broke into a mask of understanding as those in the hall laughed again. 'Con*su*mmation! I thought that you all said con*stip*ation! Harald allowed the sentence to peter out as the laughter redoubled, and Erik gave Gunnhild's hand a squeeze of sympathy as he felt her squirm at his side. 'Well, come on then,' King Harald was saying, 'bring the broom forward.' He held up his cup, upending the empty vessel and throwing the room a look of disappointment. 'The quicker we can get the whole thing over, the quicker we can return to the important business.'

Thorir hersir had been given the honour of sharing the duty with Gunnhild's brother, and the pair held the broom low as the newlyweds took the bride leap. Brands were being raised all along the hall, and Thorir and Harald Bluetooth flanked the couple as they made their way between ranks of raised drinking horns.

Soon they were through the big doors, putting the noise and reek of a thousand bodies behind them as the cool night air pecked at their cheeks. Erik's hall lay alongside that of his father, a clear statement to all of his preferred status among the sons of Fairhair, and the coiled and twisting forms of beasts and heroes which adorned the doorposts came alive as they approached beneath a serpent of flame. The night sky was a vault of stars as Erik bent to sweep his bride into his arms, and Gunnhild moved her own arms to his neck for the first time as Erik stepped across the threshold.

A solitary hearth blazed along the centreline, and Erik carried Gunnhild beyond it and laid her down upon the bed which had been moved into the centre of the room for that auspicious night. The pair quickly undressed and slipped beneath the bearskin as the witnesses ringed them with flame. Soon the final act of marriage was completed, and Gunnhild arched her back as Thorir and her brother slid the bottom sheet from beneath her. Satisfied that they had witnessed the moment that Erik and Gunnhild had become one, the men began to troop from the hall; there the sheet would be passed from bench to bench so that all could bear witness that the husband had taken his wife's maidenhead.

Erik began to move aside as the shadows returned, but to his surprise Gunnhild's calves coiled around his waist to hold him in place. 'The women who care for me tell me that tonight is fortuitous.' She teased his beard with a hand as the other floated across his groin. 'We have the whole night ahead of us, Erik,' she breathed, 'to get me with child before the sun returns.'

14

MOSKSTRAUMEN

Kolbein glanced across as he eased the steering oar amidships. 'It is up to you of course, lord, what with you being the king of Halogaland and all. I did say that I would show you it if we were ever in the area, that first day after you had shot the gap in the old *Isbjorn*.'

Erik thought for a moment, but his face creased into a smile as the memory hardened from the mists of time. 'Of course!' He gave a chuckle. 'Our first day together when we were running south to escape the retribution of Sigurd Jarl.' He chewed at his lip as he thought. 'That was...what...'

Kolbein had the answer ready. 'Twenty years ago now, when we were on our way to our first raid together, the big monastery in Brittany.'

Erik nodded. 'Landevennec; and you told me that if we were ever in the Lofotens you would take me to see the great whirlpool of Moskstraumen. That settles it. What kind of king would I be if I had never set eyes upon such a wondrous thing in my own land, the gateway to Njörðr's seabed hall?'

Erik raised the horn to his lips and blew a long note. As the styrismen on the other ships in his fleet turned their faces his way he exchanged a grin with his foster-brother on the steering platform of the *Sea Stallion* to starboard.

Erik was king of Fjordane now of course, and his old foster-father Thorir hersir collected the skat owed to both Erik and King Harald in their halls down in Rogaland. It had been a moment of great pride when he had rounded the old familiar headland, and the hall which held so many fond memories of childhood hove into view on its ledge of land overlooking Naustdal. His own father the king had gifted him a magnificent drekkar before they had left his hall to come north, and Erik's eyes wandered to the dragon headed prow as the ships began the turn. Named *Draki* after the very first dragon ship which had carried his father to victory at Hafrsfjord, only the more elaborate decoration set Erik's new ship apart from Arinbjorn's *Sea Stallion,* the other skei in the fleet, but it was enough to show the new realities of their social standing. The men of Romsdal too had answered the war arrow, and Erik lifted his gaze to watch as the snekkja *Fylki,* the Falcon, bucked and rolled in the swell as she too came on to the heading. Soon they would be joined by a final ship as the men of Halogaland met their obligations to their king, and they would begin to steer a course for Bjarmaland and war.

'How far is this place then?'

Kolbein turned back and squinted into the sun as he gauged their position. The land was little more than a broken line on the eastern horizon as the fleet had taken advantage of the benevolent weather conditions to move offshore. With the increased sea room available the ships had fanned out into a loose gaggle, and the crews had ridden the deep ocean rollers like horsemen at the gallop as they ploughed their way north. Kolbein had finished his calculations, and he centred the tiller as he replied. 'It's still early in the summer and the sun is still low on the horizon, but we are close to noon and I am certain we are drawing near. Those lands which you can just make out to north-west will be the southern tip of the Lofotens. We should reach them long before dusk, even at this speed.'

Erik laughed. 'Well, that's good news at least. I would rather not arrive there after dark!'

'It would make no difference if you did, lord. The Mokstraumen only appears twice a day, you'd sail over it and just think that it was a tricky current at any other time.'

'We had best get a move on then,' Erik replied. 'I would hate to miss my chance to knock on the sea god's door.'

Skipper Alf had edged across in the *Fjord-Ulf,* and Erik suppressed a smile when he saw the enquiring look on his old friend's face as he gripped the stern post and peered across. Despite the fact that the years spent under the tutelage of Alf and the other styrismen had honed Erik's seafaring skills to the point where he had very little to learn from any man who travelled the whale road, he still valued the old seaman's advice. Alf, if not quite of his own father's generation was not far off it, and Erik was astute enough to recognise the need in the man. Although still a skipper of reputation, Alf's usefulness was ebbing away as younger, more vigorous men learned his trade. Erik knew that it must be a difficult thing for a proud man to accept and always ensured that he gave his advice and council the attention it deserved. He cupped a hand to his mouth and called across the waves. 'We are going to the Mokstraumen.'

Even at a distance Erik could see the roll of the eyes as Alf reacted to the news, and he snorted at the old man's world weariness. He called out again. 'We will race you there old friend.'

Alf ran his eyes along the sleek hull of the *Draki,* and then back to his own ship. He turned back and pulled a face.

'Some race,' he called across the gap. 'Me and my lads in this old tub, and you in a dragon ship.'

'I will shorten the sail to give you a chance,' Erik called back.

The men on both ships were listening in and Erik could see the desire on their faces. With one eye on the crews lining both wale's he upped the stakes. 'There is a barrel of ale for the winning crew.'

The men on the *Fjord-Ulf* gave a cheer, and Erik could hear the cries for acceptance come from the little snekkja even as his own men stood-to. Alf's face broke into a soppy grin as he saw that he had little choice but to accept, and Erik called the order as the men flew to the sheets. 'Double reef the sail lads and lower the yard, halfway will do.' He shot them all a grin. 'Let's work up a thirst.'

Alf called across as the crews got to work. 'Kolbein! We had best make the finishing line the first to pass the southern tip of Vaeroy!'

They shared a grin before Alf turned away, and Erik's styrisman explained. 'The Mokstraumen occurs in the strait between the northern shore of the island and Lofoten Point to the North.' He gave a snort. 'Go north of Vaeroy at the wrong time of day and we may end the day swimming with the fishes. We have no local pilot until the ship from Halogaland joins up with us.'

Thorstein skipped up onto the steering platform, and within moments he and Erik were working the handle of the halyard. As the yard clattered down on the rakke bracket Erik threw a look outboard, watching as the crew of the *Fjord-Ulf* worked the braces, angling the spar as they hunted the wind. As the way came off the bigger ship the little snekkja bounded forward, and within a heartbeat ribald cries were crisscrossing the waves as the ships drew apart.

Despite the efforts of the wind and waves to drown them out, catcalls and laughter carried to Erik's ears as the other ships in the fleet got wind of the contest and threw their support behind the smaller vessel. The *Draki* settled down as the crewmen manning the sheets sought the wind, and the long lithe skei began to live up to her name as she slipped through the waves like a knife.

Erik raised his chin and looked out past the upsweep of the bows as Kolbein worked the steer board at his side. Alf's ship was a couple of lengths ahead, but the gap was already closing inch by inch as the slimmer hull of the *Draki* creamed the surface. The snekkjur was left astern as the pair pounded on and, raising his eyes further, Erik was surprised to see that the island chain was already beginning to grow distinct from the haze.

The *Sea Stallion* bounded past on the starboard beam, its sail full and taut, straining against the sealskin ropes which held it in place as Arinbjorn threw them a mocking wave. A voice came at his elbow, and Erik snorted as he turned to see the look on his styrisman's face. 'This is the hardest thing I have ever done, Erik,' Kolbein said with a grimace. 'Only being able to use half the sail in a race. I feel about as much use as a one legged man in an arse kicking contest.'

'Just hold your station here,' he replied with a wink. 'Alf and the rest think that they have the better of us, but I have an idea which should wipe the smirks from their faces and win us that ale.' The wind was blowing steadily from the Southwest, and Erik flicked a look outboard as the island of Vaeroy began to fill the view ahead. 'Here,' he said. 'It will be easier and quicker if I take the tiller than explain what I want to do. Besides,' he said with a wink, 'it will give you a better chance of watching the smile of victory drop from the faces of Alf and his lads.'

Erik slipped into Kolbein's place, and he braced his foot against the sheer strake as he waited for the moment. The *Fjord-Ulf* began to move across his line of sight, edging to starboard as it gave the outlying islands in the archipelago a wide berth, and Erik worked the steering oar with a deft hand as he shadowed the little snekkja's movements. Clustered along the centre line where they would have a greater stabilising effect on the long, lean craft, the crew of the *Draki* had grown quiet as the *Fjord-Ulf* held its lead, but the time had come for Erik to make his move and with a flick of the wrist he slotted into position broad on the larboard quarter of his opponent. A gap had opened up between the *Fjord-Ulf* and the first of the rocky outcrops which marked the beginning of the Lofotens, and Kolbein shot his king a look of concern. White water ahead showed the presence of underwater hazards, razor sharp rocks which would rip the bottom out of the drekkar in a heartbeat, despite its shallow draught.

Erik's eyes flicked between the spume flecked madness of the water little more than a dozen ship lengths ahead of the *Draki,* and the sail of Alf's ship as it moved to starboard and safety. He saw the moment when Alf's styrisman began to centre the tiller, ready to steer the ship back on its course to inevitable victory, and a pang of regret came as he thought that he had endangered the vessel in vain. But as he watched the top of *Fjord-Ulf's* sail the first flicker came a moment later, and he teased the tiller on his own ship to hold her steady as his plan began to bear fruit. Anlaf Crow was watchmen and he called back from his position in the prow as the ship neared the rocks. *'Six lengths of clear water.'*

The wind was blowing steadily over the larboard quarter, and Erik stared at the top of his opponent's sail as he fought down his own fear of foundering. At last, just as he thought that he would have to abandon his plan and save the ship, a shiver ran down the length of the *Fjord-Ulf's* sail as it began to luff, and the great woollen sheet collapsed against the mast as the *Draki's* own sail stole the wind. In an instant Erik had the tiller hard over, pulling with all of his might as he willed the ship to come about, and the crew held their breath as one as the tall stem post began to swing to starboard with agonising slowness.

Anlaf called again the concern dripping from his voice, *'two lengths!'* and Erik fought to calm his voice as he cried out to the crew. 'Over to the side lads, let's give her some help.' The *Draki* heeled to starboard as the men rushed to add their weight to the turn, and Erik redoubled his efforts at the tiller as a yowl beneath their feet told them all that the bottom of the ship was scraping against an unseen rock. A shudder passed the length of the ship as the keel caught, but a moment later the sea had surged to lift her clear, and Erik watched as the crew exchanged looks which told that they knew that the gods had been with them.

The outlier passed down the larboard side as the *Draki* surged forward into clear water, and Erik stole a look at the *Fjord-Ulf* as they moved away. The current had pushed the bows to the East as he had hoped once the way had bled off the ship, and Skipper Alf's crew were desperately hauling at the sheets as they hunted the wind. The sail was beginning to fill once again as the yard came about, but the momentum had been lost and everyman there knew that the race could only have one winner. Vaeroy broke the waves a few miles ahead, the big double bay on the landward side of the island clearly in view, and Erik centred the tiller as he led the fleet to the place where they would overnight.

Kolbein was back on the steering platform, and they exchanged a look as the crewmen filled the ship with nervous laughter. The styrisman made to make a comment, but his mouth gaped like a fool as his mind scrabbled in vain for the right words. Finally he gave up trying, and the pair, king and huskarl shared a tight smile as Erik spoke for him. 'Thirsty yet?'

'HERE SHE COMES.' Kolbein narrowed his eyes and peered away to the East. 'Yes,' he added, 'no mistake, that is a warship. A big skei too!'

Erik nodded with satisfaction. 'That makes three, plus the snekkjur.' He did a quick calculation as the fleet bobbed on the swell. 'That gives us just over four hundred men.' He shot his styrisman a grin. 'Even leaving an adequate ship guard that will give us enough men to hit them hard but not so many that this King Svasi will shy away from battle, especially after we have given him good cause to seek my own head over the course of the summer.'

The broad expanse of water known as Ofotfjord gaped to the East, with the sleek shape of the Halogaland contribution to his ship army breasting the waters as the rowers pulled out to join up with their king beneath a madness of gulls. 'It was a good idea,' Kolbein was saying at his side, 'that we steered well clear of Narvik.' He shook his head as he thought of the northern town. '*Kaupmen*, traders, the lot of them. They would sell their granny if the price was right.' Erik nodded in agreement. This Narvik was the furthest north of the towns which bore the same name dotted up and down the coast of Norway. It simply meant *knarr-vik*, the harbour of the trading ships, and although the locals and Erik himself as king had grown rich on the trade from the interior, those same connections with the hinterland could very well have led to his arrival in Bjarmaland being met not with surprise and fear, but a fully mustered and battle ready army.

They were up in the lands where the sun neither set at high summer nor rose at all in midwinter, but the gods had seen fit to keep the sea ice free all year round, unlike the coastlines of Sweden and Finnmark on the far side of the mountain chain men called The Keelbacks so a healthy trade had developed. The downside for Erik was that communications between the two regions were frequent and the path well trodden; they would have to move fast, despite the precautions he had taken to keep their destination secret.

The men began to cheer and beat a rhythm on their shields, and Erik looked again towards the oncoming ship. Seeing the king's pennant flying at the mast top the Halogaland ship was coming about, flashing a glimpse of her keel as it heeled over in the turn to come alongside the *Draki*. The other ships fanned out to give the newcomer sea room, and Erik recognised the bluff shape of Ragnar Jarl at the stern. A smile flashed from within the depths of his great beard, and Erik returned the gesture as he felt the warmth of the man even across the waves. The styrisman on the Halogaland ship brought the skei onto a parallel course a short hail from the *Draki*, and Erik watched as Ragnar filled his lungs. 'Welcome to your kingdom of Halogaland, King Erik. I bring you the *Orm,* the Serpent, double crewed to do your bidding,'

Erik ran his gaze along the length of the Halogaland ship. Ragnar was right, the deck was crowded with men, good fighting men, and his heart soared at the sight. That would add another one hundred and twenty or so hirdmen to the force: he had an army, despite the poor response to his war arrow from the jarl in Moerr. A single Snekkje was almost a snub, and although he realised that the district lay close to the Trondelag and Sigurd Jarl's seat of power he had expected more. It was true that his half brothers had burned in the old jarl and his men, but King Harald had taken revenge and installed the present jarl from the family line. Arinbjorn's sister Gytha was there, and Erik hoped that she was safe. It was a thing which would need his attention he was sure, and soon. 'We expected you yesterday, lord,' Ragnar was saying. 'The beacons were lit when the watchers on the headlands saw your approach.' Erik was about to answer when he saw the gleam in Ragnar's eyes, even from a distance. 'You went across to see the Mostraumen?' Erik confirmed that they had. 'What did you think?' Erik's mouth curled into a smile as he made to reply. It was obvious from the looks on the faces of the Halogalanders that they already knew what the answer would be. 'I have seen more movement on the surface of a bowl of broth,' he said to gales of laughter on the *Orm*. 'As you can see we carry a *skipsbåt* amidships, a little ship's boat which I use if I need to convene my leading men whilst at sea. We loaded it with gifts for Njörðr and set the sail to carry it to the heart of the whirlpool, but all it did was spin it around in a circle and send it right back to us!'

The crews of both ships were laughing now, and Erik regarded Ragnar Jarl as the big man waited for the ruckus to subside. Despite the warmth of the day the jarl was swaddled in the thickest bearskin, a heavy circular cloak pin at the shoulder of the type favoured by the Irish and Scots testament to the more usual destination for his summer raiding. He was an imposing sight, just the type of man that Erik needed if the raid was to be a success.

'Come up in the spring, lord,' Ragnar called across. 'The Moskstraumen is in full flow then, that's when Njörðr collects his tribute.' He furrowed his brow as he asked their destination. 'We are heading north?'

Erik nodded in confirmation. 'How did you know?'

The Halogalander flashed a grin. 'If we were heading

anywhere else you would have summoned us to Avaldsnes, lord.'

Erik exchanged a look with Kolbein at his side. It was true of course, and he hoped that the rest of the population in Narvik were not as sharp witted as their jarl.

Ragnar was pointing ahead. 'I will take us through the Tjeldsundet Strait and out into Astafjord. Once through that we will be well on our way to Finnish lands.'

15

The flames flared as a gust wormed its way beneath the shingles, and the watching men coughed and spluttered as greasy black smoke swept across the yard. 'It may be choking standing here in the middle of this shit, but it's worth the discomfort,' Kolbein said, his eyes red rimmed and streaming as the cloud engulfed the little group. He slapped the back of his neck, rolling yet another insect between thumb and forefinger before flicking it contemptuously away. 'I am surprised that the little bastards can still find a place to bite. I can't have much blood left, even if they do.'

Erik managed a snort of sympathy, but he was as sick of the blood suckers as any. He looked up at the sky and cursed again. Thick clouds cloaked the sun, the grey mantle little higher than the treetops themselves. They could put as many outlying settlements in Bjarmaland to fire and sword as they liked, but if nobody saw the smoke they may as well have stayed at home. Finns! He spat in disgust. Ragnar Jarl knew them well as did all men of Halogaland, and he recalled the man's description of their fighting abilities as he watched the clouds roll northwards. *"They'll not fight unless they really have to, lord, at least not against Norsemen. They will stand off and try and pick men off with their powerful bows, you will have to really stir them up, do something that King Svasi cannot ignore if he wishes to keep his king helm."*

Arinbjorn had followed his gaze, and Erik's foster-brother sent a ball of spit spinning into the grass. 'Even midges need to eat.'

'Well, they can go and eat someone else, the little bastards.'

Kolbein's reply drew a snigger from the group, and Erik threw a wink to Helgi at Arinbjorn's side. 'It was not a problem we had up on Jostrudal, eh?'

Helgi snorted. 'We had other problems if I remember rightly lord,' Arinbjorn's huskarl replied with a grin. 'Like how to take a piss without it snapping off with the cold.' They shared a laugh, and Erik took in his old friend's features as they did so. Helgi had been a young man when they had crossed the great mountains to repay Bolli Sigurdsson for the insult at the horse fight. But the passage of time had been kind to Arinbjorn's huskarl, and little more than a handful of grey flecks within his beard and hair distinguished him from men who had seen far fewer winters.

Erik looked away to the South. The pale sunlight was silvering the forest canopy, but the weeks spent scathing the settlements along the banks of the White Sea had used up the days where the sun never set at all as had been his intention. 'We will set up camp here for what passes for a night this far north. Get the fires going on the beach, hopefully they will drive these little bastards away too.' He inhaled to continue, but spluttered and coughed as another of the insects met its end. Erik picked the tiny black body from his tongue and flicked it away. 'We have done our harrying,' he said with a predatory smile. 'Now that we have a few hours of darkness to work with, it is time to hit them where it really hurts.'

As the leaders wandered away to pass the orders, Anlaf pushed a man down the beach towards him. Erik studied him as they came. Leather boots and breeks and the same long white shirt belted at the waist that he had seen throughout these lands. Only the whorls and lines peeping out below his cuffs set him apart as a man versed in spell work from any of the other locals.

'Another one, lord.' Anlaf called as he approached. 'There seem to be as many shaman in this land as there are common folk.'

Erik nodded. 'Did you destroy everything? Idols, warlock staves?'

Anlaf shook his head. 'I fired the hut, but this is another new one, lord. I thought that you would like to see it.' He tossed the small figure across, and Erik snatched it from the air as the Finn was forced to his knees before him. He studied the piece, turning it over in his hand as he did so. 'Are you certain that this thing is a god? It looks more like part of the hut.' The features of a human face were just about distinguishable, and the remains of branches gave passable if unequal representations of limbs; above the eyes arced brows of moss, and a long beard of lichen hung from the pointed chin. He was about to ask the Finn the name of his god when a voice made him glance to one side. 'That is Tapio, lord, he is a forest god worshipped by hunters. They leave offerings to him before they set out in the hope that he will drive game their way.' Erik recognised the man as one of the Romsdalers, come across to help. 'You know Finnish?'

'My wife is Saami, lord.' The man shrugged. 'We call them all Finns much the same as the English call every man who tumbles from the side of a longship a Dane, but they are a nation of many tribes just like us. She started off as my first wife's thrall but, well...' He flushed and pulled a lopsided smirk. 'You know how it is.'

Anlaf still stood over the captive, and he snorted before reaching down to force the Finn's head down. 'Nobody is talking to you, god botherer.'

Erik ignored the interruption. 'Thankfully not, no, Gunnhild is enough for my appetites. My father does,' he admitted with a sigh. 'It's the reason why we are the main course for the local midges this summer.' He nodded down at the captive. 'I am in a good mood, despite the flies. Ask our friend if he has any last words.'

Erik looked about as the men conversed before him. The place was like any other in this part of the world. A sandy beach stretched away to either side, the high tide mark a tangled line of bleached and wave polished tree limbs. Twenty paces from the tideline the forest was a rampart, with only the roughly hewn track which had led them to the settlement marking the presence of men. The spearman had said his piece, and he turned back to report to Erik as he fingered the shaft of his axe. 'He said that today is a happy day, lord, he will soon be with the greatest god of all.'

'Óðinn?'

'Jomal, lord,' the spearman replied. 'My wife fashioned a small idol of him at home. I am a hunter myself.' He shrugged his shoulders. 'A god is a god, only a fool would turn down a little help, wherever it came from.'

Erik spoke again as his fingertips traced the design on the axe head. 'He said far more than that...' He allowed the sentence to hang in the air and cocked a brow, and Erik was gratified to see that the Romsdaler was astute enough to supply the answer he sought.

'My name is Sturla, lord.'

'Tell me what he said, Sturla.'

The warrior attempted to bluff it out, but the tone in his voice betrayed him. 'Lord?'

'Don't worry,' Erik replied. 'I am not some milkmaid who jumps at every shadow. I am a king with far too many brothers.'

Sturla snorted at his king's fatalism. All knew that the length of a man's life was in the hands of the Norns, the three old hags who hovered over every life thread on Midgard with their shears of woe. The only control which a man had over his fate was to build a reputation which would echo down through the ages in the time which was given to him.

'He said that he has been sent dreams of this day all his life. You are the Bloodaxe and you are a king of Norsemen. But, he says, what the gods give with one hand they often take away with the other.' The Romsdaler looked uncomfortable again, but Erik insisted that he finish. He cleared his throat and pushed on. 'He says that you will be five times a king, but that you will die on a windswept fell and few men will mourn your passing.'

Erik nodded as he took a pace back and raised his axe. 'Thank him for me,' he said as he prepared to strike, 'from myself and Jomal here.' He gave his axe a look of affection. 'I have been waiting for the gods to reveal its name to me. If things are as you say, they have spoken through this Finn.'

Jomal sang its song for the first time as it cleaved the air, and a moment later the Shaman's head had spun from his shoulders. As the Finn's body slowly crumpled and blood pulsed to redden the ground, Erik ran a fingertip along the blade and flicked the droplet away. 'Five times a king,' he breathed as his eyes lit up with pride and anticipation. 'Five times! Who cares how many men lament my passing, I shall be supping honeyed mead with Óðinn and my ancestors in a hall roofed with shields.'

Erik raised his gaze, sucking his teeth in frustration as the moonlight edged the cloud with silver. Kolbein gave word to his thoughts. 'A week of solid cloud cover and now this.' Erik gave a shrug. 'At least we can see where we are going.' Ahead of them gaped the mouth of the River Dvina, the banks and forest beyond dark shapes against the moon washed sky. 'It's just a shame that we took the trouble to lower the masts.' He threw a look across his shoulder. The ships' wakes were a glistening spear aimed straight at the river mouth, the telltale ripples made by hundreds of oar blades flashing in the light. He clapped his styrisman on the shoulder. 'Increase the speed, let's use the fact that we can see to our advantage.'

As Kolbein called the change, setting the stroke with a tap of his boot, Erik stepped down from the steering platform and made his way forward. The faces of the rowers were notice-ably pinched as he passed, but he exchanged a nod with those who looked his way as the pre-battle tension twisted men's guts. 'Soon be there lads, thanks to Anlaf and his boys at least we know what lies up ahead. If we had taken one of the other channels we would have found them blocked by sunken ships.' He drew a finger across his throat and grimaced. 'Very sticky!'

Thorstein Egilsson was at the point of honour, prow man in the king's ship, and he flashed a smile as Erik came up. 'All set?'

'Yes, lord.'

Erik ran his eyes across the men at Thorstein's side. Bunched in the scoop of the prow, these were going to be the first men to board the blocking ship, and he was pleased to see how keen they looked to get started. A quick look and he saw that he approved of Thorstein's disposition, drawing a smile from the man as he told him so. Thorstein was at the point of the formation, the huskarl's axe flashing at it caught the moonlight. Spearmen bunched in his lee while bowmen lined the side strakes, ready to unleash a torrent of arrows on the enemy ship. Once their opposite numbers had been forced back the grapples would fly, and before the enemy could recover Thorstein would lead the men over the side and get among them.

The dark shapes of the *Fjord Ulf* and the *Fylki* hung back as the ships entered the confines of the northern channel, and Erik saw with a glance that the prow men were ready there too. As the flotilla rounded the final bend in the Dvina the lights of the town of Perminia came into view at the head of the bay, and Erik retreated back to Kolbein's side as he sought a better view ahead. Anlaf Crow had stayed at his side now that the first attack of the day was only moments away, Erik's standard bearer proudly holding aloft his king's new axeman war banner. Erik threw a sidelong look as the first cries of alarm carried to them from the enemy blocking ship. 'It's just as you described it, well done.'

Anlaf snorted. 'If you have to spend half a week wading through mud, sleeping under bushes and being eaten alive by clouds of those little flying bastards you make sure that you do a thorough job.' He flashed a smile. 'Believe me, lord, you don't want to be sent back to take another look!'

A last look astern and Erik exchanged a thumbs up with Helgi, Arinbjorn's own prow man settled in the bow of the only other skei there that night. Further aft his foster-brother was working the steering board to come up abreast the *Draki* as the channel widened; both of the big ships should hit the

Finnish ship simultaneously, spilling their cargo of death and destruction on the enemy crewmen in an overwhelming tide.

A rolling roar from either side told Erik that the smaller *snekkjur* had reached the riverside, and a quick look confirmed that both ships were already disgorging their cargo of warriors onto the grassy banks. Anlaf shook his head, *'look at them run!'* the contempt he felt dripping from every word, and Erik risked a glance aside to see the small knot of men guarding the blocking chain choose life over certain death, casting their weapons aside as they bounded away into the darkness of the interior.

The moon chose that moment to creep clear of the clouds, painting the river a steely grey, and Erik widened his stance as Kolbein called out at his side. *'Brace!'*

The *twang* of bowstrings drew his eyes towards the bows, and Erik watched as the first arrows disappeared into the night. A heartbeat later the *Draki* struck, and he watched as the force of the impact rocked the enemy ship back on its beam ends. Within moments Arinbjorn's *Sea Stallion* hit near the bows and the blocking ship looked for moment like it would capsize completely, but the Norwegian ships began to edge back as the way came off, and Erik looked on in admiration as the spearmen in both ships kept their discipline and awaited the best chance to wreak havoc among the men reeling before them. The blocking ship stilled, its wale little more than a hand's length from the surface as it balanced on the very cusp of keeling over, before rolling back as it righted itself. The nearside now dipped towards the cold waters, and the Finnish warriors were left fearfully exposed as the deck came up to send them tumbling down to fetch up in a heap against the side of the hull. The spears flew then, peppering the defenders to send them scrambling away in bloody confusion as grappling hooks thudded into the sheer strake all along the hull. The moment that the bows of the *Draki* kissed the enemy ship Thorstein was across, his murderous axe cutting a swathe through the panicked Finns as Erik's spearmen vaulted the gap to complete the rout.

The final few Finns were leaping from the far side of the ship as the *Sea Stallion* finally grappled to send Helgi and his spearmen leaping into the fray, but the fight was already won and Erik flashed a mocking grin across the waters as his foster-brother came back alongside. 'You can enter the temple first,' he called across the gap. 'I promise!'

The great chain which had been strung to block the waterway had been lowered by the parties on either bank, and the oarsmen on the two skei dipped and pulled as they fought against inertia to gain way. The men on the big longships were hand-picked hirdmen, the best there were, and they were soon streaking across the inner bay towards their target, the temple of Jomal on its rocky outcrop. A quick look out past the curve of the stern post told Erik that the *Fjord Ulf* and *Fylki* had already gathered up the men who had lowered the chain and were busy towing the stricken blocking ship away from the deep water channel. Axe heads flashed in the milky light of the moon as the boarders prepared the ship for scuttling, and Erik noted with satisfaction that the chain itself lay suspended across the wales of both ships as they too gained way and prepared to ditch the obstruction in mid channel.

Away to the East torches were winking into life on the high walls of the town as the keening wail of a warning horn drifted across the water, and the oarsmen redoubled their strokes as the first splash of grey lit the sky to herald the fast approaching dawn.

Erik rechecked the chin strap on his battle helm as the ships neared the bank, bending to scoop up his shield as Anlaf Crow raised the war flag high. 'Come on,' he said, bounding down from the steering platform as the crewmen began to ship their oars. 'I am not letting anyone else have the honour of being first to land.' The pair paced the deck, huskarls bunching in their wake as they approached the stem. Erik called out as he walked, and the men shared grins as they stowed the oars and took up their own weapons. 'It's been a cold night. Let us set a blaze.'

The bows rose as the ship grounded against the bank, and a moment later Erik was over the side and splashing down into the shallows, wading ashore as men began to tumble from the bow. The *Sea Stallion* grounded her keel, and Erik paused for a moment as the first of her men made the bank and began to form up into an ordered column. Arinbjorn was there, and Erik, mindful of his earlier promise indicated the way ahead with an outstretched arm and a smile.

They set off at a jog as warning horns echoed along the valley of the Dvina, but there were no spearmen to bar their way and they were swapping the dew covered grass for a stony pathway as the first lights winked into life at the temple. Arinbjorn threw Erik a look as the line of grey in the eastern sky widened by the moment. 'Someone is in for a rude awakening!' Erik nodded. 'Let us hope so. If this morning goes as planned we will be on our way home before the sun sets again.'

Ahead of them the lime washed temple and its outbuildings stood out in brilliant relief against the dark bulwark of the tree line beyond, and Erik and Arinbjorn increased the pace as they saw the men to either side begin to fan out to close off any escape routes.

A dark square appeared in an outbuilding wall as a shutter was slid back, and the pair shared a laugh as a slack jawed face appeared within it. Despite the warning howl from the nearby town the owner's sleep befuddled mind was clearly struggling to accept the evidence of his eyes, but one of the Vikings was faster and the head shot back into the shadows as a spear thudded into the wall only a hand's breadth away.

Erik and Arinbjorn, their banner men at their sides, swept into the courtyard as the men began to search the huts. They shared a look, *'straight in?'* and moments later the little group were crowding into the temple building itself. A priest was there, the same white shirt and belt as always, and a Viking pinned him to the wall with his spear as Erik ran his eyes over the figure of the god himself. 'Greetings Jomal,' he said with a wolf-like smile. 'We have come to kill your king.'

16

The cart was dragged out from the lean-to and manhandled to the base of the steps. 'In you go lads,' Erik said with a flick of his head. 'There is a kneeling figure facing you as you enter, about three times the height of a man. On its lap there is a large bowl for offerings filled with silver coins, small bars and clippings.' He glanced down at his chest and threw them a smile. 'Jomal did have this rather lovely thing around his neck, but as we are about to burn his temple about his ears it seemed a shame to leave it.' The Vikings looked at the necklace with avaricious eyes. Alternating figures of gold and amber shone in the reflected flame of their torches, the whole triple looped around their king's neck so that he too appeared to shine like the sun. 'Have a quick rummage around in there for anything else worth taking and then fire the building,' Erik added as they struggled to tear their eyes away from the thing. The men nodded, skipping the steps two and three at a time in their haste to discover what other riches the Bjarmians had bestowed upon their god.

Erik planted his feet on the lower step of the temple as

they went, and looked out across the valley. The ship guard had already rowed the four longships out into midstream, and he watched the oar blades flashing as they held their position in the river current with easy strokes. He let out a sigh at the sight, the sleek hulls standing out in dark silhouette against a field of beaten bronze as the sky horse dragged the sun into the eastern sky. It had not been the easy or popular choice to send the ships away with the town little more than a mile upstream, but he knew that it had been the correct one. He had sold his decision to them by explaining that the town was just too close by, the distance to the temple just too great; a sally could easily overwhelm the guardsmen before the men at the temple could come to their aid and then they would be left stranded in the enemy heartland, shipless and in dire straits. Only a select few knew the real reason why he had chosen to take such a risk, and Erik's hand went to the hammer of Þórr pendant at his neck as he sent a plea to the god that his bold action would lead to success.

The priests of Jomal and their helpers were lined up in the field below the complex now, and Erik let his eyes wander across the vale to the walls of the town as dawn flared and the trees filled with birdsong. Perminia wore a corona now and the brands on the high walk were beginning to be extinguished, but the field before him still lay in shadow; the next part of his plan would have to wait awhile yet.

'Here you go, lord,' a voice said. 'This will bring the colour back to your chops.'

Erik came back from his thoughts, and his eyes widened in anticipation as he saw the reason for Kolbein's joviality. 'Porridge,' he beamed. 'Any good?'

Kolbein feigned indignation at his lord's words. 'I tested some, yes,' he said. 'What kind of huskarl would I be if I handed my king poisoned porridge?'

Erik indicated the priests of Jomal as he spooned his first dollop. 'They made it?'

Both men looked down at the meadow. The men from the temple had been forced to their knees, their arms tied securely behind their backs. The sun was just peeping above the town walls, and the golden light of dawn was advancing across the grass towards them like an incoming tide.

Kolbein shook his head. 'A woman, the boys are passing her around now; she will be ready to send back to them soon.'

Erik nodded. 'That's good; a wailing, ravaged woman always upsets the other womenfolk, then they get on the backs of their men and demand that they do something about it. It's true what you said about the poison though,' he added as he shifted the hot bowl in his hand and spooned another mouthful. 'I wouldn't be the first king done in by his breakfast.'

To his rear the temple was now a balefire, and Erik moved away as the heat began to scorch his back. The men were all out now, and he stepped aside as they loaded the cart with the last of the silver before trundling it to safety.

A murmur came from the men in the army as horsemen appeared from the town gates, and Erik ran the wooden spoon around the rim of the bowl before licking the last of the food from it. 'It would seem that we have gained their attention,' he said as he tossed the empty vessel aside. 'Let's hurry things along. I don't want to give them time to stop and think.'

The town stood little more than a mile to the East, and Erik ran his eyes across the members of what was obviously a delegation as they rode forward. Half a dozen riders, each man magnificently dressed and well armed, were intended to show him honour, despite the fact that he had spent the best part of the summer singling out the kingdom's holy men and shrines for destruction. The leading men in any community they encountered had been put to death, their taxes and skat carried away in Norwegian hulls. It was a calculated strike at the very heart of King Svasi's kingdom, and Erik felt the first pang of unease that he could have underestimated the innate cowardice of the man. Anlaf was trailing along in his wake, and Erik threw a remark across his shoulder as he realised that his goading of the Bjarmian king was not yet over. 'Stay close. I want to ensure that they know I am the same man who has been terrorising them these past months.'

The sun finally cleared the walls of the town as they walked, and the line of captives was revealed to those lining the ramparts. Erik could see hundreds of small shapes crowding the spaces, and he allowed himself a smile of satisfaction that the timing of the raid had worked out so well. The Romsdaler Sturla was there, and Erik called him across as he went. 'Stay with me. I want you to tell the prisoners what I say.'

He was up on the first of the shaman now, and he flicked a sidelong glance to check on the position of the horsemen as the haft of his battle axe slipped from his shoulder. They had covered half of the distance from the town gates to the place where Erik's ship army had gathered, close enough to recognise who the men on their knees were but not so near that they could even think to protest or intervene in any way. He turned his face to the riders as he stood over the bound man, the chain of Jomal glittering like shards of broken ice on his chest as he did so. 'Hoist that banner high, Anlaf,' he said as the axe came back. The comment had caused the captive to glance his way, and Erik saw fear flash in the man's eyes as he watched the blade rise and knew that his end was a heartbeat away. The axe came down to send the priest's head whirling across the grass, and Erik placed a boot in the middle of the torso and gave it a shove. As the body fell forward and blood steamed in the cool morning air, Erik ambled behind the line of bound men. They were shifting uneasily now as he approached, but he held the nearest man's gaze in his own and offered him a small smile of encouragement. 'You are about to leave Midgard friend,' he said. 'Jomal will be watching, show him your worth.' The priest opened his mouth to reply as Sturla translated his king's words, but the axe was already in motion and his head had left his shoulders before a word escaped it. Erik paused and looked towards the horsemen. They had drawn rein, holding their position on the roadway, and despite the distance Erik thought that he saw the moment when the look of disbelief on their faces transformed into snarls of fury.

As the last of the priests met their end, a flash of pale skin beneath a shock of raven black hair so typical of the northern Finns drew their eyes back towards the compound. The men there had finished ravishing the cook, and the woman was in the throes of suffering her final indignity of the morning as what little remained of her clothing was stripped away and she was packed off towards the town with a parting slap on the arse. The watching army beat their spears against the boards of their shields as she ran, the catcalls and laughter adding another level to her humiliation. One of the horsemen put back his heels and cantered across, bending low to scoop her up before retreating to safety, and Anlaf stepped up to speak as a movement from the town caught his eye. 'The doors are opening, lord,' he said. 'It looks like we have been successful.'

'ORDER THEM BACK.'

As banner man Anlaf had been trained in the use of the

battle horn, and the huskarl blew the falling note which would send the men of the army to the rear. Satisfied that all the warriors were back within the confines of the temple compound, Erik watched as the main gate of Perminia continued to spew forth armed men. Horsemen had been the first through, only a score or so, but he had felt the concern sweeping the ranks of his own men as they watched the riders head straight to the riverbank to nip any ideas of a retreat back to the ships in the bud.

A voice sounded vaguely at his side, but he was too caught up in his own worries to pay any attention until the familiar voice snapped out again.

'Erik!'

The change in tone had done the trick, and he tore his gaze away from the enemy warriors to glance aside.

'I said stop picking at your nose, it unnerves the men.'

It took a moment for his jumbled thoughts to recognise the man at his side, but his eyes widened as the words ordered themselves in his mind. He stopped what he was doing and looked at his hand in confusion. 'I don't pick my nose.'

'Yes, brother,' Arinbjorn replied, 'you do. Every time you are worrying over something or other your hand goes to your nose. What's more,' he added with a frown, 'the men know it too; so do me a kindness and rest your hand on the handle of your sword or the haft of your axe if it needs to be occupied while you think.'

Erik did so, and he was about to share his fears with his foster-brother when he saw the thing which he had been waiting for and he gave an involuntary gasp. The head of the Bjarmian force was half way to the temple and he had feared that the man he had come all this way to slay would stay safe behind his walls, but he laughed for the release of it as the banner left the gateway and came out into the full light of the morning sun.

'*There!*' he cried as the relief he felt washed through him. 'There is the bear banner of King Svasi!' His eyes ran down to the standard bearer and he grinned like a fool. 'And that old bastard must be him!' He flashed them both a smile. 'Come on then, let's get back to the others. Arinbjorn?'

'Yes, brother?'

'You recall what the signal is when the time comes?'

A blank look crossed Arinbjorn's features and Erik's own face dropped, but he laughed again at his friend's joke as his mouth curled into a smile and he replied. 'Seven short blasts on *Gjallarhorn* there, repeated in two groups.'

Erik and Anlaf laughed at Arinbjorn's description. They were almost up with the men in Erik's shield wall, and he saw with joy that the sight of three leading men in such high spirits had visibly lifted their own. Gjallarhorn, the Yelling Horn, would be sounded at the onset of the Ragnarok by the god Heimdallr to summon the warriors from Óðinn's hall to the fight, and he clapped his friend on the shoulder as they parted to take up their positions for the upcoming battle. 'It shall not be our end of days, brother. I know it!'

The battle line drew apart as he approached, and Erik kissed the blade of his axe and threw them a rallying cry: 'Bjarmians? I shit 'em!' Erik watched with glee as faces lit up all along the line, and the ground shook beneath his feet as men beat their shields in time and chanted his eke name in reply:

'*Blóðøx! Blóðøx! Blóðøx!*'

Past the shield brothers Erik took up his position just to the rear. He had already picked out the grassy bank before-hand and he placed his feet foursquare, running his eyes across the field before him as Anlaf Crow hoist Erik's axe banner high. Thorstein took up position immediately before him, and Erik watched the enemy come closer as his own guardsmen formed a wall of steel around him. The crew of the *Draki* had drawn up to his front, each flank anchored against the solid walls of two of the temple outhouses. Neither window nor door pierced the solid screen which faced downhill from these buildings; they would be a tough nut to crack.

Arinbjorn's men from the *Sea Stallion* ran from the other end of the outhouse on the left, almost to the flames of the conflagration which was the temple itself. Erik squinted to look through the smoke and heat haze and saw that his old friend Helgi anchored the end of the line there. He allowed himself a smile at the sight as he imagined the man he had known since his own childhood, back in Nausdal. He was no doubt suffering as the heat scorched his skin and clothes, and Erik resolved to fill that skin with good Norwegian ale at the day's end. The position he held was even more difficult than normal. All those who had fought in the press of shields knew of the importance of the man on the end of the line. Turn him aside, force a way through, and the shield burg would fold back on itself. Gaps would form between shields as the line stretched, spears become entangled in the crush and the slaughter would begin.

Away to the right the men of the snekkjur, *Fjord Ulf* and *Fylki,* held the line, and Erik looked on with affection as Skipper Alf tucked his grey hair into his helm and fumbled with the chin strap.

They were set, and Erik raised his gaze to watch as the army of King Svasi arrived at the foot of the slope and began to deploy. The king himself was just arriving, and Erik watched with disbelief as men began to erect a tent there and the men of Perminia began to form a leisurely battle line. The shelter was clearly for Svasi's use, and Erik made a snap decision. He could not let the day develop into a siege for his plan to have any chance of succeeding, he had to force the issue.

'Anlaf Crow! Sound the advance.'

The huskarl blew the three short blasts, and as faces turned back from the spear hedge Erik saw the look of surprise come into them as they watched the axe banner tip forward in confirmation. Erik seized the moment; snatching up a javelin he passed Jomal back to Anlaf as he gave the men a rousting cry. *'Come on boys, let's shake them up!'*

The battle line opened up once again as Thorstein led him through. Out in the clear he called again as he strode towards the enemy.

'Hold your position. Bowmen to the fore!'

As the sound of stomping feet trailed away and the bowmen scurried proud of the line, nocked and prepared to loose, Erik and his tiny band strode on towards the enemy. In the field before him the men of Bjarmaland were hastening to form a solid defence as they stole looks of incredulity towards the Norwegian madmen, and Erik raised his gaze as he sighted towards the king's tent. The look had reassured him that the horsemen were still down at the riverside, and he tossed the javelin in the palm of his hand as he sought the point of perfect balance. A skip and a jump as he opened his body, and Erik grunted with the effort as his arm flashed forward to send the spear hurtling towards the enemy and he cried the ritual challenge.

'Óðinn owns you all!'

Erik took a backward pace, and the men of the guard opened ranks to swallow him up as they watched the javelin clear the first of the Bjarmians and tip down as it plunged to earth. The shot looked true and the little group held their breath, hardly daring to hope that the fight could be won so easily, but a Finn glanced up at the last and his shield came up to deflect the dart harmlessly aside.

Despite the danger they were in the huskarls laughed at the sight of the King of Bjarmaland being bundled unceremoniously away from his own tent due to the actions of a single man and javelin, even if that man was Erik Haraldsson. Erik showed his disdain with a sniff and a sneer. 'Time to get back, before they discover where they left their courage.' Within a few paces they were back within the bosom of the army, and Erik called out a final instruction as he stood shoulder to shoulder with the men in the front rank.

'Bowmen!'

The men raised their bows and sighted.

Erik savoured the moment as all eyes turned his way. The beginning of the battle itself waited upon his command, but the Bjarmians had seen the action and were hurrying to cover themselves with their shields. It had to be now, and Erik felt the thrill course through him as his order rolled across the hillside.

'Loose!'

The dark shafts whistled away, a blur of movement against the cool morning sky, and Erik watched alongside the men of the *Draki* as the wicked darts converged on the portly figure of King Svasi. A heartbeat before they struck the king disappeared behind a wall of hastily raised shields, and Erik joined in the laughter as they watched men hobble away or go down. 'That should rile them up, a nice tight pattern lads,' he called as the Vikings before him yelled and gesticulated at their impotent opponents. Anlaf was at his side, the axe banner held high, and he murmured his concern as was his duty. 'It is best we get back to our vantage point, lord,' he said. 'Of all the people on Midgard, the Finns are never shy to put their own bows to good use.'

Erik nodded. If the Finnish tribes were noted for magic and skiing, their prowess with the distinctive short curved bows of the eastern lands was not far behind in the minds of westerners such as themselves. 'You are right,' he said, 'we have done enough. Svasi has been humiliated. He must attack, and soon.'

The pair, king and huskarl, looked across to the West; to the place where they had run down the blocking ship and sunk the great chain. The breeze was ruffling the surface, the early morning sunlight gilding the crests as eider bobbed and dipped. The men looked back, exchanging a knowing look at the peaceful scene, and Anlaf gripped the shaft of the battle banner a little tighter as his lord heft his axe and the first horn wailed at the foot of the hill.

17

SHIELDS!

E rik's eyes flicked from side to side as he prepared to enter the fray. A quick look told him that Arinbjorn and the men of the *Sea Stallion* were holding their own, despite the overwhelming numbers of Bjarmians who were desperately attempting to turn the position. Helgi was still in place, fighting like Þórr himself as he anchored the battle line against the flaming timbers of the temple of Jomal, and Erik sent a plea to the strange foreign god that his old friend could hold out until they had the victory.

Skipper Alf's men on the opposite flank seemed to have been all but forgotten by the avenging army of Perminia, but he saw that they were holding their discipline, plugging the gap between the outhouse and the temple despite what must be an almost overwhelming desire to fall upon the exposed flank of the enemy.

Finnish bowmen were skirting the edges of the fight, weaving and ducking as they sought a target for their powerful recurved weapons. Erik had let the best of his own bowmen choose their own place to fight, with orders to pick off any of their opposite number as the opportunity presented itself. It had contained the threat, but the steady stream of wounded men he had seen struggling back from the fighting pierced by shafts told the story that the deaths and woundings from the bowmen's assault had only been lessened and not nullified completely.

The heavy thunk of an arrowhead embedding itself into wood sounded at his side for what felt like the hundredth time that morning, and he gave the guardsman a clap on the shoulder in thanks; throwing them all a heartening comment as they lowered their shields and watched for more: 'not long now lads.'

He hoped that he was right, and he fought to push any images from his mind of the hundred and one disasters which could have overtaken the others, any one of which would spell death for the beleaguered Viking force.

As if replying to Erik's fears, Thorstein's gleeful cry tore through Finnish air. *There it is!*

As Erik's face spun back to the West he was pleased to see that not one of his guard turned to follow his gaze despite what must have been an almost overpowering urge to do so, but he spoke to remind them of their duty, just in case. 'Shields! Watch for those arrows boys, it would be a shame to take one now.'

He looked out, over the heads of the crews of the *Fjord Ulf* and the *Fylki* to the Dvina channel, and his heart leapt as he saw the prow beast of Ragnar Jarl's skei carving the waters of the great river as it came on at full rowing speed. The beast heads of the other ships, the golden headed snekkjur that he knew so well, *Reindyr, Bison* and *Okse* leading the little *Tranen,* the Crane, the ship from Moerr, were clearing the confines of the northern channel and he spoke again, recalling the earlier conversation with Arinbjorn.

'Anlaf!'

'Yes lord?'

'It is time for Gjallarhorn to play its part. Let my foster-brother know that we have the Jarl of Halogaland in sight.'

The banner man let out a snort of amusement that his king could joke at such a time, and he spat into the grass to clear his mouth as the horn of Heimdallr came up to his lips. A moment later the signal was made, and Erik watched as Arinbjorn's own banner man dipped his raven flag in acknowledgment before moving it forward to signal the attack. A cry went up as the men of the *Sea Stallion* saw the sign, and Erik watched with mounting excitement as their chosen men entered the fight at last. Kept back for just this moment the wolf coats: axemen; sword men; surged forward as the battle line parted to let them through; smashing into the front ranks of the Bjarmian warriors, sweeping aside men who had thought themselves on the cusp of a famous victory only moments before like the bow wave before a ship. Erik watched as the swords and axes rose and fell, the flash of steel dimming with every passing moment as Finnish blood misted the air and darkened the blades. A final push and he thrilled to the sight as he saw they were through, curving to the South, racing to come between King Svasi and the safety of his town as Arinbjorn and the others streamed in their wake.

Erik lifted his gaze, out across the heads of the main force of the enemy, as the first inklings of the disaster which was unfolding on their flank began to cause the men there to cast worried glances back towards the safety of the town walls. Ragnar's *Orm* was already past the place where Erik had landed his force in the wan light of the pre dawn, the oarsmen beating the surface to froth as they raced upstream. The snekkjur were struggling manfully in the wake of the giant skei, but the crews were no slouches and he knew that they would be in position long before Svasi could mount a horse and make his escape. The moment had arrived to take the head from the beast, and Erik cried out as he fixed his grip on the shaft of the great battle axe.

'Now!'

A flash of pink as Anlaf's tongue flicked out to moisten his lips and the war horn spoke again. The men before him began to ease aside but Erik and his guardsmen were already moving, shouldering their way into the press as they moved to seize the moment. Thorstein led the way, the others drawing their swords, hefting their shields as they moved forward to form the wedge that men called *svinefylking*, the boar head formation taught to the Dane king Harald Wartooth by Óðinn himself.

The crew of the *Draki* had scrambled aside at last, and Erik looked into the eyes of the first of the Bjarmians and saw the moment when the light of victory was replaced by the acceptance of imminent death as he watched the boar head crash towards him. Before the man could react Thorstein's sword came down, shattering the horn plates of his battle helm to crush the skull within. As the first of the enemy fell away Thorstein pushed on, hacking down at helm and shoulder alike as the Bjarmians quailed before the onslaught.

Erik stepped across the first bodies as the men at his side hacked and slashed, widening the breach, driving away the danger from their king as they drove forward. Safely ensconced within the wedge Erik raised his head, and a surge of excitement built within him as he saw how close they had already come to the war banner of his opposite number. Bearskin clad warriors were hastening to King Svasi's side as they saw Erik's axe banner reach the rear ranks of their own shield wall. Both sides knew that it was here that the weakest fighters congregated, battle shirkers and men carrying little more than kitchen knives and wood axes to the fight, and Erik heard the telltale swoosh as Norwegian sword blades cut only air and their opponents turned tail and fled before them.

Little more than a dozen paces now stood between Erik's *svinefylking* and the first of King Svasi's bodyguard, and he fixed his eyes upon the bulk of the king as he came on. The king of Bjarmaland had chosen a slight rise in the land to plant his standard, a place where he could direct his warriors and oversee the expected victory against the raiders who had tormented his lands all summer. Ordinarily it would have been a position of strength, the height advantage enabling his men to beat down upon the heads of any attackers, but Thorstein was no ordinary warrior and Erik watched with satisfaction as his huskarl threw his shoulder into his shield and drove forward and up. The first of the bear-men staggered back as Thorstein punched into his midriff, dropping his shield instinctively to parry the blow, and he barely had time to recognise the horror of his mistake before Erik's axe smashed into his shoulder. It was a tactic they had used in fights throughout the North, from the windswept glens of the Sudreys to the sun baked meadows of Pomerania; it rarely failed, and it succeeded again. Erik pulled the blow before muscle and bone could hold it fast, hooking the warrior out of line, and the Bjarmian's cry of distress was stillborn as a following huskarl's sword chopped down to drive the last breath away.

Cries in his own tongue all around him told Erik that the main enemy line had broken, and he fixed his gaze upon the figure of the king as they cut their way towards him. King Svasi was looking anxiously from side to side as he sought an escape from the collapse of his army, but Erik saw the moment when he realised that his position was hopeless and the look of panic was replaced by the countenance of a man determined to sell his life dearly. The attack had slowed as the bearskins dug in and fought back with the determination of men well aware that their actions in the following moments would be recited in smoke filled halls for many winters, but Erik laid about with his battle axe, carving a bloody path towards the king as the thing which had drawn them to the flyblown north that spring was about to be realised.

King Svasi hefted his spear as they approached, the morning sun gleaming from the gold chased blade as it caught the light, and a mournful moan rose above the field of battle as the last of his guard was chopped to the ground and the bear banner wavered and fell from sight.

'I am King Erik Haraldsson, named by my father Blood-axe,' Erik called as their eyes met across the bloody remains of his guard. 'King Harald of the Norwegians has sent me to take the blood price for your treachery, the day that you repaid his hospitality with seith and a witch bride to share his bed. He wants you to know before you die that your daughter's sons are being killed, one by one.' He gave a snarl of triumph; 'largely by myself, his favoured son.'

King Svasi opened his mouth to make a reply, but Erik had said his piece and besides, it never paid to allow a man versed in sorcery an opportunity to cast a spell. Erik darted forward, Jomal already a blur of motion as it cut the air, and an instant later the head of the king was joining the others it had taken that morning as it fell away in a brume of blood. Twin columns pulsed from the cadaver as Erik's own guardsmen stabbed bloodied sword blades skyward in their victory, and Erik cast a look about the battlefield as the body of the king crumpled and fell.

The army of Perminia was streaming away, men showing their backs to the Vikings as they desperately sought out the safety of the town. Away to the south Ragnar Jarl and the men of the *Orm* were ashore, sweeping across the riverside to harry the flanks of the retreating army. Men were tumbling from the bows of the snekkjur to add their own spears to the slaughter work, and Erik snorted as he imagined the disappointment of the men there as it became clear that the Bjarmian collapse had robbed them of an opportunity to be in at the kill. The smaller hulls of their ships had snatched away the chance to be there for the culmination of a summer's hard work, but each man had played his part, and any who lived to see his dotage could stand a little taller when a skald told the tale, and tell any who would listen that he fought with King Erik the year he had carried scathe to the land of the midnight sun and deprived King Svasi of his head.

A cry of acclamation caused him to lower his eyes, and Erik flashed a grin in return as Arinbjorn and Helgi pushed through the crowd towards him. 'I saw it!' His foster-brother swirled a forefinger in the air and described an arc. 'I looked across just in time to see old Svasi's head spinning through the air like a top!' The pair of them laughed again as Arinbjorn jerked his chin towards Erik's axe. 'I take it that was Jomal's work?'

Erik kissed the blade, throwing his brother a wink as he wiped Svasi's blood from his beard with the back of his sleeve. 'She is a hard bitch, but she knows her work.'

A man had retrieved the head of the king and was busying himself fixing the grim trophy to the point of its own war banner. Moments later he was at Erik's side, and the cry of triumph rolled around the battlefield once again as it was raised alongside Erik's own. Erik's guard still flanked him despite the overwhelming victory, and he was pleased to see their eyes quartering the field, searching out any sign of danger; aware that even a wounded man or lone bowman could still snatch disaster from the very jaws of their success. Together they walked the few feet to the top of the mound and looked away to the East. The last remnants of the beaten army were nearing the town gates, the same portal they had marched through to expected victory only a short time before. Ragnar Jarl had drawn up out of bowshot of the men on the walls and his men were yapping at the heels of the beaten Finns, herding them like so many sheep lest they stop to think and decide to make a last stand. Despite the arrival of the other ships and their crews, the Vikings were spread out over a large area; a determined counterattack spurred on by the watching women and children lining the walls could easily cause them unnecessary casualties. The day was won, and Erik found that he approved of the wisdom of his jarl.

A cough sounded at his elbow, and Erik looked down to find one of Skipper Alf's men waiting for permission to speak. Erik shot him a grin as the euphoria of the moment swept him up, despite the nagging voice at the back of his mind which was trying to warn him that all was not as well as it had seemed a moment before. 'Hall!' he said at the sight of the man's pinched expression. 'Cheer up. We won the day!'

Hall grimaced, but forced a smile. 'Congratulations lord, no man in the army ever entertained the thought that you would fail to lead us to victory.'

Erik caught the mood at last, and the smile fell from his face as he realised why the man was stood before him. 'Alf?'

'The Skipper is too weak to move, lord. He respectfully asks if you could spare him a moment at the time of your greatest victory.'

RAGNAR JARL SUCKED at his teeth as he turned Erik's question over in his mind. Finally he exchanged a look with his styrisman, and Erik saw the doubt which passed between the Halogalanders before he turned back and gave a shake of his head. 'I cannot recommend that we try lord,' the jarl said with obvious reluctance. 'I would be failing in my duty to you if I did.'

Erik made to question them again, but the looks on the faces of those of his crewmen who were closest to him told him that they too sided with experience over foolhardiness.

Ragnar opened his hands and gave a shrug. 'Even if the gods allow us to double the cape we should be thrust into the teeth of the gale. There is no land between there and the shores of Iceland, the rollers are as high as gable ends, even on what passes for a calm day this time of the year. With this?' He shook his head. 'We shall be little more than drift-wood before the day is out.'

Erik nodded that he understood. 'So we make for a shel-tered bay and set up camp for the winter?'

The ghost of a smile lit Ragnar's face for the first time in days as he saw that his king was coming around to his way of thinking. He gave the side strakes of the ship a pat. 'Build low walls and we have ready-made roofs. We can use your little *skipsbåt* to fish the waters of the bay when the weather allows it and the men can hunt the forests. We already have some provisions aboard, and the big ship barrels we can top up with melted snow for fresh drinking water. I doubt that even Ski Finns will dare to attack an army such as this, even if they discover us before the spring.'

Erik looked out beyond the mouth of the bay which Ragnar called Varangerfjord to the ocean beyond, and gave an inward sigh as he looked again on the windblown chaos there. Rollers as dark as slate were driving northeastwards, witches fingers of spray and spume flying from the crests.

There was no way that his flotilla could beat westwards against such power. 'Have you a place in mind?'

Ragnar indicated to the West with a flick of his head. 'If we follow the coastline the fjord narrows. It is a sheltered spot and off the beaten track, ideal for our needs.'

The first autumn storms had hit early that year. They had hardly buried their prows into the rollers beyond the White Sea when the first wintry showers had come on from the North. Within days the droplets had turned to sleet, sleet to snow as they had beat their way northwestward; Erik's hope that the coastline would begin to trend to the South dashed with each headland doubled. The prevailing wind had slowed their progress to a crawl, and each night when they had pulled the ships ashore to make camp they had covered a little less distance. The hours of daylight were growing less and less with each passing day, and it was no longer unusual to make camp for the night within sight of last night's stopping place. They had barely edged into the calmer waters of Varanger-fjord when the gales had redoubled. It was impossible to sail into the teeth of such fury and everyman aboard knew it; Ragnar's plan was the only one which offered a reasonable hope of survival, and Kolbein worked the steering oar to bring the *Draki* into *Orm's* slipstream as the crews ran out the oars and began to brail up the sail lest the gale shred them to ribbons.

By the afternoon of the second day land appeared to the Northwest as their journey neared its end, snow capped peaks above a mottle of reds and golden browns as the fauna of the North prepared to endure the coming freeze. The gales had lessened as they rowed, but everyman was a seasoned seafarer and none were fooled. Once the season of storms had begun the next blow would follow soon after; heavily laden and built for speed, the long narrow hulls of the skei in particular would be lucky to survive. A last night's stay on the indented shoreline which edged the southern limit of the fjord and they were striking out across the calmer waters of the inner bay. Unlike the low lying coastline which they had clawed their way along thus far the land here climbed away towards the uplands, and soon Ragnar was leading the ships towards a small sheltered cove.

Erik looked about him as the sound of keels grating on gravel filled the air. The cloud cover had thickened that day, moving down to shroud the distant peaks in a mantle of grey. The snow would move down the flanks by morning, the giantess Skadi, the winter huntress, would already be skiing the heights. They would have to move fast.

18

FIMBULWINTER

E rik rolled onto his back and stared at the arch of the ceiling for the thousandth time, tugging the russet fur of a musk ox up to his chin as the winds howled and sighed outside. He was thankful at least that his own bolthole was roofed by the long, sleek hull of a skei. Unlike many of the others, huddled together beneath the upturned hulls of the snekkjur, the rowers in the larger ships sat upon their own sea chests while at sea not the thwarts, the cross beams which braced the hull and doubled-up as a rowing bench. This small mercy at least allowed them to stand almost upright while sheltering from the ferocity of the northern winter. But while no man there would describe either as the height of comfort, everyman agreed it was preferable to an eternity spent in Njörðr's hall of the drowned, which had been the almost certain outcome had they not taken Ragnar Jarl's advice and abandoned their attempt to drive their hulls into the teeth of the storms.

Despite his surroundings Erik found that he was smiling as he ran his eyes around the space. Dully lit by the guttering light of a single seal blubber candle, the grunts and farts of almost a hundred men were sounding all around him, turning the air in the upturned hull of the *Draki* into what he was sure he would have considered a lethal soup of fumes at any other time. All of the ships had been carrying bundles of furs home from the lands which bordered the White Sea: bear; white fox; reindeer; even a goodly number of the highly prized furs which the folk in Christendom called miniver. The furs had been put to good use that winter as blankets to help ward off the cold ground and colder air as they slept, and Erik snorted as he imagined the thoughts of the eventual owners in the South if they ever knew.

Raised a few feet from the hard ground on walls of logs and turf, the hulls had made excellent shelters. Interior fires of course were impossible due to the build up of smoke in the cramped space, but the bungs which sealed the oar holes could easily be removed when the weather allowed to let a modicum of air and light into the dwelling space. The deep cold was still a problem, but Ragnar and his northerners had explained how they always heated rocks from the seashore around the cooking fires when living off the land this far north, and each man had used the hot stones to heat his bed for a good part of the night.

The scrunch of snow beneath booted feet drew Erik's attention across to the thick bearskin which covered the doorway, and he watched as the pale northern light threw a jagged rectangle across the sleeping men as the cover was drawn aside and quickly closed again to conserve the heat. The guard hesitated for a moment as his eyes grew accustomed to the gloom before picking his way carefully across to the place where the king lay.

Erik pulled himself up, rubbing the sleep from his eyes as the man came across and knelt at his side. 'It has happened again, lord.'

Erik's expression betrayed his surprise, but the spearman nodded his head and grimaced. 'It's unmistakable.'

'I will be along,' Erik replied as he fished about for a boot. As usual Anlaf and Thorstein were alert to anything which concerned their lord, and the pair were already waiting at the doorway when Erik arrived there. They exchanged a look but kept their thoughts to themselves as Thorstein held the bearskin aside for the others to exit the shelter. In the open Erik made his way across to the rear, loosening his breeks to take the first piss of the day. Moments later the others were at his side, and Erik gave a shrug as the three men made deep holes in the snow. 'There is no need to rush, Alf is not going anywhere in a hurry.' Bladders emptied, the three crossed the open space between the shelters to the place where a small knot of early risers had gathered. The group looked up, taking a rearward pace as they recognised the king for who he was. Erik surveyed the grave before flicking a look up at the man who had summoned him. 'This is how you found it?'

The guard nodded. 'Yes lord, I thought that you should see it before we replaced the stones.'

Erik drew in a deep breath as he ran his eyes across the scene. 'We carried Skipper Alf's body away with us for a reason,' he said finally. 'Not so that he could be dug up and carried away by animals. What do we think? A bear?'

'That is the only animal that I can think of that has the strength and guile to come here and move the rocks aside, lord,' the spearman replied. 'I know that there are few men standing watch,' he added defensively. 'But I cannot see how something so large would get by us, not with last night's moon.'

The mention of the moon caused his companions to exchange worried looks, and Thorstein spoke at his side. 'Bears could be up and about at this time of the year, lord,' he said with a glance towards the lightening sky. 'But why would a bear bother trying to dig up a corpse when we have fish down there on the drying racks?'

Erik looked down towards the beach. Half a dozen frames had been constructed as soon as they had set up camp, several months before at the start of winter. Despite the occasional dangers posed by sea ice and the permanent darkness of midwinter, men had been using Erik's small ship boat to fish the waters of the fjord almost daily. Only the onset of really severe weather had kept them hunkered down in their shelters until the blizzards blew themselves out. The constant supply of fresh fish, added to the reindeer and seal meat which the hunting parties had brought in, had not only kept them fit and hale but their spirits high through the dark months. Now with the spring almost upon them, just as thoughts were turning back towards hearth and home, a new problem was rearing its head. Erik looked again at the men gathered around him. He could sense that something was going unsaid, and he asked them to put words to their thoughts. The men looked at their boots as they waited for another to speak, but eventually their discomfort drew a reply. 'The moon was full lord,' one said with obvious reluctance.

Anlaf answered the statement with a laugh, but another of the hirdmen finally rediscovered his tongue and backed up his friend. 'It's been a month since the last time, lord. The moon was full then too and we *are* in Finnmark.' The man cast a furtive glance towards the nearby hillside before continuing. 'Who knows what moves about out there in the shadows?'

He was about to scoff at the men's fears when he realised that it was a thing which could quickly cause problems. Hundreds of men in the prime of life had been cooped up all winter, men used to a life of sea raiding and outdoor work. Even the smallest thing could set them to bickering among themselves like fishwives; he needed to show that he was taking their worries seriously. 'Anlaf, you remember the man who spoke Finnish? Where we killed the shaman with the little wooden statue of the hunter's god last summer?'

'The Romsdaler who helped you speak to the priests at Perminia? Sturla?'

'That's him,' Erik replied, 'the one with the Saami wife. He seems to know a lot about this kind of thing, nip down to the *Fylki* and get him up here. Maybe he can help lay these lads' fears to rest.'

Erik began to move the stones back onto Alf's temporary grave as Anlaf trotted down to the Romsdal shelter. He had in mind the perfect place for the old Skipper's remains; it was the sole reason that Alf's body had not joined the other Norwegian dead on the battlefield pyre outside Perminia the previous year. Sealed inside a cask of ale Alf had been left to overwinter in a hole dug from the permafrost, where the extreme cold would help to preserve the remains until they could carry it home in the spring. The other men pitched in, and the stones were already back in place when Anlaf returned with the spearman. 'Here he is, lord.'

Erik shot him a smile of reassurance. 'We may have a problem, Sturla. We think that a bear is trying to dig up Skipper Alf.'

Sturla looked from Erik to the gravesite and back again, and the king's heart sank a little as he recognised that he was not going to receive the answer he had hoped for. The Romsdaler sucked his teeth as his eyes flitted across the ground before them. 'That is not bear work,' he said finally with a shake of his head. Sturla walked to the far side of the mound, and they all watched as he raised his head to scan the hillside. Thorstein attempted to lift the mood, but his lighthearted comment only seemed to darken it. 'The boys here think that we have an *eigi einhamir,* a man not of one skin; a shapeshifter.'

Sturla seemed not to hear, and Erik watched the fear begin to creep into the men as they followed the hunter's progress. Suddenly he fell to his knees, and laying his head low to the ground proceeded to blow the loose snow from the track. 'Here it is,' Sturla said as he traced the outline of a footprint with a forefinger. 'A dusting of fresh snow blew in to cover his tracks, but this is where he came in.' He raised himself to his knees and shook his head. 'It's not a bear; too short. But it's too big for a man and the wrong shape for a wolf.' Sturla splayed the fingers of his hand above the footprint to prove his point. 'Besides,' he added squinting up at them, 'what sort of man would be walking about barefoot in the snow?'

Erik decided to confront the problem as he watched the colour drain from the hirdsmen's faces. 'There are four hundred of the meanest bastards I have ever clapped my eyes upon within pissing distance of this spot, men who destroyed an army in less time than it would take to describe the attack. If we have a shapeshifter, I think that he will rue the day that he decided to invite Skipper Alf to dinner.'

The first smiles lit the faces of the men at the graveside that morning, and Erik called across to Sturla as he climbed back to his feet. 'Tell us what you know about these things, and I will decide what is to be done.'

Sturla brushed the snow from his hands on the seat of his breeks as he came across and pulled a face. 'There are three types lord. The ones that cast a spell so that they appear to be something they are not we can obviously discount.' Erik raised a brow in question and Sturla explained his reasoning. 'If that was the case, the footprints would be recognisably man-like. Then there are those whose spirits go forth, we call them sendings, but their body remains elsewhere in a trance.'

Erik nodded as he began to take up the thread of the thing. 'Which we can also discount, because spirits don't leave footprints, man-like or not; so you think that it is the third kind then?'

Sturla nodded. 'There are those versed in shamanism who by donning the skin of a beast, take on the attributes of that animal. It's usually a bear or wolf, a bit like our berserks:'

> *'When thou, as a wolf,*
> *wanderest in the woods,*
> *knowing not good fortune,*
> *nor any pleasure,*
> *having no meat,*
> *save rivings of corpses.'*

Erik made a comment as the faces of those around him dropped again. 'Where did *that* come from?'

'It's something that my old ma used to chant on winter nights, when the moon was full lord.'

Thorstein cut in as Sturla smiled innocently. 'It must have been fun in your house. I will lay odds that your father was a hunter too. I bet he used to disappear for weeks on end every winter up onto the fells?'

Sturla looked surprised. 'As a matter of fact he was, he taught me all I know; he never stuck around during wintertime.'

Thorstein kept his face deadpan as Erik stifled a laugh. 'Funny that…Who would have thought?'

'Well, last night was the second night of full moon, so it will still look full tonight,' Erik said. 'Do you think that our *nátt-ganga* will return?'

Sturla teased his beard as he thought. 'Now that the weather has warmed up a bit from the depths of winter, it does look like our night-walker has picked up the scent of death. We call this full moon the Hunger Moon at home but up here it goes by a different name, the folk here call it the Wolf Moon.' He nodded as he reached his conclusion. 'He will be back.'

'Good, the days are lengthening and the seas should be calmer by now; we will float the ships tomorrow and be on our way. That leaves me just tonight to skin the bastard, Wolf Moon or not.'

ERIK SHIFTED on the stool and pulled his cloak a little tighter. All was still and calm down in the clearing, and he rocked from arse cheek to arse cheek as he sought to restore the blood flow, cursing himself again that he had not thought to bring one of the furs along to soften the seat. Sat in his hole on the hillside every part of the compound fell under his gaze, and he watched as the burly figure of Thorstein paced the shoreline, the moonlight reflecting dully from helm and spear point as he tramped another lonely circuit. He fought down a yawn and checked the position of his spear once again. The moon was low in the West now, casting the long shadows of the upturned ships away to the East; even at this time of year the dawn must be close.

The large island which they had been forced to call home for the duration of the northern winter was connected to the mainland by a narrow causeway; it was perfect for defence, the monster would have to cross here if he was to make another grab for the body of his friend, and in doing so he would have to move directly across his line of sight. Erik would emerge from cover and cut off the fiend's retreat as the

hue and cry was raised and armed men erupted from the shelters. Whether the *ganga* stayed to fight or turned to flee
mattered little; he would fall to their spears one way or the
other.

Erik was about to turn back to face inland when a movement caught his eye, slight, all but unseeable, almost as if the
shadows themselves had taken on life. His head spun back
around to search out the gloom, but nothing moved save his
huskarl pacing his lonely beat. Erik stared hard, but the darkness in the lee of the larger ships was as black as jet itself.
Thorstein was approaching the point where he would pass
from view as his route took him past the drying frames, out
beyond the hogback arcs of the skei to round the eastern end
of the island.

Erik stared again: nothing.

He was about to turn away when he realised that a small
part of the darkness was denser, more solid than that which
surrounded it, and he squinted into the gloom as his mind
attempted to make sense of the image his eyes were sending
him. Suddenly he had it as the unmistakable outline of a
snout hardened from the background, and before he was even
aware that he had moved Erik was out of his hollow and
running hard. With what little tree cover there had been
removed over the winter to feed Norwegian fires the winds
had scoured the snow on the hillside to runnels, and soon Erik
was on the well beaten track which led down to the crossing
place. In a heartbeat he was across, calling out a warning to
Thorstein as the spearman became lost from view. Men were
beginning to tumble from the doorways as Erik couched his
spear and shot between two hulls, crowding in his wake as he
burst out into the darkness beyond.

Erik dropped into a fighting stance as he waited for his
eyesight to become accustomed to the murkiness, bracing

himself to receive the attack he was sure was just moments away. A figure moved towards him and he tensed his muscles for the fight to come, but the flicker of moonlight on steel caused him to stay his thrust, and a moment later a familiar voice hailed him from ahead. 'I have seen nothing, lord. He has not come past me.'

Erik snapped out a reply. 'He is here, I saw the outline clearly.'

Dozens of men were pouring through the gaps between the shelters, spreading out across the strand and crowding protectively about their king as they too searched the shadows for the attacker. Erik's mind swam, the beast was among them, he knew deep in his gut that it was, and a cry from further down the beach brought them all running towards the northern perimeter.

'Here, lord! It's here!'

Erik pushed through the crowd and rushed towards the sound, hefting his spear and loosening the peace bands which secured the handle of his short seax within its scabbard as he ran. Within a few paces he was up with the man, and he scanned the shadows for a glimpse of his opponent as the others fanned out along the foreshore.

'Where?'

'This must be what you saw, lord,' the man replied, 'this old pelt.' He gave the wolfskin a contemptuous flick with the point of his spear. Erik looked as men began to chuckle and joke in their embarrassment. The skin of a wolf hung balanced on a pole, its lips drawn back into a snarl as it regarded them through the rheumy eyes of the dead.

Something was wrong. His father had told him that no man remained a king for very long if he failed to develop a sense of danger, even while surrounded by lesser men who played the fool and thought it a good way to spend their days sinking their face in ale horns. 'Back!' he cried. 'None of us are wind drying wolf pelts. This is a trick!'

Erik thundered between the whalebacks of the upturned ships, breaking out into the moonlight just as the gangly form leapt clear of the grave. Erik checked his stride as the moonlight played upon the figure for the first time, and the breath caught in his throat as his eyes locked with those of the *náttganga*. The beast curled its lips back in a snarl, but if the action was intended to make him stand his ground it had the opposite effect. Erik roared with anger and burst into a run, drawing back his arm to hurl his spear with all his might at the inhuman form straddling his old friend's grave. The spear cut the night air, and Erik's heart leapt in his chest as he watched it dip towards its target. At the final moment the monster threw itself aside, and Erik watched in anguish as the missile glanced off a rock and disappeared into the gloom. He drew his seax and raced across the clearing hoping to bring his tormentor beneath his blade, but the fiend was already across the causeway and drawing further away with every bound.

Erik drew up at the midpoint of the raised track and watched his enemy go. To his surprise the thing paused at the place where he had spent the night, just long enough to cock a long leg and piss into his old hiding place. Turning back, it cut the chill air with a final snarl and loped away into the darkness.

Thorstein's voice sounded at his side as they watched him go. 'It's a good thing that you swapped poor old Alf for that seal carcass. Who would have thought that a night-walker would be such a crafty bugger?'

19

HALFDAN'S CUNNING

'Well,' Ragnar said. 'We made it back in time for the spring tide, just like I said we would.'

Erik turned and pinned him with a look. 'Thanks to you.'

The jarl of Halogaland snorted and shot his king a grin. 'Somehow I think that Erik Bloodaxe would have seen off a king of Finns without my help.'

'Your modesty does you credit, Ragnar,' Erik replied. 'But we both know that's not what I meant. I was all for pushing on home last autumn, even when the seas were breaking over the wales of the Snekkjur and the rollers were prow beast high. If I had blundered on into the teeth of those storms it would have been both myself and the rest of my army who were guests of Njörðr, and not just the old Skipper there.'

The comment caused both men to look out beyond the fire-drake headed prow of the *Draki* to where the sleek hull of the *Fjord-Ulf* was edging closer to the centre of the great whirlpool with every moment. The flames were roaring now, the mast a wand of flame as the pair, ship and master, neared the end of their final voyage together.

They had left the place which they had been forced to call home for the winter a few days after the last attack. With the underside of the ships easily accessible the men had used the short daylight hours of the previous months to careen the hulls, removing every trace of the barnacles and other creatures which had made the lower strakes and keels their home over the course of the cruise. Freshly caulked, cleaned and repaired, the ships had quickly put the fjord behind them as they made for the open sea and home.

For once the sea god had been in a benevolent mood and they had made good time. Within the week they were back within the necklace of offshore skerries which gave the country of Norway its name; safe from storms and hurtling southwards in their rejuvenated hulls, the men had watched with renewed interest as the moon had waxed above them. Sturla had told them that this month it was the Crow Moon which would shine in the night sky: the man was popular; knowledgable; a skilled hunter. Erik had been delighted when he had accepted his offer of a place within his personal hird.

The light of the Crow Moon had changed the waters surrounding the Moskstraumen into a steely bowl, with just the darker shapes of the hulls of Erik's fleet and the saw-toothed ridges of the mainland and islands which ringed the bay to contest the night with the flames. The *Fjord-Ulf* was gaining speed as they watched, now bow on to the churning waters, and Erik thought back to his conversation with Ragnar, back at the beginning of the campaign. *'Come up in the spring, lord,'* Ragnar had said then. *'The Moskstraumen is in full flow then, that's when Njörðr collects his tribute.'* They had not thought then that the tribute would be Skipper Alf and the *Fjord-Ulf,* the very same pairing they had raced across the surrounding seas on the far-off day. The sea god had turned away their tribute at that time, but Erik was certain that Njörðr would be satisfied tonight once he saw who and what had moored alongside his sea floor hall.

A hush fell over the watching men as the bows of the *Fjord-Ulf* pirouetted on the spot, and the stern scattered an arc of glowing embers as it gyrated through the night sky. Gaining speed as it neared the boiling centre of the Moskstraumen, the wave tops were painted red as the pyre teased out to larboard and the little ship nosed down. A sudden jerk and the waters were cascading over the bow, and Erik watched as the snarling wolf head which he knew so well slipped from the sight of men. Almost vertical now, the flames cleared away just long enough for the awestruck men to catch a glimpse of the body of their old friend surrounded by booty and the trappings of war and then he was gone, the keel slipping beneath the waves as Njörðr reached up to embrace his offering.

Erik caught his breath at the potency of the scene which was unfolding before his eyes, and a heartbeat later all that remained on the surface was a pall of smoke and steam. To a man the crews at their benches stared pale faced at the scene as the breeze teased the brume apart, and Erik turned away as Kolbein called the stroke, the rowers bent their backs, and the ship began to pull away.

'IT'S NOT the welcome we were expecting, that's for sure.' Erik followed the points of light from hilltop to hilltop as they winked into life. 'Surely they must recognise us for who we are, so why are they lighting the warning beacons?'

Thorstein clicked his tongue as he too watched the signal fires begin to smoke. 'Do you want me to get the men battle ready?'

Erik nodded. 'Look to it. There is no telling what we are going to find when we arrive at Avaldsnes.'

Anlaf had been conversing with Kolbein as the big man worked the steering oar, and he added a comment as Thorstein began to move down the ship. 'King Harald could have died or been overthrown while we were away, lord. We have not put in at a town or even stopped to share news with fishermen all the way down the coast. It's been a long year, and it's not like we were in the South where traders carry news from port to port with their cargoes.'

It was true Erik thought as the men began to dig into sea chests and slip into mail shirts, they had been out of reach of any news from home since the previous springtime. His father could have died, been overthrown by one of his brothers or even be away from home on some foray or other. He brightened a little at the thought; even in his dotage, King Harald Fairhair was never slow to crush any opposition to his rule. 'You are right,' he replied. 'We should have been more cautious on the way down but what is done is done. I was eager to get home and I made an error of judgement.' He glanced down at the battle horn which never left Anlaf's side. 'Make the signal to the other ships.' He looked outboard, and despite the uncertainty of the moment Erik thrilled to the sight as the flotilla ploughed the home waters of Karmsund. Even without the *Fjord-Ulf* and the ships from Halogaland, Romsdal, Moerr and Arinbjorn's *Sea Stallion* this was a powerful force of battle hardened warriors, fresh from a stunning victory in the North. Most of the men had been together now for more than two score years, and they knew each other better than they did the members of their own families. He spoke again as the sound of the signal horn began to fade. 'The king has already named me as his heir. Let us hope that if my father *is* dead that one or more of my brothers has seen fit to usurp my gift stool,' he said with a snarl. 'It will save me the trouble of hunting them down.'

Thorstein returned and held out his king's brynja, and Erik waggled like a landed fish as he thrust his head and arms inside and the mail shirt slipped down his body with a metallic swish. He looked outboard again as he fixed his baldric back into place. The ships had cleared the strait and were turning into the landing place, the jetties and boathouses of Avaldsnes coming into plain view ahead as sails were shortened, oars run out, and the momentum bled away.

'Well, there is no shield army there,' Thorstein said as Erik fixed his helm into place and fumbled with the straps, 'and that looks like Helgrim Smiter and a few of his lads come down from the hall. They must have recognised us at last. It doesn't look like we will have to fight our way ashore at least.'

Erik looked as the remaining snekkjur, *Okse, Reindyr* and *Bison* moved in to flank the *Draki,* before twisting to call across his shoulder to his styrisman, confident that the smaller ships would hold their station and steer clear of the wharf. 'Beach her, Kolbein. The tide is out and I don't want us to have to clamber up onto the jetties when we are unsure of our welcome.' He threw his banner man a look as he took up Jomal. 'Anlaf, make the signal to form a battle line.'

As the notes rang out Erik and Thorstein walked towards the bow, the king raising his voice so that all could hear as he went. 'A last shield wall and then a night on the ale. Let's make it a good one!'

The oars were being shipped by the time the pair reached the bows of the long skei, and Thorstein gripped the handle of his shield as he prepared to protect his lord. The big battle axes were two handed weapons, devastating in a confined space, but their defensive qualities were almost non existent the moment that an attacker got within the arc of the swinging blade and it was then the duty of the axeman's right hand man to step up and counter the threat.

A slight tremble beneath his feet told him that the keel of the *Draki* had finally come into contact with its home shore after a year away and Erik was over the side, the first man in the army ashore as was right. As he waded the shallows Thorstein came to his side, and a quick glance to left and right told him that what had only moments before been little more than a stony strand devoid of life was now a seething mass of warriors as the ships disgorged the fighters. As the men reached the high water mark the shields came together with a crash, and Erik walked proudly forward as the battle cry thundered out.

'*Blóðøx!*'

The leader of King Harald's guard had left his companions and was walking towards him, and Erik was pleased and a little relieved to see that he was not only alone and unarmed but smiling widely. Thorstein and Anlaf Crow eased away a pace as the man approached, and Erik rested the great haft of his axe on his shoulder as he hailed him. 'Helgrim Olavsson! This is not the homecoming we expected, warning beacons and deserted strands. What news have you brought us?'

Helgrim's smile was replaced by a frown. 'I apologise lord, many things are not as you left them. You father...' His voice trailed away, and Erik could see the man struggling to find the right words. Finally Helgrim shrugged as he came to realise that there was no easy way to describe the king's condition. 'Your father's mind is addled, lord,' he said sadly. 'But we sacrificed to the gods for your safe return,' the huskarl added with a tight smile, 'and here you are.'

'How long has he been like this?'

'Ever since the autumn, lord. As the days grew darker so

did his mood, until the black cloud seemed to overwhelm him completely. There was some talk that the jarls should invoke *attrœðr* but your wife Gunnhild set herself against it, arguing that they should await your return as it was well known that you were the king's declared heir.' Erik's eyes widened in surprise at the revelation. If Harald had been declared *attrœðr* he would have reverted to the legal status of a child. It was a necessary safeguard in a society where honour and status were jealously guarded, where a drunken remark by mad uncle Thorkil at the Thing could spark a feud which would cost the lives of kinsmen yet unborn. But it was not without its dangers, as patriarchal powers waned and sons grew impatient for their inheritance. Erik's brother the king in the Trondelag would likely have been declared High King, and Erik would have returned to almost certain death. 'She is one of the few who can get any sense from the king,' Helgrim added. 'The bairn probably helps...' Helgrim winced as Erik looked at him in astonishment, before King Harald's huskarl cleared his throat. 'I apologise lord, it was not my place to break the news. You have a son born just after Jule; he is hale and hardy, everybody loves him.'

Erik nodded. 'There is no tougher fighter than a mother who fears for the life of her child. So all this,' Erik said with a wave of his hand. 'Sour faced spearmen and jumpy signallers. With the king ailing and me away and unable to protect my family, you were expecting a visit from Sigurd Jarl and my brother Halfdan the Black?'

'We didn't know what to expect lord,' Helgrim admitted as they began to make their way towards the hall of the king and the ship's crews began to relax and follow in their wake. 'The last we heard was that you were raiding in the White Sea, after that,' he gave a shrug, 'nothing. We knew that you would be victorious if you could tempt the Finns to take the field against you, but the storms came early last autumn so you could have been lost at sea.'

'Thanks to Ragnar Jarl we found a sheltered bay, hunkered down and sat them out.'

'That must have been a long winter, lord,' Helgrim Smiter replied with a look of pity. 'Holed up for months with nothing to do.'

Erik shared a look of amusement with Thorstein and Anlaf. 'You would be surprised. Finnmark offers up some unique distractions.'

They had reached the steps to the hall and everywhere he looked Erik was greeted by smiling faces. The hall steward came through the doors as they reached the top of the stairs and Erik was pleased to see the general happiness thereabouts reflected in the man's face. 'The king is sleeping, lord,' the man was saying. 'I will wake him and tell him that you have returned.'

Erik shook his head. 'Our meeting can wait, there is a boy nearby who has yet to meet his father. See that my men are found places on the benches while I introduce myself to my son.'

Erik skipped back down the steps, angling towards the hall which had been his father's gift when he had declared him heir to the high seat of the Norwegians. Anlaf and Thorstein dutifully followed on, but Erik paused and shot them a smile. 'I think that I can manage this lads. It has been over a year since we enjoyed the pleasures of the hall, go and make up for lost time.'

'If there is any chance that you are unsafe, our place is with you lord,' Anlaf replied. Thorstein added a comment of his own as the trio neared the hall. 'He's right, lord.' He cast a look around. People were emerging from the buildings again now that they were sure that Avaldsnes was not coming under attack; they had all seen the smoke from the warning beacons tainting the skyline and it was a good indication of just how fraught things had become at the very heart of the kingdom while they had been away. Erik saw the sense in their concerns and gave a curt nod. 'Wait for me outside then, I shan't be long. I want to be there when the king wakes.'

The doors were ajar and the steward lowered his head as the master of the hall gained the steps. Erik saw the door-posts, the rich carvings gleaming in the sunlight and he knew that he was finally home after the long year away, and he drank in the view ahead as he passed through the portal into the building itself. At the head of the room his high seat stood framed by the twin posts carved in the images of Óðinn and Þórr. Set a foot lower Gunnhild rose from her own high seat as he entered, stepping forward to offer her lord a horn of mead and congratulate him on his safe return from war.

Erik felt a pang of desire as he looked upon his queen. A pale shift overlaid a *hangerock,* an apron-dress of vibrant blue wool. Heavy gold brooches fastened the straps at her shoulders between which beads of amber, glass, silver and gold festooned the front of the gown. Topped off by a headdress of woven gold thread the sight caused the man, so long starved of female company, to catch his breath in anticipation of what was to follow.

He pushed such thoughts from his mind with difficulty and flashed a smile in greeting before taking the horn and draining its contents. 'You did well to await me in the hall,' he said as he lowered the vessel and cupped her chin with a palm.

Gunnhild replied in a steady tone, but her breath had quickened as much as his own at their closeness. 'I am not some scatty wench who cannot control her urges. I am the daughter of one great king and the wife of another.'

Erik bent to kiss her tenderly on the lips, and his face broke into a smile as they parted. 'Did I miss anything while I was away?'

Her lips pouted in mock indignation, but laughter danced in her eyes as she replied. 'You have been told!'

'Accidentally; Helgrim Smiter welcomed us on the strand and it slipped out.'

She snorted. 'That's not how I remember the birth!'

They shared a laugh as Gunnhild beckoned to the shadows. A maidservant came forward, and Erik's heart leapt as he saw his son for the first time. He indicated that the servant hand the boy to his mother with a flick of his head. 'I shall name him Gamli, but I will hold him for the first time when I take him upon my knee and acknowledge him as my son, tonight in the hall before the king and the men of the hird.' The boy reached out and gave his father's beard a tug, and Gunnhild chuckled as a fistful of bristles came away. 'He's strong!' Erik exclaimed as he moved out of reach. 'Just like his father.' He dropped his gaze to the lad's groin. 'Does he take after me in other ways?'

Gunnhild hooked a little finger and flashed a roguish smile. 'He is definitely Norwegian, lord.'

Erik snorted as Gunnhild handed the boy back to the wet nurse. Slipping her hand inside his own, she began to lead her husband towards the rear of the hall as her features took on a darker mien. 'Did Helgrim tell you anything of the difficulties we faced while you were away, Erik?'

'Yes, I have yet to meet my father but he walked me up from the landing place. I got the impression that he wanted the opportunity to talk to me alone before I reached the hall.'

She nodded. 'Helgrim has been useful to us, I am sure that he is trustworthy. There were others whose loyalty I am less certain of.' She turned her face to him and he was surprised by the coldness in her eyes. 'When you failed to return last year some men talked of invoking the law of *attrœðr* and having your brother Halfdan made king. As soon as I gave birth I made arrangements for our son to be carried to my father in Jutland if our position grew more serious.'

Erik was about to tell her that he already knew about the plot, but he paused as he realised that Gunnhild had not included herself in the plans to flee. 'And yourself?'

Gunnhild looked puzzled at the question, and Erik could see that she had never given a moment's thought to her own safety as she replied. 'My place was here Erik, organising the defence of your hall.'

He gave her waist a squeeze of affection as they reached their private chamber. Stepping inside Gunnhild was finally free to remove her headdress, and Erik thrilled to the sight as her flaxen hair tumbled free. 'Which others?' he said as they embraced. She put a finger to his lips to stop the questions as she pulled him down onto the bed. 'I know their names. Some are no longer a threat to anyone, others I can use to deceive Halfdan's supporters if we ever have the need.'

Erik looked at her fondly. Gunnhild was the most beautiful woman he had ever laid his eyes upon; now it was obvious that she was fox cunning too. Allied with his strength and battle prowess, who could hope to stand against them?

She spoke again, interrupting his thoughts. 'Come,' she breathed as she loosened his belt. 'Our enemies are growing bolder Erik; let us add another kinsman to our ranks.'

PART III

KONUNGR

20

Harald Fairhair settled back into the depths of the chair and let out a low sigh of contentment. 'I love this seat Erik,' he purred. 'When you are a king you spend so long on benches, high seats and saddles that to feel the softness of a deep fleece beneath your arse is worth a purse of silver.'

Erik kicked back, taking a pull from his ale cup as the last of the servants closed the door behind them with a thunk.

'It is good to have you back son,' the king said. 'There is something important that I need you to do.'

Erik's ears pricked up. 'Sigurd Jarl?' he suggested hopefully. 'He is scheming against us father. He has turned my brother Halfdan the Black against us and means to deny me my birthright, the king helm which you promised shall be mine alone.'

Harald gave his son a quizzical look. 'Sigurd is an old friend, we fought together at Hafrsfjord.' The king's face brightened as his mind drifted back to the day. 'Did I ever tell you about the fight? What a day that was!'

Erik cut in, eager to discover what plan the king had in

mind. 'Yes lord, you have, many times. It was a great victory, every man of worth throughout Midgard has heard the tale.'

Harald ploughed on regardless, tapping out the metre of the poem which recalled the event on the arm of the chair as he spoke:

> *'Listen ring-bearers while of Harald I tell you,*
> *the mightily wealthy and his manful war-*
> *deeds.*

> *Words I overheard a high-minded maiden*
> *speaking, golden haired, white-armed,*
> *with a glossy-beaked raven.*

> *Wise thought her the valkyrie who welcomed*
> *men to the bright-eyed one-'*

King Harald took another breath and Erik grabbed his chance. 'You said that you need me to do something father.'

His concentration broken, Harald's mind came back as if from a dream. 'I did?'

'Yes father, something important. Was it to do with the men in the Trondelag? Sigurd Jarl and King Halfdan? They conspired against us while I was away in the North.'

'You were in the North?'

'Yes lord,' Erik persisted, 'we killed King Svasi there. You remember, the warlock king of Bjarmaland, Snofrid's father. I offered up his head to you before the warriors last night in the hall.'

The mention of his old wife's name seemed to finally cut through the fog of ages which clouded the king's mind, and Erik felt a pang of pity despite his frustration as he saw tears begin to form at the corners of his father's eyes. 'Yes, I do remember now,' Harald said sadly. He shook his head and held Erik's eyes with his own. 'Don't ever grow old, Erik,' he said with a sigh. He looked down at the hands which had wielded a sword and hurled spears on that far-off day, carrying the fight against Thor Haklang; felling the great berserk with a blow of his war axe and leading his huskarls across the wale to clear the ship of hated foemen. Erik's gaze followed the king's, and he too sighed as he saw the ravages of time laid bare there.

King Harald spoke again, and his eyes narrowed with hate as he recalled the reason why he had summoned his intended heir. 'All the sons I have sired are Óðinn wolves,' he spat as his knuckles whitened on the arm of the chair. 'Some have done questionable things, the gods know that I have done so myself. But only Rognvald Straight-Boned has done shameful things.'

Erik's own eyes widened in surprise. 'My brother in Hathaland?'

Harald nodded. 'Another of Snofrid's whelps. There are not many left now, and this one is the worst of a bad bunch.'

'Men say that he is a warlock like his grandfather,' Erik said. 'It is true then?'

'It is even worse,' the king replied with a look of disgust. 'He is a seith-man, he practices female rituals and is *argr,* unmanly. I have learnt that he will be leading a gathering of likeminded sorcerers a week after the midsummer *blót* at a remote hall in Hathaland. I will not suffer such a son to live, Erik.'

ANLAF PUCKERED his lips and shifted from side to side. 'A week in the saddle! It's a shame that we could not take the ship, we would have been there by now.'

Erik threw him a look. 'Yes, we would have arrived far quicker but my brother would have been long gone.'

'Maybe it would not be such a bad thing, lord,' Anlaf replied earnestly. 'Eighty sorcerers, all worked up into a slavering madness following the midsummer *blót*.'

Erik gave a snort of amusement as the horses trotted on. 'You have the beginnings of a verse there. See if you can finish it on the way, that should take your mind off angering the gods.'

Anlaf shook his head at his lord's good humour. 'I should think that we are too late to worry about that. We have spent a lifetime killing priests and desecrating churches and temples. Even if they were foreign gods, I doubt that they will look too kindly upon it.'

'Why should they care? We know that the gods fight wars as do men. Óðinn led the Æsir in the very first war against the Vanir. When neither could overcome the other both sides spat into a pot. From this was created the very first man, Kvasir. So you see,' Erik said, 'man was created from war and we follow the gods' example; why would they disapprove?'

The pair drew rein as they crested the rise and looked out across the treetops to the hills of Hathaland. 'It's a gentle country,' Erik said as the column came to a halt on the lee. 'Far too good to waste on seith-men, whether Óðinn likes it or not.' Summer was at its height now, and only the scattering of lakes glinting like jewels in the sunlight broke the carpet of green all around. Beyond that in the middle distance, the expanse of Randsfjord shone like burnished silver in the light of a westering sun. 'We shall ride down into the vale and spend the night beside the first lake we reach,' Erik said. 'I doubt that anyone will come this way, even with the lighter nights, and we cannot risk any of the settlements down on the main road this close to Hov. All it would take is one man with a rowboat to cross the fjord and warn our friends, and a week spent in the saddle will have been for nought. At least down there we can water the horses and light fires without fear of being seen.' He patted his belly. 'A few spoonfuls of hot food would go down just fine after another day spent chewing on wind dried fish and oat cakes!'

They had departed Avaldsnes and been ferried across the waters of Karmsund the previous week. Erik had shadowed Harald as the old man performed the duties of king and godi at the Thing, many clearly thought for the final time. To his surprise his father had been in fine fettle, and the years seemed to roll way as the bonfires were lit and the folk jumped hand in hand through the cleansing flames. The midsummer gathering had been a great success, and Erik had felt more than a little relieved that his father appeared to be more like his old self as the crew of the *Draki* had climbed the valley side early the following morning and made their way to the east.

Keeping to the ridge tops and rarely travelled pathways to avoid the settlements which lined the route, they had nevertheless made good progress thanks in large part to the length of the northern day. Now they were almost within striking distance of the hall at Hov, and Erik clicked his tongue, urging his mount forward with a dig of his heels as he led the army back down into the shadows of the greenwood. Soon they were there, and the first fires were already flickering into life as men unsaddled weary mounts and led them to the lake-side. The needs of the horses satisfied, men gathered about him as he prepared to share his plans before they dispersed to eat.

The trunk of a tree lay hard against the track, the insect ravaged bole testament to the length of time which had passed since it had fallen foul of some long forgotten autumn blow, and Erik hauled himself up as he waited for the chatter to die away. Close to the lake the air was a haze of midges, and the king shared a smile with his shipmates as he slapped at his neck, rolling the thing into a bloody ball before flicking it away. 'That is something we are used to at least,' he joked, and the men shared his laughter as they recalled the voracity of their Finnish brethren the previous summer. 'I will not keep you lads,' he began as they waved the pests away. 'I just want to outline the attack before we settle down to eat. We can pull back a little towards the trackway at least; this far from any settlements, we should be able to use dampish wood on the fires to smoke the bastards out.'

The men shared a smile as Erik began to outline his plan. 'We are near the northern end of the fjord now, and we will get as much rest as we can as soon as we have eaten. At first light we move off. Good roads skirt both sides of the fjord, but they don't come together until they reach the crossing place on the River Etna half a day to the North. That's obviously too far away to be of any use to us,' he said as his eyes swept the gathering. 'An hour's ride away on the far side of this wood, the waters of the fjord come together at a pinch point where the nearness of the far bank makes it little different to a river crossing. We swim the horses across, pick up the road south and follow it to Hov as fast as we can.' Erik ran his eyes across the upturned faces of the warriors to see if any questions were forthcoming. A man raised his chin and Erik indicated that he go ahead. 'Do we know the layout of the hall, its surroundings and if they can expect any help from nearby?' Erik nodded in reply. 'I spoke to men, back in Avaldsnes before we left. They told me that the building which the seith-men will be using for their witchery lies in a secluded clearing on a heavily wooded slope, so we will have both cover and plenty of time to make sure that none of these fiend escape us. It is more a large farmhouse than a king's hall, with the only door up near the end of the long wall which opens into a room for boots and wet clothing. To the left of this, beyond an oaken screen, lies the main room where we can expect to find our friends.'

'We are not just going to burn them in then, lord?' the man said with obvious surprise.

Erik shook his head. 'I want to make sure that we leave no man alive. It's bad enough if a normal man survives to plan his revenge.' He shot them a smile, and a rumble of laughter rolled around the lakeside as the men exchanged knowing looks. Every man there knew the story of Bolli Sigurdsson's death, the reason for it and Sigurd Jarl's ongoing hatred for their lord. 'But I don't want to leave a single warlock alive to cast spells against me or my kin.'

'So, we are going into the building then?'

Erik nodded. 'We are going in. Once we are sure that they are all dead and there are no others lurking in any outbuildings we will fire the place before we leave.'

Erik furrowed his brow to invite any further questions, but the warrior nodded that he was satisfied with the answers he had received and no others were forthcoming. 'Watch out!' Erik warned them with a stab of a forefinger. 'I am told that these sorcerers are well versed in weapon craft despite being *argr*. Keep your wits about you and I am confident that any man here will have the beating of them, but these are dangerous men nevertheless. I want them dead before they can reach for their weapons.' He threw them a smile, and a rumble of laughter came back in reply to his concluding words. 'Much less chicken claws, powdered bat wings or rune staves.'

·   ·   ·

'HERE HE COMES,' Thorstein murmured. 'About time too.'

Erik could hear the concern in his old friend's voice and gave him a nudge. The huskarl shrugged. 'Sorcerers, seith-men and the like; I had enough of them in Finnmark, I just don't like 'em.'

Erik looked beyond the big man, along the tree line to the rest of the army. Hung back in the sun dappled shadows only the odd glint of steel revealed them even up close, and he relaxed a touch as he switched his gaze back to the horseman.

The latest addition to his hird was on foot, Sturla smiling a greeting to someone as yet out of sight around the front of the building; Erik clicked his tongue softly as his hopes that all those inside would be sleeping off the rituals of the previous night were dashed, and he gripped his spear a little tighter as he waited for the moment to dart forward from cover.

It was as well that the Romsdaler had thought up the plan Erik mused, as he watched the man walk free of the cover of the building out into the morning light, or they would have blundered directly into him. It was not the first time that Sturla's knowledge of the habits of such men had been of use, both in the far North and here at home in Norway. The men had begun to only half jokingly call him Sturla Godi because of it, and the nickname was beginning to stick.

Out beyond the farmhouse Sturla was wearing a frown as he bent to lift the foot of his horse, running a hand over the hocks as he described some fictitious ailment to the seith-man. As the man went down onto one knee to examine the foot Sturla straightened his back, stared hard into the wood-land beyond the building and gave a curt nod. It was the sign that there were no other men in the open, and Erik was moving in a heartbeat. All along the tree line men were bursting forward into the open, pouring forward in an unstoppable tide of leather and steel as they raced to round the farm-house and gain the only door before the alarm was raised.

Erik looked up just as Sturla brought a hand axe down onto the unsuspecting head of his helper, his legs pumping as he gained the side wall of the farmhouse and swung around the corner. The door was ajar, just where he expected it to be, and Erik ducked inside as Thorstein and Anlaf followed close behind. Like all such rooms this wet room had a floor of stone sets, and Erik slid across to the inner door as he scanned the interior for opposition. His glide had brought him up with the inner doorway, and he leapt the sill beam as he brought his spear around to parry any possible attacker. A sea of faces were turned his way, and he thrust out with his weapon as the nearest man began to recover from his surprise. The spear slid easily into a mouth which had been opened to yell a warning, but the shaft was wrenched from his hand as the man threw himself to one side in a forlorn attempt to dodge the strike.

Erik drew his sword as he stepped further into the room, scything a path through the panic-stricken men there as the rest of his warriors burst through the door, yelling their war cries. Men who had only moments before been slumbering after their late night sorcery and spell working fell back in terror before the sudden clamour and violence of the attack, and Erik led the men further into the building as he sought to end it quickly. A man had turned his back as he made a desperate grab for one of the swords which lined the wall; Erik brought his own blade crashing down to lop off the arm before the hand could close around the handle.

Everywhere his own men were pushing forward as the enemy began to fight back with what came to hand. A smoul-dering log crashed into his arm as he moved forward again, and Erik twisted to face the attacker only to see him go down with Thorstein's spear embedded in his chest. The weight of their attack had forced the defenders back against the far wall of the room, and although they were beginning to snatch up what arms they could from the walls and benches the crush of bodies was making the act of fighting back almost impossible for them.

Erik stepped aside as his men swarmed forward to finish the slaughter in a flash of steel, and Thorstein and Anlaf moved protectively to his side as he ran his eyes across the men opposite. Despite the fact that they have never met, the man he sought was unmistakable when his face hardened from the scrum; a head taller than any of his companions, the man had the shock of flaxen hair which was typical among the king's sons, and Erik called out above the din as he began to force his way across. 'Rognvald Straight-Boned!'

The king of Hathaland jerked his head around at the sound of his name, and Erik tore his helm from his head, freeing his own hair as he came. Straight-Boned recognised his attacker as a half-brother for the first time by their shared features, and he called out as the circle of men around him continued to shrink back under the force of the attack. 'I am Rognvald Haraldsson, king of Hathaland. Which brother are you?'

'I am Erik Haraldsson, king of Halogaland, Moerr, Fjordane and Romsdal and I have come to take your life, seithman.'

'Our father will kill you for it.'

'Our father ordered it.'

Erik saw the horror of the realisation that his own father had ordered his death flit across his brother's face for a heartbeat, but the iron will which flowed through the blood of all the sons of Harald Fairhair reasserted itself, and Erik felt a pang of regret that he had to kill the man despite his dealings in the dark arts. The feeling was gone in an instant as the two

Haraldsson's glared at each other across the hearth, each man rolling on the balls of his feet, dropping into a fighter's stance as he sought an opportunity to strike.

Erik could sense his huskarls hovering a short distance away on either flank, and more of his men were beginning to detach themselves from the fight as those at the rear of the press began to run short of opponents. Straight-Boned could sense the ring of enemies closing in too, and Erik glanced across to the place where the last of the Hathalanders were being hacked into meat as he saw just how desperate his brother's situation had become. Rognvald snatched at the chance to kill his tormentor as Erik had hoped that he would, leaping the glowing hearth and raising his sword for the killing stroke. But the look had been a ruse, Erik was faster and he ducked inside strike, sweeping his own blade low to open his brother's thigh from knee to hip as he crashed past.

Anlaf jumped back as the warlock king's leg folded under him and he crashed to the floor, and Erik turned quickly to hack the heavy blade down onto the back of his brother's head before he could recover.

Erik turned his face away as Rognvald's body shook in its death spasm at his feet. Anlaf met his gaze, and Erik pulled a grimace as his huskarl recognised the anguish there with a nod sympathy. Unlike Halfdan up in the Trondelag, Rognvald had never conspired against him nor given any cause to suspect that he may, and Erik sent a plea to the gods that he need never kill a kinsman again.

The fight was won, and Erik called out as his men moved among the wounded and the last of the Hathalanders were finished off where they lay. 'Fire the place,' he said with a frown. 'Let us put as much distance between us and this lich-house as quickly as we can.'

21

BJORN THE FAR TRADER

'Tunsberg!' Kolbein exclaimed as the town came into view. Erik's styrisman drank in the smell of the sea and turned to flash his lord a smile. 'It's been far too long, Erik. We should have journeyed here long ago.'

Erik ran his own eyes over the town and bay as they waited at the edge of the wood for the men to come up. It had been an easy ride down from Hathaland through a landscape dotted with farms and hayfields, but the horses were all but done-in following their exertions of the previous weeks and the men's weariness was not far behind. The town which was their goal now in sight, the mood lifted as men's thoughts turned to a weeklong rest before a leisurely ride back to Rogaland.

Anlaf was at Erik's shoulder, and he gave voice to his thoughts as the party watched the comings and goings of ships in the great bay below. 'It's a rich land, lord. Such wealth can buy many spears; Kolbein was right, we should have visited before now.'

Erik snorted at his banner man's caution. 'My brother has not earned the eke-name Farman, the far trader, by being a mighty warrior. King Bjorn would rather sit in his hall and grow rich taxing merchants than go Viking.' He shrugged. 'As long as he recognises my right to rule when the time comes it's a thing which suits us both. He can live an easy life free from my interference, just so long as the ships carrying my share of the profits tie up at Avaldsnes each year.' He nodded towards the axe banner which hung limp in the still summer air. 'Keep that furled, we are not an invading army.'

Erik hauled at the reins, and the horse turned a slow circle as he addressed the column. 'Remember that we are guests here. Look and act like king's men while we are at my brother's hall and around the town; any fights or drunkenness and I will abandon you to King Bjorn's judgement.' As murmurs of disappointment came from the men, Erik exchanged a look of amusement with Kolbein. 'They will get over it, I am sure that our reception will forestall any such behaviour. Come on,' he said, putting back his heels, 'let's get down there. I have spent long enough in the saddle these past few weeks.'

The column trotted free of the tree line, and out onto the sun drenched farmland which ran down to the town. Fields of spelt and rye drew away to either side of the roadway, with the smattering of barley cropping close to isolated brewhouses serving to sharpen the riders' thirst as much as the dusty air. Spirits were as high as the pillowy clouds above them as the final mile of their journey went beneath the hooves of their mounts and the walls of Tunsberg drew closer. Soon they were there, and Erik reined in as the worried looking spearman at the gate came across. 'Welcome to Tunsberg, lord,' the guard said with an unconvincing smile. 'King Bjorn is waiting to greet you at his hall. If you follow this road straight through the town you will see the fortress on your right.'

Erik nodded in reply, exchanging a look of concern with

Thorstein at the brusqueness of the welcome as they passed through the gate into the town itself. Erik's prow man spoke as they drew out of earshot. 'Something is up. Either they already know about the burning and think ill of it or something has happened at home. Either way,' he said with a heavy look. 'We had best keep our wits about us, and watch for any hint of trickery.'

'They cannot know about Rognvald yet unless Bjorn also has second sight,' Erik replied. 'Besides my brother only has eyes for a profit, and why would anyone from Hathaland race to tell the king of the Vestfold anyway?' He raised his chin to look along the way ahead. Everywhere the squat homes of the lower orders peeped out beneath a fringe of mossy thatch, but the walls were in good shape beneath a lick of lime wash and the children who ran thereabouts looked rosy cheeked and well fed. A line of workshops lined the road itself, gaudy signs advertising to all the type of wares available for sale or barter within. In the distance the waters of the fjord sparkled in the sun beneath a mantle of cawing gulls, the halls of the merchants and better sort dwarfing those inland as they took advantage of the freshness of the sea air and closeness to their ships and warehouses. Tunsberg bore all the signs of a well ordered and prosperous town, and Erik put his fears aside as he thought on the amount of skat it would deliver to his treasury in Avaldsnes when he succeeded to the high seat.

The wall of rock which had lent the town its name rose to their right, and Erik coaxed his tired mount away from the main road and up the final rise as the town fell away beneath them. Gaining the summit the road approached the stronghold of the kings of the Vestfold; spearmen were gathered at the entrance to a magnificent hall, the fineness of their arms testifying that these were unmistakably king's men, and Erik knew that he had finally arrived at the town house of his brother. The hall steward came forward, the practiced easy smile of such men already beginning to rile Erik as he saw that his brother had remained within. The man opened his mouth to speak a welcome, but Erik cut him short. 'I was told at the gate that King Bjorn was expecting me. Was I misinformed?'

'The king awaits you in his hall, lord,' the steward answered in the oily tone common among their sort. 'He has asked me to welcome you to his kingdom and convey you to his presence.'

Erik was not alone in sensing the tension in the air, but he held out a hand to stop Anlaf and Thorstein as they moved to his side and returned his own best false smile to the steward. 'Lead on,' he said. 'We have had a long, hard journey and my brother's offer is welcome to our ears.'

Erik dismounted, recovering his shield and spears from their carrying places as his men clattered onto the yard to his rear. He could still sense the outrage that their lord was being treated in such a high-handed manner, and Erik growled a warning as they followed the steward towards the hall. 'It appears that we may not be among friends here after all, but keep your tempers in check. If we are treated with dishonour there will be a reckoning, but unless we are in danger that time is not now.'

A quick headcount told Erik that the men in the courtyard were evenly matched in numbers and quality, and a sense of foreboding crept over him as the steward flashed his greasy smile once again. 'The king extends a welcome to yourself and ten of your closest hirdmen, lord. The rest of your party will find that tents have been provided for their use; perhaps they would like to make a start pitching them while you talk with the king?'

Even a man versed in the duties of a go-between was

clearly struggling to suppress a trace of mockery from his tone, and Erik had the unfamiliar feeling that the situation was slipping from his control. His men drew up as they awaited his reaction, but he turned back and forced a smile of reassurance as he ordered them away. Erik sensed his senior men bristling at his side, and he spoke softly as his brother's spearmen looked on gleefully from a distance. 'Whatever he says, whatever the provocation you keep your hands well clear of your sword handles. Clear?'

They murmured that they understood with obvious reluctance, and Erik led the small group up the steps to the inner room of the hall itself. The steward gestured towards their weapons, indicating that they stack them in the racks there before entering the hall itself. It was custom everywhere; large numbers of heavily armed men contained within the confines of four walls could be the cause of unlimited trouble even without the addition of copious quantities of strong drink, and the carrying strap of his shield slid down his arm as he laid the board aside with a heavy heart. His spears and battle axe joined the pile as the others followed his example, but Erik shook his head as the steward held out a hand to receive his sword. 'Don't presume to take the sword of a king,' he growled. 'Or the king's personal guard.' The anger and hostility he felt was obvious from the tone, and Erik was pleased to see that the man's training had been thorough enough to recognise when to relent.

They came through the inner doorway and into the hall itself, and Erik took in the grandeur of the hall as he strode towards the figure reclining on the high seat at the far end. It was an impressive hall, cunningly carved and gold bedecked, but Erik was in no mood to appreciate the beauty of the place as he fixed his stare upon his brother. To his relief the hall was all but empty of others; spearmen flanked the king's high seat pillars and a dozen others sat at their ale to either side, but the echo of their footsteps only seemed to add to the unreality of the moment as the steward ushered Erik to his place.

It was clear now that Erik and his men were unwanted guests, and he was no longer surprised when King Bjorn failed to rise in greeting at his approach, but it was all that he could do to contain his anger when he realised that he was being shown, not to a seat of equal standing with his brother, but that of an honoured guest. Erik paused just long enough to make his feelings plain at the slight before sitting down and regarding Bjorn across the hearth.

Erik's huskarls took their places at the bench alongside their lord as thralls and serving wenches carried out jugs of ale and mead to set down before them. The drink was welcome at least, and the men slaked their thirst as the two kings exchanged the formalities expected of them. News and forced pleasantries flighted between them, but it was not long before the subject of their father's health came to the fore.

'And how is King Harald?'

'Ailing,' Erik replied. 'It will not be so long before he sups sweet mead in Óðinn's hall.' He took a sip of his own drink and fixed his gaze upon his brother. 'I shall be king of Norwegians then, and I shall remember my friends.' Erik paused for a heartbeat to reinforce his statement. 'And those who have thought it a day well spent to mock me.'

'Maybe you will not be king?'

Erik was taken aback. 'You would seek to go against the wishes of our father?'

Bjorn gave a hollow laugh before adding with a hint of menace. 'When Harald Fairhair is in his Howe he will have no will, who is to say what fate the Norns have in store for any of us?' He leaned forward and a look of exasperation came to his face. 'Why are you here, Erik? I am king here, that's why my seat is higher than yours. There are other kings in Norway and powerful jarls; somehow I don't think that this inheritance which you seem to believe is your right will be so easily gained. If our father is as wan as you say you should be at his side. Stay this night and prepare to leave on the morrow.'

Erik raised his brow in surprise. 'You deny a kinsman shelter?'

'No,' Bjorn replied steadily. 'That would be unworthy of any man, much less a king.'

'My horses are spent,' Erik explained. 'They were pushed hard to cross the mountains from Rogaland. They require rest before they return, a week would be ample.'

Bjorn shook his head as the matter came to a head. 'That is out of the question. I know the reputation of your crew, two nights shall be more than enough. Neither the townsfolk nor their king could suffer such a band of cutthroats to live among them any longer.'

Erik ignored the remark, conscious as he was that they were all in his brother's power. 'Give me a skei in the morning then, and I shall be on my way.'

'I have none to give.'

'I saw several at the quayside when I arrived.'

'They are my own ships. I need them to keep the coastline here free from Vikings.' Bjorn gave a smirk as an idea came to him. 'I am sure that I could provide you with a knarr. A cargo vessel will be a bit cramped for a company the size of yours, but you don't have so far to sail after all.'

Erik's patience was about to give out when Anlaf murmured at his side, and his eyes narrowed as he repeated the suggestion. 'Maybe a knarr is not such a bad idea.' He paused to give his brother the opportunity to betray his surprise and delight at the thought of the humiliation before adding with a hard stare. 'It is the time for you to deliver this year's skat to our father in Avaldsnes. I could save you the trouble.'

To Erik's delight the suggestion had clearly wrong-footed Bjorn, but the king of Vestfold recovered quickly. 'It is no trouble. I shall fulfil my duty without your help.'

Erik glowered. 'You don't trust me?'

'No,' Bjorn finally admitted. 'I don't trust you.'

Erik rose to go, and the sound of wood scraping against wood rolled around the great space as the benches were pushed back and both sets of warriors stood with their hands resting on their sword hilts.

'You have my thanks for the entertainment,' Erik said as he stepped from the dais. 'I am glad that we understand one another. I will be on my way within two days, until then we will camp on the outskirts of the town.' He gave his brother a hard stare. 'I shall pay with silver for supplies from the surrounding farms, and trouble you no more.'

'THIS IS ACTUALLY A GREAT IDEA,' Thorstein said as he stripped the meat from another rib with his teeth and sent the bone spinning away into the reed bed. 'Who wants to stay in Bjorn's pissy hall anyway?'

It was late evening, and the heat had finally gone off the land as the men of Erik's hird sat in contented groups idling away the last of the day. As promised Erik had sent men around the local farms as soon as the tents were pitched and the horses corralled, paying top price for bread, cheeses and freshly brewed ale from the delighted farmers and alewives there. A nugget of hacksilver had brought in a head of beef which the happy farmer had slaughtered and cut up on the spot, and now the men chatted in groups or watched the antics of the wandering birds as swifts and martins swooped and capered inches from the ground. Anlaf had the keenest eyesight in the group and the conversation fell away as they saw him stretch his neck and look away to the North.

'Is that our boy?'

The lowering sun was a ball of fire on the hills to the West, and Anlaf squinted and shaded his eyes with the shelf of his hand: 'yes that's him.'

Erik nodded before calling across to a group of men lounging nearby. 'Sturla!'

The Romsdaler jumped up and hurried across. 'Yes, lord?'

'Nip down to the bank and tell the swimmers to prepare to move.'

The others were pulling themselves to their feet, the idle chatter forgotten as they became men of war again. Erik motioned for them to remain where they were, strolling across to pluck another hunk of meat from the kettle. 'Stay there for now lads,' he said as he licked the hot juices from his fingers. 'But get back into your brynjur now that the sun has westered.'

The horseman had left the road and taken to the fields in his haste to report to his king, and the senior men exchanged looks of anticipation as the great chest of the beast parted the rye before it like the bow wave of a ship. As the sound of men donning mail coats filled the air the rider slowed to a halt before them and slipped to the ground. 'King Bjorn left the berg through the western gate a short time ago, lord,' he blurted out. Erik held up a hand before he went on. 'Slow down Olvir,' he said as he bent to fill a cup from the ale tap. 'Here drink this, and then report your news in a calm manner.' He flicked a look over his shoulder as the last of the swimmers shook the water from their hair and began to dress.

'These boys know their business, they are not easily spooked. But one day we may be at the head of an army of levy men, farmers, shepherds and fishermen, and they want to see that their leaders are confident of victory not racing about like their arse is on fire.'

The young scout took the cup and drank, his eyes scanning the group of battle hardened veterans as he ordered his thoughts. Thorstein threw him a wink, and the boy visibly brightened at the gesture of support as he lowered his cup and calmly resumed his report. 'King Bjorn and fifty men left the far gate of the berg and took the western road out past the head of the fjord.'

'Did he see you?'

'No lord, I stayed within the woodland the whole time they were in sight.'

'You are from these parts, where do you think they could be heading?'

'The king has a hall on the far side of the bay, lord,' Olvir explained. 'At a place called Saeheim. I couldn't follow him without leaving cover, but they were heading directly towards it when I last saw them.'

Anlaf threw Erik a look. 'It would make sense if those riders earlier were carrying the war arrow to the nearest hersar. If your brother thinks that he only has two days in which to overwhelm us here before we leave, it would be a good place to muster.'

Erik nodded. 'You are sure of the numbers?'

'Yes lord, they rode two abreast so it was easy to tally.'

Erik opened his mouth to ask another question, but Olvir anticipated and supplied the answer before he could speak. 'There are normally twenty or so men at the hall lord.'

Erik rubbed his nose as he thought. The numbers should

be roughly equal if he moved fast, and a plan was already beginning to form in his mind.

'It will be twilight soon,' Anlaf said, interrupting his thoughts. 'Miles from home, deep in a hostile land; any sane leader would slip away under the cover of darkness and live to fight another day.'

Erik looked up, and a smile spread across his features as he recognised that they already knew his decision.

22

FIGHT AT SAEHEIM

The horse snorted again and pawed the ground. The rider looked shamefaced as Erik glared in his direction, calming the animal with a stroke of its neck as the king looked back towards the East. The lights of Tunsberg glowed dully on its mount; high above a gibbous moon silvered a screen of shredded clouds. Squares of light perforated the darkness around Saeheim as the inhabitants took full advantage of the warm night to put shutters of wood or scraped hide aside, and Erik cursed again beneath his breath as he waited for the telltale flames to wink into life.

'Not long now, Erik,' Anlaf breathed at his side. 'Even as we sit here, Kolbein is hunched over his fire steel.'

A moment later the first flicker showed in the dockyard below the town, and Anlaf flashed a smile of triumph as his king looked back and arched a brow. The war band walked free of the shadows as the fires began to take hold in the East, and Erik turned his head to address the men as they began to jog across the meadow towards the first of the buildings. 'Hit them hard, lads,' he snarled, 'and leave none living. They thought to redden their sword blades with our blood in the morning. Let us show them how killing should be done!'

After an hour spent wincing at each and every whinny or cough the fall of feet and soft swish of mail sounded thunderous in Erik's ears, but the need for concealment was thankfully past and a moment later the first cries of alarm came from Saeheim as Kolbein's handiwork was spotted by the guards there. The men instinctively increased the pace as rectangles of amber light showed where doors had been flung open, and Erik pointed to left and right as the hall of the king reared up before them. A figure stood silhouetted by the light within, and Erik cried a dedication to Óðinn as his spear punched the first man to die back into the room and his men bayed their bloodlust like hounds at the kill.

Sturla and a few others had been given the task of firing the thatch, and Erik recognised his brother's panicked cries fill the air as they emerged from a nearby hut carrying their torches. 'Out! Out! I will not be burned in my own hall like some wretch!'

The first fighters to exit the building were quickly cut down by Erik's men before they had the room to wield their sword, but soon the pressure began to tell and the crew of the *Draki* began to bow back on itself as more and more of Bjorn's men fought their way out of the trap. Sturla and his men were circling the hall, thrusting their brands deep, and soon the roof was aflame from gable to gable as the tinder dry thatch became a torch.

A warrior darted from the crush and Erik dodged aside, recognising the moment when mail links gave way under his powerful upward stab and the sword blade slid into belly and gut. Another reared up an arm's length before him, a bearded snarl beneath a fringe of steel; Erik brought his own helm crashing forward to shatter teeth and nose into a bloody mash as Thorstein's arm shot forward to carve the grim rictus of a smile into his throat. Erik stepped forward into the gap, ribs snapping like sun dried twigs beneath his heel as the man fell at his feet. Bjorn was still not in sight, and he called out above clash of steel and roar of flames as he sought out the man whose insults had brought them to this place. 'King Bjorn? Bjorn Haraldsson? Erik Haraldsson has come to this place to put an end to our squabble!'

The fallen were piled so high in the courtyard now that the newly killed were unable to fall to the ground, some being attacked again and again by Erik's men until the lopping off of the head or a limb proved to the blood crazed attackers that they were no longer a threat. Thorstein and Anlaf Crow were at Erik's side, and the trio waded through the carnage as they hunted for Bjorn. The building was an inferno now, long sinewy flames roaring skyward and casting an orange glow over the dead and living alike as they turned over bodies with the toe of a boot or heel of a spear.

Erik glanced at the hall as they worked their way across the courtyard. The doorway through which the men of the Vestfold had raced to their deaths only a short while before was a dragon's roar of flame as the fire fed hungrily on the warm night air. Twin windows set within the long wall of the hall had become the monster's baleful eyes, nobody could be alive inside by now; Erik began to fear that his brother had brought shame upon the family of Harald Fairhair by choosing to die within rather than face his assailants, when a cry drew him across to the eastern side of the hall. Sturla was there with Thorgils, a weather-beaten Orkney man, his face bearing the look of a man sat downwind at his oar as a crew-mate pissed over the side. Erik glanced down at the body of his brother and gave his killer a reassuring clap on the shoulder as the man began to apologise for the killing. 'You did me a service Thorgils,' Erik said as a wave of relief swept across the crewman's features. 'No man wants to be remembered as a brother killer, whether that death was deserved or not. Here,' he said, sheathing his sword and handing his spear across to Thorstein for safekeeping. 'Help me to mark his wounds. I will have to describe them to his father and I want him to know that he died like a man.'

As Thorgils tugged the king upright, Erik released Bjorn's belt and worked the brynja from his torso. A flick of his short seax opened up the shirt beneath, Erik tearing the thing away as he looked upon the body of his brother. Nicks and grazes covered the front of Bjorn's body and a spear thrust to the chest had clearly been the Vestfold king's death wound; but his back was as white and clear as newly poured milk, and Erik laid a hand on the side of his brother's face and looked into eyes glazed by death. 'All I wanted was to rest my men and horses. Was even that little thing too much to ask of you kinsman?'

THEY HAD RARELY SEEN the waters of Karmsund so empty of shipping, and Erik had ordered the men to don their war gear as the final few miles went beneath their bows. King Bjorn's belligerence had taken Erik and his men by surprise, but once the king had paid the price of his hostility Erik had determined that any opposition to his high kingship was best faced down while he was on the spot. There had been amusement at first as the hersar of Vestfold had reached the muster only to discover that the fight was over. Erik had insisted that the men swear allegiance to him before sending them away with fine gifts, but the obvious shock and dismay with which the death of their king had been greeted by high and low born alike was disquieting. Added to that, Bjorn's wife had managed to spirit their young son Gudrod away to safety with King Olav of Ringerike, Bjorn's full brother. As yet the lad was young and no threat, but lads had a habit of growing into vengeful men; it was a situation he was sure he would need to return to in time. While Erik had been away wooing the folk of the Vestfold the summer ripened and waned. Now, it would seem, his absence may well have caused his enemies closer to home to seize their chance.

The mood lightened a touch as the ship put her bows beyond the final island before the anchorage and the man stationed in the prow cupped hands to make his report. 'It's almost empty lord,' he called, the relief obvious from his tone: 'two…no…three warships and a dozen knarr.'

Erik exchanged a look with his senior men. They had taken the best two longships from the harbour beneath Tunsberg, filling the hulls with treasure from the hall on the berg which he claimed as his own by right of conquest. Two skei crewed by the best of his men were a powerful force, but if Halfdan the Black *had* taken advantage of his absence to install himself as high king at Avaldsnes he could have expected the rest of his hird to be put to the sword and the town filled with enemies. Erik's feelings of anxiety came down a level but the emptiness was still a mystery, and he called on the rowers to pick up the stroke as the ships swung on their keels and pointed their prows to the land.

Thorstein was keen-eyed, and the big warrior laid a hand on Erik's sleeve as men began to appear on the foreshore. 'That is Ulfar Whistle-tooth, lord; and Gauti Thorodsson off the *Bison.'* Smiles broke out all across the steering platform as the others saw that it was true. 'Well, that is our worst fears quashed,' Erik said. 'Let us get ashore and discover what we have missed this summer.'

Erik's eyes flittered across the townscape as the ship

neared the jetties. Despite the appearance of two of his styris-men, the events in Vestfold had taught him to be more cautious at all times. It was clear that if the news of his coming had travelled a little quicker before him, Erik would have been greeted with overwhelming force when he had emerged before Tunsberg. It would have been Erik and his men lying bloodied on the field, and if that had occurred he was in no doubt that the assassin's blade would have found Gunnhild and little Gamli before the summer was out.

The dragons edged alongside, and ropes were tossed ashore as men came to make her fast to the jetty. Erik was first ashore, and he fixed his gaze upon a distant point as he waited for his mind and body to recover from the constant pitch and roll of the sea. His bodyguard came up and he allowed their bodies a moment to remember the sensation of firm land beneath their feet before leading them on. The boards resounded as the men stomped ashore, and the clatter of steel replaced the squawking of gulls as the crewmen crossed the wales.

Ulfar and Gauti waited on the dockside wearing faces wreathed in smiles, and Erik returned the gesture as they gave voice to their happiness. 'Welcome home, lord,' they beamed. 'It has been an eventful summer.'

'So we can see. How is the king?'

'At the head of an army, lord,' came Ulfar's stunning reply. Erik was taken aback, and Ulfar gave a snort and gestured towards King Harald's hall. 'Perhaps your wife is the best one to explain, Erik. She has taken up the reins of kingship here while your father is in the North.'

Erik crinkled his brow at the news. 'A woman reigning in Norway? If it was any other, I may have been surprised…'

Gauti added a comment of his own as the men chuckled at the absurdity of the situation. A nation full of kings fighting like rats in a sack was in reality being governed by a young Danish queen. 'She has become widely respected for the quality of her rede and judgement while the king has been away, lord. She will know far more about kingly matters than us.'

Erik nodded his agreement. 'Yes, it is best that I discover how the world upended itself while I was away.' He flicked a look across his shoulder at the body of his hird, lolling around now that any threat had disappeared and eager to get to their cups. 'Make sure the boys are entertained in the main hall while I talk with Gunnhild.'

Erik took off, angling towards the familiar walls of his own hall before the pair could answer. Folk were venturing from the buildings of Avaldsnes as word went around who the unfamiliar longships contained, men and women alike dipping their heads in supplication as he walked the final few yards and entered his home for the first time since high summer. Gunnhild was sat on her high seat as two men stood before her cap in hand, but she rose and shooed them away when she saw that Erik was home. As the hall steward and his helpers began to usher the supplicants from the building, Gunnhild crossed to the door of their private bower and disappeared inside.

As he had hoped, his wife had freed her hair when he arrived and the pair embraced, kissing hungrily as the tensions of the summer evaporated for them both. As they came apart Gunnhild buried her face in his hair and inhaled deeply. 'Mountain air and sea spray,' she murmured before kissing him again. 'How I yearn to ply the seas, to be free like a man.' Their closeness had revealed another thing to Erik, and his face broke into a smile as he ran his hand across the fullness of her belly. 'Yes,' she said with a look. 'Freedom is not the only reason for women to envy men.' Her swollen belly had cooled Erik's ardour and his mind came back to his father. 'Where is the king? What have I missed?'

'King Harald is in the Trondelag,' she replied with a look of triumph, 'leading a host against Halfdan the Black.'

Erik returned a look of disbelief. 'When I left him he could barely remember his own name.' His face suddenly took on a frown as he remembered that not all of Snofrid's sons were yet dead. 'Is there witchcraft involved?'

'Sit down Erik,' she said as she called for ale to be carried in. 'There is much to tell.'

Erik took the opportunity to remove his baldric and sword, prising the boots from his feet as they awaited the drink. He sat there kneading his soles as the ale arrived, luxuriating in the cool air and the ability to spread his toes after a week spent in dank sea boots.

The maid departed, and Gunnhild passed a cup to Erik as any good wife should as the servant closed the door with a click of the latch. 'You recall that I noted the names and faces of all the men who were keen to have your father declared *attrœðr* when you were thought lost in Bjarmaland?'

Erik nodded that he did. She had refused to divulge the identities to him and it had threatened for a time to come between them, but a beery talk with Anlaf and Thorstein had made him see the sense of it. Knowing his temper better than anyone, they all knew that it was unlikely that Erik could have concealed his feelings towards them and the chance to use their loyalties against them would have been lost.

'I kept to the king's hall after you rode away.' Gunnhild smiled, clearly proud of her guile. 'I always took Gamli with me; the men love to make a fuss of him and it helped to make me look like a soppy lovesick woman. The same men started to ask where you had gone. In roundabout ways of course,' she said, 'but it was clear to anyone who was not just there to

dull their senses with ale that it was more than a casual interest. I let slip once or twice that you had travelled up to Moerr
by horseback rather than take ship, as you wished the folk in
outlying districts to see their king and you were keen to take
advantage of the summer weather to hunt the high moors on
the way. A week after you left I hired a shipload of men and
sent them to Solvi to air and freshen the hall there and to
await your arrival. High summer passed and we learnt that
Halfdan the Black had crossed Dofrarfell, ringed the hall in
one night and burned in the men thinking that they were you
and your huskarls.'

Erik nodded that he understood. Bjorn Farman had
warned him that his efforts to take up the king helm from
King Harald would be far harder than he had hoped. He had
no doubt that Sigurd Jarl in Lade was also behind this attempt
on his life. Not only had he burned in the jarl's own son many
years before but Sigurd was foster-brother to Halfdan and
another brother of Erik's, Gudrod. The whole of the Trondelag was a hotbed of enemies; he could only hope that his
father's miraculous rediscovery of his mind and vigour could
help him to whittle down their number before the old man
died.

Gunnhild was in full flow now and Erik knew that it
would be futile to attempt to get a word in edgeways, so he
leaned forward to top up their ale cups, settling back to
congratulate his father once again for choosing such a woman
to wed his intended heir. 'When news of the attack reached
your father he raged and raged, it was as if Þórr himself had
sent a lightning bolt to clear away the fog which had
enveloped his mind. He immediately sent forth the war arrow,
and within days the watch fires on the hills opposite mirrored
the stars above each night as more and more men came in.
Ships filled the sound,' she went on as Erik watched the

excitement dance in her eyes, 'and within the month a mighty host was clearing the headland and turning their prows to the North.'

Gunnhild paused to gulp down ale, and Erik took his chance to ask more questions. 'Have we heard anything since then? Has my father brought Halfdan to battle?'

'The last we heard was a week hence,' she replied. 'Halfdan has gathered his hird, men and ships, and camped on the southern shore of Trondheim Fjord, at a place called Stad. King Harald Fairhair,' she said proudly, 'has put ashore at a place known as Reinsletta on the shoreline opposite.' She pulled a smile of satisfaction as the success of her manoeuvring was laid before her husband.

'You did well,' he purred, 'very well. You are a shrewd and canny woman. I shall gather my hird and set sail for the North at dawn.' His lips drew back into the smile of a wolf as he totted up the number of fresh fighters available to him. 'I will take the three skei, if I am sailing to war it will be in my own ship *Draki*. If I give the two Vestfold ships to Ulfar and Gauti and their crews, I can add some of the spearmen from here to make up the numbers needed to work the larger ships.' Gunnhild flashed a savage smile of her own as her husband revealed what had detained him so long out east. 'Bjorn Farman will never trouble us again, so there is no eastern threat for them to guard against. That way I can add three hundred spears to my father's army.' He smiled again as Gunnhild sidled across and began to brush her lips against his neck. 'If the gods will it, we should have cleared out the nest of adders which is the Trondelag once and for all by the time that the harvest is in.'

23

HARALD'S BANE

Nerves were stretched as taut as bowstrings as the lookout in the bow called back again. 'I can count twenty sail now, with more ships coming on in their lee.'

Erik cupped a hand to his mouth and called an instruction. 'Olvir! You proved the value of your eyesight outside Tunsberg. Get yourself up the mast and tell me what you can see.'

As the Vestfolder scurried aloft, Erik turned back to the men at his side. 'We need to find out the identity of this fleet, and soon. If we are about to be faced by a victorious Halfdan on the way to Avaldsnes to claim his prize, we still have time to put about.'

Thorstein set his face into a frown as Kolbein stretched his neck to peer around the sail. 'We could take them on Erik.' The huskarl looked outboard at the other ships as they buried their heads into the swell, rose again and surged forward. Despite the high seas barely a misting came inboard on any of them. 'The men of the Vestfold may not be up to much in a fight, but they know how to build a ship. Both of the skei we took from Tunsberg are high sided and well found, and the *Draki* is the finest ship that I ever set foot upon. With these crews,' he said with a look of pride, 'we could clear the decks of the leading ships, kill the leaders and then fight our way clear.'

Erik's eyes scanned the horizon as he thought. The *Draki* had been in the naust, the boat shed where it had resided since the previous winter, but it had been the matter of a few short hours work to rig her and bend on the sail, and she had been ready to put to sea before the sun had set that evening. Despite their affection for their own ships, the little snekkjur *Okse* and *Bison*, Ulfar and Gauti had been over-proud when given the command of the two Vestfold skei. Their crews supplemented with some of the men that King Harald had left to guard Avaldsnes Erik's war fleet, though small in number, was a force to be reckoned with. Desperate to reach the Trondelag before the fighting started they had left Karmsund at first light the previous day. Ignoring the safety of the leads and channels of the North Way they had beat out to sea and picked up the prevailing wind. With the full force of the westerlies now behind them and free from the danger of rocks and shoals, they had pounded north night and day until the southbound fleet had appeared across their track. Now it would seem the gods were asking him to choose between a glorious death in battle or ignominious retreat.

'I know what it is, lord,' Thorstein said as he stepped in closer. 'You have responsibilities now, Gamli and a wife with child, but a king cannot let that sway his judgement. You cannot ask men to leave their farms and families to fight for you if you are unwilling to leave your own. Besides,' he added with a smile. 'From what I know of Gunnhild she already has a fast ship rigged and ready to sail in the harbour. If Halfdan did appear in Karmsund she would be on her way to her father and brother as soon as the beacons were lit, and he would spend the remainder of his days watching the southern horizon waiting for avenging Erikssons to appear there.'

Erik too looked out to the long sleek forms of the dragons as the huskarl spoke, the shields lining the strakes glistening in the sun. Most of the crewmen were his own huskarls, and a thrill ran through him as he saw his own bloodied axe emblem decorating their shields staring back at him. 'You are right old friend,' he said with a clap on the big man's arm, 'today is a day for war.' Energised by Thorstein's words, Erik called across to his banner man. Anlaf Crow was already preparing himself for the fight to come, running a sharpening stone along the edge of his sword blade with long careful strokes. He looked up, and Erik realised with satisfaction that he too had never given withdrawal a thought. 'Signal to the other ships; we are attacking!'

'I HAVE TO SAY,' King Harald said as they watched the flames saw back and forth. 'That I have never been prouder of any of my sons than I was at that moment.' His rheumy eyes took on a deeper gloss as his mind pictured the three drekkar cleaving the swell as they closed with his mighty fleet, the blood-axe banners of his favourite son dragon-tailing from the mast head as the howl of war horns haunted the waves.

Erik poked about in the embers with a stick, and the two kings watched as the fiery sparks and smoke-blackened smuts curled up and became lost in the night air. Sat on a beach in Moerr while the noises and smells of an army filled the air all around, he still could not quite believe that he was alive. Erik turned his face to Harald and the old man recognised the despondency written there. 'Still,' Erik replied as he puckered his lips and sought to push the feeling aside. 'I wish that Halfdan or Sigurd Jarl had somehow slipped past you in the night and made a dash for the South, hoping to draw part of your army away from the Trondelag.' For a moment Erik's mind was back on the steering platform as the *Draki* led the three powerful longships on a Valkyrie Ride to Valhöll. Sails straining, shrouds singing as the big ships took the rollers like war horses at the gallop, Erik glowed with pride as his own mind's eye saw again the decks aglitter as men threw on brynja and helm and gird themselves for war. Eventually, he perked up enough to shoot his father a wan smile as he tossed the blackened stick away into the darkness. 'Peace...' he said shaking his head. 'Of all the outcomes which had occurred to me on the journey north, peace was the only one which escaped me.'

'Believe me son,' Harald said. 'Peace was the last thing that I wanted.' He pursed his lips and shook his head. 'This was my final chance to die a warrior's death Erik,' he said sadly. Harald Fairhair spread his sword hand as well as he was able but it was still little more than a claw, and Erik felt a pang of guilt that he had acted so boorishly when his father, the man who had bequeathed him a kingdom and roused himself from senility to lead a host north on his behalf, had had his own hopes of a hero's death snatched away by a cruel twist of fate.

Erik nodded at the king's hand. 'Could you have wielded a sword?'

Harald shrugged. 'Helgrim Smiter managed to wedge the handle into my palm, but I doubt that it would have stood up to hard fighting.' He threw his son a wink and a cheeky smile, and Erik thrilled as he saw the man he remembered from long ago resurface for an instant. 'I had my spear to hand though, so I had all my angles covered.'

'So, who was this Guthorm Sindri then? A man who can single-handedly prevent a war.'

'A gadabout,' Harald replied. 'He came to my hall, ooh...' Harald scratched at his beard as he thought. 'It must be at least twenty, twenty-five years ago now: when you were at foster with Thorir hersir. He spent the winter with us and his word play was the talk of Rogaland. When spring came I asked him to stay, but he said that he had other places to visit, other people to see. Mindful that my enemies would seek to bring shame upon me by labelling me a stingy host I offered to let him choose anything from my gift hoard, but he refused and I never saw him again until a few days ago.' Harald paused to pull the bearskin which lay about his shoulders a little tighter as the cool of the evening began to gnaw at his old bones, and Erik too shivered a little inside as he felt that he was watching the dying flames of the great fire which had forged the first kingdom of the Norse guttering as his words floated away into the night.

'And this wandering poet just walked into camp one day and told you to lay aside your war plans and sail home?' Erik asked incredulously.

Harald laughed into his beard. 'I said that Guthorm Sindri refused payment in gold and silver, I never said that he refused payment. Before he left he said that we would meet again one day, and on that day I would honour his boon and grant him his wish. Men have told me that Guthorm spent the last winter in Halfdan's hall as he did my own, and asked for the same payment for his verse. Men went between the armies and told us these things so you can see, we were both honour bound to accept his wishes. Halfdan was to remain king in Trondelag and you, Erik, were to be left in peace. If either of you conspired against the other it would be your bane.'

Erik had listened, enraptured by his father's words. It was clear that the great king had little time left on Midgard but he was thankful that, despite the fact that Harald had been denied a fitting end in battle by the vagaries of fate, the attempt on his own life at Solvi had somehow served to clear away the fog of age which had clouded his mind and allow the true Harald Fairhair one last tilt at life. That energy seemed to be draining away like ale from an overturned cup, and Erik threw a last comment at his father as the old man began to doze. 'Still…a poet,' he said with a shake of his head. 'I live in a world where a woman rules from Avaldsnes, wordsmiths ask armies to put away their weapons and go home, and they do!'

Harald Fairhair raised his chin from his chest, the whiteness of his beard splaying like the long clouds which girded the mountaintops of home and threw his son a wink. 'When one-eyed wandering poets ask you to honour their wishes Erik, it's usually a good idea to do so.' The old king closed his eyes again and settled back into his chair as the rigours of the past few weeks spent on campaign began to overwhelm him. As Erik began to realise the implication behind his father's words, the old king opened an eye and murmured again. 'Particularly if they have not aged a day in twenty winters!'

Erik's mind wandered as the skald warbled another verse. If the king was to go to Valhöll he reflected as he sank another mouthful of the Jule ale, at least he would be spared the constant repetition of the tale of the fighting at Hafrsfjord. Earlier that day Harald had sprinkled his new grandson with water at the temple and named him for himself, but even Erik's newest son had caused little more than a flicker of light to shine from the darkness which now enveloped the king.

It had quickly become obvious to Erik that the hours

spent around the fireside, that night on the strand in Moerr, would be the last time that he would hold a meaningful conversation with his father. Helgrim Smiter had told him that the king's vigour seemed to seep away the further they sailed from the Trondelag; by the time the fleet had crammed the bays of Karmsund, Erik had looked on sadly as the old man had struggled back to his hall on the hill. If it really had been Óðinn who had breathed life into the king and intervened to put a stop to the conflict, it was clear now to Erik that the wandering god had moved on again, that the days of Harald Fairhair were drawing rapidly to a close.

He glanced across to the figure of his father, and a feeling of guilt crept over him as he realised that he was growing more anxious every day for the old man to ascend to the Allfather's hall of heroes. If the kingdom was a ship it was adrift off a lee shore. Storm clouds were gathering, and the rocks and skerries waiting to rip the bottom from stem to stern were his brothers. The king, the helmsman, had lost his way and needed to be replaced if they were to steer clear.

Halfdan and Sigurd Jarl had been emboldened by the weakness of King Harald, and had stopped sending their half of the tribute south the moment that they heard that Harald had confirmed Erik as his heir on their return. Traders said that Halfdan now sat upon the high seat which had been Fairhair's at the hall there. In the East, Bjorn Farman's full brother Olav had added Vestfold to his own kingdom at the same time and taken Bjorn's son into his care. The boy was still too young to be a threat Erik mused as he watched the skald prance and sing, but the lad would soon grow to manhood; given the chance. The income from Vestfold, from the whole of the Vikken had dried up too. He needed to go to war, this spring, or starved of the income from the wealthiest areas of Norway the rump of the kingdom still under his control would wither and die.

MEN WERE STRAINING to hear and the godi was doing his manful best, but the words were being snatched up and thrown away across the strait almost before they could clear his beard. Arinbjorn mumbled beneath his breath, despite the certainty that the spirits were swirling around them. 'We could have done it tomorrow. When a man lives for nigh on ninety winters, I am sure that his ancestors could wait another day to share a horn with him.'

Erik pushed the hair back from his face for the umpteenth time that afternoon and raised his gaze to the sky. Iron grey clouds were scudding across a sky flecked with sleet. 'No,' he said as he thrilled to the sight. 'If Þórr had to be elsewhere with his lightning bolts, I can think of no better way for the gods to announce their presence.'

The last breath had hissed from the lips of King Harald Fairhair the previous week. Erik had immediately received the oath from Helgrim Smiter and the rest of the king's guard and set the thralls to work opening the mound of his grandfather at Haugar on the opposite side of the bay. It had taken far longer than he had hoped to dig away the western end of the Howe to reveal the deck of the ship due to the frozen ground; but as soon as the burial chamber had been exposed to the light of day for the first time in generations, Harald's body had been put aboard his own ship and rowed the short journey across to his final resting place.

'It's a funny thing,' Arinbjorn said as the priest slit the throat of another horse and the blood pulsed out to slosh about the foredeck. 'We are looking at what remains of your grandfather Halfdan the Black as we lay our plans to kill Halfdan the Black.'

Erik snorted, despite the solemnity of the occasion. 'When you live as long and produce as many sons as my father, it must become difficult to think of new names for them all.'

Thorir hersir added a remark of his own as the next horse, its nostrils flared in terror, was manhandled down into the grave. 'That may be a problem you get to know yourself lord.' The three men shared a funny look, and smiles broke out on their faces regardless of the solemnity of the occasion. Despite the fact that Erik had been a king for several years now it still seemed unnatural for his old foster-father to defer to him and call him lord. 'It's true then, Gunnhild is with child again?' Arinbjorn's brow shot up as he asked the question. Erik nodded, and a self satisfied smirk lit his features. 'She seems pretty sure.' He flashed them a smile. 'And she should know by now.'

'What with looking after your father and all, I am surprised that you found the time. It must have been distressing, your father suddenly dying on her like that.'

'I am surprised that she lasted as long as she did. Being tired and sickly herself and taking care of the king.' He buried his chin into the folds of his cloak as a cold gust took his breath away before continuing proudly. 'But she is a fighter. Nothing she does is for herself, everything is for the good of her kin.'

What had been sleet only a short time before was thickening by the moment; soon driving snow would make the ceremony in the burial mound all but invisible to those not within the confines of the hollow itself. Erik indicated that they leave the rim and walk down as the last of the horses was led down. The final animal to be sacrificed to the gods that day would be despatched by the hand of the new high king of the North Way, and Erik threw a glance towards the great white ox as he unfastened the linen peace bands which held his short seax secure in its scabbard. The deck of the old warship was awash with blood, and Erik ran his eyes over the treasures which would accompany Norway's greatest king to the afterlife as he waited for the last of the horses to grow still.

Harald Fairhair lay on a wooden bed beneath the pelt of a great white bear, the dragon headed posts a whirl of intricate carving. Shields encircled the bed, their own designs adding to the splendour of the whole while spears and swords, ritually killed by the priests, lay scattered about. Gaming boards, tuns of ale and southern wine lay alongside flitch of swine and joints of beef.

The horse had kicked its last, and Erik withdrew his seax as the ox was led aboard. He instinctively reached out as the beast came alongside, brushing the pads of his fingertips along the coarse hair of the animal's snout as the priests tugged its head down by the nose ring. A dark baleful eye widened before him as he gripped the handle of his blade to saw through muscle and tendon, and Erik stepped smartly back as the blood gushed at his feet. The ox was the last to die that day, and Erik turned to lead them towards the ship which would carry them back across the icy waters of the bay.

Mourning for King Harald would last for seven days, after which the death ale would be drunk and Erik would be confirmed as high king. He paused on the lip of the hollow as the wind once again plucked at his hair and clothing, throwing a last look across his shoulder at the man who had made him a king. He had now been made king twice over; if the shaman in Finnmark was right, at least three more king helms still awaited him before he too would lie alongside his father and grandfather in the mound.

Perhaps the kingdoms of Trondelag and Vestfold were two of them, or maybe a yet greater prize awaited him? The ships had dispersed since Harald's return, back to fjords the length of the West lands, but the war arrow would draw them from the nausts like serpents awakening from their winter slumber and he would lead them to war and see.

24

'Ragnar Jarl is coming Erik,' Thorstein said with a frown. 'And he is not smiling.'

Erik sighed and filled another cup to the brim. 'He has not smiled for a week.' He cocked his head and looked up at his huskarl. 'Another ship bearing ill tidings from home?'

'Not that I know of, but it is the usual reason.'

Erik clicked his tongue in frustration as Thorstein made a suggestion which was only partly in jest. 'Maybe if we stationed guard ships at both ends of the sound we could turn the traders away?'

Erik threw him a pained expression. 'I know that you mean well old friend,' he said. 'But not only will we collect no skat at all, but those same traders will take their wares either north or east and pay that silver to our enemies.'

A shadow fell across the doorway, and Erik looked up and threw his jarl a beatific smile. 'Ragnar! I was just saying to Thorstein. I wish that I had someone with more to their conversation than *skjald-borg* and tits to share a cup of mead with.'

To his credit the Halogalander forced a smile, despite the

worries which were becoming more obvious with every passing day. He came forward, reaching out a meaty hand to grasp the cup. Sinking the drink in one, he held the cup out for a refill. As Ragnar watched the golden liquid pour from the spout, Erik spoke again. 'Has another ship arrived from the North?'

Ragnar blew out through his nose and nodded sadly; 'yes lord fresh in today.'

'From Halogaland?'

The jarl nodded again. 'I wish that shield walls and tits were my only concerns. Things are taking a turn for the worse, Erik.' His brow creased into a frown and he studied the floor as if reluctant to continue.

Erik encouraged him with warm words, despite the fact that he was dreading hearing what must surely follow. 'Ragnar,' he began, 'old friend. Of all the men who have sworn an oath to me since my father made me a king, none have proven more loyal in council or steadfast in battle. Were it not for your advice returning from Bjarmaland I should not be standing here now, so I am not only honour bound to listen to your woes, but keen to help in any way that I am able.'

Ragnar brightened a touch at his king's words, but it was clear to all present that it was an onerous duty that he was bound to perform as he lifted his chin and spoke again. 'Lord,' he croaked, before clearing his throat and trying again. 'Lord king. I must ask your leave to remove my ships from your fleet and sail for home.'

Erik had expected as much and he nodded immediately, much to the jarl's surprise. 'You have my permission to travel and my blessing. No man here in Avaldsnes has displayed more loyalty towards me than you.' Erik snorted and exchanged a look with Thorstein and Anlaf at his side. 'How did we feel when we were outnumbered on a hillside, cut off from our ships and we saw the prow beast on the *Orm* come clear of the Dvina channel?' Erik's huskarls nodded their agreement as Erik went on. 'If you are needed at home, go now,' he said earnestly. 'If their king cannot come to their aid, it is only right that their jarl and hersar act on his behalf. Is the cause the same as before?'

'The situation has worsened lord,' the jarl replied. 'The traders in the fjords have been forced to remove the goods from their warehouses and carry them inland. This saves their stock but ruins trade, so they still suffer almost the same depredation. Now that they have destroyed our trade, the Trondelag ships have moved offshore to harry the fishing fleet.' He grimaced, running his gaze around those present to allow the enormity of the problem to sink in. 'Not only will we lose a good part of our trade goods, but many will face starvation this winter if the fish are not cured in time. Sink or carry away the fishing boats themselves...' The jarl let the sentence hang in the air before shaking his head sadly. 'Halogaland faces devastation, lord. We will have no kingdom left to save, far less tax.'

Erik nodded. 'You must gather your men and leave for the North as soon as you are able. Any king's first duty is to the safety of his subjects and I would be no king if I allowed otherwise. As you know, circumstances dictate that I cannot be there yet in person so you will have to act on my behalf, but tell every man, woman and child that their king is coming and will make their southern neighbours pay for their actions as soon as he is able.'

The change in Sigurd's demeanour was palpable, and the jarl's eyes shone with gratitude as he offered his thanks. As the leader of Erik's most northerly province hurried off to gather his men, the king cast a look at his own most trusted men and hissed a curse.

. . .

THE LAST STERN post became lost from sight behind an arm of land as Arinbjorn turned to Erik with a scowl. 'Who would have thought that young Gudrod would have turned out to be such a competent king?' Erik glared, and his foster-brother cleared his throat and quickly backtracked. 'It's a family trait Erik, like falling to your sword.'

'Who would have thought that the death of my greatest enemy would have caused so many problems?' Erik gave a snort of irony as the horses walked on. 'Halfdan the Black gasps his last and drops dead suddenly at a feast, and all it does is delay their attack. That means,' he said as he looked out across the sound to the mainland, 'that not only do I have to feed and pay for an army to camp within the sound for a whole summer, draining a treasury of funds which are not being replenished due to the war. But that my enemies can use the time to scathe and weaken the lands which are loyal to me while my strength ebbs.'

'You do know that the enemy are blaming the death of your brother on Gunnhild, lord?' Arinbjorn asked.

Erik shrugged. 'Well, they hate us. Why would they not try to use every trick against us that they were able? They seem to have conveniently forgotten what the consequences would be if Halfdan broke the agreement with our father brokered by the skald.'

'And that she murdered King Harald?'

'Because she was caring for him when he died? After they had raised armies against him hoping to do the very same thing? How do you know this?' Erik spat the question before he was able to contain his rising anger at the way the war was progressing. It was not the fault or wish of Arinbjorn or any other of the men who had rallied to his cause that things were not going according to plan, and his shoulders slumped as he turned his face to his old friend. He opened his mouth to offer an apology for his outburst, but Arinbjorn beat him to it. 'There is nothing to apologise for Erik, if anyone knows you it is me.' He held Erik in his gaze as he spoke again. 'Erik, you know that I am loyal to your cause. Nothing will ever shake that conviction. However part of that loyalty and, I hope, friendship, is that I must be free to offer you advice or information which you may not wish to hear. A king can find any number of men to stroke his ego and laud him far and wide, but we both know that those men will be loitering at the rear or far away when the war horn sounds.'

Erik had been watching Anlaf Crow and Thorstein swimming in the shallows at the foot of the hill with Thorir hersir's men Helgi and Horse Hair Gisli, splashing about and acting the fool for the washer women nearby. Further out a small boat was crossing the strait as his foster-brother spoke. There was something about the way the rowers were bent over their oars that looked out of place as men went calmly about their business, but he had taken in his friend's words and he turned back with a self-deprecating smile. 'You are right, if I cannot listen to well meaning advice from my friends I would be no king but a tyrant. Tell me what you have heard and I can counter their lies.'

Arinbjorn slid from the saddle and flexed his legs. 'You will have to give me a moment,' he said as he turned his back to the wind before loosening his trews to piss into the grass. 'There is a lot to tell, and this can't wait.'

Erik dismounted and followed suit, and the chuckles turned into full bellied laughs as each eyed the other and tried to piss the furthest. As the golden arcs were snatched up by the wind to spatter the hillside, the simple pleasure caused the cares and duties of adulthood to fall away, and they were back rampaging in the hills above Naustdal for a welcome moment. 'The heather will colour the hillside here soon,' Erik said as he finished and tucked himself away. 'The island of Kormt is well known for it.'

'Yes,' Arinbjorn replied as his mind came back to the business at hand. 'The summer is almost spent. It looks as if we will not get our war until next year after all. We will have to release the bonder soon to gather the harvest. High King or not,' he said with a look. 'Only tyrants would insist that the farmers serve in the levy at harvest time, it is against ancient law and custom.'

'Next year it is then. We can crush them in the spring. For now tell me what you have learnt, it may help us in some way.'

'Well,' Arinbjorn replied, 'the main thrust of it is that they are suffering under the intolerable yoke of Danes.'

'Because of Gunnhild?'

Arinbjorn shrugged. 'Partly; she is undeniably the daughter of King Gorm, but they are also spreading the rumour that she practices seith.'

Erik crinkled his brow in surprise. 'They think that she is a witch?'

Arinbjorn shrugged. 'It doesn't matter what the leaders believe, but if the bonder begin to consider that your wife is not only a witch but a Danish witch...' He paused and shot Erik a look. 'Well, you can see how bad it looks. Not only did King Harald die in her care, but the man who had just tried to burn you in keeled over and died with no warning. One moment he was at his cups with his warriors, the next he was choking and gasping on the floor.'

'As Óðinn warned he would if he conspired against me. Either that or the stupid bastard choked on something.'

Arinbjorn narrowed his eyes. 'Do you think that this skald really was the Allfather?'

Erik shrugged. 'Everybody has to be somewhere. My father seemed convinced.'

'But you can see how easily they could use the Danish connection against you. You know how much the folk of the Fold and the Vikken have suffered under the Danes over the years. Show them any hint of weakness or disunity and the sea is a cloud of sail, either come to scathe the land or stay to rule. The gods know the people thereabouts have suffered both horrors at Danish hands for as long as men can recall.'

'So,' Erik replied, 'my wife is a Danish witch. Is there anything else I should know about?'

'Erikr Danøx.'

Erik narrowed his eyes. 'Erik Dane axe? A lot of men use the long hafted Dane axe, I do so myself. Is he a berserk?'

Arinbjorn laughed. 'Some would say so!' He pointed a forefinger and poked Erik in the chest. 'It's what they are calling you!'

Erik was about to scoff at the absurdity when he paused as his mind began to tease apart the weave of the thing. Finally he nodded as he had to admit to himself that the accusation contained more than a grain of truth. 'I have underestimated our foemen,' he admonished himself with a scowl. 'They are a wily bunch. I may be a son of Harald Fairhair, but I was the only child of his queen Ragnhild Eriksdottir and I am named for her father, a Danish king in Jutland.'

Arinbjorn nodded. 'So we have a half Dane, married to a Dane who they say dabbles in seith. Said half Dane just killed two of his brothers who were kings in the Vestfold and Hatha-land, and the Dane they say used her witchy powers to kill another of her husband's brothers who stood in their way, not to mention the much loved high king of Norway who refused to die quick enough.'

Erik's features took on a frown as his foster-brother ran through the situation. The boat with its frantic rowers had reached Kormt now and men on the jetty were pointing in his direction. As he watched a figure detached itself from the group, threw itself onto the back of a horse and began to gallop in his direction. Arinbjorn had noticed him too, and he shaded his eyes against the late summer sun as he watched the rider come on. 'It's Kari Hallsson!' he exclaimed suddenly as he shot Erik a look. 'You remember Elk Kari, Erik. He led you across Jostrudal when you burned in Bolli Sigurdsson, the Lade jarl's son. Let us hope that he brings us good news, he is not a man to make a fuss over nothing.'

The pair watched with mounting dread as Kari goaded the horse up the rise. Both men knew that if the mountain man carried news of an impending attack on them, it could scarcely have arrived at a worse time. Within a short while he was before them; the same widely spaced eyes, bulbous nose and easy smile which Erik recalled from his youth as he dipped his head, jumped to the ground, and took a knee as he waited for permission to speak.

'Kari, it is good to see you again after so long,' Erik greeted him with a smile, despite his fears. 'Two score years is a long time, but I am glad to see that a life on the fells has been good to you.' He hauled the man to his feet and smiled. 'You have news for us; spit it out and we shall deal with the consequences, good or bad.'

'The men of the Trondelag are on the move lord king,' Kari announced in reply as he whipped the leather cap from his head and wrung the sweat from it. 'Thorir hersir sent me to keep an eye on the passes between Trondelag and the Vikken at the beginning of summer and report to you here if either army made a move. Well, they have. A month ago King Gudrod passed through Upland with his hird. I tailed them for a couple of days to make sure of the heading before questioning a few country folk as to their destination.' He gave them a shrug and a gap toothed smile. 'Women like me, always have. They always tell me what I want to know, it's a gift.'

Erik snorted. 'Well, that's debatable. But carry on, what did these lovelorn women tell you?'

'They all said the same, lord,' Kari continued proudly. 'King Gudrod was on his way to meet with King Olav in the Vestfold, to pledge their loyalty to each other and make plans to rid the country of the Dane axe. That's you, lord,' he added happily.

Erik and Arinbjorn exchanged a look as both men immediately realised the importance of Kari's report. 'So Gudrod and Olav are in Tunsberg together, now?'

Kari nodded. 'Yes, lord, they must be. I had to cross the highlands to get here and they had a far easier road to travel, even if their numbers would slow them down.'

Erik felt a thrill course through his body as he realised the opportunity which was presenting itself as if from nowhere. 'This is very important,' he said as he fixed the hunter with his gaze, 'think carefully before you answer.' Kari nodded. 'You say that Gudrod was accompanied by his hird. Are you certain there were no men of the levy among their number or following on behind?'

'Yes lord, I am certain, there is no way that even an old country boy like me could confuse the two. One lot are warriors in magnificent war gear, with fine horses and built like trolls. The other are bonder and fishermen armed with the tools of their trade and a hardened leather cap and jerkin if they are lucky.'

Arinbjorn nodded at Erik's side. 'It makes sense. This time of year, approaching the end of summer, the men are needed in the fields. You don't need me to tell you that the law states that levy men must be released to harvest the crop.' He cast a look across the glassy waters of the sound to the hills opposite. Every night the number of fires burning there told the same story. Men were beginning to take the long trek home as the period of their enlistment came to an end.

Erik slipped a gold ring from his arm and passed it to the dumbstruck hunter. 'Here, this is a mark of my appreciation for all that you have done for me, now and in the past. Take yourself down to my hall and eat your fill, while I discuss with Arinbjorn how to react to your news.' As Kari went to remount his horse Erik called across as a thought pushed itself to the fore. 'Before you do, Helgi and Horse Hair Gisli are down by the water's edge.' He pointed the group of swimmers out as the huntsman pulled himself into the saddle.

'Yes lord, I can see them.'

'My men Anlaf and Thorstein are with them. Hurry down and tell them to send the fastest ship available to tell the jarl of Halogaland to return with the utmost urgency. Do you understand?'

Kari gave a curt nod as he hauled the head of his mount around, casting another look of disbelief at the ring gracing his forearm as he set off back down the hill. Erik turned to Arinbjorn as a hundred thoughts swirled through his mind, until a few began to coalesce and form themselves into a single word:

'Attack!'

'What if Gudrod has returned home by the time we cross the mountains?'

'He will still be there, I am certain of it,' Erik replied. 'Kings can't just drop by, say a few hellos, make a few plans and then piss off home. There will be feasts, skalds, weapon play and a good deal of drinking. Besides, we will not be crossing the mountains.' He ran a finger across his tongue and held it high. 'A westerly, blowing nice and steady as we found out when we were spraying the hillside,' he said with a smile of triumph. 'It usually does at this time of the year.'

Arinbjorn nodded as he caught on. 'And they cannot sail home even if they were given ships by their generous host, because they would have to beat against the prevailing wind far out to sea or sail right past us here. It would be quicker to walk back to the Trondelag.'

'Attack now and we have them,' Erik said as the light of victory began to shine in his eyes. 'Our lands here are safe because we know that the men needed to fill Gudrod and Sigurd Jarl's ships are away in the South. They are shorn of the levy due to the harvesting, and no doubt made groggy by a month of drinking and debauchery. Get the men on the ships, and as soon as Ragnar returns with his Halogalanders, we sail.'

25

THE HARRYING

Sailcloth strained, shrouds and stays thrummed as the *Draki* buried her prow in the swell, climbed the next roller and surged ahead. Spray and windblown spume curled eastwards from wave tops silvered by the light of the moon as Erik cast a look astern. If anything the conditions were just *too* perfect for their headlong dash to the Fold. The westerly blew strong and steady through a night made day by the full moon which shone from a cloudless sky. The way ahead clear any fears of collision with other ships or land had melted away, and Erik's fleet had bent on sail and flown as men tried to snatch a few hours sleep wherever they could find a space. But the same conditions which allowed them to sail through the night were also scattering the fleet as the long, lean hulls of the skei surged ahead, and Erik knew that there was only one thing to be done. 'It's no good,' he said before sending a ball of phlegm spinning out into the void. 'We will have to rein the old girl in if we are not to arrive piecemeal.'

'It's a shame,' Kolbein replied. 'But it's the right decision lord.' The styrisman cast a look back across his shoulder as he held a steady course. Half a mile astern the snekkjur were bounding the waves; they were not a problem, they would be up in no time once they reached the entrance to Tunsberg Fjord. Astern of the powerful warships the mast tops of the karvi were now only visible each time that the *Draki* breasted the swell, the fuller, shorter hulls of the craft which made them such fine workhorses no match for their sleeker brothers when it came to all out speed.

'How long ago did we double Lindesnes and steer nor-eastward, half a day?'

Kolbein wrinkled his nose as he thought. 'A bit more?'

Erik cast a look outboard. Ten miles or so off the larboard quarter a dark line marked the islands and skerries which girded the rich farmlands of the Vestfold. Men there slept soundly in their beds or tossed and turned as troubled minds wrestled with the everyday concerns of life, still unaware that the coming dawn would render such things footling.

'No,' he said. 'There is no shame at all. The gods are working for us old friend. Shorten sail and we can gather our wolf pack for the final run in.' His teeth flashed white in the moonlight as Kolbein called the order and men leapt to work the sheets and priare. 'We have a day of fire and steel ahead of us.'

THE WARRIORS WATCHED with amusement as the styrisman on the boat worked the steering oar back and forth, his indeci-sion reflected in the movement of the craft as the stern of the little knarr wagged its tail like a dog. Finally they recognised the moment when the boatman knew he must trust his fate to the gods, and he turned the knarr seaward hoping to bluff his way through the warships unscathed.

The *Draki* was in the van where a king's ship should be, and Erik snorted at Kolbein's remark as he ordered the crew to back their oars; the trader threw them a cheery smile and raised a hand in greeting. 'He must have the balls of Þórr himself; the cheeky bastard!'

Erik had dressed for battle as the first grey light of the false dawn had scored the eastern sky. Now the sun was up and he shone like the morning star itself; a king of Norway in his war glory. The whole was meant to intimidate as much as protect him from sword's bite or the thrust of a spear, but the man in the ship below him seemed unfazed and Erik felt himself warming to him as he called out across the gap. 'What cargo, chapman?'

'Ship's stores mainly, lord. Sealskin rope, barrels of nails and pitch.' He raised his chin and indicated towards the front of the hold, 'plus a few ells of wadmal for the lassies.'

Thorstein had stepped up onto the steering platform, and he made a comment as they ran their eyes over the trader's stock. 'Pitch, rope and a few lengths of wool cloth; nice and smoky.'

The comment caused Erik to raise his head and he swept both shorelines with his gaze. Columns of thick dark smoke were climbing into the late summer sky from both banks as Arinbjorn and Ragnar harried the farms and settlements there, and he allowed himself a smile of satisfaction as another petal of flame blossomed into life. Men standing guard on the high walls of Tunsberg would be pointing their spears to the South as the dark cloud stained the horizon, and the young kings would be hastening from their bowers as the wail of signal horns drifted across the berg. The timing of their arrival had been gods-given, allowing Gudrod and Olav enough time to gather their hird, but not enough to muster the levy. Even though outnumbered, honour would force them to confront the Vikings doing scathe on their doorstep, and Erik congratulated himself as he turned his gaze back to the knarr. 'Can you all swim?'

The styrisman's shoulders slumped visibly as he realised the implication of the king's words, but he quickly recovered his wit and Erik fought back a smile as the man threw his arms wide and screwed up his face. 'This is all I have in the world, lord,' he pleaded, 'my ship and my sons here.'

The two lads whipped off their leather caps and wrung them to rope, and Erik finally chuckled as he saw that they too had the flogged hound look of their father down to perfection. Erik fished inside the purse that hung at his waist and pulled out a length of gold the width of his thumb. 'Something tells me that you have the wits to be worth far more than a leaky old tub and a few ells of homespun, but no matter. Here.' he said, tossing the treasure across. 'Buy yourself a bigger knarr.' He flicked a look at the two lads and back to the father. 'And put some aside to pay off outraged fathers when they come calling, demanding compensation for their daughters' loss of marriage prospects.'

The gold disappeared inside the trader's shirt and the trio slipped into the water as silkily as otters, striking out for the nearby shore as men jumped across to set the fires. 'Quickly does it lads,' Erik called. 'My brothers are waiting for me and it's rude to be late.' It was the work of a few moments for men well used to plundering Christendom, and soon the spearmen were scrambling back aboard as the *Draki* got underway and the first wisps of oily smoke curled skywards.

THORSTEIN RECOGNISED the long drawn out island midstream from their homeward journey following Bjorn's death, and he turned to his king as a hand moved up to check the chin strap of his helm. 'We pass that and we are into the final run-in Erik,' he said. The king nodded. 'I recognise it myself.'

Anlaf as banner man was at his lord's side, and Erik gave him the nod that it was time to call in the Vikings for the final attack. As the strident notes drifted across the waters of Tunsberg Fjord Erik moved down the ship, swapping smiles and cheery banter with the crewmen as they rechecked their straps and armour and gave a final edge to spear, sword or axe blade.

Arinbjorn and the men of Fjordane had passed from his sight as they doubled the island, but no new lines of smoke were staining the sky to larboard and Erik's stomach gave an involuntary kick as an image of his foster-brother hurrying the men back to the ships flashed through his mind. To starboard Ragnar Jarl and his Halogalanders had already made their hulls, the oarsmen curling their backs as they beat the mirror smooth waters of the fjord to foam.

The snarling prow beast of Erik's ship cleared the island, and the king of Norwegians retreated the few steps to the tall stern post as he looked back with pride at his war fleet. Ragnar's ships were closer, the gaudy war banners which topped each mast hanging limp in the still airs, but a quick look to his right showed that the men of Fjordane were coming up fast. The sky to the South was storm black as the higher winds teased the smoke columns apart and Erik grunted with satisfaction; short of spears or not, no man could hope to ignore such a challenge in his heartland and expect to remain the king. Olav and Gudrod *had* to abandon the safety of the berg, they *must* come out and fight.

Ahead of them the fjord doglegged to the left before straightening out for the final mile; it would force Ragnar out wide, giving Arinbjorn the opportunity to make up the distance before they hit the beach, and Erik turned back, reassured that his disposition was sound. The turn was coming up fast as the rowers swept the lithe warship forward with easy strokes, and Erik strained to catch the first glimpse of the enemy shoreline as Kolbein hauled at the tiller and brought the *Draki* onto the final heading.

The head of the fjord came into view, and then as they grew nearer still the fortress of Tunsberg itself perched upon its rocky outcrop. Away to the left, just beyond the rise, lay the place where they had surprised King Bjorn as he drank to Erik's humiliation and raised a horn to the nearness of his death. Well, Erik had shown the upstart why Harald Fairhair had chosen him above all his other sons to follow in his footsteps as high king of the Norwegians, and he would do so again; here, today, at this place.

A breath of wind returned to the balmy airs and the crack from above drew Erik's eyes to the mast top. At long last his blood-axe banner was in plain sight; there could be no doubt now in the town up ahead who was coming to visit fire and sword upon them, and as if in confirmation Thorstein gripped his arm as he exclaimed with delight. 'There, Erik!'

A gaggle of horsemen were galloping from the town gate towards a grassy knoll at the midpoint between Tunsberg and the place where a river emptied into the fjord. Erik narrowed his eyes, and a kick of excitement mixed with relief flooded through his body as he saw that the battle flags of Vestfold and the Trondelag streamed above them. It was all the confirmation he required as to the identities of the riders who rode beneath them, and he clapped Thorstein on the arm as he skipped down from the steering platform. 'Come on,' he said breezily. 'Or you will miss the fun!'

The fjord widened as it approached its head and Erik threw a look from side to side as the strand crept closer. Ragnar's *Orm* was there, the jarl busy in the bows as he prepared to lead his men ashore. Arinbjorn's *Sea Stallion* had made up the lost ground and now lay off the larboard beam, and Erik's foster-brother glanced across to shoot him a smile as Helgi and Horse Hair Gisli moved to his side with expressions as grim as Óðinn himself. Thorstein moved forward, rolling his shoulders for the hard work ahead, but Erik placed a hand on his huskarl's shoulder and gave it a squeeze. 'I am to be first man ashore today. It will give our army a fillip to see their king the first man to vault the wale, and it will send a shiver through the enemy ranks when they see how keen I am to come to grips.'

Thorstein took a backwards pace and threw his lord a wink. 'They might think that, Erik. But we both know that I will be a pace away. If any danger threatens, I will be at your shoulder.'

A cry came from astern, and Erik's attention returned to the field ahead as the oarsmen put on a spurt of speed for the final run in. More and more men were streaming from the berg, crossing the skyline like a great silvered serpent as they hurried across to form up beneath their kings' standards, and Erik was suddenly overcome with a feeling of disgust that it had come to this. Their father Harald Fairhair, the greatest Norseman who had ever lived, had chosen Erik to follow him as high king of the Norwegians. That the king had seen something in him that made him rise above them in his estimation was neither here nor there; Erik had never intended nor threatened to remove any of his brothers from the kingdoms which had been granted by their father. But jealousy had made them conspire against him; now he was the Half Dane, *Erikr Danøx*, the father of witchlings. Good men, blameless men, fellow Norwegians would die for their greed, and a resolve came upon him that he would wipe his brothers from the face of Midgard.

The beach was filling his view now, and a moment later the keel shushed the sand before driving hard aground. Erik was up on the wale and leaping into the shallows as the sound of oars clattering to decks filled the strand like rolling thunder, and splashing ashore he took a moment to take in the scene. Longships were driving ashore all along the beach, their prow beasts: dragons; wolves; bears; snarling at the spirits which inhabited the enemy shore as the morning sun blushed them to red-gold. Erik was already moving as the men began to tumble from the hulls and in a few paces he was off the sand, gripping his shield a little tighter as he drew his sword across his body and the ground firmed beneath his feet.

Thorstein and Anlaf Crow were the first to reach him, and the banner man planted Erik's blood-axe sigil in the soil of his enemies as the war cries of his army filled the air. Satisfied that they had reached the place of battle unscathed, Erik raised his eyes to the hillock as he began to plan his attack, but Thorstein stiffened at his side and he scanned the hillside for any sign of danger.

A horseman had seen the war flag and detached himself from the crowd, hoping to cut the head off the enemy snake and win the day before another blow could be struck. Peeling off from a group of latecomers the rider was already close, and the sound of hoofbeats were loud in his ears as he watched the warrior prepare to launch his spear. Thorstein threw himself before his lord, raising his shield to parry the throw, but Erik had other ideas and he barked an order as he darted forward.

'Stay here!'

Before the men could acknowledge his order Erik had burst forward into a run, and the breath sounded loud in his ears as the gap to the horseman shrank. The man released but

Erik's tactic had taken him by surprise, and although he attempted to adjust the angle of the throw before he let fly the dart deflected harmlessly off the rim of his shield. Erik dodged back then, dropping the board as his opponent struggled to draw his sword. Erik watched as the blade came free, but the look of triumph which flashed across the rider's face when he saw that the enemy king was shieldless lasted little more than a heartbeat as he threw himself forward onto the grass. Erik's head tucked under, and he rolled as the horseman drew rein and attempted to bring the king back under his blade, but Erik was rolling back to his feet and his own blade swept across to sever the horse's leg at the hock. As the horse went down with a scream of pain and the rider attempted to leap clear Erik was pivoting, scything the sword back and across to take the man in the small of the back. All the anger and frustration Erik felt towards the actions of his brothers was channelled into the blow, and he felt the blade bite through mail and flesh before coming to a halt as it lodged itself deep within the rider's hip bone.

As the shrieks of man and horse died away Erik realised for the first time that a deathlike silence had descended upon the field as the men of both armies watched the fight. Óðinn would give the victory to the man most deserving of it whether through bravery or just cause, and the waterfront exploded with noise as Erik walked forward to send his opponent across the rainbow bridge. Thorstein and Anlaf were hurrying across to their lord's side now that the victory had been gained, and Erik raised his gaze to drink in the sight as hundreds of men stabbed the air and beat a staccato thrum on their shield as they celebrated their king's victory. 'It is time to return lord,' Thorstein was saying as he flicked a worried look over Erik's shoulder. 'We are too close to the enemy.'

Erik looked. His huskarl was right he was barely beyond

spear shot, but he had seen the effect that the victory had had on both hosts and he sheathed his sword as he reached behind his shoulder to the place where he carried his battle axe. 'You lads stay with me,' he replied. 'I have a better idea.'

As the pair took up position on either flank Erik walked down to the place where the horse had come to rest. The wounded animal was still attempting to rise, and Erik looked deeply into the dark pools of its eyes as he placed a foot upon its neck and raised Jomal. The axe flashed in the sun as it swept down to take the horse's head in an echo of King Harald's horse sacrifice, the day that he had gifted Jomal to his heir on a distant strand. The significance was not lost on those present, and Erik stooped to collect the head from the spreading pool of blood and began to make his way back towards the shore. Men there had realised what he intended, and an oar had been retrieved from one of the ships and was being driven into the ground by the time that he had returned. He gave the men a nod of recognition for their quick thinking as they returned to their friends, and Erik fixed the head in place as Anlaf raised his banner high.

As the field once again fell silent Erik, as king and godi of the nation, cut runes into the shaft of the oar before fixing the head of the horse to the landward end. The head was now pointing uphill, directly at the place where Gudrod and Olav's standards were teased out in the fitful breeze, and Erik spoke the curse as the men of both hosts nervously fingered talismans and charms.

'Here I set up a *niðstang* to curse Gudrod Haraldsson and Olav Haraldsson.

'This curse pole I turn also on the spirits who dwell in this land that they may wander, not reaching nor finding their home till they have driven out the pretenders and taken up their rightful king.'

26

BATTLE AT TUNSBERG

The enemy had quietened since he had set up the scorn pole, but they were still drawn up in a strong defensive position. The river and a smaller bay off to the right acted to squeeze the land into a bow shaped peninsula, with the beach-head at the point where the hand grip would be. The bowstring was formed by the armies of Gudrod and Olav, with the kings themselves occupying the′ higher ground almost dead centre and the wings anchored to the river and bay at either end. Given enough time to pack the higher ground with men, Erik was certain that any competent war leader could hold the position all day long, pinning the invaders in place until he had weakened them enough to finish them off; he had to hit them like a thunderbolt before that could happen.

The howl of a war horn drew worried glances to the North. Caught out of position it would be a hard run race to return to their respective armies should the enemy launch a downhill attack, but Erik rolled his eyes and turned back with a snort of derision as he saw what has happening there. 'If they think that unleashing the dogs will turn the tide for them they had best think again.' He turned his face from Ragnar Jarl to Arinbjorn Thorirsson and back again. 'Þórr sent winds to drive our ships eastwards and his father Óðinn gave me victory over the horseman. The gods have allowed us to seize the advantage, and I am not going to throw it away by letting our men's battle zeal drain away.'

Arinbjorn thought that he already knew what his foster-brother had in mind, and his face was aglow with excitement as he said the word. *'Svinfylking?'*

Erik shook his head; 'not one, three.' He continued as the howls and screeches of the Eastland berserks began. 'Because we split up to scathe the fjord we arrived here already deployed in our divisions. All we have to do is form up and charge. It looks as if we still outnumber them, but who knows what the hill is concealing from us? What I do know,' he continued, 'is that the longer we leave before we attack, the more chance there is that men will arrive to bolster their position, and the more chance that our boys will begin to lose their battle fervour.' The trio looked across at Erik's army. The men there were still abuzz after their king's single-handed victory over the galloping spearman, but they would begin to calm with time and all three leaders were experienced enough to recognise that the time to strike was now.

Erik pinned Ragnar with a stare as the jarl's eagerness to get to grips with the enemy set him shifting from foot to foot in anticipation. 'As I said before we outnumber them for now, but who knows how long it will be before the men of the levy reach the field? The swine array was gifted to men by Óðinn himself, and my victory over the lone horseman will have shown those men on the hill which side the war god favours.' He pulled a lupine smile as the challenges rolled down the hillside from the men lining the ridge. 'Now I have cursed them too, so let us see how long their resolve lasts once we get among them. Drive along the bank of the inlet and outflank them; turn in and roll them up. If you can break through into the rear all well and good, but make sure that you pin them in place and cut the road to the berg.' Ragnar gave a grim nod by way of reply, and Erik switched his gaze to his foster-brother. 'Arinbjorn, you do the same on the left. Watch out for the river though, you don't want to end up fighting with your backs against it if they prove to be stronger than we expect. I will head straight up the rise towards my brothers' flags. The fighting will be hardest, but as soon as the banners go down the slaughter can begin.' Erik threw them both a grin. 'What? You thought I was going to share the glory?'

The pair laughed at their leader's joke and their own confidence, although never shaky, strengthened a little more. 'Remember,' Erik said finally with a snarl which drove the smiles from their faces. 'Gudrod and Olav die today. If Olav was foolish enough to think to blood his own son here, then we can try to get him too…and Bjorn's boy,' he added as an afterthought. 'But they will be sauce on the meat. Gudrod and Olav die.'

The trio clasped forearms before Ragnar moved off to begin forming the battle wedge of the men of Halogaland. Arinbjorn had to move across to the left flank of the army, and he called across his shoulder as he trotted away past the lines of catcalling warriors and the odd bared arse. 'Keep you eyes open for the wolf warriors, brother. They have a nasty bite!'

Erik flashed a smile in return. 'I will throw them a stick. It works every time!'

Thorstein and Anlaf were waiting impatiently for his return and he threw them a comment as he came up. 'You can relax now lads, I am back.' The pair exchanged bashful smiles at their lord's words, both men loathe to admit just how anxious they were anytime that Erik was away from them when danger was near.

'Svinfylking!' he called. 'Get it organised!'

Erik ran his eyes across the men of Rogaland as they began to shuffle into place. The face he was seeking hardened from the crowd surrounded by his men, and Erik called out as he looked across and saw that Arinbjorn was already in position and itching to lead the army of Fjordane uphill.

'Helgrim Smiter!'

The man turned his head as he heard the shout. Harald Fairhair's old huskarl had been among the first to pledge his oath to Erik when his lord took the rainbow path to Valhöll, and Erik had always had it in mind to show his gratitude when the right moment presented itself. That day had come, and Helgrim's face lit up like the morning sun as his king called out so that all could hear. 'Will you honour both myself and the memory of my father by leading the swine array this day?'

'Yes lord!'

'Well, lead on. We have not a moment to lose.'

The wedge began to form as Helgrim took the lead and his two doughtiest warriors stood shoulder to shoulder at his rear. As the next three men formed up behind them and the wedge began to take shape, Erik strode free of the line so that all those on the field could see him. Anlaf Crow planted his war banner at his side so there would be no mistaking the man as any but the king of Norwegians, and Erik raised the bloodied axe above his head and roared his battle cry.

'Blóðøx!'

The answering cry shook the ground beneath their feet as the army of the West roared in unison, war horns blared and Helgrim Smiter took the first pace forward of the advance.

Three times the battle cry rolled across the hillside, and each time the answering roar grew louder until it petered away to be replaced by the steady tramp of booted feet. The formation opened up to admit the king as it passed, and Erik and Anlaf joined Thorstein, Kolbein and Sturla Godi tucked in to the rear of old King Harald's men.

Erik looked across to the place where the Halogalanders were moving off beneath their lurid flags and banners, watching in fascination as men left the beach and the formation swelled by the moment until it became a tidal surge of leather and steel. The hillside was gentler there, far less steep than the climb which faced Erik and his men of Rogaland, and Erik took a last look as the northerners increased the pace and began to draw away.

Westwards the men of Fjordane had already put the low lying riverside behind them and were moving to outflank the men on the hill, and Erik felt his calf muscles tighten as the land before them trended upwards. Erik's head swept from left to right as he judged the perfect moment to order the charge. Each *svinfylking* was advancing across contrasting ground; it was one of the things which made the peninsula such a wonderful defensive position, and Erik tried to push down the thought as he wondered how many men had died on the hillside in the days since Óðinn had started the first war. It was imperative that the three fists hit the enemy wall at the same moment; punch through the hard outer shell and they could spill out and attack the soft belly of the enemy, or be fought to a standstill and it would be the invaders who would die and the assault would fail. Thankfully in Ragnar and Arinbjorn Erik had two leaders who had fought all over the northern lands and beyond, and he watched in admiration as the two men adjusted the pace of their own advance to help bring that about.

A hundred and fifty paces ahead the wolf men and bear shirts were being driven into a frenzy by the closeness of the enemy and their unwillingness to be overawed by the howled threats and gyrations. Beyond them the shields of the eastern armies came together with a crash which resounded across the hillside as snarling faces jabbed spears and beckoned them on to their deaths.

The point was fast approaching when he would have to order the charge regardless of whether the armies were in position or not, and Erik's head flew from left to right as his mind weighed how the distances and angles would affect each prong of the attack. Go too soon and the slope would sap the men's energy, weighed down as they were by mail and helm and struggling for footing within a crush of warriors. The attack would begin to lose momentum at the critical moment before they hit the enemy line; leave it too late and that momentum would never have time to develop.

Shields were raised as the first arrows began to spatter the formation, any moment now and the berserks would attack; Erik had waited long enough, and he placed his trust in Óðinn as he growled into his beard: 'Anlaf Crow!'

The banner man was poised and waiting for the order, and he snapped a reply before raising the horn to his lips: 'Ready!'

'Signal the charge!'

The doleful howl was greeted by a cheer as the westerners picked up their feet and gathered speed. Erik thought to check on Arinbjorn and Ragnar, but the thud of steel on wood made him think better of it as Thorstein moved an arm to pluck an arrow from the sky. Erik peered ahead, across the bobbing heads of Helgrim and his men as the gaudy shields and banners lining the ridge grew to fill his vision.

The berserks were bounding down the slope, their faces

contorted by hate as they sought to close the distance before the swine head could get into full stride. With the run of the slope to aid them it seemed only a matter of moments before the men to Erik's side and front were bracing themselves to receive the attack, and Erik watched in fascination as the nearest bear shirt prepared to throw himself upon their spears. At the last moment, just as it seemed that the man must become empaled upon the fence of spears the berserk leapt into the air; twisting like a whirlwind, the thick bearskin brushed the spear points aside as he crashed through into their midst. Men were bowled aside by the force of the strike, and before he could move Erik found himself staring directly into face of the slavering madman. Before the bear shirt could recover his balance Erik had planted his spear into the soil, freeing the hand to move across and snatch at the handle of the short seax which lay across his belly.

Men said that berserks' minds were Óðinn-giddy when the madness was upon them, barely aware of reality, their bodies unfeeling and impervious to pain; but Erik saw the flash of recognition in this man's eyes that he was face-to-face with the high king of Norway which gave it the lie. The crush of bodies told against him, and Erik felt panic begin to sweep through him as he realised that his arm was jammed hard against his side, but a heartbeat later the berserk's look of triumph was replaced by shock as the point of a dagger emerged from his mouth in a spray of blood. A hand reached forward to tug the bear head back and away, and within moments the warrior's unprotected head had disappeared beneath a flurry of blades as the man was hauled to the ground and finished off.

Erik looked about him as the immediate danger passed, and he was pleased to see that the last of the attackers was suffering a similar fate. If Erik had died in that moment the day would have been lost; without their king and leader the armies of the West would have had no reason to fight on. But there was no time to dwell on the fact, and spurred on by the massacre of the berserks the men of the *svinfylking* let out a cry, threw their shoulders into their shields and charged home.

The opposing armies came together with the crash of rolling thunder as Helgrim Smiter hacked and hacked, driving the swine head deep into the ranks of the easterners as the men behind him stabbed and slashed, punching out with their shields as they widened the breach.

Erik stepped over the first bodies as he too reached the old front line, raising his eyes as he sought out his brothers' banners, and he felt a kick of joy as he saw just how close Helgrim's attack had carried them. The war flag of Vestfold was little more than a dozen paces ahead of him, and dropping his gaze he saw the man who must be Olav for the first time. Despite their kinship the two had never met, but the magnificence of his arms and the way that the guard were drawing about him confirmed to Erik that this must be the king.

Up on the Ridgeline now Erik could see what he had suspected all along; the enemy shield wall had been stretched painfully thin in the brothers' attempt to hem the invaders in, denying them the opportunity to turn the flank until reinforcements could arrive. But he was nearing the high point now, and a quick glance across to the East told Erik that Ragnar's northern army had brushed the defenders aside with ease and were turning inward to roll up the line. To the West Arinbjorn and the men of Fjordane were still out of sight, but the backs of the furthest defenders were coming into view as the line began to curl back on itself and Erik knew that it too was doomed.

Erik dropped his spear and the hand went to the haft of his war axe, but he hesitated as he saw that the enemy were still fighting hard. Jomal could easily cut a swathe through them to the king but the war axe was a two handed weapon, and he would need to break free from his own men before he could bring the devastating power down upon the heads of his foemen. The hand moved back down to his side, and he raised his voice above the din as he drew his sword and hefted his shield:

'*Ready?*'

Growls came at his shoulder in affirmation, and Erik raised the sword and cried his battle cry as the men before him took a pace aside:

'*Blóðøx!*'

The shout was taken up, and the wedge surged forward again as Erik lowered his head and threw himself at the men facing him. A face flashed into view as he shouldered his shield, widening the breach, and Erik saw the look of dismay in the man's eyes that the Bloodaxe had chosen him of all the men on the hillside to receive his first attack. It was the look of a man who knew that his death was upon him, that the three hags of destiny were at that very moment poised to snip his life thread with their shears of woe, and a moment later Erik had brought reality to that fear as his sword blade drove down through helm and skull.

Step forward, shove again, and Erik was across the body of the first to die and hacking down on the heads of his foe with all the power and control honed to perfection on the hayfield before Thorir's hall so many summers before. Withdraw, stab, step up and hack again. The enemy were beginning to wilt under his attack, and Erik could sense that one big push would see them break. Thorstein and Kolbein were at his side, the shadow of his axe banner shading the men immediately to his fore showing that Anlaf Crow was a pace behind, and Erik roared his battle cry again as he barged a spearman aside.

He felt a spear blade snag in a link of mail, and he was twisting aside before the point could worm its way through as Thorstein brought his sword blade down to take the assailant's arm off at the elbow. Kolbein was scything a path towards the place where King Olav still stood beneath his banner, and Erik dropped his sword, reaching behind him to grasp the haft of Jomal as a space opened up before him. The shadow of his war banner retreated from the faces of the men opposite as Anlaf moved back to give his lord room, and Erik wound his body, the great curved blade of the axe whistling gleefully as it too cleaved the air. The first sweep took two heads clean off, the faces still showing looks of surprise and horror as they bounced away across the turf. Men were falling back under the pressure of their assault, the rearmost beginning to cast longing glances towards the safety of the distant tree line.

To Erik's left Helgrim Smiter and his men had broken the line, spilling out into the rear to double the crest and cut the king's line of retreat. The men of Vestfold and Ringerike had seen it too, and they broke before they too could be swept up in the net like a shoal of silver herring. Suddenly the hillside was filled with running figures as panic swept Erik's foemen, and men threw aside weapons and armour, anything which would hinder their headlong flight.

Erik turned back as the king's guard, doughty warriors to a man, drew close to their lord and prepared to sell their lives dearly. The hilltop belonged to the men of the West, twin arms sweeping around to engulf the stout hearts beneath their proud banner. Away to the East the scene was being repeated as the army of Halogaland flowed like a tide around young

Gudrod and his Tronds, and the men of both sides paused from the slaughter as they watched Ragnar Jarl overwhelm the last opposition there. Steel shimmered in a rapidly decreasing ring until the battle flag of Trondelag juddered and fell, rose again to flash in the morning light, and was beaten down for a final time.

Erik sniffed his satisfaction at a job well done and turned back. Locking eyes with King Olav for the first and last time, he spat on his palms, hefted Jomal, and walked forward.

27

HAKON

E rik Haraldsson, by Óðinn's will *Konungr* of the Norwegians, bent low and pressed the dagger home. As the wounded man's head went back and the last breath rattled and died in his throat, the king held his gaze as the light there began to fade. The ropes of gut the Vestfolder had been holding in slid to the turf as the strength left his arms, and Erik stepped away as the stench of innards washed over him. The hilltop was a mass of tattered and bloodied bodies, and Erik ran his eyes across the scene as his guards clustered protectively at his side. Some lay contorted in death, the terror of their final moments etched upon their features; others looked deceptively peaceful, almost as if they had chosen a bad place for a nap. Some sat bewildered as they watched the lifeblood drain from their wounds to darken the soil beneath them; others crawled to find a quiet place to spend their final moments on Midgard, as the animal which exists in all men forced itself to the fore.

Erik's men laughed and joked with their friends and kins-men, scarcely able to believe that they had faced an army of fellow Norsemen and lived to tell the tale. Some of course had not, while others compared wounds and still more held out arms and bared chests for their kinsmen, the wonder on their faces telling the tale: not a scratch.

As men began to make piles of the plunder, Erik strode across the hillside towards the place where they had watched the war banner of Trondelag fall. Ragnar Jarl watched him come, the smile on his face betraying the pride he felt at his part in the victory. The Halogalanders parted before the king, smiles and chants, *Erik! Erik!* following him as he walked the final few paces and the jarl dipped the captured flag in defer-ence. 'Welcome lord,' he said as Erik ran his eyes across the carnage there: 'congratulations on your victory.'

Erik snorted, throwing his arms forward to draw his greatest jarl into an embrace. 'The victory was as much yours as mine old friend,' he said as they came apart. 'I shall never forget.'

The Halogalanders cheered again as the king raised their jarl's arm high, and the cheering redoubled as men carried forward the flags of Rogaland, Fjordane, Vestfold and Ringerike to add to that of Trondelag and Halogaland itself. Erik's eyes sparkled with pride as Anlaf Crow raised his own personal axe banner alongside the flags of the kingdoms as he savoured the moment that he had worked so hard to achieve; to unite the lands of the Norwegians under the rule of one king as Harald Fairhair had willed it.

'You will want to see the body of the king,' Ragnar said as Erik lowered his arm and the men went back to plundering the dead.

Unlike Olav, Vestfold's usurper king who now lay gore spattered nearby with Jomal embedded in his skull, Erik had met his brother Gudrod on numerous occasions when he had accompanied Halfdan the Black and Sigurd Jarl to King Harald's hall at Avaldsnes. But looking on the faces of dead kinsmen was a thing which he had grown accustomed to, and Erik gave a curt nod to indicate that the jarl lead on. Ahead, a bloodied ring of death lay where the king's guards had fallen fulfilling their oath, and not for the first time that day Erik felt a pang of regret that such men had been forced to give their lives for such an unworthy cause.

'We have not touched Gudrod's body,' Sigurd explained as they walked. 'We wanted to wait until you decide what you want done with it.'

It was the first time that he had considered the disposal of his brothers' bodies, and he surprised himself as he answered with barely a thought. 'They were both sons of Fairhair and kings by right, acclaimed as such by ancient law at their respective Thing. That their ambition got the better of them rightfully cost them their lives, but the shame should not sully them in death. We will throw up earth,' he said as he looked about, 'here, on the ridge line where they fought and died. Men not yet born will see them as they travel the roadway or look across the vale from the berg and say; 'look yonder to the place where Gudrod and Olav Haraldsson rest in their mounds; hacked down by their brother Erik Bloodaxe their rightful lord, as Óðinn willed it.'

They had continued picking their way through the dead as Erik spoke, and as he finished he realised that they were already standing over the body of his brother. Erik looked down at the cut and hacked about remains but, in truth he felt little emotion. He had been the only child borne to Ragnhild Eriksdottir, the only son born to the daughter of a king. As well as his numerous wives, Erik's father had sired countless sons on women the length and breadth of Norway, high born or otherwise. 'I am glad,' he said with a sigh. 'Norway has enough enemies without fighting among ourselves. I will sacrifice to the gods at the Thing and give thanks that the only Haraldsson's left alive live content in their kingdoms.'

'Will you want to harry the Vestfold?'

Erik clapped his jarl on the shoulder. 'I may,' he replied with a knowing smile. 'These people need to realise that I am their king and no other, but you shall not be counted among my host. Take your Halogalanders home as soon as you are able. With any luck the threat from the Trondelag died on this field today, but you and your men have shown me nothing but loyalty going back beyond the fight in Bjarmaland and I would be no worthy lord if I kept men from their homes a moment longer than necessary.'

Ragnar brightened. 'Will you invest the berg?'

Erik shrugged. 'I will pitch tents for a couple of days and see if they are wise enough to throw open the doors. It will be a shame to burn such a fine and wealthy town, but their future is in their own hands. Then I will ride through Olav's lands and take the submission of the leading men before sailing back to Rogaland before the winter storms set in.' He smiled. 'The jarls and hersar will be lying on the ground hereabouts, surrounded by those of their hird who were not born fleet of foot. There will be many places in need of a new lord, men of proven worth and loyalty. I will think on it over the winter and reward those who have been steadfast in their loyalty to me in the springtime.' Erik smiled again as the reality of a kingdom shorn of opposition to his rule came upon him. 'We have forged the future of the kingdom here Ragnar, here on this thrall's tit of a hill. With my warlike brothers dead or cowed into obedience nothing can stand in our way.'

ERIK WIPED the ale from his chin and held the cup out for more. 'Hakon is back?'

Gunnhild nodded. 'He is in the Trondelag, at Sigurd Jarl's hall in Lade.'

'Of course he is,' Erik replied, 'he is a kinsman of the jarl.' Gunnhild narrowed her eyes in question and Erik explained. 'Hakon is one of my father's by blows, a son born out of wedlock to a distant kinswoman of Sigurd. Harald sent her away when she fell with child and Sigurd took her in. He sprinkled the child with water, accepting him into the family and gave him the name of his own father, Hakon.'

'So why is he here now, with three ships full of English warriors?'

'A few years back my father received an embassy from King Athelstan in England, offering to make common cause against the Dublin Norse who were making trouble for him in Northumbria.'

Gunnhild snorted. 'I know all about Northumbria, my brother Harald has a hall just south of there, at a place called Torksey in the Five Boroughs. They will never accept rule by the southern English kings, the land is populated by Norse, Danes and English in equal measure.'

Erik shrugged. 'Whether the inhabitants like it or not, their wealth and location means that the English and Scots will always covet their land. That wealth could also build an army to threaten the king here in Norway, so it was also in my father's interest that the Dubliners be kept out. The two kings exchanged gifts, Athelstan sent a magnificent sword, and Harald gave the English king a purple sailed dragon ship in return to seal their alliance. Hakon's fostering with Athelstan was part of that deal, and I can see now that Sigurd used it to remove his kinsman from harm's way here in Norway.' Erik shook his head as Athelstan's forethought began to reveal itself to him. 'Sigurd thought that he was being guileful, but he had more than met his match in the English king.'

The king chuckled as his mind went back to a far off strand, and he smiled at Athelstan's cunning. 'When I was in Northumbria one of their leaders, a churchman called Wulfstan, was interested in gaining my support. He sent a man called Oswald Thane to share his fear that Athelstan was planning to instal Hakon as under king in York and annex the kingdom, but it would seem that he had a far greater king helm in mind for the boy. Only last summer he sent a fleet to harry the Scottish coast, all the way up to the Norwegian land of Katanes, only a strait away from Orkney itself.'

Gunnhild's eyes widened as she began to tease apart the wider implications of the plot. 'Henry the Fowler, king of the East Franks; his eldest son Otto is married to Athelstan's half-sister, Eadgith. This is all part of the Christian fightback. Henry's army is pushing north into Jutland, keeping my father and brother busy and away from causing trouble in Frisia and England.'

Erik's jaw dropped as the machinations of the Christian princes was revealed to him. 'So Athelstan gets a free run at Northumbria, browbeats the king of Scots, and the two southern kings also get the chance to serve their God by supporting the first Christian to sit upon the high seat of Norway.'

'Then you need to kill Hakon this year,' Gunnhild snapped. 'And make sure that Sigurd Jarl pays the price for his disloyalty.'

Erik pondered her words for a moment but shook his head. 'It will have to wait until the spring, I have just released the levy to salvage what they can from the harvest. I asked a lot of them to fight for me in the Vestfold so late in the summer, I cannot recall them now.' He shot her a wink and pulled her close. 'What can a fifteen year old and three shiploads of Englishmen do against the mighty Bloodaxe?

There will be time enough to shoo this whelp and his Christian nursemaids from the kingdom when the campaigning season comes around again.'

KING ERIK STOMPED BACK into the hall, and faces were turned to the floor as he swept the room with a withering glare. Even Gunnhild paled in the heat of the king's anger, but she knew that she had a duty to perform and she did it well. Walking forward, the queen took up a horn of mead and cleared the room with a look. 'Drink this,' she cooed, as the men and servants hurried through the doorway and cast nervous glances their way. 'We have faced tougher times together and come through unscathed; we shall do so again.'

Arinbjorn, alone among the men who had accompanied Erik from the Thingstead had remained, and he cleared his throat softly as he sought permission to speak.

Gunnhild's eyes went from Arinbjorn to Erik and back again as she awaited her husband's reaction, and the king inhaled deeply as the mead began to cast its spell. 'Barely a half of them,' he muttered sadly. 'My power is seeping away by the day.' Erik walked across to the pitcher and topped up his drinking horn. Gunnhild and Arinbjorn exchanged a look as he did so, and both realised with a start that they were witnessing Erik lose faith in his ability to inspire men for the first time in his life.

Gunnhild attempted to rally her man as the realisation that her children were in grave danger came upon her. If Hakon could wrest the kingdom from Erik they could all pay with their lives. 'You have seen off far harder men than this stripling,' she said. 'What is so different this time?'

Erik had finally noticed that Arinbjorn alone remained in the hall out of all his followers, and he made a gesture that the man explain on his behalf as he slumped down in the high seat and took another gulp.

'Sigurd Jarl has persuaded Hakon to hand the bonder back their allodial rights. It was the wellspring of Harald Fairhair's power.'

Gunnhild looked askance, and Arinbjorn explained. 'Allodial rights allowed the farmers to hold their land and the goods on it in absolute ownership, free to dispose of as they choose and completely without payment of rent or service to an overlord. When Harald Fairhair was winning the land in his youth he made it law that all ancestral lands and other inheritances belonged to him alone. In return for remaining on their land or carrying out their trade all bonder, great or middling had to pay skat to the king.'

Gunnhild nodded. 'I can see why Hakon's popularity is sweeping the land like a heath fire. Why did King Harald make such a law? The Norwegians are notorious for their love of independence and self reliance, it could only end like this.'

Arinbjorn took a sip from his own cup before continuing. 'As the old kings were killed or driven from the land and Harald's kingdom grew it became impossible for him to attend every Thing, so he appointed jarls over each district to act as his representative. A third of the skat raised came to the king's treasury, here in Avaldsnes, and the rest went to keep the jarls and the hersar below them. In times of war these men, men like myself, had to supply the king with huskarls or hirdmen depending on his wealth and status; sixty for every jarl and twenty each for every hersir.'

Erik had been listening and he broke in with a comment of his own. 'It was a good system, fair and just; the farmers and other freemen paid a little but they gained the security of a well ordered kingdom. Gone were the days when Vikings could scathe a coastline and be away with their booty and enslaved before the local ruler could organise a response. Even the Danes and the Swedes thought twice before they harried the Vikken or set foot across the Gota River because they knew that they would be faced by the king's host before they could get very far.'

'And the incessant warfare which had weakened Norway in the days of many kings was over,' Arinbjorn added.

'Warfare is one thing,' Gunnhild said, 'but a man's gods are altogether different. I may be a Dane by birth, but I know the men of Norway now as well as my own. Even the basest woodsman would never turn his back upon the true gods for a handful of silver. If Hakon thinks that he can get the Norwegians to bow down to this Christ, I think that he is in for an unpleasant surprise.'

Arinbjorn's great frame shook with laughter. 'Forgive me for saying so queen, but you have never wanted for silver, nor food or much else I am thinking. It can mean the difference between life and death for most. They will keep the silver, mumble a few words to the Christ if they ever have the need, and then go back home to their own shrines and sacrifices.'

Erik saw the queen's expression darken at his foster-brother's words and a realisation came upon him. Maybe this was the way that kings toppled from their high seat; not the death he had given his brothers, a king's death on the field of battle ringed by the bloodied corpses of his oath sworn. But bit by bit, cut by cut, as support seeped away and men, even unwittingly, began to lose their dread. He shook away the thought with difficulty. This was Arinbjorn after all, if anyone had earned the right to speak freely in their presence it was he. But he had recognised Gunnhild's look of shock at the impertinence, and he asked the question which was begging to be asked before she could snap a reply. 'So, what's to be done?'

Arinbjorn's laughter trailed away to be replaced by a frown. In truth Erik suspected that the situation was quickly becoming hopeless, but he valued his oldest friend's advice more than any other and he needed to hear that he felt the same. 'Hakon and Sigurd Jarl spent the winter and early spring travelling from hall to hall, Thing to Thing. Everywhere, in the Trondelag, Upland and down in the Vikken he was taken as king as soon as his proposal to free the bonder from taxation was aired. He elevated Bjorn Farman's son Gudrod to his father's old high seat in the Vestfold, and made Tryggvi Olavsson king in his father's kingdom of Ringerike. The gods!' he exclaimed with a shake of his head, 'men are even saying that Hakon looks so much like his father that he is Harald Fairhair reborn! Everything they do, they do to win support, here and now, regardless of the cost in the future.'

'And they are still pushing the Danish connection I hear. Erik Daneaxe and his Jutland witch,' Erik said as he rose from his seat. 'Well, I trust to my axe be it Danish or Norwegian, and I will not flee from a child without a fight. Let us send around the war arrow regardless of the numbers at the Thing, and take the fight to them.'

28

A WORLD TURNED UPSIDE DOWN

The wooden latch went up with a clack, and the fallow bloom of a candle flickered to light all but the deepest recesses of the little room as the door creaked open. The old archbishop let out a gentle grunt of amusement, and he recognised the look of gratitude that washed across the face of the young scribe as the letters revealed themselves again on the page before him. As the monk moved from candle to candle, touching each wick with the taper to push back the winter shadows, Wulfstan relaxed as he allowed the smell of beeswax and smoke to carry his mind back to the far off days of his own youth. Every churchman, high or low, had started his new life bent forward transcribing passages from one sheet to another, be they mundane legal writs, king's judgements or the beautifully illustrated ecclesiastical passages which graced the great churches and monasteries. That so many had been destroyed since the pagans had begun their attacks on Christendom he reflected with a snort of irony, was part of the reason that he was in this place. That and the trouble he had caused, offering one Norseman after another the Northumbrian crown in a bid to keep the kingdom independent of the grasping southern kings. King Eadred had finally seen no other recourse than to carry him away to the South coast, as far away from his own land as he was able, and Wulfstan allowed himself a smile as he recalled the struggles of the unfortunate monks tasked with his instruction so long ago: he had always been a bit of a scoundrel.

As the elderly brother bobbed his head and made his way from the room Wulfstan, Archbishop of York, took a sip from his cup and threw the man before him a fatherly smile. He had become carried away by the cut and thrust of his tale, and it was clear now that the scribe had been hard pushed to keep pace with his wittering in the gathering dusk. Bloodshot eyes stared back at him across the vellum, but the lad's expression betrayed his keenness to continue and he asked the question anyway although he already suspected the reply. 'Shall we leave it there for today? You look all in.'

Wulfstan was not to be disappointed, and he smothered a smile as the monk shot back a retort. 'Perhaps we could just finish this part of King Erik's tale, lord? If you think that we can squeeze it in before we break for vespers?'

Outside the rooks had finally quietened as the short winter day drew to a close, but the dogs had taken to yowling again and the pair exchanged a look of gratitude and amusement as a man growled a curse and a yelp cut the air.

'Yes,' he replied. 'If we forego supper beforehand, I think we can just about make it…'

GUNNHILD HAD TOLD herself that she would march smartly to the ship without a backwards glance, head held high, chest thrust proudly forward as her own mother had taught her so many years before; but the sight of Erik pulled her up short, and her eyes misted over despite her promises. She had never regretted her marriage to the bluff northerner for a moment; the gods knew that she had only escaped a marriage to a prince in East Frankia by the skin of her teeth. But she had never been really sure that she truly loved him until this moment, when all around were downcast, their hearts and courage in their shoes; Erik filled the waterfront like Þórr himself: like a king. Unconquerable and full of life her husband was marching towards the gangplank, laughing, hailing one and all; looking for all the world like a man out for a summer jaunt on the waters of the Sound.

Gamli, their first born marched at his side, the lad's face shining with the pride he felt to be in his father's company after so long away. Recalled from foster with a trusted hersir in Halogaland, the man had made his excuses and sent the lad on ahead promising to follow on when he had settled some business or other. Erik had accepted the news graciously as was to be expected of a great king, thankful that he had the lad back at all. But all those there knew that the only time the two men would meet in the future would be if they found themselves glaring across the rim of a shield.

'Halogaland!' If the word had been a dark hair fished from her broth, Gunnhild could not have spat it out with greater venom. Overcome by the enormity of the events she was witnessing on that warm summer morning a maid made the mistake of glancing her way, but a withering stare drove the girl's eyes back to the floor where they belonged: Halogaland.

It had been the moment that had broken Erik's will to resist, the closest Gunnhild had ever come to seeing the steel which flowed through the Bloodaxe's veins buckle when Arinbjorn had reported the news to a silent and fearful hall. The banners of Halogaland, and of Ragnar Jarl too, had been seen alongside those of Trondelag, Upland, Romsdal, even

Moerr. They already knew that Hakon and Sigurd Jarl had not waited until Erik was ready to appoint replacement jarls and hersar to Vestfold and Ringerike and had stolen a march. Only Fjordane and Rogaland remained loyal, but even here support was lukewarm at best. Gunnhild sighed, despite her promises to herself. Arinbjorn's brusqueness had been worth more to Erik than her denial. He had been right about this Christianity all along: woodcutters; smiths; farmers and the like. What price a dunk in a chilly stream if it helps to fill the bellies of your children and get them through another year?

ERIK PLACED his hand upon his son's shoulder and threw him a heartening wink. 'Take a good look around,' he said. 'This is the home of the king of Norway.' He raised an arm to point away to the North, pushing down the sense of shame which threatened to overwhelm him as he did so. 'You see that barrow on the skyline?'

Gamli shaded his eyes and followed his father's tree trunk of an arm. 'The lefthand one, father?'

Erik nodded, 'yes, the biggest one. That is the Howe of your grandfather and his father before him. When the wind howls like a wolf in heat and the moon shines like a Serkland dirham they come from the tomb to look out over the Sound, sinking horns of mead and swapping tales of the old days. Mark it well,' he said as the wonder of the thing drew the colour from the lad's cheeks. 'One day you will lead men here, and when your ancestors next settle down upon their lofty perch to sink a draft or three, a new king will sit in the high seat at Avaldsnes and men will call him Gamli Hakon's Bane.'

Gamli nodded with all the earnestness of a boy keen to make his father proud, and Erik exchanged a look and a wink with Arinbjorn as the last of the huskarls trooped aboard the *Draki*. 'Go on, son,' Erik said. 'Lead your kinsmen aboard, and remember what I said. These lands are our lands, paid for with the blood of our ancestors.'

Foster-brothers from way back the pair watched him go, and Arinbjorn sucked the air through his teeth with a whistle as his mind wandered back over the years. 'Who would have thought that it would lead us here?'

Erik's brows dipped in question and Arinbjorn went on; 'the fight.'

'What fight?'

Arinbjorn shook his head and threw him a look. 'The horse fight, back at the Gulathing; when we took an axe to Bram.'

Erik snorted as his mind drifted back to that far off day. 'Bram,' he said, the affection he felt at the memory taking him by surprise. 'He was a good horse, a real fighter!'

'Yes,' Arinbjorn said. 'He was a good fighter, but the horse fight led to Bolli Sigurdsson's killing. You made an implacable enemy that day, and by a roundabout route it has led us here.'

Erik's deep laugh rolled around the quayside, and the warriors sat at the rowing benches or lounging forlorn where they could find space on the decks of the longships exchanged looks of wonder at the sound. Gunnhild had reached them, sandy and ruddy haired bairns swirling around her skirts like the waters of the Moskstraumen itself, and his heart gave a kick as he recognised the pride in her eyes despite the grimness of the day. She shook her head in disbelief as he threw her a lascivious leer, but he could see the love there and his heart swelled with pride as he recognised just how lucky he really was despite it all.

'Maybe you should have let it go?' Arinbjorn said. 'You might still be king of the Norwegians if you had.'

Erik pulled a face. 'Sigurdsson deserved all he got. If I could go back to that time I would not change a thing.' He looked at his foster-brother and poked his chest with a finger. 'And neither would you Arinbjorn Thorirsson, for all your well meant words. Come,' he said, 'it is time we were away. Hakon's host cannot be far off, and I have at least three more high seats to fill before the Norns snip my life thread.'

'What do you mean, three more high seats?'

Erik threw an arm around his old friend as they trod the jetty. 'I thought that you were there? In Finnmark when the shaman lost his head and Jomal gained a name.'

'Oh, I was there,' Arinbjorn snorted, 'like as not swatting smaller pests. If the shaman told you anything about the future Erik, he did so out of mischief; it was a curse, and I don't want to know. No man should know his fate, that is for the Norns to decide and no other.' Arinbjorn pinned his lord with a look, switching the subject to more immediate matters as they came to a halt between the gangways. 'Is it time then?'

'Time for what?'

'Time to let us all in on the secret of our destination.'

Erik laughed again. 'Just follow my stern post; I *can* promise you though that we sail not into shameful exile, but to war.'

Arinbjorn's face lit up at the disclosure, and he turned to share the news with the men crowding the *Sea Stallion*. Arinbjorn's glee was reflected among the warriors sat ready at their oars, backs straightening, chins rising again as the news spread, and the leaders gripped forearms and each wished the other gods-speed as they boarded their ships. The news was passing from ship to ship, and men who dragged their feet on the way down from the hall found the spring return to their movement as hawsers were slipped and the ships began to pull out into deeper water.

The big skei were the first to reach mid channel, and Erik looked on proudly as they peeled off one by one and turned their prows to the South beneath a cloud of gulls too numerous to count. Heavily laden the knarrs tucked in behind, the tubby trading craft waddling into position as the snekkjur came out to form a screen to their rear. Thorstein watched as spars clattered aloft, sails were unfurled and oars stacked amidships for the journey. 'The knarrs are sitting low in the water, lord,' he said with a frown. 'Imagine if one went down.'

Erik snorted. 'I would pretend that it was a sacrifice to Njörðr.' He threw his huskarl a wink. 'Rather that than gift the contents of my treasury at Avaldsnes to Hakon and my turncoat countrymen when they arrive.'

The wind came on from the North, sails bellied, pennants snapped, and before the sun had reached its zenith in the southern sky Skudenes, the rocky tip of the island of Kormt, was disappearing astern.

Gunnhild and the children had settled amidships and Erik, despite the gravity of the moment, found that he was chuckling happily watching the boys play rough and tumble with his men. It was a glimpse of a truth which victory would have denied him, and he recalled the pride he had felt at the admiration in young Gamli's eyes back on the jetty. Real wealth was not measured in the number of spearmen at your beck and call, nor the size of your gift hoard; it could be found everywhere, even in the shabbiest shack. His mood lifted another notch as he shifted his gaze outboard, filling his lungs with salty air as he thrilled to the sight of the fleet porpoising south under a cerulean sky.

The huskarls had gathered on the steering platform, and as the wide inlet which led to Hafrsfjord opened up on the larboard quarter Anlaf Crow spoke for them all. 'So, we shall be fighting this summer?'

Erik nodded, and the men thrilled as they saw his eyes flash in anticipation. Anlaf exchanged a look with the others as they waited for Erik to outline his plans, but after a while they realised that they were waiting in vain and the huskarl pushed again. 'Did you have any particular foe in mind, lord? Or are we just waiting to see who crosses our path?'

Erik came back from his thoughts, and the steeliness they saw caused the battle hardened warriors to blanch as all the good humour of moments ago was chased away. 'Christ men,' he growled. 'The kings of England and Frankia thought it a fine thing to topple a king, to buy another man's gift stool with his own silver. But Óðinn protects his own; the tafl pieces are moving now, the game has just begun.'

AFTERWORD

Despite falling firmly within the period when historical records were becoming widely kept throughout Europe, the people of Scandinavia were still overwhelmingly illiterate at this time. Christianity with its monastic seats of learning and record keeping had barely begun to make the first tentative inroads into a society which still modelled itself on the heroic culture of the older Germanic and Celtic north. What little has come down to us today of the lives of the men and women who inhabited the North in those far-off days is fragmentary and conflicting. Those written within Scandinavia itself were written hundreds of years after the events they describe, with even the simple matter of dating a reign proving to vary widely from one source to the next in a region which was late to adopt the Christian calendar. Luckily I could use two raids which can be dated with certainty using contemporary sources, the sack of Landévennec Abbey in 913 and Athelstan's punitive expedition into Scotland in 934 to bookend the narrative in this book. Most histories have Harald Fairhair dying around the year 933, so this was ideal.

One of the primary sources for Erik's life is the Saga of

Egil Skallagrimsson, more often known as Egil's Saga or simply Egla. First written down in Iceland in the thirteenth century, almost certainly by the scholar and lawspeaker Snorri Sturluson, Egla purports to tell the story of an Icelandic farmer/skald/warrior. A large part of the tale concerns Egil's conflict with Erik Bloodaxe and especially Gunnhild. Most of what we think we know about Erik and Gunnhild comes from this, but the truth is that there is little independent evidence that Egil existed at all outside of these tales, much less that he almost single-handedly won the battle of Brunanburh for King Athelstan of England. It is a great story, as are all the Icelandic sagas and I recommend that you read it if you have not already done so, but to attempt to use this to reconstruct a history of Erik Haraldsson's life would be pure folly, and I decided at the outset to leave the character out of my tale completely. Snorri Sturluson was a leading politician in thirteenth century Iceland, often *the* leading politician, at a time when King Hakon IV in Norway was looking to incorporate the commonwealth of Iceland into the realm. Initially a supporter of the king Snorri had a falling out which led to his assassination, but it is important to bear in mind what type of man Snorri was when reading his works regarding Erik, Gunnhild and Hakon, the king who even shared the same name as that in his own day, a man Snorri knew personally.

Gunnhild herself, known to later history as the Mother of Kings, is a character with conflicting origins. Some sources, notably Egla and Heimskringla, both probably written by Snorri Sturluson, say that she was the daughter of a minor nobleman in the north of Norway. I have chosen what I think is the far more likely background for this remarkable woman, that she was the daughter of King Gorm the Languid, later known as Gorm the Old, in Denmark, sister no less to the equally famous Harald Bluetooth. One of the earliest sources certainly back this up; commonly known as Ágrip, a history of the kings of Norway thought to have been written around the turn of the twelfth century. Erik himself had family connections with this part of the world through his own mother, a daughter of another Danish king after whom he was likely named. That Erik Haraldsson was not only provided with a spouse by his father from Denmark but was the only one of the king's many sons to marry into Royalty, also serves to support the claim he was Fairhair's intended Successor, as does the fact that he was fostered in the household of Harald's own foster-brother Thorir Hroaldsson. The final piece of evidence supporting this would be the name of Erik and Gunnhild's first born son, Gamli. King Gorm is still known in Denmark as Gorm den Gamle, old Norse Gormr gamli. It would not only honour Gunnhild's father to name the child for him, but the continuation of a family tradition would serve to illustrate the feelings of respect and affection which the histories and sagas say existed between Harald and his son Erik.

All the sources agree that Harald Fairhair sired a prodigious number of children and lived to a ripe old age. The number of legitimate sons he produced vary from eleven to twenty according to which source you read, and there were many more born to various women of all social backgrounds. If Harald had died sooner there seems little doubt that a man of Erik's qualities would have succeeded to the High Seat almost unchallenged; that the king lived to a venerable age was, to Erik's position at least, unfortunate.

I have given Harald Fairhair the honour of naming his favoured son Bloodaxe, but the truth is it is far from certain that Erik carried the name within his lifetime. Ágrip again is the first to record the epithet which is usually explained by the ruthlessness with which Erik dispatched his half brothers as he sought to keep the crown, although another source, Fagrskinna, ascribes it to his success as a Viking. The truth is that we will never know for certain, but as all the sources agree that Erik was Fairhair's choice to succeed him I thought that I would hand him the honour.

As mentioned above, the raid and sack of the Benedictine monastery at Landévennec in Brittany occurred in 913 which fitted my timeline perfectly. Christian religious houses were often sited on remote coastlines, and as I have attempted to show precious metals were not the only riches they contained. Important members could be ransomed, the younger monks were well fed and usually disease free, perfect fodder for the slave markets throughout Europe and beyond.

Heimskringla tells us that Harald sent five fully crewed ships to Thorir's hall in Naustdal when Erik turned twelve years old and became a man in law, with instructions that he go Viking and prove his worthiness. He spent a total of eight years raiding all around northern Europe before setting off to Bjaramaland where he 'won a great victory.' King Sveri and his daughter Snofrid were as they appear in our tale; the Finns were always renowned in early medieval Scandinavia for their witchcraft and dark magic and Erik could very easily have been acting on his father's orders. The overwintering on the return journey was my own addition to the timeline, as was the attacks of the shapeshifter. From the vantage point of our twenty-first century world such things can appear absurd, but the truth is that the population of early medieval Europe and beyond believed that such things existed and people sometimes see what they expect to see. Most people have heard of the condition known as 'cabin fever,' and this would be a similar experience.

The Mokstraumen is far better known now by the simplified name given it in "A Descent into the Maelström," a short story written in 1841 by the American writer Edgar Allan Poe. Whether Njörðr was still swapping seafaring yarns with Skipper Alf there he fails to mention.

The attack on Erik's hall at Solvi by Halfdan the Black really occurred, so the hall burnings and subterfuge were certainly not carried out solely by Erik as they are usually portrayed. Another of the sagas, Orkneyinga Saga, contains the following line which supports this: "When they grew up the sons of Harald Fairhair turned out to be very arrogant and caused a lot of trouble in Norway, bullying the king's jarls, killing some of them and driving others from their estates."

King Harald did rouse himself for one final campaign in defence of his chosen heir and battle was avoided in the way I have written by the actions of a wandering skald named Guthorm Sindri. Whether he was really Óðinn in disguise I will leave it to you to decide, but again it was just the type of thing that the god would be expected to do and he was the god of poetry after all.

The barrows of King Olav and King Gudrod can still be seen outside Tønsberg where they fell in battle against their half brother Erik, but as we have seen, even remote Norway did not exist in a vacuum. Other kings in foreign lands also schemed and plotted and Erik paid the price.

Although it is never mentioned in English sources, it seems very likely that Hakon Haraldsson was fostered at the court of the English king Athelstan and that his return at fifteen years of age was sponsored by the Christian king. Hakon's forlorn attempts to introduce the religion to pagan Norway is another tale, but Sigurd Lade-Jarl was his strongest supporter and it seems to be true that Hakon had kinship to the jarl on his mother's side. The horse fight and burning in of Bolli Sigurdsson I introduced to literally fan the flames of hatred felt by the jarl towards Erik, but it is as likely that the ties of kinship and a desire for a return to the old days of independence for the regions could have sufficed. Whether Sigurd was behind the restoration of allodial rights to the bonder is unknown, but all of our sources agree that this happened and that Erik's support evaporated with it. Rather than fight an unwinnable war Erik chose exile, and it is to those adventures that we turn our attention next.

Thank you for buying and reading Bloodaxe. If you enjoyed my tale could I ask that you help spread the word by leaving a review on Amazon, Goodreads, social media or elsewhere? Even a line or two are enough to influence Amazon's algorithms, it really does raise the profile of the book. Independent authors must survive without the advantages of publicity departments and agents, so it is the best way that you can support our efforts beyond the actual purchase itself. I read and appreciate every review and respond to all communication usually within the day.

Cliff May
East Anglia
March 2018.

CHARACTERS

Anlaf Crow - Erik's huskarl and banner man.

Arinbjorn Thorirsson - Son of Thorir hersir and Bergthora. Erik's foster-brother.

Bergthora - Wife of Thorir hersir.

Bjorn Farman - Half brother of Erik and under king of the Vestfold.

Bolli Sigurdsson - Son of the jarl of Lade.

Erik Bloodaxe - Favoured son of Harald Fairhair.

Elk Kari - A hunter and guide in Fjordane.

Gauti Thorodsson - Styrisman on the *Bison*

Gamli Eriksson - Erik and Gunnhild's eldest son.

Gorm the Languid - King of Danes, later called Gorm the Old. Father of Gunnhild.

Gudrod Haraldsson - Succeeded his brother Halfdan as king of Trondelag. Killed at the battle of Tunsberg.

Gunnhild Gormsdottir - Erik's wife. Daughter of King Gorm the Languid and sister to Harald Bluetooth.

Guthorm Sindri - A one-eyed itinerant skald.

Gytha Thorirsdottir - Sister of Arinbjorn.

Hakon Haraldsson - Fostered and sponsored by King Athelstan of England to return to Norway on Harald Fairhair's death in an attempt to introduce Christianity to the kingdom.

Halfdan the Black - Erik's half brother. Under king of the Trondelag.

Helgrim Smiter - Harald Fairhair's leading huskarl. Leads the swine head charge at the Battle of Tunsberg.

Harald Eriksson - Erik and Gunnhild's son.

Harald Fairhair - High King of Norway. Erik's father.

Harald Bluetooth - Son of Gorm the Languid and brother to Gunnhild.

Helgi - Thorir hersir's huskarl.

Horse Hair Gisli - Thorir hersir's huskarl.

Hrolf the Ganger - A son of Rognvald Eysteinsson jarl of Moerr. Now settled at the mouth of the River Seine in West Frankia.

Kolbein Herjolfsson - Erik's huskarl and styrisman on first the *Isbjorn* and then the *Draki*

Olav Haraldsson - Under king of Ringerike. Killed at the Battle of Tunsberg.

Olvir - One of Erik's hirdmen. A native of Vestfold.

Oswald Thane - Archbishop Wulfstan's representative in Northumbria.

Ragnvald Straight-Boned - Warlock King of Hathaland, burned in by Erik.

Skipper Alf Karisson - Styrisman on the *Fjord Ulf.* Killed in battle at Perminia.

Sigurd Hakonsson - Jarl of Lade.

Sturla Godi - A Romsdaler. A member of Erik's hird.

Svasi - King of Bjarmaland, father of the Harald Fairhair's queen, Snofrid.

Thorfin Ketilsson - Styrisman on the *Reindyr.*

Thorir Hroaldsson - Hersir at Nausdal.

Thorstein Egilsson - Erik's huskarl and prow man.

Ulfar Whistle Tooth - Styrisman on the *Okse.*

Wulfstan - Archbishop of York, Northumbria, England.

PLACES/LOCATIONS

Avaldsnes - Karmøy, Rogaland county, Norway.

Dofrar - Dovre, Oppland county, Norway.

Gulen/Gulathing - Sogn og Fjordane county, Norway.

Hafrsfjord - a fjord in the Stavanger Peninsula in Rogaland county, Norway.

Hestad - Gaular Municipality in Sogn og Fjordane county, Norway.

Hov - Oppland County, Norway.

Jelling - Vejle, Syddanmark, Denmark.

Jostrudal - Jostedal, Sogn og Fjordane county, Norway.

Kormt - Karmøy, Rogaland county, Norway.

Lade - now a district in Trondheim, Norway.

Landevennec - Landévennec, Finistère department, Brittany, France.

Lindesnes - Vest-Agder county, Sørlandet. The southernmost point on the Norwegian mainland.

Narvik - Nordland county, Norway.

Nausdal - Sogn og Fjordane county, Norway.

Perminia - Archangel, Arkhangelsk Oblast, Russia.

Solvi - Selvik, Midsund, Møre og Romsdal, Norway

Saeheim - Sem, Vestfold county, Norway.

Tunsberg - Tønsberg, Vestfold county, Norway.

ABOUT THE AUTHOR

I am writer of historical fiction, working primarily in the early Middle Ages. I have always had a love of history which led to an early career in conservation work. Using the knowledge and expertise gained we later moved as a family through a succession of dilapidated houses which I single-handedly renovated. These ranged from a Victorian townhouse to a Fourteenth Century hall, and I added childcare to my knowledge of medieval oak frame repair, wattle and daub and lime plastering. I have crewed the replica of Captain Cook's ship, Endeavour, sleeping in a hammock and sweating in the sails and travelled the world, visiting such historic sites as the Little Big Horn, Leif Eriksson's Icelandic birthplace and the bullet-scarred walls of Berlin's Reichstag.

Now I write, only a stone's throw from the Anglian ship burial site at Sutton Hoo in East Anglia, England. Bloodaxe is my tenth novel, following on from the success of the concluding book in the bestselling king's bane series, The Scathing.

ALSO BY C. R. MAY

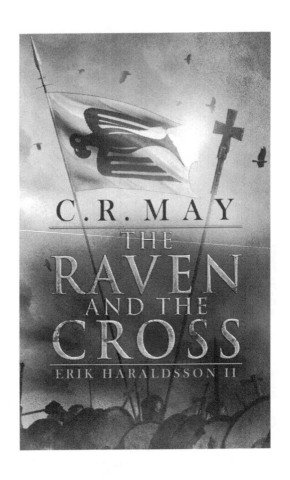

THE RAVEN AND THE CROSS

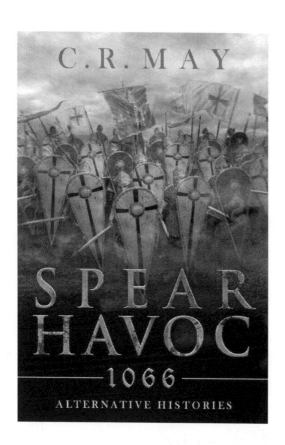

SPEAR HAVOC

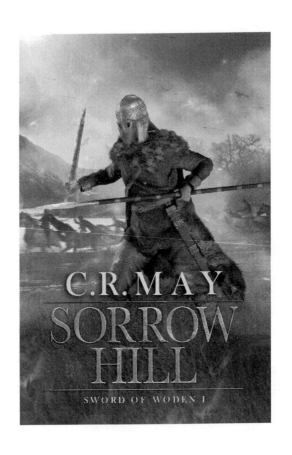

SORROW HILL

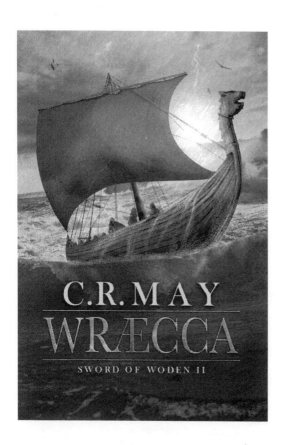

WRÆCCA

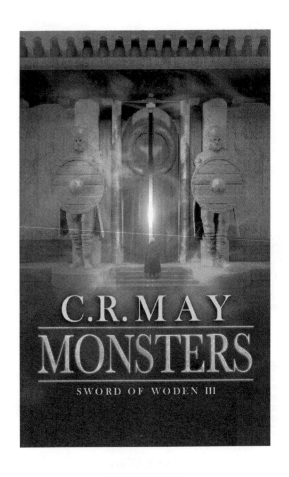

MONSTERS

C.R.MAY

DAYRAVEN

HYGELAC'S RAID

DAYRAVEN

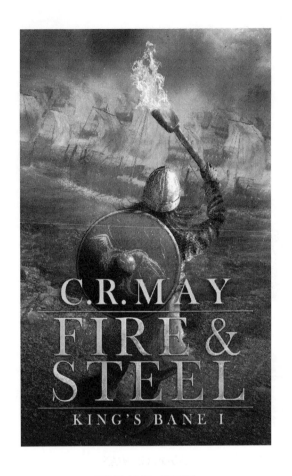

FIRE AND STEEL

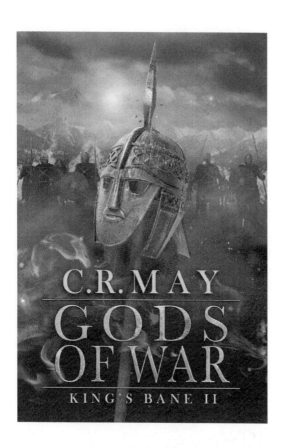

GODS OF WAR

THE SCATHING

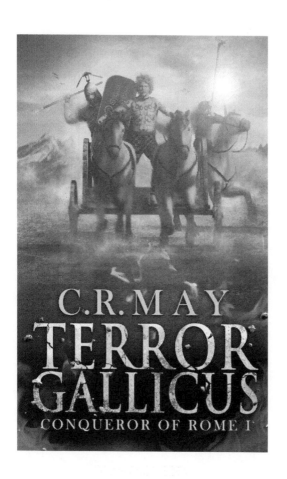

TERROR GALLICUS

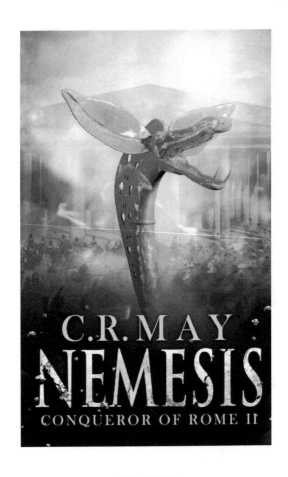

NEMESIS

Made in the USA
Monee, IL
05 May 2020

29865787R00199